only
in
new
york

Melissa Hill is a *USA Today*, No. 1 *Irish Times* and international best-selling author living in County Wicklow, Ireland. Her page-turning contemporary novels of family, friendship and romance are published worldwide and translated into twenty-six languages, with many adapted for film and TV.

Follow her on Facebook and Instagram: @melissahillbooks

Also by Melissa Hill and published by HQ:

Keep You Safe
The Summer Villa

MELISSA HILL

only in new york

HQ

ONE PLACE. MANY STORIES

HQ
An imprint of HarperCollins*Publishers* Ltd
1 London Bridge Street
London SE1 9GF

www.harpercollins.co.uk

HarperCollins*Publishers*
Macken House, 39/40 Mayor Street Upper,
Dublin 1, D01 C9W8, Ireland
This edition 2025

1
First published in Great Britain by HQ,
an imprint of HarperCollins*Publishers* Ltd 2025

ISBN: 9780008699598

Set in Sabon LT Std by HarperCollins*Publishers* India

Printed and bound in the UK using 100% Renewable
Electricity by CPI Group (UK) Ltd

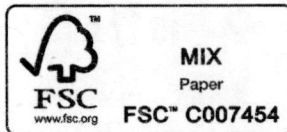

FSC
www.fsc.org

MIX
Paper
FSC™ C007454

For more information visit: www.harpercollins.co.uk/green

To Kevin & Carrie,
with all my love.

Chapter 1

HANNAH

Welcome to my humble abode!

Thank you soooo much for taking care of my new home – happy to know that the place will be in safe hands without me. Sorry that some rooms are not quite ready yet, but still lots of space to enjoy (no parties though, please – leave that to me!).

Know Sara's filled you in on everything already, but just another quick reminder that the marble guys are coming on the 15th (before they install it, just make absolutely sure it's Calacatta and bookmarked as ordered), and a couple of Peacock chairs (sooo retro, just WAIT 'til you see them!!!!) and an Eames lounger are scheduled to arrive at the end of the month, along with some A/W collab drops (but not too many, I promise) that I so appreciate you taking care of.

The refrigerator is packed with the good stuff and you're welcome to borrow whatever you like from my closet while you're here so go nuts (though maybe not my shoes and def not my top-shelf purses, 'K?). Or anything that takes your fancy from the PR drops, go right ahead too (our little secret).

Just Snap or message Sara if you need anything or have any questions, though idk the time difference in Europe might make things tricky but hey . . . hope you settle in OK and enjoy being back in NYC!

Courtney XOXO

PS Ignore the crazy old dinosaur next door – guy was so peeved that the co-op let me buy into the building that he spent the ENTIRE YEAR complaining about construction noise! No doubt Sara's told you all about the stupid lawsuit already. So much for friendly neighbours, huh?)

Hannah Ryan looked up from the note, still trying to take in her new surroundings and couldn't help but seriously question her life choices. Here she was, mid-thirties and having to start her life over in another city, and a girl a decade her junior outright *owned* a newly refurbished Classic Six, one of two penthouse floor apartments in a landmark building on NYC's Upper East Side.

She knew that 'classic' referred to the pre-war era when apartments of this ilk were built, and 'six' to the total number of rooms; a living room, formal dining room, separate kitchen, two full bedrooms and what would have once been servants' quarters located near the kitchen and with its own bathroom facilities.

These homes were also famed for the architectural touches popular during the same period: hardwood floors, spacious rooms, high ceilings, eye-catching mouldings, grand entrance galleries and hallways to separate the spaces.

In short, Hannah was standing in a piece of New York history.

And while she might be leaving her LA life behind to start over on the East Coast, thanks to her client's magnanimous offer at least she wasn't homeless.

New York-based social media superstar Courtney Wilde was a priority client of Hannah's employer Lotus PR, and whom she herself handled as West Coast liaison. The influencer had recently departed for a three-month-long tour promoting her latest book, *Empower*.

A few weeks ago, not long after Hannah's world had been upended, prompting her transfer to the company's New York office, she was meeting with Courtney at the Beverly Hills Hotel when she received an urgent call from her realtor informing her that the Brooklyn shoebox she'd initially set her sights on had fallen through.

'And there's nothing else?' Hannah cried, crestfallen. Couldn't *anything* go right for her these days? 'No, no Manhattan is way out of my budget.'

Courtney had obviously been eavesdropping and when Hannah hung up, she said, 'I'm gonna be nosy, OK?'

'Sure.'

'You need somewhere to stay in NYC?'

'You might say that,' Hannah admitted, biting her lip, unwilling to get into the specifics of her personal life. 'It's a little awkward because my ex . . . well, let's just say I needed to get out of Dodge, so I asked for a transfer. And a change is as good as a holiday, yes?' she finished brightly, hoping Courtney wouldn't push for specifics. 'But I'm not having much luck with finding somewhere.'

Thanks to her recent out-of-the-blue relationship implosion, Hannah had jumped at the chance of a fresh start at the company's New York arm. But not so much at the prospect of wading into the city's real estate market.

Courtney wrinkled her nose sympathetically, which managed to make her look even more adorable. 'That sucks. Tell you what – why don't you crash at my new place while I'm in Europe? I'll be gone for a few months and it's pretty much ready to go, save for some last-minute construction tweaks, furniture deliveries and stuff. And

I *hate* the idea that no one's lived there for so long. Coming back to a space that's been vacant for a while . . . the vibes are usually so wonky, you know?'

Hannah paused, unsure how to answer. On the one hand, a temporary place to stay while she got settled would be a lifesaver, but finances were an issue and there was no way she could afford the rent in that part of town.

'Naturally,' Courtney continued, 'I'll be paying *you* to house-sit – or apartment-sit, I guess,' she grinned.

Which was how Hannah currently found herself (temporarily) living the dream in one of two top-floor apartments in a salubrious building on the Upper East Side. She let out a low whistle, impressed afresh at her surroundings. To be fair, the apartment's original state must surely have been magnificent in itself – but soon after Courtney bought into the 72nd Street property, her manager had pronounced it 'criminally unsuitable for his client's aesthetic'.

From what little Hannah knew of the period, it seemed the interior designer had stayed true to the original pre-war architecture while giving it a glamorous mid-century modern flair. The original beams and columns were kept along with the solid floors, creating a nice sense of continuity between the old and the new. The walls were also painted white to provide a neutral backdrop for the newly installed fixtures.

Custom-built storage units meant there was ample space for the influencer's quirky travel artefacts, art sculptures and photographs, but they also provided a warm, inviting touch. The wood grain blended seamlessly with the classic mouldings, columns and zig-zag walnut parquet flooring, creating a sense of subtle harmony between contemporary and traditional.

The bedroom Hannah would be using was also updated with

modern features while still honouring the original period's charm. A tufted headboard complete with LED lighting was installed to give the bed that luxurious boutique hotel feel, while the walls were painted in a muted shade of blue to create a tranquil atmosphere. A plush neutral carpet provided a soft, cosy touch.

This room alone was about the same size as her very first box-room apartment in Greenwich fifteen years ago when she'd first emigrated from then-recessionary Ireland as an unemployed young woman hoping to find a career path in the US. And now, after almost a decade in LA, she was once again starting over in New York. Not *quite* back at square one (at least she'd managed to hold onto her career, if not her reputation), though right now it sort of felt like it.

Walking back through a living room that felt large enough to host an NFL football game within its confines, Hannah still couldn't help but wonder if she was in a dream. Though after the scenario she'd just left, *anything* would seem like a dream.

Before she could go any further down that disaster-strewn path, and determined to keep her spirits up, she continued her tour of the space, moving through to the small kitchen and marvelling at the state-of-the-art chef's kitchen, dazzling aluminium pots and pans hanging over the prep area island currently awaiting its aforementioned Calacatta marble countertop finish.

It was every chef's idea of heaven. But Hannah was a little uncertain about whether or not she was allowed to use it and made a mental note to go back over the house rules Courtney's assistant Sara had mailed across when making initial arrangements.

Not that it mattered. She was a tragically terrible cook and there was no shortage of great places to eat in this town. Which would also encourage her to get out there and help meet new people – as it was, she knew she'd spent far too long licking her wounds and eating her feelings in the form of Ghirardelli's hot fudge sundaes. It was time to start living life again.

She smiled dolefully. Still . . . baby steps. Passing by a mammoth Sub-Zero stainless steel refrigerator, Hannah caught sight of herself in the reflective surface and regarded what she saw with a more critical eye. While she would never in a million years be considered influencer material like Courtney, she knew she looked decent enough not to send kids (or New Yorkers) running away in terror when they saw her.

Petite in stature, with shoulder-length chestnut hair and wide blue eyes, it was all too easy to underestimate her, and very many people did. Hannah smiled. She liked that, the way appearances could be deceptive; and it was something she utilised every day in her PR manager role.

She left the kitchen and ambled back into the living room. The main living space was also brought into the modern era with a few carefully selected pieces of furniture. Sleek, low-profile sofas in shades of grey and blue provided ample cosy seating, with a round ottoman and a couple of mid-century modern pieces for enjoying those incredible Central Park views, and the Dakota building directly across.

The yet-to-be-delivered Eames lounger Courtney had mentioned in her welcome note would surely be the piece-de-resistance in here. To finish off the space, an elaborate art-deco chandelier was installed in the centre, adding a bit of twenties sparkle and glamour.

Belying that era was a beyond-state-of-the-art media system capable of replicating an IMAX experience that even put some LA movie mogul pads to shame. Along with smart lighting and climate control systems, with programmable thermostats and automated shades. Hannah had no idea how much the media installation alone would cost, but suspected it must surely be a few years of her salary, plus maybe tossing in selling an organ or two on the black market. Let alone the price of the apartment itself.

What must it be like to be one of the richest social media stars of your generation? That was something Hannah would never know – and that was fine with her really. In her line of work, she routinely dealt with the top of the elite mountain – the one per cent's one per cent.

While many of the younger so-called tastemakers she'd worked with back on the West Coast – mostly bored rich kids – were narcissistic, demanding and completely out of touch with the rest of the world ('away with the fairies', as the Irish expression went), Courtney Wilde was a surprising exception to the rule.

The twenty-three-year-old millionaire had become a voice and role model for millions of young women around the world, with a successful online platform that combined her passions for fashion and finance. While the majority of retail and lifestyle influencers typically sought out IV lines direct to followers' pockets to enrich themselves, Courtney Wilde conversely used hers to empower her audience with knowledge and wisdom about money and financial independence. Her mission to help younger women become financially literate and learn how to pay for their purchases through careful savings and clever investments instead of becoming slaves to credit was a powerful one that was both fashion-forward and financial-savvy.

Dior or Front Door? (blow money on designer stuff or use it to buy your own home) was the catchphrase that had captured the imagination and gone viral, thrusting Courtney's atypical fusion of fashion and finance into the spotlight. And one which the young lady had utilised herself, with spectacular results, since this gorgeous penthouse was merely one element of a significant property portfolio.

Hannah wished someone like Courtney had been around when she was that age, particularly in her younger years growing up as a bookish, painfully-shy teenager in the rural Limerick village from which she hailed. A small farming community that offered few opportunities for glamour or social variety, about the only adolescent role models she had back then were gleaned from books and TV, and much of her life advice via Jean Luc Picard in *Star Trek TNG*.

Make it so . . .

She chuckled. Truly a galaxy apart from the largely confident go-getting youth of today.

Even possessing a smidgen of that kind of moxie could've meant that Hannah might also have been much better placed to take control of her situation after everything imploded in LA. Her ex, Rob, remained in the Brentwood walk-up he owned, rendering her homeless practically overnight.

So she was doubly grateful for the opportunity to get a true taste of the good life, temporarily at least. There was only one minor wrinkle in the entire situation – the neighbours' issue mentioned in the welcome note.

Hannah learned from Courtney's assistant Sara that a group of residents in the building had lodged a lawsuit against the co-op board for allowing the influencer to buy into it.

When word initially got out that she had made an application, apparently the cantankerous old guy living in the adjoining penthouse had insisted that they couldn't allow some 'attention-seeking airhead' to upset the social dynamics in the building. But evidently the group's wish to have Courtney's bid denied was refused. As were their subsequent submissions about construction noise, odours from the fresh paint or insistence that the planned renovations would not only go against the architectural integrity of the landmark building but structural too, and they were all going to die when it caved in around them.

Hannah knew that such co-op disputes could be the stuff of legend in NYC, with residents routinely fighting board members and each other for myriad reasons (ironically the very opposite of co-operative), and she could well imagine why the arrival of a millionairess bright young thing into the prestigious building might put much older and well-heeled noses out of joint.

Sara had quickly brushed away Hannah's initial concerns by assuring her that the matter was now in the hands of the legal eagles, and there was nothing to fear from any personal encounters. But maybe once the neighbours met Courtney in person, she'd disarm and charm them too? Well, they certainly had nothing to fear from introverted Hannah anyway. No wild parties or noise of any kind – she wasn't even the singing-in-the-shower type.

Nope, while she was here, she just planned to lay low, pick up the pieces of her life, and most importantly, she mused, gazing out at that picture-perfect Central Park view, make the most of the incredible gift she'd been given in one of the greatest cities on earth.

As she stood by the window, watching the light slowly fade over the park and cityscape beyond, Hannah felt optimistic for the first time in months.

She'd been in Los Angeles for so long that she'd almost forgotten the exhilaration Manhattan could evoke, and was appreciative of the opportunity to experience it anew from such an incredible vantage point. Opening the sash window a little, even fifteen floors up the air was suddenly filled with familiar sounds of the city – honking horns, laughter against the murmur of traffic and a million conversations – and, at that moment, Hannah felt a profound reconnection with the place she'd once called home. This very same vibrant energy had once helped her shake off those youthful small-town inhibitions and encouraged her out of her shell to become the mature, self-assured person she was now. She felt a lump in her throat. Or used to be.

With luck, New York would work that same magic for her again.

She had been away from the city for so long and yet it still felt like no time had passed. Her instincts were correct to leave LA. She had come to the right place to lick her wounds, heal her heart, and she was more than ready to start a new life in the city that never sleeps.

Heading back out to the foyer to collect her bags from where she'd dropped them in awe on arrival, Hannah noticed that something had since been slipped under the door. A piece of paper and a handwritten note:

P-2,
I'm still getting your stupid 'fan mail' shoved in my box downstairs. I know this might come as a surprise to someone who lives in their own perfect Barbie bubble, but there are two penthouses up here. I've been marking it as Return to Sender, but soon I'm just gonna start shredding. So tell your herd of bazillion idiot sheep to stop sneaking their crap into the lobby. Or even better, tell 'em to go to hell.
P-1

Hannah's eyes widened. So much for nothing to fear from the neighbours. Seemed they were still engaged in active battle.

Chapter 2

The fifty-something building supervisor Julie, who looked remarkably like Meryl Streep, had personally introduced herself upon arrival, assuring that she was on hand if Hannah needed any help settling in. On Monday morning, Hannah quickly sought her out in the hope of borrowing a standard phone-charging cable since the penthouse's charging stations had been customised for tech at least three iterations ahead of her own phone.

When she mentioned the note from next door, Julie burst out laughing, shaking her head. 'Ed just doesn't know when to quit. You've gotta admire that, right?'

'Well, with the lawsuit and everything, I really don't want to step on anyone's toes . . . ' Hannah replied since she couldn't be certain whether Julie might be involved in the residents' dispute. In her line of work, diplomacy was a given and she'd always been a pro at poker face. Which could often be a blessing or a curse, depending on the situation.

'Look, a lot of people in this building can be a pain in the butt, but he's actually a pretty decent guy. Always gives out a great Christmas bonus. I think he's just one of those old-school types who doesn't like the way the world is changing around him and it makes him cranky.'

'Well, I know that type all too well,' Hannah admitted. 'My grandfather was similar – gruff, no-nonsense, always talking about the way things were back in his day. Typical Irish male of his generation. From what I can tell from that note, though, the difference is that my granddad wasn't so . . . angry about it.'

'I think Ed's just lonely actually.' Julie shrugged. 'Always used to be pretty friendly but now that I think of it I rarely see him around these days. Likes his privacy. Seems he gets all his groceries delivered online and doesn't go out much, or have many visitors either. Poor guy probably doesn't have anything to do all day but go online or watch the news, which would make anyone miserable,' she added, rolling her eyes.

'You might be right,' Hannah demurred. 'I went over and knocked on the door a couple of times over the weekend, wanting to introduce myself and assure him I'd be there to take care of issues with mail or anything else on Courtney's behalf, but he never answered.'

Julie shook her head. 'A lot of people here went *crazy* when they found out that her application had been approved. You'd have thought that the board had announced that we were opening up a petting zoo in the lobby and turning the roof into a stage for Cirque du Soleil.'

'I don't get it. Life's too short, isn't it? And Courtney's great.'

'Well, like they say, the rich are different. And some people take longer than others to get with the times.'

'Case in point?' Hannah held up her charger and grinned. 'I suppose I really need to think about upgrading. And I don't have an excuse either, being so close to the mothership,' she chuckled, referring to the famed Apple store at the top of Fifth Avenue, a few blocks down.

'Yep, like it or not, time moves on.'

'Speaking of which . . . ' Hannah checked her watch, 'I need to get going for work. But first, coffee. Where's the nearest Starbucks around here?'

'Oh, there's a much better place just a couple of blocks down. Frank's – been around forever. Does the best cinnamon rolls too.'

Hannah smiled, her mouth watering already. 'Perfect, thanks for the recommendation.' She popped the rolled-up wire in the pocket of her blazer. 'And the charger.'

Manhattan was ablaze in the morning sunshine as she stepped out of the building onto the bustling Upper East Side during the commute rush. The city rose before her like a phoenix, its sheer magnificence almost too much to take in all at once.

Cars and bicycles moved briskly along the streets, while purposeful pedestrians carrying coffee cups and briefcases filled the intersections and overflowed into doorways as they hurried past one another.

There was a unique energy here that always filled Hannah with a sense of awe, and as she glanced around she couldn't help but marvel at how much the city had changed over the years, all the same. So many shiny new skyscrapers – colossal edifices of glass and steel – towered above the lower-rise brownstones and older ornate construction so prevalent in this part of town.

The sidewalks were full to bursting with people – rich, poor, and everything in between – all hustling and bustling with their own unique purpose and destination. It was as if every person walking by had gathered together their hopes and dreams and poured them into this town, suffusing it with life. She knew exactly how that felt, having done it herself all those years ago.

As Hannah ambled along in the sunshine, her skin prickled with a sense of optimism and anticipation. Everywhere she looked were signs of spring – vibrant blossoms of tulips and brilliant yellow daffodils, heralding warmer days to come. And as she continued her journey along the edge of Central Park, the recreational space looked even more alive with its unique display of colour and beauty.

Unable to resist ducking inside for a bit on her way, the more beautiful everything became. The trees were in full bloom, displaying their lush greens and cherry blossom pinks in contrast to the bright-blue sky. And surrounding it all stood so many classic landmark buildings from old New York – intricately detailed brownstones and mansions, a marked contrast to the modern skyscrapers towering above them. It was always here within the confines of this verdant space that she truly felt the energy and beauty of the city. A quiet oasis amid the chaos.

That was something she'd definitely missed in a car-centric city like LA, and while there were some wonderful individual neighbourhoods there, there was no replicating New York's unique combination of conversations, laughter, or dizzying array of sounds and smells. And today, as Hannah wandered through it, the city felt more than just a place of nostalgia – it was a new beginning, a fresh start that held as much potential as it did uncertainty.

Anything could happen here.

Hannah found the local place Julie recommended without issue. A narrow premises not much wider than its double-door entry, Frank's was tucked away between a cigar store and what looked like one of those pet pampering places for Park Avenue pooches.

She headed inside, finding to her relief that for this hour of the morning, there was surprisingly no line, just a couple of customers waiting on orders and oh my, *what* was that mouth-watering smell . . .

'Are those fresh?' she gasped, approaching an old-style wooden and glass display cabinet filled with the most delectable pastries and sweet treats imaginable, but indicating the cannoli in particular. Yes, she wanted to try the cinnamon rolls Julie recommended, but oh was she a goner for fresh cannoli . . .

'Made just this morning,' replied a booming voice from behind the counter, a heavyset man in his mid-fifties who she guessed must be the titular Frank. 'What can I get you? Or should I say how many?' he chuckled, dark eyes twinkling.

Hannah laughed. 'I'd love to say them all but I think that might be pushing it. Just one for now, and a coffee too, thanks. Black, no milk or sugar.' Since this didn't seem to be the kind of place that offered macchiatos, lattes and such. Which suited her perfectly, since too much choice made her head spin.

'Sure, let me ring you up and pickup's just this end,' Frank said, indicating further down where some other patrons stood, drinking coffee or waiting on their orders.

There were a couple of tiny tables and an empty pair of stools lined up at a full-length window just inside the door, and Hannah thought how nice it would be to sit there for a bit and watch the world go by outside. She made a mental note to do just that at the weekend maybe. Frank's seemed like one of those charming old-style people-watching spots that had been around forever. And she was pretty certain that, given the opportunity, the man himself would have a story or two to tell.

'That'll be six dollars and ten,' he said and Hannah duly lifted her wrist to tap with her watch.

But Frank shook his head. 'Sorry, cash only here,' he apologized, pointing to a nearby sign on the wall that she'd failed to register.

The downside of old-world charm.

'Oh! Sorry, I didn't think to bring any with me. You don't do card payments, even?' she blustered, reaching into her purse on the off-chance there might be a couple of bills in her wallet. It was just for something to say though, since Hannah knew she didn't have any cash on her and, in truth, rarely used it anymore. 'Sorry, I'll need to cancel it then,' she admitted, crestfallen. And she truly was. That cannoli looked (and smelled) *incredible*.

'I got it,' mumbled someone who'd just come in behind her, a guy – around her age, she guessed – shuffling along with a cane.

'Oh, thanks, but honestly, there's no need,' Hannah was quick to protest.

'It's not a problem. And believe me, I know how hard it is to leave one of those behind; they're my favourite, right, Frank?'

He chuckled at the proprietor who seemed unperturbed, as if customers offering to pick up the tab for complete strangers was par for the course in here. And since this guy seemed like he was a regular, maybe it was.

'Truly, you don't have to—'

'It's fine. Besides, nobody leaves cannoli in Frank's,' he added, green eyes crinkling, and in a tone reminiscent of that famous line in *Dirty Dancing*, and Hannah had to smile too. It was one of her favourite movies.

'Well, thank you, I really appreciate it. And I'll pay you back – maybe drop off the cash later to pass on or whatever.'

'It's just a couple of bucks, forget about it.'

She stole a closer look at the guy. Having ordered for himself, he proceeded hesitantly along to the register. Leaning awkwardly on the walking aid, he dug some cash out of the back pocket of his jeans.

Tall and sturdily built, with a broad chest, sandy-coloured

hair and a couple of days' growth on his (nicely chiselled) chin. Outdoorsy type, definitely not a Park or Madison Avenue suit, and way too much muscle to be tech or stockbroker, but who knew these days?

Back in LA, Rob had probably spent more time at the gym than he had with her, Hannah admitted to herself wryly. Her ex was extremely body-conscious and careful about what he ate.

But there was something about this guy's build that suggested his bulk was genetic as opposed to pumped. She wondered too about the cane and whether the necessity for that was also genetic, or just temporary.

But wow oh wow, those eyes. Deep pools of green with golden flecks that, when focused on you, were enough to turn anyone to mush. And they were focused on Hannah now while she remained there, still a little dumbstruck that such a fine thing had picked up the tab for her morning snack. The snack currently still waiting for her to collect at the other end. So really she should stop daydreaming and just get a move on.

'Well . . . thanks again, I really appreciate it and . . . I'll pay you back, honestly. Like I said, I'll call back with the cash, or return the favour sometime?' She smiled. 'That's if you come here often or . . .'

Oh, for crying out loud, just stop talking.

'Sounds good.' His eyes crinkled up again, this time in amusement, and realizing she was babbling, Hannah hurriedly moved to the pickup point, deciding to just get the hell out of there. Probably just a combination of first-day work nerves and unfamiliar surroundings that were making her so tongue-tied and discombobulated, she told herself, getting a grip. Because now he seemed to think she was flirting and she definitely wasn't.

Was she?

Eager to get moving, she grabbed her stuff off the counter and whipped backwards, not realizing the guy had since come up right behind her. Completely distracted, Hannah barrelled straight into his cane, sending it flying into the air, and her saviour off-balance.

Time seemed to stand still for a moment and she watched in horror as he scrambled (and failed) to recover his footing, before crumpling to the ground.

'Oh my god, I'm so sorry! Here, let me help you, give me your arm . . .' Mortified beyond belief, and horrified that she might have hurt him, Hannah dropped her stuff and grabbed at his shoulder, wrenching his arm back as he hoisted himself up on one knee and attempted to steady himself against the register. 'Oh my god, sorry, I'm such an eejit.'

'You OK, man?' Frank had since hurried out from behind while the other customers looked on with mild interest.

'I'm fine,' the guy insisted, wincing in pain, or was it embarrassment?

'Just . . . take my arm, OK?' Hannah insisted. 'It's grand, I've got you.'

'I said I'm fine . . . ' he repeated through gritted teeth, his complexion reddening, and she noticed his eyes had turned a much darker shade of green now, emerald almost.

Frank duly pulled across one of the window stools, and the guy leaned back against it, stretching his right foot – the bad one obviously – out in front of him, while his face twisted in agony.

Shite, what had she done? Hannah stood there uncertain of what to do next, her mouth open and closing like a fish, her hands jittery. Her instinct was to keep apologizing but there was little point in that. She'd done enough.

'Can I get you a drink of water or something or . . . ' She trailed off awkwardly, realizing everyone was looking at her now. 'I really hope you're OK, but just know that I feel *terrible* and . . . '

The look of frustration he shot her suggested that Hannah's repeated protests weren't helping. To say nothing of the fact that the entire incident seemed all the worse for the fact that he was being so kind and doing her a favour.

No good deed goes unpunished . . .

'OK, well . . . thanks again.' Raising her coffee cup in one final attempt at an apology, Hannah backed out the door and onto the city street, grateful to be swallowed up by the pedestrian masses.

And escape Cannoli Guy's now considerably less friendly gaze.

Chapter 3

Later that same evening, Hannah stared at what was supposed to be baked salmon with teriyaki sauce, but the blackened material in front of her didn't look like something anyone should eat. While she was great with meal prep, somehow she always managed to lose track of time after putting everything in the oven and so her culinary creations always wound up blackened – except for the ones that were supposed to be. Conversely, for some reason, those ended up underdone.

'So much for "foolproof",' she muttered, scraping it all into the garbage.

And that had been pretty much the theme of the day.

Following that terrible start at the coffee place, she'd struggled to regain her composure.

The same company notwithstanding, it was still difficult starting over in a different location, with a brand-new working environment, and new colleagues too. While everyone in the Lotus office in Rockefeller Centre had been quietly welcoming, and her new boss Wes, had assured her she'd settle in in no time, Hannah still knew she had a lot to prove. And she wasn't sure either whether the rumour mill had managed to follow her over to this side of the country. Nothing had been said, of course, but since it was the same company she guessed it was probably only a matter of time.

Which would inevitably make her office-newbie getting-to-know you opportunities much trickier. Hannah winced at the thought.

Well, regardless of recent personal wobbles, when it came to the job she knew she was one of the best in the business and, social challenges aside, was definitely champing at the bit to get started on her new client list to truly prove her worth.

Her stomach rumbled. She'd grabbed a bagel at her desk between a succession of welcome meetings, and save for that and this morning's cannoli, she thought – cringing afresh at the memory – she'd had very little to eat and was starving.

Having burned through most of Courtney's delectable Dean & DeLuca stash at the weekend, she scrolled through her phone in the hope of finding a takeout option that could deliver at warp speed. Just then, it buzzed in her hand.

Seeing the Caller ID, she grinned. 'Hi!'

'Hey East Coast,' her best friend and sadly former colleague Zoe, greeted. 'How'd your first day go?'

When she and Hannah first met at Lotus PR's Century City office all those years ago, the Texan redhead had been very standoffish and aloof. At the time, they were the only women in their department on a male-dominated floor. Hannah had made repeated attempts to be friendly but had been met with nothing but resistance. She'd decided she probably wouldn't ever get close to renowned ballbreaker Zoe Maxwell but just didn't have it in her to stop trying to break the ice at least.

One day, during a meeting, a senior executive had jokingly suggested that if they really wanted to land a client they'd been pursuing for months, Zoe might consider combining business with some good old-fashioned pillow talk.

Hannah had stood up before she'd even realized it and glared at the guy, her heart pounding.

'Is that something you consider part of your own repertoire?' she'd challenged, before she could stop herself.

To his credit, the executive's face had turned beet-red and he'd looked properly ashamed. And after stammering out an apology, he'd proclaimed the meeting adjourned.

As Hannah was leaving the office that evening, Zoe had caught up with her at the elevator.

'You know, you didn't have to do that.'

She'd shrugged. 'I know.'

'Why did you then?'

'We're the only two women here – if we don't have each other's backs, who will?'

Zoe had stared at her. 'You really believe that?'

'Why wouldn't I?'

'I don't know where you've been, but in my world, people aren't out there helping each other. They're all just doing whatever it takes to get ahead, and if that means stepping on someone else regardless of gender, that's just the price of entry.'

'Well, then you need to get out of that world,' Hannah had advised her, 'and spend a bitta time in mine.'

That had been the beginning of a wonderful friendship, and it was the only regret Hannah had about leaving LA. Zoe was currently visiting her parents in Canada, and while Hannah secretly hoped she might stop over for a visit on her way back, Zoe's hatred of New York was legendary.

'It was . . . good,' she said, answering her friend's query about her first day. 'Though they're already pawning me off with the lost causes.'

Hannah had no illusions that she'd waltz straight into the New

York office and get handed prime accounts. Instead, she'd have to earn her chops by handling some of the company's newer or lower-priority clients.

'That won't last once they figure out what a prize you are. For example, there aren't many people I know who could charm a millionairess into letting you crash at her brand-new pad.'

'It wasn't like that and you know it. But it's been such a godsend all the same. I don't know how I can ever repay her.'

'So what's the place like? I hope Courtney hasn't turned it into a grown-up Barbie Funhouse.'

'Dreamhouse, you mean. And nope, very tasteful – incredible actually, like something from a movie. And if you come and visit you can see for yourself.'

'If I ever make it out of here alive, you mean. Honestly, I love my folks, but being back in this town is like being in a different century.'

Hannah could relate to that big-time. She hadn't been back to Limerick in almost a year and whenever she did return home for visits, the insular village somehow always served to regress her to that same insecure young woman she'd worked so hard to leave behind.

Since the pandemic, her parents, both now pushing their seventies, were reluctant to travel, which meant visits across the Atlantic to see her were sadly a thing of the past.

'Ha, speaking of a different century . . . ' She went on to tell Zoe about the old guy next door, the only snag in her newfound dream setup.

'Well, there you go then.'

Hannah frowned. 'What do you mean?'

'PR is quite literally your job. If you want to find a way to pay Courtney back, there's your chance. Hit him with a charm offensive and pave the way for some positive neighbourly relations?'

'I don't know . . . with a lawsuit in the offing, the last thing I want is to step on any toes.'

'Oh, come on, getting people on side is your speciality, so you'd be doing Courtney a huge favour. Think of it as a side hustle, something to get your teeth into until you're off probation and assigned more interesting talent than the dregs. Honey, I've seen you in action. There isn't a man alive who can resist your legendary Irish charm. So why not work it on Grandpa next door?'

Chapter 4

WARD

The ice rink was alive with energy, from the booming cheers of the crowd to the echoing clangs of sticks colliding with the puck; the tension electric as opposing players skated around the ice, both determined to get the upper hand. A thrilling matchup, Panthers against Falcons, two of the biggest ice hockey teams in the league.

The Falcons were inching ahead, their team working together as a cohesive unit to advance the play. The Panthers were putting up a good fight, but their energy was starting to flag as the third period unfolded.

Ward McKenzie's heart raced as he skated on the ice, feeling the full weight of a thousand pairs of eyes on him. He had one shot, a chance to bring glory and redemption to the Panthers if he could put the puck in the net in time.

The frigid air engulfed his face like a blanket of icy needles as he dashed towards the goal, determined not to miss this shot.

The roar of the crowd seemed to peel away at his confidence but he pushed forward, visualising every next move in his head. The blades of his skates cut through the heavy layer of frosted ice as he raced towards his destiny, nothing standing between himself and victory but this one defining moment.

He had to make it count.

Then suddenly it all went wrong. Just as Ward shifted position to take the shot, he felt a sudden jolt of pain as his knee gave way beneath him. He stumbled and crashed inelegantly to the ice, the puck sliding harmlessly away from him.

The crowd gasped, a hush falling over the rink as he clutched at his knee in pain.

He'd blown it. In more ways than one.

Two of his teammates skated over to help him off the ice, their faces a mixture of disappointment and sympathy. Ward's emotions remained between confusion and defeat while he struggled to comprehend what had just happened.

As he limped off, he felt the mood of the crowd shift from hopeful anticipation to stunned silence. Could almost feel the disappointment emanating from the stands, and he knew that the Panthers' chances of winning were done for. He glanced at the scoreboard and his heart sank even further. He had let his team down, and there was nothing he could do about it.

Ward gingerly made his way toward the locker room aided by the medical trainers, barely aware of their words of comfort and sympathy as he replayed the events in his mind. He had been so close; he had seen the goal, had felt it within his grasp . . .

When they finally reached the locker room, he undressed and removed his equipment, wincing as he tried to put weight on his injured knee. He slowly made his way to the trainer's table and sat down, grimacing afresh as the medic examined him.

'It's not good, man,' he said. 'It looks like you've torn your ACL. We'll have to get you to the hospital right away for surgery.'

Ward nodded numbly, his heart sinking as the realization of what had just happened truly began to sink in. He had been so close to making that winning shot.

But it was too late. He had let his team down, and he had let himself down. He'd been presented with one chance to prove himself, one chance to show the world that he still had what it took to compete at the highest level, and he had failed.

Story of his life.

★

'So how's rehab coming along?'

Ward's jaw muscles tightened. His agent was *not* going to be happy about what he had to say.

'There's been a bit of a . . . setback,' he admitted.

Bernie Pitwell stared at Ward's leg, his eyes even more enlarged by the thick-lens glasses he wore. 'You're kidding me?! What happened?'

'Think I came off the crutches too early. Knee went weak and I took a tumble. Nothing too serious; just an unexpected setback, that's all.'

'I see,' the agent murmured, looking distinctly uncomfortable. 'But that's not good, man, not good at all.'

'You're telling me.'

Twelve weeks since the injury and he was still reliving that godawful game almost every waking moment. Hell, not even every waking moment. He'd dreamed about it again last night, and it was so real, it was as if it was happening all over again. But no matter how much Ward hoped the dream would change, it always ended the same way.

Failure.

Bernie sat forward. 'OK, I came here today to run something by you, but now with this . . . additional development, I don't think there's a choice involved. 'Management's . . . not thrilled.'

'I'm not thrilled either, Bernie. But I didn't ask for a busted knee to keep me off the team for three months.'

And possibly more now, thanks to that goddamned fall.

'It's not just your absence – it's what's been going on during that absence too. The board is . . . concerned.'

Ward sat forward, his eyes wary.

'Bernie, if there's one thing you and I both agree on it's that you never have to toss me a rainbow when you want to give me a hand grenade. There is nobody out there truly concerned about Ward McKenzie – other than you and Coach Lewis.'

'About your reputation, I mean.'

'My reputation? I've been sitting on the sidelines, bored out of my mind. OK, so I admit I might've been going a little overboard on some fun stuff, but it's no big deal.'

Bernie looked pained when he said, 'Like that time you had Johnny push you in a wheelchair through Times Square at three in the morning, the two of you half-naked and pumped up on booze and painkillers?'

Ward burst out laughing at the memory of that wild night. 'He was Forrest and I was Lieutenant Dan.'

'Doesn't matter. You can't do that stuff, make fun of disabled people, I mean.'

'What the hell, Bernie?' he said, incredulous. 'They're characters . . . from a *movie*. What, so even made-up people are getting offended now? And hey, I was using that chair for a while too, and *I'm* not getting all up on my high horse about it.'

The world truly had gone crazy.

'I hear you, but that's how it came across online. And there are way too many examples of similar stuff you've done over the years. While once upon a time, your little . . . stunts were sort of overlooked, the world's changed, plus you're older now and supposed to be more mature. A good influence. Fact is, if you want to get back on the ice and keep playing for the Panthers at this stage of your career, you're going to have to make some changes.' Bernie peered at him. 'And maybe use a razor now and again and get a haircut. You look like shit.'

Ward sighed defeatedly. Well, one thing was true; he didn't feel the same as he used to back in the day. The hangovers were definitely longer and more brutal.

But since his knee got busted, he was going out of his mind with boredom.

'OK. I'll tone it down. Definitely. You have my word, Bernie.' He ran a hand over his chin. 'And clean up too if it helps.'

His agent grimaced. 'That's just for starters, I'm afraid. And your word's not going to be good enough this time.'

'What are you talking about? Since when is my word not good enough?'

'Since that incident at the karaoke bar?'

Ward snorted, shaking his head. 'The guy was talking trash about Jimmy Buffett, Bernie. America's greatest folk singer ever and a goddamn hero. What was I supposed to do?'

'Behave like an adult?'

'Oh, come on! All I did was give the asshole a little shove but it was like I threw him off the roof or something. It won't happen again, OK?'

Bernie gave him a long look, then licked his lips. 'There's something else.'

'OK, I know that look and it's never good. What's going on?'

'Management has intimated that you're already on thin ice, so to speak,' he said carefully, and Ward's stomach dropped. He knew his game had been off the last couple of seasons, and yeah since hitting mid-thirties was starting to slow down, but he was still far from being put out to pasture just yet. Physical therapy on the knee was going great and once he got a clean bill of health, he was itching to get back out on the ice and prove that he still had it.

But thanks to that latest goddamn tumble, his recovery would be delayed by a few more weeks.

'The Panthers want to fire me? Is that what you're saying?'

'Of course not; contractually they can't fire you for a busted knee. But we don't want to give Craig Sumners or the top brass ammunition in any other areas . . .'

'You're going to have to spell it out for me, Bernie,' Ward said. Was the team owner losing faith in him because of the injury, or something else?

He hated all this dancing around. Why couldn't anyone just come out and say what was on their minds anymore? What the hell happened to straight talk and home truths?

After a pause Bernie said, 'Coach Lewis and I both agree that you need to get your reputation cleaned up—' he inhaled '—so I went ahead and hired a public relations firm.'

Ward's eyes widened. 'You're kidding. You know how I feel about PR, Bernie. Why would you do something like that?'

'Because you leave me no choice. If you want to salvage what's left of your playing years, you're going to have to change your attitude and fix your image. We've pretty much discovered that you're not able to handle that on your own,' he said pointedly. 'Which is why we're hiring professionals.'

Ward snorted. '*We're?* You mean I have to pay for this shit too?' But as much as Bernie loved him, he knew his agent wouldn't be doing this out of the goodness of his own heart. 'Professionals,' he repeated, disgusted. 'PR people are nothing but a bunch of leeches, you know that. Clean up my image? All they're gonna do is try to turn me into someone that I'm not. I'm WildCat McKenzie, damn it.'

'You'll still be WildCat McKenzie,' Bernie soothed. 'Just a shinier, more public-friendly version.'

Chapter 5

HANNAH

Hannah straightened up and double-checked her reflection in the bedroom's full-length mirror, before leaving for a preliminary meeting with the first of her newly assigned client list in the New York office.

The dregs, as Zoe described them.

And yes, while this particular motley crew – mostly comprised of up-and-comers and almost down-and-outers – weren't the most glamorous bunch, that didn't mean Hannah was going to give them anything less than her best.

Most people went around wearing a public mask, showing the world only the side of them they wanted to be portrayed. Hannah still did it herself, at work especially, and there were only a few people for whom she dropped the cool, calm collected persona to reveal the real her.

Ironically, a major part of her job was to find the person beneath – the inner part that was truly who they were. And with luck, and mostly some gentle coaxing, help the client feel comfortable enough to show their authentic selves to the world. It was the part she loved the most too.

Because Hannah knew first hand how empowering it was to escape the clutches of outside expectations to truly be at ease with yourself. Like she finally had after leaving small-town Ireland.

As with all her clients, she wanted to make a good first impression, but since this was an evening meeting, she needed a change of clothes after a full day at the office. So she went with professional but casual – her hair pulled back into a ponytail, a salmon-coloured blazer and a crisp white shirt beneath, jeans and metallic mid-heel slingbacks. Then opened the top button of her blouse, figuring it looked a little less austere considering she was meeting an athlete, who tended to be more relaxed about dress codes. She'd never worked with an ice hockey player, before though.

'McKenzie isn't just a hockey player, honey,' Zoe tittered when Hannah initially ran through the client list with her over the phone. 'The stories about that guy are legendary.'

'Really? Can't say I've ever heard of him.'

While Lotus PR's West Coast office represented countless athletes, Hannah's interest in sports just about extended to the games she used to go to with Rob.

'Yup, he's a legendary jerk. Cute though.'

Great.

Intrigued, she'd briefly scanned McKenzie's online presence in the meantime, though as a general rule, Hannah preferred not to know too much about any client ahead of meeting them in person, so as not to cloud her judgement.

But even basic research on the athlete seemed to suggest that her friend had a point. The most cursory online search suggested a boozing womaniser with a penchant for brawling and shooting his mouth off. 'WildCat' McKenzie didn't seem to have that great of a player achievement record to support such an inflated ego.

No personal social media that she could find either, but that was a good thing, given his apparent lack of decorum. Nor professional photographs other than generic team shots in full player garb and helmet, or blurry snapshots and video footage taken by the public of McKenzie falling out of bars and getting into drunken scrapes. Clearly, she had some work to do to turn his reputation around, and she figured that her new bosses were truly testing her mettle with this guy. WildCat indeed.

Hannah picked up her purse and headed for the foyer, whereupon she spied another note beneath the door.

Another delivery for you downstairs. Next time somebody calls on me to take a package meant for you, I'm gonna hurl it out the window. P-1

She stood there for a moment, mentally counting to ten.

Great – not only did she have to tackle an egotistical Neanderthal for work, but at home needed to contend with another entitled male who, age aside, still hadn't figured out how to behave like an adult.

Story of her life.

She tried her best to keep an open mind, but the moment Hannah entered the Hell's Kitchen bar McKenzie had suggested – or rather *insisted* upon – for this evening's meeting, she found her initial estimation of the guy sink even further.

The place was a dump; dark, nasty-smelling and full of TVs with the sound up so loud she could barely hear herself think. Which was probably exactly why he'd chosen it. But he presumably hadn't reckoned on Hannah's heritage and that, unlike Zoe who detested Irish bars, she was right at home in places like this.

As the barman eyed her with interest, she gazed around and quickly spied a guy wearing sunglasses and a Panthers sweatshirt at a corner booth. Even through the shades, she could feel his insouciant gaze on her as she approached. There was the faintest hint of a smirk on his lips and Hannah took a deep breath, determined to remain calm and professional. She was still a bit rattled from the latest note from P-1 and now having to deal with an overgrown schoolboy who clearly wanted nothing to do with her was rubbing salt into a wound.

When she reached the booth she smiled, hand extended. 'Ward? Good to meet you. I'm Hannah Ryan from Lotus PR.'

He barely glanced up as he limply took her outstretched hand, which instinctively got up her nose. *Deep breaths, Hannah*, she muttered inwardly. But then, looking closer at his clean-shaven face, or more to the point spotting the pair of crutches poking out from beneath the table, a sudden jolt of recognition shot up her spine.

'Oh!'

And to her horror, Hannah realized that the Good Samaritan who'd offered to pay for her coffee (and whom she'd repaid by tripping), and her brand-new client, were one and the same.

He seemed to have come to the same realization at the same time, whipping off his sunglasses in surprise.

'Cannoli Girl?'

Hannah nodded shamefaced. 'I'm so sorry I . . . I had no idea.' She dropped her hand and slumped down across from him in the booth, unexpectedly rattled now.

'Is this some kind of joke?' he said, his voice sounding more like a snarl.

'More of a coincidence, I think,' she replied, nowhere near loud enough to be heard over the blaring TVs projecting various sports games in session. She raised her voice. 'Believe me, this is as much of a surprise to me as it is to you.'

'I doubt that.' His arms were folded and his stance was even more closed than before.

She could hardly blame him.

'Look again, I'm so sorry about that morning,' she began, attempting to bury her discomfort and get things back on track. 'You were being so nice and—'

'I was in a hurry and you were taking too long,' he said gruffly. 'Nothing to do with nice.'

The kind, good-humoured guy she'd encountered that day was a world apart from the closed, indolent one sitting across from her now. And given the circumstances, Hannah knew she needed to summon every ounce of diplomacy in her power.

'So how is . . . everything?' she asked, indicating his crutches. 'I know you're recovering from a knee injury so I truly hope the fall didn't set you back or anything . . .'

He pulled them up defensively. 'It's all good, just a tumble, nothing to worry about,' he insisted, but recalling the pain on his face that day she knew that wasn't true. The tough guy act wasn't fooling her. Then she remembered that she was here because the guy's career was on the slide, so maybe he was also afraid to admit to any injury setbacks for fear it might damage his career prospects any further. And since she herself had been the root of his latest woes, the stakes for saving Ward McKenzie's career had suddenly become a whole lot higher.

She swallowed hard. *Great.*

'That's good to know,' Hannah said, rearranging her features into a reassuring smile and deciding to change the subject. If they had any hope of successfully working together, she needed to get Ward to trust that she was there to help. 'So while we didn't get off to the best start that morning, I take it you know why I'm here today?'

'Not exactly,' he growled, still unwilling to meet her gaze. 'My agent says you're supposed to make me into someone that the Panthers aren't ashamed of.'

'That's one way to put it,' she admitted, 'but not entirely accurate. My job is to help Ward McKenzie find out who the real Ward McKenzie truly is and help reveal—'

Eyes wide, he cut her off with a burst of laughter.

'You're kidding me, right? Did you actually just say that? No offence, Emma, but I know who the hell I am.'

'Hannah,' she corrected him.

'What?'

'You called me "Emma". My name is Hannah.'

'OK. Whatever. Doesn't matter. What does matter is that you're wasting both of our time. This is the real Ward McKenzie.' He stabbed a finger at his chest.

'Really?' she asked, and this time she couldn't help but keep the annoyance out of her voice. 'You admit to being an overgrown frat jock who gets drunk and acts the maggot in public?'

The smirk disappeared and he was quiet for a beat. When he spoke again, there was a dangerous edge to his voice.

'Here's the deal – I'll admit that I'm not everyone's cup of tea, OK? Some people might say that I'm an . . . acquired taste. Whatever. The thing is, Emma, I'm not about to change who I am just so you can boast that you managed to tame WildCat McKenzie. Do I go overboard sometimes? Hell, yeah. It's who I am. When I show up somewhere, people know what they're going to get – a guy who's fun, a little bit dangerous and who knows how to have a good time.'

'That's it?' she asked. 'That's what you're proud of? That's how you want to be known. Why not the guy who was kind enough to help out a random stranger with her cannoli order?'

He rolled his eyes.

'I told you – you were holding things up and making me late. And come on, what kind of person doesn't have even a couple of bucks on them?'

'Well, what kind of business doesn't take electronic payment?'

'The kind that maybe can't afford to?' he shot back. 'Frank's place has been around for years – it's a family business, but he won't be there much longer if the tech bros get a piece of everything he sells.'

She had to admit that maybe he had a point there. The rent in that location alone must have been eyewatering.

'And you have eyes yes? You didn't see the sign?'

'Obviously I didn't.' Hannah felt riled up and embarrassed all over again. 'And I'm so sorry for holding you up to the point that you felt the need to pay for my stuff. Though I can't imagine where you could've been rushing off to,' she added, unable to resist the jibe.

'To physio,' he retorted. 'An important session as it turned out, thanks to you.'

'Oh, so you admit that you *were* hurt then. What happened to the tough-guy act?'

'What happened to minding your own business?'

Annoyed with herself for allowing him to unsettle her like this, Hannah glanced around looking for a server, hoping to get things back on a more even keel. 'Have you eaten? The least I can do is buy you dinner to apologize and pay you back for the cannoli too. You're right, it was incredible.'

Though she had been too embarrassed to go back to Frank's ever since. And now truly hoped that this place wasn't cash only also.

'I'm good. But you're wasting your time if you think you can tap your way out of this one too.' Her face must have revealed what she'd been thinking because he chuckled and shook his head. 'Good luck with the apocalypse.'

'Ah, a conspiracy theorist, I see.'

'Just because someone has a different opinion they're automatically a conspiracy theorist? When did the world turn Borg?'

OK, Hannah *definitely* hadn't pegged this guy as a Trekkie. And felt herself automatically soften towards him. He truly was full of contradictions. 'Well, cash aside, if you're that paranoid about being monitored,' she pointed out teasingly, 'I'm assuming you have a smartphone, rendering all this caution pointless anyway?'

'Nope.' He reached into his pocket and took out an old-style flip phone that Hannah didn't think was even operational anymore, sliding it onto the table.

Yep, conspiracy theorist, for sure.

'Well, it's pretty apparent that you don't trust easily anyway,' she murmured.

'Hey, aren't you supposed to be working for me or something? So what's with the attitude?'

He was right; McKenzie was supposed to be Hannah's client so what was she thinking, practically goading him like this? Cursing herself for being so unprofessional, she bit down hard on her lip, trying to bring her emotions back under control. Barely a half-hour in his company and this guy was already getting under her skin.

This wasn't like her. At all.

'It's not an attitude. Part of my job is taking charge of how you present yourself to the world, and surely you yourself would admit your current media persona leaves a lot to be desired . . .'

He chuckled mirthlessly. 'I know that you might find this hard to believe, you being in the PR game and all, but I really couldn't give a damn what anyone thinks of me. I refuse to bend over, for the media or anyone else. *That's* who I am.'

Now Hannah tried to bite back a smile at this rather vivid illustration of her job description. This guy was unbelievable. But belligerence aside, she also couldn't deny how that mesmerising gaze turned upon her was making her feel . . .

Get a grip, Hannah.

'OK then. Forget . . . bending over for the moment,' she added, unable to keep the amusement out of her voice. 'Why don't you just go ahead and tell me more about who you think you are, and we can go from there. Who is Ward McKenzie?'

He leaned back, arms folded and glared at her as if taken aback by her change in stance. This time she looked into his eyes without flinching and after a few moments, he spoke again.

'OK, you want to know who I think he is? We can go there.' He leaned forward, squarely meeting her gaze in return, and even in the dim light she could still see those golden flecks in his eyes – if anything they seemed more pronounced. 'He's the kind of guy who doesn't put up with any media bullshit and the last thing in the world he's gonna do is roll over and play dead for anyone – on or off the ice.' He shrugged then, dropping his gaze to the table. 'Does he drink a little too much? Yeah – now and then. If he's out with the guys and he's having a good time, he might get a little rowdy. Guess what? There's nothing wrong with that. We all need to blow off steam now and then. Granted, that might not be something that you're familiar with, Public Relations *Emma*, but out there in the real world, people do that all the time. Anything else you want to know?'

Those goddamn eyes again. But Hannah refused to blink or, worse, show any emotion. 'You also have a reputation for being something of a womaniser . . .' she challenged.

Something else flared in them then, passing too quickly for her to identify before Ward dropped his gaze and looked down at his watch.

'I've got physio,' he muttered, but she knew he wasn't telling the truth. 'As I'm sure you can appreciate, my recovery is my priority at the moment. So do your worst, Emma. Just don't expect me to be something I'm not.'

She bit back yet another retort at the intentional misuse of her name but figured there was no point.

'Fine,' she said with a pasted-on smile, picking up her purse, only too happy to escape if not McKenzie, then the deeply discombobulating way he was making her feel. 'I'll be in touch again once I've come up with some ideas.'

Assuming that was even remotely possible.

Chapter 6

WARD

Driving out of the city, Ward did his best to keep his attention on the road. The last thing he needed was to get into a car accident or something. The next thing he knew, the internet would be claiming that he'd been high or drunk off his ass when it happened.

Damn, but he hated the modern world sometimes. Sure, technology gave people all over the world the chance to reach out and connect. That was a good thing. It also gave people from all over the world the chance to insult and tear each other down and he hated *that*.

Especially how the online world came after him and tried to tear him down over the years. Deciding that he was a bozo womaniser, shallow and basically a complete moron. The truth didn't matter. Nobody cared about the truth.

He thought again about Cannoli Girl. So yeah, *that* was a surprise. And not an entirely unpleasant one, to be fair. While he was still pissed at her for knocking him over that time, Ward had to admit that he liked the way she'd come right at him from the start just now. In the past, other so-called media people typically tried to immediately 'bond' with him and act like they were his friend to get him to jump through whatever hoops they decided he needed to.

She, Hannah, hadn't tried to play him though. She also hadn't backed down when he'd pushed, which he had to respect too. Though he cringed afresh that her first impression of him had been such a weak-ass one, falling over in Frank's like that.

She was *definitely* easy on the eye too, which of course he'd noticed that first time also. Cute as a button, but despite her tiny stature and baby blues, he got the sense that she didn't take any shit.

Still, Ward was long enough in the game to know how the PR play went. She might just be better at her job than the others. He suspected that their initial encounter had confused her somewhat too. Understandable. Considering the shit show that was his current public persona, it was a world apart from the guy who'd paid for her coffee last week.

The stupid nice-guy stuff that always let him down.

It had been almost six months since Melanie left him. He'd met his photographer ex when she was taking team shots for an online sports magazine. Tall and blonde with hazel eyes, she'd immediately charmed him with her sense of humour and her blasé attitude about his jock status.

Things had started slowly, but once they'd started progressing, it had been pretty rapid and Ward had fallen hard. Before he knew it, he'd even found himself beginning to think about an actual future with her.

Like all good things though, it had come to an end. One night, when they were in his place watching TV, she'd turned to him and said, 'There's something I need to tell you.'

He still remembered how his stomach had tightened and he'd felt nauseous. Whenever anyone said something along those lines, it never, in his experience, led to a good outcome. 'What's going on?' he'd asked.

Melanie hadn't met his gaze. That was never a good sign either. As he'd sat there, waiting for her to respond, he'd felt his heart racing. He'd known right then, that they were through.

'I've been offered a job in Chicago,' she'd said. 'It's a permanent position at a magazine and the pay is double what I'm making right now. There's so much opportunity for advancement too.'

His mouth had suddenly gone dry and it had taken him a few moments to answer. 'OK. And how do you feel about long-distance relationships?' he'd managed to ask.

Her bittersweet smile had told him everything he'd needed to know.

'I've been down that road before, Ward. Maybe it works out at first but before you know it, we're drifting apart.'

'We won't know until we try, though,' he'd suggested stupidly. 'Just because something didn't work out in the past doesn't mean it's going to always be that way. For one thing, you're dealing with me now and I won't let you down.'

Melanie had given him the sweetest smile he'd ever seen, tears welling up in her eyes, and she'd leaned against him.

'You're a nice guy, Ward, but I just don't see it happening. I'm going to be busy getting everything set up, and you've got the new season coming up too . . . Maybe when I'm properly settled in you can come and visit and we can talk about it?'

By now, Melanie should have been settled in. If she'd wanted to make things work, she'd have picked up the phone and they'd have discussed things. There had been no phone call. There had been no discussion.

A nice guy.

Ward wasn't stupid. She'd moved on. She'd started her life over in Chicago and that life hadn't included him.

To the public, he was as Cannoli Girl had just described him: an overgrown frat boy womaniser, living up to his on-the-ice moniker and tough-guy reputation.

In private he tried to be a decent guy, but that didn't seem to get him anywhere.

And worse, now he was past his prime and benched with an injury that showed no sign of getting him back on the team anytime soon. His coach was losing faith, his agent was losing faith, and if things didn't change soon, his career would be lost to him too.

Hannah said she wanted to improve his image. The problem was Ward knew deep down that improving his image meant being the other guy – the *nice* guy.

And that never worked out well.

Chapter 7

HANNAH

When Hannah returned, still rattled from her second unexpected encounter with Cannoli Guy, the building's evening doorman, Bruno, was on shift. A friendly New Yorker in his sixties, he greeted her with a smile then reached down to pick up an oversized skincare hamper, setting it on the countertop.

'Delivery for Courtney. Mistakenly dropped up to penthouse-one by the courier earlier when no one was here,' he said, raising an eyebrow, 'who sent it back down with some choice words and this note.'

Hannah's stomach dropped as she read the words, which were pretty much a carbon copy of the note she'd received earlier. She'd intended to pick up what was evidently one of Courtney's PR drops, but hadn't had a chance to do so any sooner, so what was the guy's problem?

'Ugh,' she groaned, frustrated. 'Why is it that when some people get old, they get mean and sour and just seem to hate the world?'

Bruno gave her an odd look and Hannah worried then that she might have insulted him.

'Age has nothing to do with it,' he said. 'It's just his personality.'

'Well, thanks so much for keeping it safe,' she muttered, picking the package up and heading to the main elevator. 'Have a great evening.'

Riding back up to Courtney's apartment, Hannah thought about what Bruno had said. Was it possible that P-1 was just mean and angry by nature?

Rob always used to tell her she was way too naive about human nature and that, given the chance, people nearly always tried to screw you over. But her ex existed in a world driven by competition.

She sighed. Though he was definitely right about her being naive.

As she set down the hamper and went to input the apartment entry code, Hannah glanced toward Penthouse-1 and, without thinking too much about it, strode over and knocked on the door. Then knocked again. Obviously, he was home. She could hear music coming from inside. The guy – Ed – was ignoring her.

Oh no wait he had mobility issues, she recalled, wincing at her impatience, so of course it would take him that bit longer to answer the door. But still, no reply.

Hmm . . .

Hannah scooted back to her own door.

One way or the other, she was going to make sure P-1 responded to her.

A little later, Zoe called again for a catchup.

'You caught me right in the middle of making Rice Krispie buns,' Hannah told her friend.

'Yikes, what's the occasion? Or should I say, who made you mad?'

Whenever she was feeling anxious or off-kilter, Hannah resorted to making a beloved Irish childhood treat that was impossible to mess up – a simple mixture of Rice Krispies and melted chocolate poured into paper bun cases and left to cool in the fridge. And, after today, she was definitely both.

'I thought I'd take your advice and try to break through next door's walls,' she retorted airily.

Zoe laughed. 'You truly cannot stand someone not liking you, can you? It's cute, of course, but it can also be a little intense, and I'm talking from experience here. You take people-pleasing to a whole new level.'

'I'm not *that* bad,' Hannah argued, though the comment hit a nerve. 'I just think that maybe Ed is angry and lonely because no one's taken the time to get to know him, so he's turned away from the world. It's like that movie with Tom Hanks, where he plays that grumpy old dude who's actually got a heart of gold?'

'Unless it's a movie with Momoa in it, I have no idea what you're talking about. Anyway, if he's that ornery maybe you might want to take it slow all the same? Some folks don't like other people butting into their lives. New Yorkers especially.'

At this, Hannah found herself smiling.

'But,' her friend conceded with a sigh, 'if you're truly going to engage in one of your culinary charm offensives, then I also know that poor guy doesn't stand a chance. Literally. Just try not to poison him, OK?'

'Very funny.'

But the call (and the baking distraction) had the requisite effect of lifting her spirits, and a little later, once the treats had sufficiently cooled, Hannah clutched a plate of Rice Krispie buns, her pulse quickening in anticipation as she once again approached her not-so-friendly neighbour's door. She could still hear muffled sounds coming from inside, like the TV was on or something, but when she knocked there was still no response. Undeterred, she took a deep breath and decided to scribble a quick note of her own, once again calling on her trusty diplomatic skills.

> Sorry about the recent mistaken deliveries – guessing the delivery people don't realize there are two of us up here. Made these Rice Krispie buns as an apology? Hope you like chocolate. :)
> P-2

Then carefully folded the slip of paper and slid it under the door, leaving the plate outside by the architrave. But just as she was about to leave, she heard footsteps approach and a burst of panic shot through her as she realized her neighbour must have company.

Hannah hurried back to her own door, not wanting to meet him for the first time in such circumstances, or perhaps needing to explain to complete strangers (perhaps even more of the angry residents' group?) why she needed to make a peace offering. With the lawsuit in the offing, she also needed to remember she was on somewhat delicate ground here.

Back in her apartment, she was running water for a pre-bedtime bath accompanied by a long-awaited glass of wine when the doorbell rang. The unexpected intrusion startled her, to the point that she almost spilled her wine.

Ed from P-1?

Having since changed out of her work clothes, Hannah looked down at her current attire of fuzzy pink robe and a pair of comfy rainbow-coloured socks. She debated whether she had time to go and change back into daytime clothes, then decided against it. Actually, it was probably a good thing she looked so non-threatening, it meant there was less chance of anyone yelling at her.

But when she opened the door, there was no one to be seen. She was about to close it again when she looked down and saw her now-empty plate resting on the carpet. The treats were gone, and in their place was another note.

Thank you. At first, I had no idea what the hell you'd put on my doorstep so to speak, but these were something else. The perfect combination of crunch and chocolate. Rice Krispie buns, you say? Just what my soul needed, actually. Seems like you're a woman of many talents after all.

So, I'm going to be honest here. I know your generation seems to permanently live online and thrives on being in the spotlight – as you can probably guess, I'm not a big fan of social media stuff. I'm one of those guys who likes the safety of people not knowing who I am or what I do every minute of the day.

I've been in the spotlight myself once or twice in my time. Not quite the same thing I know, but either way I didn't like it.

So anyway, thanks again for the treats. Made a bad day a helluva lot better – and I guess I should say that I'm sorry if in the past I came across as a total jerk. I'm not a total asshole.

Maybe just a half-asshole.

P-1

Hannah put down the note and smiled. *Result.*

She wasn't sure what she'd been expecting, but it wasn't what she'd just read. There was humour and intelligence to the message that completely caught her off-guard.

'*A half-asshole.*'

Smiling afresh, she grabbed a pen.

Dear Half-Asshole,

I'm glad you liked them. If I'm being honest (and I am), they're about the only thing I'm able to cook without totally destroying it.

I actually agree with you about the online world. People are a lot braver when they can hide behind their words and don't have to see the results. There are times when I've been hurt by what someone's written about me and I've had great intentions to track them down and confront them face to face. (Of course, I'd never do that because I'm a total chicken really.)

Don't think for one minute I like any kind of attention either. You know how when in school the teacher called on you to read something out in front of everyone? I used to hate that. I had this one teacher who'd always call on me to read out my English homework. My stomach would clench into this tight ball of worry and my mouth would go dry. The weird thing was that once I started reading, it wasn't that bad at all.

I suppose my worry was more about the idea of reading than the actual reading.

It's nice to hear from you though, and if you'd like to chat more that would be lovely since we're neighbours now. Or if you're someone who feels more comfortable communicating at arm's length, I completely understand. Too many people wanting to get into your business can be overwhelming, I know that only too well.

Either way, I'll be baking more Rice Krispie buns. :)
P-2

Chapter 8

WARD

'So apparently, they want to start with a piece on you for Fur Parents Magazine . . .'

Ward frowned at his phone, bleary-eyed.

'She wants me to wear fur? I thought we were supposed to be improving my image here, Bernie. How about a Coors commercial or something?'

'It's not about wearing fur, you idiot,' his agent told him. 'It's about dogs and cats and stuff.'

'Right – but I don't have a dog or a cat or . . . stuff.'

'That's why you're doing this. Hannah wants to reveal a gentler side of you that hasn't been seen before. It's going to make the public realize that there's a living breathing person inside that tough-guy shell. So she's suggested a visit to this animal shelter—'

'No.'

'What do you mean, "No"?'

'Look, while I agreed to do this whole "image reboot" crap you wanted, what I'm *not* gonna do is pretend to be someone I'm not. And definitely not some wimp drooling all over an ugly ass dog and talking to it like a baby and shit.'

There was a long pause. And when Bernie spoke again, Ward heard the no-nonsense tone in his rep's voice.

'Hey, you've got to meet me halfway here. Just meet with the PR people, do a couple of minutes of pretending to be fascinated with the animals, and then you're out of there. They run a couple of cute pictures that go viral, and hey presto, the bad boy stories eventually get resigned to history. What have you got to lose?'

'Gee, I don't know – other than my dignity, what *do* I have to lose?'

'Just knock it off, man. You can play Mr Macho with everyone else, but you and I both know the truth.'

Hanging up the phone, Ward dropped his head back on the pillow and winced at the familiar ache that, no matter what he did, didn't seem to be abating.

By rights, he should have been completely healed and back on the ice by now.

He'd been doing everything he'd been told to do by the team physio – but thanks to that recent tumble, it seemed as if he was worse off now than when he'd first busted it during the game. He pushed himself out of bed, wincing at what felt like lava shooting down his leg. Then stood there for a moment taking several deep breaths, before he slowly navigated to the bathroom.

Opening up the medicine cabinet, he shook a couple of pills into his hand and tossed them into his mouth. He ran some water into the plastic cup he kept by his toothbrush and swallowed the pills. Then glanced at his reflection in the mirror and what he saw repulsed him. There was a haunted look in his eyes – a quiet agony he couldn't ignore. He'd seen that look before but never in his own reflection.

A cold feeling formed in his gut and he took a deep breath, realizing there was yet another bitter truth he had to face.

★

When Ward showed up at Carver's Steakhouse in the East Village a little later, most of the pain had subsided – but he was still feeling a little shaky as he walked. He glanced around until he spotted a dark-haired muscular figure who looked like he could once have been an athlete, but was now past his prime. Which was exactly what he was.

When Ward reached the table, Johnny – his friend and ex-Panthers teammate – stood and went to give him a strong embrace.

They both sat down and the waitress came over to get their drink order. Johnny went with a scotch on the rocks and Ward chose club soda.

His buddy raised an eyebrow, his dark eyes curious. 'What's the occasion?'

'Just trying something new. Thanks for coming, man.'

'Hey, always there for you – just like you've always been there for me.'

Johnny's mom had passed away from cancer eighteen months ago when he was still with the team. It had hit him hard and he'd spiralled very quickly. The Panthers' owner had wanted to get rid of him, but Ward had stepped in and told the coach that he'd handle things and get his teammate back to where he needed to be. With the knowledge that if he didn't make that happen, they would probably both be gone from the team.

For five solid weeks, Ward had been Johnny's babysitter/best friend/confidante and all-around go-to person.

That infamous Times Square Forrest Gump thing with the wheelchair Bernie mentioned was one example of a related blowout, and some innocent badly needed fun for his buddy. But of course the media had to turn it into something sinister.

In the end, Johnny had duly pulled himself back to where he needed to be for one last season before retiring.

'So, how's the knee coming along?' Johnny asked now. 'Physio and pills doing the job?'

The question was asked matter-of-factly but the concern in his friend's eyes suggested he knew something was off.

'Well, I've been on the meds for a while and I think I've reached the point where I probably don't need them for the pain anymore,' Ward admitted, then sat forward a little, 'but I think that I might still need them. If you know what I mean.'

A brief nod. 'Yeah. I know. So, what's the game plan? Tell me what you need and I'm right there, dude. You thinking of going the rehab route?'

'Hell, no. If that got out, I'd probably get cut from the team for good. I was thinking of something a little more . . . discreet.'

'Gotcha. You want to handle it on your own but with some backup, am I right?'

They fell silent as the waitress brought their drinks; once they'd ordered food, Ward spoke again, 'Any ideas?'

Johnny sipped his drink, his brow furrowed and, after a moment, he slowly nodded.

'I know someone. Ex-nurse now working as a personal trainer and she's damned good. She can't get you pills or anything but can keep an eye on you physically, and if she feels you might be heading into trouble, make sure you handle it.'

'She can be trusted?'

Johnny laughed. 'Shelley's like a sister to me. We were neighbours back in the day, and if she still hasn't ratted me out for some of the shit I pulled growing up . . . trust me — you're in the right hands.'

Chapter 9

HANNAH

'**A**ny idea when your guy's going to get here? Or should I say, *if*.'

Hank, the animal shelter manager, wore a dubious expression as he ran a hand through the thick thatch of hair exploding from his head.

'I'm sure he's just running a little late,' Hannah apologized, feeling her face heat up as she and the accompanying photographer waited inside the foyer of Fur Parents.

She'd told McKenzie's agent what time he needed to be here and was assured he'd make it. But the guy was now over an hour late and she was getting anxious. Not to mention embarrassed. She'd set this up on behalf of the agency, and it made her look bad.

At that moment, she saw her errant client come into the building. The hockey player wore jeans and a t-shirt that were designed to look casual, but she suspected cost quite a bit of money, and showed off his athletic body to the best possible effect. Biceps in particular, *whew*.

Hannah swallowed hard. Quickly recollecting herself, she also noticed his pronounced limp as he shuffled towards them. Despite his protests in the bar, there seemed little sign of improvement with the knee injury given he was still on crutches. And she couldn't help but again feel guilty about that . . .

Lifting his sunglasses, he gave them both a brief nod.

'Sorry, I'm a little late.'

'You were due here an hour ago,' she pointed out.

'Right – that's why I just apologized. So, what's the game plan? Am I supposed to look at all the cute little doggies and kitties and make appropriate "awwwwww" sounds and all that baby-talk bullshit?'

The shelter guy shook his head and Hannah glared at Ward, her initial softness at his vulnerability very quickly disintegrating.

'Hey, I'm here now, right? So how about you just do whatever it is you need to do to make people think that I'm more than just some moron jock, yada yada.'

Hank shot a look at her that seemed to suggest, *Good luck with that*.

'OK, so here's what we've got planned,' she told him. 'As you say, the idea is to shoot a couple of photos with some of the animals. Since you don't do any of that "baby-talk bullshit", we're just going to go with some still photography. I'll distribute the shots to some key media outlets and work from there. How's that sound?'

'Like torture,' he grunted, rolling his eyes. 'Come on then, let's get it over with.'

The photographer kept trying to get Ward to make a reasonable attempt at showing some emotion as he held some kittens, but it was no use. The same sour expression persisted for the most part, and when Hannah tried to get him to lighten up a little by playing with them he dug in his heels even further.

'Just so we're on the same page, I hate this crap, OK? This isn't what I do. Sure, I like puppies and kittens, who wouldn't? But I'm not the kind of guy who spends time in an animal shelter being all cuddly with the inmates.'

Hannah rubbed the back of her neck. 'Just maybe give me something – *anything* – to work with here?'

But still, he behaved like an automaton. Exasperated, she suggested they give up on the cattery and head to the dog section, which she hoped might appeal more to his macho instincts, when she noticed him pause next to one of the cages.

'What's that?' Ward asked Hank, indicating an adult cat that had seen much better days. Missing much of its brown and orange body fur, one of its ears was matted with blood and a portion of its face had fluff growing back in patches.

'Stray we caught the other night. She's a real scrapper, that one. Took three of us to pin her down for a vaccination shot.'

While Hank was talking, Hannah watched with interest as Ward went over to stand in front of the cage. The cat's ears were flat against its head and a suspicious growl emanated from its throat.

He turned back to the shelter worker. 'What's going to happen to her? Is she going to be put up for adoption too?'

Hank shook his head. 'Nah. She's too wild for that.'

Ward looked at him. 'In other words, because it isn't all cute and cuddly like the others you're just going to put it down? That how it works?'

'I know it's not ideal but the shelter is at full capacity,' the rescue manager sighed. 'It's a shame but she's just not adoptable. And as you can see, there are lots of others out there who are, as long as we have the room to keep them.' He shrugged. 'That's just how it works. Law of the jungle.'

Chapter 10

'. . . And the next thing I know, he's lecturing the shelter manager on how wrong it was to let the animal be euthanised just because it wasn't going to play the part of a cute and cuddly pet.' Hannah was telling Zoe all about her latest encounter with Ward McKenzie. 'Hank couldn't get us out of there fast enough. I doubt I'll be bringing another Lotus client back anytime soon.'

Her friend chuckled. 'You've got to admit – the guy has a point. Don't think he was just talking about the cat though, if you know what I mean.'

'Oh, I know exactly what you mean. He's already implied that if I insist on trying to make him into something he's not I might as well put him to sleep, too.'

'And how did you reply to that?'

'I told him it was something I was seriously considering,' Hannah said archly. 'He just doesn't trust me, but maybe after what happened in the café who can blame him.'

She'd debated telling Zoe about her and McKenzie's embarrassing first meeting but figured it would better illustrate the additional layer of difficulty in having him as a client. And she also didn't want to risk her friend picking up on any of the . . . confusing reactions he invoked either.

Especially when Hannah didn't yet understand those herself.

'You need to consider where he's coming from. I'm sure he's

dealt with plenty of PR people in the past and you know how some of us are. The key to success often *is* to have people pretend to be something they're not. Give the public what they want.'

'I already told him I'm not that kind of publicist,' Hannah protested.

Zoe guffawed. 'Oh, that you're *different*? I'm sure he hasn't heard that before either. Just give it time. He'll come around. They all do.'

'I hope so. Though I'm beginning to wonder if McKenzie might truly well be a lost cause,' Hannah mumbled, keen to change the subject. 'On the other hand, at least I'm making progress with P-1.'

'Excuse me? Is that some kind of AI assistant Courtney has? Like the one in the *Iron Man* movies?'

Hannah laughed at the notion. 'No, the old guy next door I told you about? As I thought, seems he's shy about dealing with people in person and he wrote me a note – a nice one this time – to thank me for the Rice Krispie buns. Turns out his bark is worse than his bite. So yesterday I sent over another batch.'

There was a long pause until Zoe finally said, 'There are times when I really do worry about you.'

P-2,

Thanks for the second helping. I think these might have been even better than the first, which I would've thought was impossible.

You're right when you say that I prefer not to deal with people face-to-face. Better to avoid snap judgements. And I'll admit I might have been guilty of that myself already.

As we've already established, I can be a grumpy ole bastard. And I know that's supposed to be a bad thing but why is that? The way I see it, a grump is someone who speaks his mind and points out when something is stupid or someone's being an idiot.

Sure, I could keep my mouth shut, but what's the point of that? Maybe part of the problem with today's world is that people are afraid to tell it straight anymore, terrified to point out when the emperor's wearing no clothes.

Believe me, there are a lot of naked emperors parading around these days.

P-2

Chapter 11

WARD

'Goddamnit I'm coming. Just gimme a chance.'

The doorbell rang again and Ward hobbled across his living room to answer it. To find a gorgeous woman dressed in yoga clothes standing there. Tall, lean and athletic with dark hair in a long ponytail and olive skin, her huge brown eyes looked him up and down as she moved past and uttered, 'You look like hell.'

Well, she wasn't wrong about that. He'd only been off the pain meds for a few days and already found it impossible to think about anything else other than when he'd be able to take another.

'Excuse me? Mind telling me who the hell you are?'

'Shelley, the one Johnny sent.'

When Johnny had told him he was sending someone over to help him navigate what he was going through, his friend had been insistent that Ward committed to the process one hundred per cent.

'Anything less, and you're just going to be wasting everyone's time – and Shelley's a girl who doesn't like having her time wasted.'

But Johnny hadn't told him that the physical trainer looked like *this*. Easily five foot nine and with such a hot body, in any other situation, Ward would hit on her, only for the fact that she was there to help him and Johnny had warned him about any funny business.

To say nothing of the fact that she also looked like she could easily beat the shit out of him with one hand.

'Yeah,' he told her now. 'I feel like hell too.'

Shelley looked around his place, taking in the sparse furnishings, trophy display on the sideboard, plasma TV on the wall and closed curtains, and when she turned back to him, she said, 'Yeah, this is about what I figured.'

He scowled. 'What do you mean?'

'I got filled in on your backstory, so I already knew what I was going to find here. Turns out I was right.'

Ward felt himself start to get annoyed but he took a breath. 'What were you right about?'

'About how the reason you got yourself a problem is because you spent your whole life learning how to run from pain. Look at this place – it's comfortable and safe. Nothing to chance. That's why you went for the pills. They keep you comfortable and safe too, right?'

'You don't know the first thing about me, lady.'

Her eyes narrowed. 'My name is Shelley and that's how you'll address me. Anything other than that and you might as well watch me walk out that door.'

The two of them locked gazes until finally, Ward slowly nodded.

'I need your help so I'd rather you stayed.'

'Good. Johnny also told me you were smart. Looks like he was right about that too.'

Later that day, Ward crouched to his knees outside the open door.

'Hey, I get it, OK?' he coaxed softly. 'I know that you're scared right now. You're in a new place and you don't have the slightest idea what's going on. Well, I can tell you this much – you're safe here. You got yourself a new home. Just come out when you feel like it. No pressure.'

Moving slowly, he placed an open can of tuna on the ground and stepped backwards. A pair of watchful eyes flickered back and forth between him and the tuna, and then the cat hissed and he chuckled.

'Yeah, I hear ya. You don't know me, so why the hell should you trust me? I get it. If there's one thing I've learned in life, it's that there's no one out there you should trust, really. Everyone's out for themselves and that's pretty much the way it's always going to be.'

Ward thought about Hannah again, but for some reason, the image rehab thing didn't get him as riled up. At first, he'd resisted the idea of having a PR lackey handle him, especially this one.

But following the exchange about the ill-fated feline at the shelter that day, she had maybe gotten the point and stopped trying so hard to curate this fake image of him to sell to the public.

Or just given up probably.

Now, that same calico-patterned cat tentatively stuck her head out from the carrier and sniffed the air in his apartment. He pulled out a pouch of wet cat food from his pocket and opened it, setting it down near the tuna. She sniffed again and inched closer to the food but still seemed wary.

Ward continued to speak softly to her, reassuring her that she was safe. 'It's OK, girl, I've got you.'

After a few minutes more, the animal finally mustered up the courage to come out and cautiously approached the food. She ate hungrily, her eyes still darting back and forth between Ward and her meal.

Progress . . .

He smiled, relieved that she was now out of the carrier at least.

He sat down on the floor and watched her eat, still speaking softly to her. She seemed to be responding to his words and he thought that maybe she was starting to relax a bit.

While he waited, he decided he might as well grab a snack himself since between this and Shelley's appearance earlier, he hadn't had time to pick up food on his way to the shelter.

That day of the PR thing, once Hannah left, he'd gone back and asked the manager about adopting the stray. The guy, Hank, hadn't had a problem with it, but she'd needed more shots, a little more time to heal and her fur to grow back a bit before she could leave. So Ward had picked her up earlier.

'Seems like that old wives tale about calico being lucky is true,' the shelter manager commented, following up with a nature lesson about how the cat's tri-colour black, white and ginger colouring happened purely by chance. Ward didn't know anything about that; he'd just felt the need to help the wretched thing.

Now, he reached into his jacket and pulled out the leftover pretzel piece he'd had in the car on the way. Almost as soon as she spied the snack, the cat's eyes lit up. She immediately stopped eating the food and slowly inched closer to him, her tail twitching in anticipation.

'Seriously?' He laid down a piece and she immediately shot out a paw and whipped it back to her. Then began to demolish it, her eyes still glued to him in warning.

'Well, what do you know?' Ward laughed softly, amazed at how well the name suited, given her colouring. 'Pretzel it is then.'

Chapter 12

HANNAH

Hannah was trying out another 'foolproof' recipe and things weren't going well.

About as well as her supposed fresh start in NYC.

She had an incredible place to live in the most exciting city on earth but wished she could spend more time exploring it, or simply luxuriating in this gorgeous apartment, instead of spending time trying to figure out how she was ever going to prove herself to her new bosses and get away from the client list from hell. And try to sidestep the inevitable whispering amongst her new colleagues.

With regard to her clients, there was the narcissistic up-and-coming teenage singer-songwriter who made Veruca from *Charlie and the Chocolate Factory* seem positively angelic, an equally demanding girl-about-town who, having been cosseted by her adoring parents all her life, had illusions of becoming the next Kardashian, and, despite having never lifted a finger, expected Hannah to deliver her a readymade paparazzi following.

And then there was McKenzie.

If there was one thing that Hannah had learned from a young age, and which obviously helped as a PR strategist, it was how to read people. Usually, she was exceptionally good at it but now and then, she came across someone who wasn't quite so easy to figure out. Macho bluster aside, there was something about the guy that eluded her. While so far he'd been a royal pain in the ass, there was also a vulnerability to him that she couldn't ignore.

The fact that he was so easy on the eye and had such an unsettling effect on her was possibly clouding her judgement also, and that was the *last* thing she needed just now.

She'd caught another brief insight into what she suspected was his true nature at the animal shelter that day.

Clearly, Ward had seen something of himself in that ill-fated cat – something wild that didn't want to be confined, refused to be tamed. The problem was that Hannah didn't want to tame him anymore. That wasn't her job.

But to prove to her new bosses that her professional reputation was justified, she had to overhaul his car-crash image and rebrand him into a likeable, more accessible kind of athlete. And according to his agent, if she didn't do what she'd been hired to do, he was in danger of being cut from the Panthers permanently.

Since the stubborn tough guy side wouldn't let her in though, she needed to figure out another way to get a proper handle on him and . . .

Hannah's head snapped up when suddenly she heard a sound coming from somewhere inside the apartment.

She instinctively picked up a kitchen knife from Courtney's funky little knife holder, a stainless steel figure with knives sticking out of various body parts voodoo-style. Moving slowly to the doorway, she peeked into the living room before tiptoeing through, trying to better make out the direction of the noise. Which weirdly, sounded like people talking, followed by a dramatic burst of . . . was that music?

Hannah exhaled as all at once she realized what it was. The

sound was coming from the TV in Courtney's room. One that she had accidentally discovered when she'd first arrived was motion-activated. In fact, all media in the apartment was; a supposed benefit of the younger girl's state-of-the-art entertainment set-up.

She'd gotten a similar fright when, upon entering her assigned bedroom on the first night here, the TV had automatically flickered to life like it did in a high-end hotel.

To save her nerves, and following some help from Courtney's assistant Sara, she'd since deactivated the sensor in the rooms she was using. But since Hannah had no cause to access the influencer's bedroom unless expressly required, there'd been little need to do so in the primary suite. So what could have activated it now?

Tightening her hold on the knife again, she moved slowly through the living room in her stockinged feet, noting the front window ajar from when she'd opened it earlier upon her return from work to let in some fresh air. There wasn't enough of a gap for anyone to have slipped through the opening though, to say nothing of the idea that it would have been impossible for an intruder to scale the fifteen-floor building height in any case.

Unless Ed from next door had finally decided to pop over the terrace divider and introduce himself? Though 'terrace' was overstating it, the horizontal ledge beneath the windowsill was barely wide enough to hold a planter.

Thanks to Hannah's chocolate offerings, she and the old man seemed to have come to a sort of truce in the interim, exchanging notes with a little more frequency and even some camaraderie. She guessed he'd have softened up enough soon to the point that she could introduce herself in person, but for the moment was simply happy with no more complaints. But her neighbour coming through the window for a visit was highly unlikely given his age and mobility issues and anyway, why wouldn't he just knock on the door like a normal person?

Her head spinning with the various possibilities, most of which were too outlandish to truly consider, Hannah crept slowly toward the entrance to Courtney's room. Her breath hitched when from the doorway she spied a dark shape sprawled out on the bed . . . indolently licking itself.

'Where the hell did you come from?' she sang, a mixture of surprise and relief flooding through her.

The cat looked back at Hannah with pure disdain, evidently annoyed at being interrupted. Brown and orange patterned, it was old and scrawny enough to be mistaken for a stray, save for the thin red collar around its neck.

Clearly, it hadn't just wandered off the street and decided to scale the fifteen-floor height in through her open window. Though Hannah didn't know much about cats, so maybe anything was possible. Still, wherever it might have originated, she couldn't let the animal remain there on Courtney's pristine Egyptian cotton bedding. For one thing, its fur would shed all over the white comforter.

But who did it belong to?

There was no mention of any cat when they'd been making preliminary housesitting arrangements or indeed since, and now that she thought about it, wasn't this a pet-free building? Regardless, this kitty could not stay where it was, contentedly sprawled out on Courtney Wilde's bed.

Hannah approached, and the cat immediately stood, arched its back and hissed.

Great, she thought wryly. *Yet another hostile reception.*

These days, it was becoming a pattern.

Chapter 13

WARD

For a few moments, Ward was tempted to just ignore the buzzing phone but he knew his mother too well.

Irene would keep calling until he finally wore down and answered. By that time, she would have worked up a head of steam as to how he was always doing things to annoy her (which he wasn't) and provided her even more ammunition for whatever bee she happened to have in her bonnet.

'Hey, Mom,' Ward greeted and even he heard the stiffness in his voice. He took a deep breath and tried to lighten it. 'How are you?'

'I'm fine, thanks for asking. I just got off the phone with your Aunt Helen and she wanted me to say "hello", so here I am – saying "hello".'

'How's she doing?' he asked, trying not to let his hackles rise. He already had a feeling where this was going.

'Oh, she's the same as she always is. Kept going on and on about some guy she's falling for online, and I tried to tell her not to forget that it might be some scam that she's falling for, but she didn't want to hear that. She didn't want to listen. Why in the world is that? Why don't people ever want to listen anymore?'

For as long as he could remember, Irene McKenzie's problem

with the world was that she knew what was going on more than anyone else, but no one ever wanted to listen to her.

'You know people – they already have their minds made up about things and that's all there is to it.'

'It's like when I used to tell you that you needed to go to college and get yourself a business degree. I would tell you over and over and over again to get a business degree. Did you ever listen, though? No – no, you didn't. You just wanted to play stupid games all the time.'

'Mom, that "stupid game" I play got you a nice house and a very nice lifestyle,' Ward retorted, careful to keep his tone casual.

'Maybe,' Irene replied, 'but you can't keep doing it forever, can you? You've already been out for months. And what about when you're too old to play or worse, the Panthers dump you altogether? You'll wind up bagging groceries at Walmart.'

'Mom, with my investments, I'm confident I'm going to dodge that bullet.' He forced a chuckle, willing himself not to rise to the bait. But somehow his mother knew exactly how to hit him in his weak spot. And in all honesty, bagging groceries sounded like a fine old job to him.

'Guess who I ran into?' she asked then, completely ignoring what he'd just said. 'You'll never guess.'

'I'm sure it's someone who doesn't listen to you,' Ward muttered.

'Jerry Thornhill. You remember Jerry, he was in your class at high school. The two of you used to be so close. Then you just stopped hanging out with him – probably because you had your mind filled with ice hockey nonsense and—'

'So, how is Jerry, Mom?' he interjected, hoping to get the conversation over with as quickly as possible.

'He's fine. In fact, he's more than fine. Turns out that he's now

CEO of a major corporation and he's doing really well. *Really* well. He's married and he has two beautiful children. He showed me pictures of them. They're absolutely lovely.'

'Great, well, I'm very happy for Jerry. Thanks for the update,' Ward murmured, preparing to hang up.

Irene was not about to go down without a fight, though.

'So like I said, if you'd taken my advice and gotten a degree in business or something else worthwhile, you could be right where Jerry is now — with a beautiful wife, lovely children and a steady career.'

He'd had a shit day withdrawing from the pain meds and this was just about the last straw. 'Hey, Mom, here's a fun fact for you,' Ward replied, 'Jerry Thornhill — that guy that you admire so much — date-raped a girl our last year at high school, and Daddy's money kept it quiet. So, while I was playing my silly little game, good ole Jerry was out there ruining some poor girl's life.'

There was a long pause until finally in a quiet voice, his mother said, 'I'll give your best to Aunt Helen in return.'

An hour later, he was still fuming.

Nothing he did was ever good enough for her and the fact that he refused to follow the path she wanted for him kept the two of them at odds.

His father, whom Ward had never met, had walked out on Irene when she'd announced that she was pregnant, apparently. Forced to raise a child on her own — albeit with some financial assistance from her parents — his mother had made sure that her son never forgot that he was the reason she was alone in life.

Or that she reached for the bottle so much.

'If I hadn't gotten pregnant, my life would have been a whole lot different, but that's simply the way things are,' she'd told him a million times. 'Still, no use crying over spilt milk.'

Chapter 14

HANNAH

P-2,

Well, even if you never learn how to cook anything else, as long as you keep making these, I'd say that you've secured a spot in my bunker in the event of a zombie apocalypse. Glad too that you agree with my advice about speaking your mind. The real challenge, of course, is learning how to communicate without losing your composure.

Have you ever been in an argument or a debate with someone and you've just made a really good point and the person you're arguing with also realizes that it's a good point and they lose their temper? That sucks, doesn't it? The moment that happens, the argument or the debate shuts down – and that's never a good thing. It's healthy for people to have different ideas and experiences and not be afraid to share them.

Obviously, if you're dealing with a total idiot (and I've dealt with my fair share of them), there's no point in trying. Other than that, when you keep your composure, you'll find that you can have a worthwhile conversation and even learn something. Course, all that completely flies out the window when it comes to family members . . .

Smiling a little as she read Ed's latest note, Hannah listened to her client's phone ring out and was readying to leave yet another voicemail when she heard the voice pick up.

'Yeah?'

Nice.

'Ward? Hi, it's Hannah,' she greeted pleasantly. 'How are you?'

There was a pause and when he replied, it sounded as if she'd disturbed him.

'Been better, I guess. Please don't tell me that you've arranged another cheesy photo op because we both know that the last one didn't work out so well.'

'No, nothing like that. But I was thinking about what you said before, about trying to make you into something you're not. And you're right.'

'OK . . .' He seemed taken aback and more than a little wary.

'So I think it's important that you and I get to know one another better, maybe brainstorm a bit on what you're comfortable with sharing that might help turn your image around?'

There was a pause and when he spoke, this time there was an underlying tension in his voice.

'You know, that's kind of funny when you think about it. All this going around and talking about "my image". You know how that makes me feel? Like it's just an illusion, like it's not real. The problem is that everyone else thinks it's real – and after a while, it's easier to just go along with the image you've been assigned rather than being the person you really are.'

Taking a deep breath, Hannah held the handset away from her mouth, trying to keep her composure. *Surprisingly deep for a jock though.*

'Like I said, I'm not trying to project anything false. I just want to—'

He cut her off. 'What you want is to make it seem like I'm a better person than I am, so you can get paid. I get it. So when do you want to do the brainstorming thing?'

She wanted to protest further but decided it was just easier to move things along.

'I was thinking that if the timing works maybe I could pop over to your place later and get a better sense of—'

'The park,' he stated abruptly. 'Seventh Avenue entrance. This afternoon is good.'

'Well, I was actually hoping that maybe seeing you in a more relaxed environment at home—'

'I'm at home on the ice. And that's out of the question at the moment,' he added bitterly. 'Sorry, but I value my privacy and I don't like anyone in my personal space. What I do like is the park.'

Hannah exhaled. 'Fine. The park.'

Ward hung up and immediately felt bad. He knew he'd been a little rough on Hannah just now, and even though he was in serious pain and even more irritable after talking to his mother, that was no excuse. She was just doing her job in trying to make it seem like he was a decent human being.

The problem was that he *wasn't* a decent human being. If he was, he wouldn't always wind up alone, no matter how hard he tried.

One of his therapists (of which there had been too many) told him that he had avoidant attachment issues – which meant he wanted someone to share his life with but when he had had someone like that, he'd tended to push them away.

'OK, so if I want to share my life with someone and I find

someone that I can spend my life with, why would I push them away?'

'You push them away because it's what you're used to. Although it's painful to break away, it's even more painful to navigate a relationship where you haven't been abandoned.'

Ward wasn't so sure about that, but it was as good an explanation as any for why there was this huge, gaping hole in his life. Even as a kid growing up he'd always felt like an outsider, like he didn't quite fit. And as he got older, the world began to feel even more off-kilter – kinda like everyone else in the game was able to play it without thinking, yet nobody had given him the rules. The only place he'd ever felt truly at ease, all the parts working easily and in synch, was on the ice.

For the most part, people and how they behaved remained a mystery to him.

When Melanie had come along, he'd begun to think that his luck might be turning. The two of them had seemed like a great match – both able to focus on their respective careers and still have time for each other. If she'd given them a chance, he was certain he could have made things work. She hadn't given him a chance, though.

Maybe it was time to face some cold, hard facts, like his mother said. He was fine in the short term obviously, but if it went further than that, it seemed as if he was destined to be alone.

Too late, Ward realized that he shouldn't have answered the phone or started thinking about Melanie. He was already in physical pain and now he could add emotional pain to the mix – and that was dangerous.

He needed to take the edge off but he'd sworn to Johnny (and

Shelley) that he'd stay off the pain meds. There was no way he'd go back on a promise to his friend.

But while Ward had promised that drugs were off the table, there was nothing to say he couldn't fall back on a little something else.

Chapter 15

HANNAH

Hannah stood at Central Park's 7th Avenue entrance as arranged, and checked her watch. McKenzie was running late again. The guy was really beginning to test her patience. She shouldn't have to work with someone who didn't respect that her time was important.

She wandered into the park and sighed, deciding to take a load off while she waited. One of the reasons she hated client meet-ups in public spaces was that the blasted benches might as well have been designed by experts in medieval torture.

Five minutes sitting on one and she was almost ready to confess to being a witch. Then rearranged her vexed expression when she saw that her client had decided to grace her with his presence. She pasted on a relaxed smile as McKenzie ambled toward her.

No, wait, he was shuffling. Yikes, the injury really wasn't getting any better, she mused, biting her lip. As he drew closer, however, she saw that he was unshaven and his eyes were bloodshot. He sat down next to her – although 'sat' was too generous a way to phrase it. He all but collapsed and it was then that she caught a distinct whiff. Beer and something else too . . . was it *fish*?

Hannah wrinkled her nose, wondering why she'd been worrying about his initial appeal that first time in Frank's potentially clouding her judgement. Appearances truly could be deceptive.

'You're late,' she stated, despite not wanting to get things off to yet another bad start.

'Is it that I'm late – or you're early?' he asked, grinning stupidly as if he'd just made some kind of brilliant point in a courtroom.

'So how are you?' she asked, biting back her frustration that this meeting was surely another wasted effort on her part. 'Knee playing up again?'

He straightened up suddenly. 'I'm good. Had some more physical therapy earlier and it . . . uh . . . took a lot more out of me than I expected.'

'You sure you're up for this then?'

'Yeah. I'm just a little wrung out, that's all. Though maybe I should grab a coffee.'

'There's a truck just over there. You stay there and rest a bit and I'll get it,' she offered.

'Hey, don't do me any favours. I don't need anyone to baby me.'

'I'm not *looking* to baby you,' Hannah shot back sharply, despite her best intentions, Ed's words about not being afraid to speak her mind popping into her brain all of a sudden. Then she bit her lip. 'I was just trying to be considerate.'

'Yeah, well, if you were being considerate, you would have agreed to meet me in a bar again like the first time and listened when I told you that I wasn't interested in any damned makeover.'

'Oh, for feck's sake will you give it a rest? For the hundredth time, I'm *not* trying to make you over. Far from it. After that pointless day at the shelter, I'm just trying to get a better handle on what *you're* happy to share about yourself. Simple as that.' She took a deep breath, annoyed with herself. Losing control of her emotions like this was unlike her, but there truly was something about McKenzie that somehow always seemed to unnerve her.

He snorted. 'And what if someone doesn't want to share anything? What is it with people having to know everything about everyone these days? Speaking of which,' he added gruffly, 'I didn't realize you were Irish.'

Despite herself, Hannah smiled. So many years of living in the US had dispelled much of her accent, but it unfailingly resurfaced when she was riled.

She worked to get the conversation back on track. 'It's you that we're here to discuss. Like it or not Ward, you're a talented pro athlete in a successful team – and that puts you in the public eye. I know you manage to get *some* benefits out of being a celebrity,' she added, referring to his womanising reputation. 'But having a public profile comes with a price. So maybe level with me a bit.'

He didn't seem to be listening though. In fact, he was beginning to sweat and his pallor was now a worrying shade of grey. Yikes.

'OK. Just . . . stay there, and I'll grab us a coffee. And maybe some water?'

Looking as bad as he did, Hannah wasn't sure whether it was a good idea to leave him alone, but she knew he'd surely have something to say about it if she refused.

When she came back with the drinks, the two sat in silence for a moment drinking their beverages, until Ward spoke again.

'I never wanted to be famous, you know. I just liked playing ice hockey. No, I *loved* playing – and the more I loved it, the more time I spent doing it and the better I became.' He shook his head. 'Next thing I know, I'm having scouts approach me and one thing led to another. Before I knew it I was a "professional athlete" and everyone seemed to think that entitled them to a piece of me – either money or my autograph or my time, and yeah, even my goddamn body.' Hannah tried to ignore his pointed sidelong glance as if trying to unsettle her. 'It was like I wasn't even myself anymore. Just some kind of . . . commodity. And that's why I hate this crap. I'm not just a product, a cereal box that needs rebranding.'

'That's not why I'm here though,' she said, now resisting the urge to put a gentle hand on his shoulder. 'I genuinely want to help you. Your agent said you're on your last chance with the team and—'

He shook his head. 'That's only 'cos of my injury. Once I'm good, the top brass don't care what I do off the ice.' But Hannah could tell he was trying to convince himself more than her.

'Regardless, you want to consider income potential down the line too,' she encouraged. 'Endorsement deals, maybe some TV work. An athlete's playing life – no matter how good they are – has an expiry date; I'm sure you know that.'

'I'm into some stocks and real estate, I'll be OK.'

'Maybe, but why not kill two birds with one stone? Get back on the team, yes, but there's another game you can play just as well. You think you already know the rules, but honestly, there are lots of different ways to win at that too. I just need you to trust me and let me guide you through. Like a teammate, a wingman or whatever.' She laughed. 'Sorry, I'm not familiar with ice hockey.'

'You want to turn me into some new improved fake version of myself? Take some pictures of me at an orphanage this time – doing a "Make A Wish" tour or something?'

The mocking smirk was back on his face as he spoke, and again remembering Ed's words of wisdom about straight talking, this time Hannah set aside her restraint.

'Maybe I could set up a camera crew at an AA meeting instead. How does that sound?'

He stared at her, eyes wide with surprise at her tone or the words, she wasn't sure.

'I'm not an alcoholic,' he growled with a much sharper edge to his voice too. 'Yeah, right now, I've got some booze in me. So what? I'm having a rough morning – or afternoon. I'm not sure which it is if you want to know the truth. But having a beer doesn't make me an alcoholic. Being Irish, you of all people should know better than to make that kind of leap.'

He was right. Realizing that particular jibe had truly upset him, Hannah just as quickly backtracked, feeling all over the place herself now. How did this guy so effortlessly scramble her best intentions purely by proximity? 'I'm sorry. That was unprofessional and unacceptable and I shouldn't have said it. And yes, I've had enough fightin' Irish stereotypes thrown at me over the years,' she added, nodding softly. 'And people making assumptions. You're right, it's not fun.'

He stared at her for a few moments and there was something else in his gaze this time, as if they'd finally arrived at a kind of impasse. He wasn't lying; while he was definitely in pain physically there was more there too. Whatever it was, it again made something in her soften.

Bloody hell, Ward McKenzie truly was a conundrum.

His level of emotional intelligence was unexpected for a jock, and Hannah also got the sense that despite all the tough guy talk, he was lonely. Plus she still couldn't forget how charming he'd been on their first encounter, to the point that she'd been completely flustered.

But then she recalled all those articles and mentions of him boozing and scrapping and pap shots with women of varying ages and items of clothing. Didn't necessarily mean anything either she knew, though it bothered her that she kept thinking about it.

'Hey, success always comes with a price,' Hannah remarked gently, 'but no one believes it until it happens to them.'

He looked at her then and she saw a flicker in his eyes as he met her gaze. Uncertainty, coupled with hesitation about whether or not to trust her? Then he snorted and reached for his crutches to stand up, as if still in two minds whether to stay and listen or walk away.

But somehow he misjudged his footing and next thing Hannah knew he'd crashed to the ground, this time landing square on his face.

'Oh!' she cried out, rushing over, unable to believe what had just happened.

Again.

Before she could reach him though, he'd pushed himself back up, his face red with embarrassment and he held his hands out as if to forcibly keep her away.

'I'm fine!' he growled. 'Don't worry about me.'

With that, he stormed off, leaving Hannah to stand there wondering which version of this guy actually was the *real* Ward McKenzie.

And why she felt so inexplicably drawn to find out.

Chapter 16

WARD

Ward would have done a better job of indignantly leaving Hannah there, but he'd landed on his bad knee and the pain shooting through it had almost made him want to break down and cry. Not to mention the embarrassment. Good thing he'd managed to keep it in. The thought of showing weakness, especially around her, was too much.

He just couldn't *believe* that it had happened again. What was it about this girl that meant he kept falling flat on his face in front of her?

When he'd first shown up, it had only taken him a few seconds to realize that Hannah was . . . embarrassed for him. Pitied him, even. That led to him being embarrassed and when that happened, it somehow always turned into something else.

There was no denying there was something about her that made him feel as if he needed to be better. Ward already knew he didn't have it in him to be different, but when she was near him, he kinda wanted to be.

It was confusing as hell.

Leaving the park, he limped back toward home, his knee exploding in pain and decided that from now on, it was best to just forget all about this PR bullshit and focus on the kind of rehabilitation he knew best. He was staying off the meds and, thanks to Shelley, making better progress physically too.

He'd be back on the team once his busted knee was good, of that he had no doubt. Lighting lamps and leaving behind in a spin-o-rama all the damned confusing emotions Cannoli Girl seemed to evoke.

Chapter 17

HANNAH

That evening, Hannah was exhausted when she returned from a long day at the office and still reeling from yet another unproductive encounter with Ward bloody McKenzie.

All she wanted to do was pour herself a ginormous glass of wine and get into a nice hot bath. Unfortunately, when she reached the building, the super met her in the lobby, an unreadable expression on her face.

'I got a call complaining about noise in your apartment this afternoon,' Julie told her. 'Someone having a party?'

Hannah blinked, confused. 'What? There was no party. For one thing, I was at work all day . . .'

Julie shrugged. 'All I know is that Ed kept yelling about how entitled people are these days, that there are no manners left in the world and that if I didn't insist you keep the noise down he was going to call the police.'

'Seriously?' Hannah gasped. 'There's just no way that . . .' Then she broke off and slowly shook her head as the realization came to her.

Julie noticed. 'What is it?'

'The media system in the apartment is motion activated. It must have switched on while I was out.' She'd mistakenly left the window slightly ajar this morning and Hannah's new feline friend must have paid her another visit. Although 'friend' was stretching it. Not knowing the first thing about cats, she'd offered it some milk the other night and while it outright refused that, she fared better with some leftover pretzel, which weirdly it seemed to relish.

'But if you weren't there, how was it activated?'

Shite . . .

Too late Hannah realized that she couldn't very well tell Julie that a stray cat had been wandering around the penthouse in her absence. Not when it was a pet-free building and some of the residents were already gunning for the newbie occupant. She was treading on dangerous ground.

Hannah shrugged easily. 'It's super sensitive. Happened the other night when a breeze blew in through the window, even. Don't worry. I'll try and take care of it with Ed and explain. We've been getting to know one another a little better lately, and just when I thought I was getting somewhere . . . ' She grimaced.

'Maybe the nurse was there this afternoon or something,' Julie mused. 'She comes in a couple of times a week and that always puts him in a bad mood.'

Hannah looked surprised. 'I've never seen anyone go in or out of P-1. Or him for that matter.'

'It's got a private elevator.'

Of course. Made sense if he had a wheelchair. Luckily the building had street-level door access alongside the swirling pedestrian revolvers common in New York construction of the same era, and thus no need for dedicated street ramps outside.

'Really? Does Courtney's manager know?' she asked. 'Probably not – or he'd want one for her, too.'

'It was an old feature since when this place was first built. The original occupant was some Broadway actor who liked to shall we say, entertain young ladies, but didn't want the public to know about it – so he had a private elevator installed.'

'Wow. I can't even begin to imagine what it must be like to have that kind of money.'

'More than that,' Julie grunted, 'I can't even begin to imagine what kind of a creep needs a private elevator to hide women.'

On the way back up to Courtney's apartment, Hannah felt even more discomfited.

Now she was back at square one with the neighbour getting ornery and threatening to call the police. And just when she thought she was getting somewhere.

She knew she had to tread very carefully all the same. The very idea of the police showing up at Courtney Wilde's building would have tabloids and gossip websites salivating. Which would not look good for her superstar client's brand, or indeed the ongoing lawsuit. Like Hannah tried to tell Ward earlier, that was how *this* game was played.

So where the neighbours were concerned she needed to try harder than ever to keep the peace.

For Courtney's sake if nothing else.

Chapter 18

Dear Ed,
Sorry about the noise earlier, but I can assure you I wasn't having a party or anything. It was just the media system and, honestly, you won't believe this, but . . .

Hannah was about to explain all about Courtney's snazzy automated system when her phone rang and she saw it was Ward McKenzie's agent.

Great. What now?

She set down the notepad. Ed's apology would have to wait.

'Hello, Bernie. What can I do for you?' she greeted pleasantly.

'Well, for starters, you can tell me why my client wound up on five different tabloid sites this evening claiming he was stoned off his ass in Central Park in broad daylight?'

Hannah's initial reaction was confusion – until she remembered Ward's fall in the park earlier. Some clout-chasing passerby must have had their phone out.

Shite . . .

'I was there actually, and that's not how it happened. We were having a meeting and he tripped over something on the path. That's all. He wasn't stoned.'

There was a long pause.

'Was he drunk?'

OK, that was putting Hannah in a spot. She could tell the agent the truth and not get in trouble – but it would probably get Ward in trouble. Still, since technically Bernie was the agency's client and she was only working with the athlete on his behalf, it was also her responsibility to tell him what was going on.

Out of loyalty to both, she decided to skirt the issue.

'I'm sure it was just the knee playing up. We were outside and I wasn't close enough to smell his breath or anything . . .'

Her gut told her Bernie didn't believe her – but she hoped that he at least trusted she was doing the right thing for his client.

'Look, I'm going to be honest with you, Hannah. Ward . . . well, let's just say he's a challenging . . . client.'

Understatement of the century . . .

'He's got a reputation for being difficult and irresponsible, but I'll stand right in front of you and tell you that's not who he is. He's one of the good guys but he does his best to hide it from people.'

Exactly as she'd thought.

'Why would he do that though?' Hannah asked, hoping for a better insight into the ongoing puzzle that was the athlete. 'Why *wouldn't* he want people to know that he's truly a good guy, as opposed to the asshole reputation he has?'

It was a few moments before Bernie answered.

'I guess one of the first things you learn in sport is that weakness gets taken advantage of – and he's always tried to make sure nobody thought he was a pushover. And that crossed over into life.'

Common for athletes to take lessons they learned on the field into real life, Hannah knew. But that wasn't the way the world worked and the most successful ones – the true greats – knew that.

How could she persuade Ward that learning to trust her might well be the key to winning *this* game?

Chapter 19

WARD

'You're doing good,' Shelley assured when Ward had finished another round of sit-ups. 'Really good.'

She released his ankles and he gave her a nod, wiping off his sweaty face and neck with the towel lying on the floor beside him.

'Thanks,' he said, meaning it.

'Wow. That might be the nicest tone you've ever used on me. What's the occasion?'

He got to his feet, wincing a little as he stood. He'd drunk about a gallon of water after leaving the park earlier but, hurt pride aside, was feeling a hell of a lot better after his latest embarrassing encounter with Hannah.

Though crappy about the way he'd handled it. But for some reason he turned into the worst version of himself when around her. And that was not a good sign, because Ward knew it meant that deep down he really did give a shit about what she thought of him. So straight into self-destruct mode he went.

Now, chastened by some long overdue self-reflection, he looked at Shelley. 'I just wanted to let you know how much I appreciate what you're doing for me. I know there are times over the last couple of weeks when you probably wanted to just walk away, but I'm glad you didn't.'

She shrugged. 'Johnny said that you were worth it. I'll admit I wasn't sure at first, but I've changed my mind.'

'What else did Johnny tell you about me?'

'He said that you had your heart stepped on right before you got injured and that you were probably in a fragile place – and that you'd hate being in that place and that would make you into a mean and ornery jerk but that wasn't who you were. And that if you felt threatened, you'd probably try to hit on me and I had his permission to kick you in the nuts if you did.' She chuckled and then glanced at the litter tray. 'But when a so-called big tough guy like you brought home Pretzel, it told me everything I needed to know.'

Despite Shelley's dubious assessment of him overall, Ward had to smile.

The rescue had settled in even better than expected, even though he didn't even know where she was right now. Hank had told him that since she was a stray, in order to settle in to his place she would also need the opportunity to roam outside to fully establish her new territory. She wandered off a lot – where to he had no idea – and just came back when she felt like it, or mostly when she wanted to be fed. Pretzel lived by her own rules and that was fine by him.

His phone chimed then, and when he flipped it open, he saw it was a text from a Panthers teammate with an accompanying link.

Hey man. You OK?

Frowning, he looked at Shelley. 'Can I borrow your phone? Something I need to check online.'

He didn't know what was going on, but he had a bad feeling. Had he been fired from the team and nobody'd told him yet, maybe?

93

'Of course.' She handed the device to him.

Forwarding the message to her number, Ward duly clicked on the link to find an unflattering image of himself on some online gossip site. Beneath the headline '*McKenzie Back In His Favourite Position*' was a still of him splayed head-first on the ground in the park earlier.

'Goddamit . . .'

'Everything OK?' Shelley asked, concerned.

'No. No, it's not,' he growled, deleting the message and handing her back the phone. 'Hey look, you can see yourself out, right?' Ward stormed past her and into the bedroom. 'I need to make a call.'

Hannah answered on the second ring.

'I was just about to—'

'You're supposed to be working on rehabilitating my reputation? Well, I'm not the brightest guy in the world but I've got a feeling that pictures of me flat out on the ground like some wasted loser might not be quite the image we're going for here.'

'Before you say another word, your agent already called about this. I could have told him the truth but I didn't think that would serve you well, so I sort of fudged as to whether you had been drinking. The fact that those photos are out there has nothing to do with *my* job, Ward. But maybe everything to do with the fact that you showed up drunk in the park.'

She had a valid point, he knew, so inhaling a deep lungful of air just like Shelley taught him, he forced himself to take a few mental steps back. Trying again not to be an ass to someone he liked.

'Yeah, OK – I'll admit that I probably shouldn't have had that second shot before I left, but I was in kind of a bad place and . . .'

'Seems to me like you're always in a bad place, Ward,' Hannah interjected in a tone that brooked no nonsense. 'And you don't need to be.'

'What do you mean?'

'One of the reasons I prefer to take client meetings in private is for the very thing that just happened. It's New York, for feck's sake; there's always someone around to see something you don't want them to see. That's also why I asked to have our conversations somewhere other than a bar.'

'OK, so maybe next time we could maybe meet at your place or . . . '

'I'm staying at a friend's,' she said quickly, while Ward tried to ignore why he wasn't outright resistant to the idea of another meeting with her. 'Why not set up something at *your* secret lair?'

He let out a surprised laugh. 'Secret lair? Now you're making me sound like a Marvel supervillain.'

'Well, actually you're wrong because Marvel doesn't have any supervillains. DC's the one with the supervillains. Marvel's got the best heroes but DC's got the best villains.'

He raised an eyebrow. 'Don't tell me you're a comic book nerd too . . . '

'I am, as it happens – and thanks a million for calling them "comic books",' she said in a distinct Irish accent this time, and the smile in her voice made him smile too. 'I hate when people say graphic novels like they're trying to make them sound more . . . edgy or something. Pretentious. If you're embarrassed to be a comic book nerd, then get away from around me.'

'You might be the first woman I've ever met who took such an impressive stance on comic books . . . ' he chuckled. 'And hey, I'm sorry for earlier, I shouldn't have taken off like that. And for how I spoke to you, I was out of line and . . . I get that you're just trying to help, it's just . . . ' Ward reddened. He really was out of practice at this nice-guy stuff.

'No apology needed. I understand. But maybe you need to understand that I've no time for people who portray themselves as something they're not. So now that we're being honest, Ward McKenzie,' Hannah challenged, laying down the biscuit, 'deep down, which one are you: graphic novel, or comic book?'

Chapter 20

Hannah's parting words rang in Ward's ears long after the call ended. He never lacked for words – on or off the ice; he was the epitome of a chirper. Except for right then.

Graphic novel or comic book.

Was she right? Had he purposely created this overly macho, alpha-goon persona? When he'd first turned pro, his coach had drilled in the notion that the slightest show of weakness at face-off meant that your opponent already had you even before the puck hit the ice.

It was a lesson he'd taken to heart and had pretty much lived by ever since.

But as Hannah pointed out, the real-world game was played by different rules. Was he making things harder than they needed to be? Worse yet, his mind hesitated before it drifted down a different avenue, was he playing the hero or villain in his own story?

He picked up his Nokia again and studied the device. Another way of trying too hard to be above the fray with the choices he made? Going against the grain by rote. Or was he just a wannabe bad boy in possession of a stubborn streak and chip on his shoulder – a pathetic duster people secretly rolled their eyes at and laughed at the moment he left the room. He shuddered at the notion. That *definitely* wasn't how he wanted to be seen – and the very possibility of it being a reality made his stomach roil with embarrassment.

At that moment, he heard the soft patter of furry feet and a faint *meow* before the cat landed on the armrest of the couch following a stealthy jump. Pretzel eyed him inquisitively, a knowing look on her face. As if she understood the conflict waging inside his head. And he was pretty sure he saw the damn cat roll her eyes.

'I see you judging me. Not cool, after all I've done for you.'

The feline turned away, tail straight in the air, clearly showing Ward what her thoughts were on the matter.

'At least you're honest.'

His head slumped back on the headrest and returned to his thoughts.

OK, maybe he could stop resisting so much and just go along with this for the moment. See what Hannah suggested next. He didn't have to like it, but it truly did feel like she was being sincere in wanting to help him. If playing along meant that he could get back in Panthers' management good books and back on the ice, life should go back to normal, right?

Because that's all Ward truly wanted. To continue playing the sport he loved for as long as he could. That was always his priority. So if he felt confused about who he was as a person now, the waters became a whole lot murkier if he had to contemplate who the hell he would be if he wasn't a hockey player.

He also had to admit that the idea of working with Hannah felt a hell of a lot better than actively working against her, like he'd done with other PR people in the past and which he was ashamed to admit, with her thus far too. She did seem genuine, like she actually cared.

And when she looked at Ward it was right in the eye, not somewhere beyond his shoulder like other people did when he didn't immediately live up to expectations. Could he actually trust her? Was *this* a shot worth taking?

Ward exhaled and suddenly coming to a decision, he picked up the phone again and flipped it open.

Pinging out a quick text message to Bernie, he kept it brief.

OK, I'll do as she says from now on. Doesn't mean I'm gonna like it though.

He pressed send and then waited for his agent to respond.

A minute passed, then two, then four. No response. The churning stomach roiled again and he belched a little, tasting the alcohol from earlier.

He knew Bernie was pissed at him for yet another public mess-up. And he needed his agent to be on-side. Besides Johnny, who had no sway with the suits, Bernie was the only true advocate outside of the team he had left. The last thing Ward needed now was for Bernie (or worse, Coach Lewis too) to also start seeing him as a liability and concede to Hannah that there was no fixing him and she shouldn't bother.

Especially when he'd finally decided to play nice.

He felt the cat stir again and approach on his left-hand side. She crawled right up onto his chest and took a seat like a monarch getting comfortable on her throne. Ward met her gaze, the cat's amber-flecked eyes boring into his as if he were the biggest idiot on the planet.

'Yeah? What do you want?'

She tilted her head as if confused by his apparent stupidity, then chirruped and extended a paw, swatting him across the chest.

He barked a laugh. 'So, I'm gonna be told what to do on all

fronts now, huh?' He edged her off his chest and pulled himself up. 'OK. I get it. You're hungry. Let's get you fed. Great, now I'm taking orders from a cat, too.'

Ward climbed off the couch and Pretzel followed in his wake, pleased that he was smart enough to take a hint and jump in line.

Chapter 21

HANNAH

Hannah couldn't help but feel vindicated. Like she'd just made a strategic gambit (she had no idea of the hockey equivalent) and now Ward McKenzie was scrambling to figure out a way to rethink the defensive play he'd been relying on so far.

'About time,' she muttered satisfactorily, turning her attention back to the apology note she'd been writing to her neighbour. She was confident that she'd hear from the athlete again soon and that this time her errant client would approach her with his tail firmly between his legs.

Seems there was indeed no substitute for straight-talking.

Picking up her pen, Hannah reviewed what she had started to write.

> Dear Ed,
> Sorry about the noise earlier, but I can assure you I wasn't having a party or anything.

Nah, she thought then. Better not to address him by his first name. Too familiar and potentially inflammatory. He'd only ever referred to her as P-2 . . . evidently considering her just a number as opposed to an actual person, so she'd play by the same rules. And she shouldn't apologize off the bat either for something she wasn't guilty of. It was one thing being diplomatic, but she wasn't going to kowtow to him either.

Tearing up the note she'd already begun, she started over.

Dear P-1,

About the noise earlier, I can assure you I wasn't having a party or anything like that. It was just the media system and maybe you won't believe this, but the apartment has a motion-activated system and I'm still trying to get a handle on it. I think there might be a glitch or something, because it's been coming on erratically in rooms I don't even go into.

She thought about the stray cat on Courtney's bed that time and once again decided not to mention that little tidbit. Since the building was pet-free, the cranky old guy would not look kindly upon the presence of her feline friend. Nor keep it a secret from the building super or fellow residents, especially if they could use it as further ammunition in their complaint.

Unless the cat happened to be Ed's?

Unlikely if he was such a stickler for the rules though. Yet in her experience, many people – often rich ones from a certain generation – tended to believe that rules applied to everyone else but themselves. Hannah bit the end of the pen, trying to decide whether to mention an animal's potential role in the ruckus. Nah, probably safer to wait until she knew the guy a little better.

Assuming that ever happened.

Since I was working all day and only just got home, I'm guessing that a spider, dust bunny or something small – a flying insect maybe – could've set off the motion sensors and switched on the TV or music system. Again, I can assure you that there was no raging party and I'm the only one here. Unless this place has a ghost I don't know about . . .

A little humour always went a long way. But now to butter him up a little.

I completely appreciate that peace and quiet is important to you and all the residents in this building – it is to me too. I am a great fan of keeping things on an even keel. A huge part of my job is about doing exactly that, ensuring smooth sailing at all times, with no feathers ruffled. A sense of equilibrium is paramount.

All that being said, I hope that you can accept my explanation. Today has been quite the day for me – as I am sure it has also been for you – so maybe let's chalk this down to the fact that technology sometimes has a mind of its own. And you can rest assured that nothing nefarious was going on in P-2 today and you won't hear a peep from me going forward.

P-2

PS I'm now off on the hunt for swinging spiders and dancing daddy-long-legs or whatnot.

Hannah folded up the note and headed to the door, opening it as quietly as she could, then tip-toed into the hallway and slipped the piece of paper under Ed's door, determined to keep good on her promise about being silent.

It wasn't until she was back inside Courtney's with the door firmly shut behind her that she allowed herself to exhale.

What a day . . .

Chapter 22

Hannah awoke the next morning feeling refreshed and renewed after a good night's sleep. Her thoughts drifted to yesterday and she threw her legs over the side of the bed, determined to make this day a better one.

Padding barefoot into the kitchen, she flipped on Courtney's thankfully-electric designer kettle (she hated those stovetop whistling ones), reached into a cabinet for a mug, took out the treasured box of Barry's teabags she always kept in stock and waited patiently for the water to boil.

Then out of the corner of her eye, she spied a piece of paper beneath the door and raised an eyebrow.

'Must be a night owl . . .' she muttered as she picked up the note, crossing her fingers that next door had accepted her explanation and things were back on more cordial ground. The electric kettle flicked off, indicating the water was ready.

But first, tea.

Sitting at the kitchen island with a steaming cuppa in front of her, Hannah unfolded the note and smoothed the paper on the makeshift countertop surface.

Motion-activated sound system? Is it really so hard to just flip a goddamn switch? Is your generation seriously that busy and important, or lazy, that using even a remote control is too much trouble these days? What type of idiot wants to have TVs and stuff blaring when they walk into a room? When did silence become something everyone tries to avoid? Who knew we would be living in such a stupid time in history.

All right, I accept your apology. Not cutting off my nose to spite my face here – I wouldn't want to stop the Rice Krispie train.

Hannah couldn't help but laugh. Apology? She'd gone out of her way *not* to apologize. This guy really was an out-and-out contrarian and reminded her *so* much of her granddad. A former Irish army man who brooked no nonsense and, now that she thought about it, was probably the one who'd primed her expertise in dealing with . . . difficult personalities. Tucking into her breakfast of oatmeal and blueberries, she pushed the note to the side and turned her attention to her phone, the screen listing a slew of incoming alerts; one of them a message from none other than Ward McKenzie.

Aha.

She was curious to know if he had spent the previous evening stewing over her insinuation that he was vapid and fake, or if he had come to his senses and realized he might indeed have a conundrum on his hands – one she could play a key role in solving if he would only play nice.

Yeah, I'm a comic book. But I take your point that I've been parading around as a graphic novel for a while, OK?

Then a follow-up message: You pick a place this time and I'll be there.

Hannah smiled. Quietly confident that the hockey player would come around, she'd spent some time last night reading up on the game and its fun but mystifying lingo, readying herself for checkmate.

Or as Ward would surely say, *slap shot*.

Chapter 23

WARD

A week or so later, Hannah looked around McKenzie's place in Lower Manhattan with some surprise. She wasn't sure what she'd been anticipating, but it hadn't been a cramped one-bed furnished with stuff that looked like it came from the local Goodwill.

'Not what you expected, I take it?' he asked.

She shook her head. 'I came here expecting to see some shiny interior-designed bachelor pad aimed at proving that you were a man of taste and means. Instead, I just see what looks like any other ordinary city shoebox.'

'Spoils the narrative already?' he teased, unable to keep some of the sarcasm out of his voice. 'Relax, this is my old place, the only apartment I could afford when I first moved here and signed for the Panthers. I've got a couple of other rentals in the city too. Believe it or not, I'm pretty decent at real estate investment.'

He hardly ever came back here though – it was more of a crash pad for whenever he was out with Johnny, or somewhere for his mom to stay the few times she'd come to visit. There were some good memories here – but there were some bad ones, too.

In this space, he reverted to the hopeful rookie he was – before success came along and everything changed so fast it was as if he was caught up in a dream.

The place was minimally decorated but comfortably furnished with chairs, a couch and a basic bedroom set that was simple and functional. Once upon a time, that was the kind of person Ward was too; simple and functional.

Things changed, though. People changed. He had definitely changed. There were times when he'd find himself looking in the mirror and wondering who in the hell the stranger looking back at him was. He wished things could be simple again – that he could be the guy he'd once been (minus the money problems obviously). That wasn't how the world worked, though. No rewinding life back to where you'd been happiest. All you could do was look to the future and hope some was waiting for you there, too.

Today Hannah's hair was pulled back in a ponytail and she had on a sunshine-yellow blouse and jeans. Her white trainers were the kind anyone could buy in their local Walmart but for some reason, on her, they looked expensive. She had a way, he realized, of bringing out the best in everything around her.

Today he'd even arrived early for their meeting. It hadn't been on purpose, though he couldn't help but feel it was a better look than what he had offered her before – showing up late or drunk. He had even taken the time to shave.

While he was still having some trouble with his gait, at least he looked fresher and had benefited from a sober night's sleep, determined to lay off the booze for a bit too.

Ward told himself he was doing all this to impress Hannah professionally, but looking at her now, sitting all cute and comfortable amid his stuff like she belonged there, his mind wandered to what it might be like to share life with a girl like her.

But just as quickly stopped himself. Now *that* was dangerous play.

She chuckled. 'Actually the more I think about it, I see how I can make this work. I asked you to show me a side of yourself you'd be happy to share with the world, and that's what this place is. You could have showcased some macho bachelor crib more fitting to a pro player, but that's not what you did. Instead, you chose to meet me somewhere from your past – a place representing a time when life was simpler.'

He continued to be surprised at how goddamn perceptive she could be too.

Had he deliberately picked this place to meet, one that downplayed the image the world had of him? Had he gone out of his way to highlight, not to the stupid public but to *her* – that he was, deep down, just an ordinary guy?

She took out her phone and set it down on the small coffee table between them. Ward could see onscreen some app designed to mimic an old-style pocket-tape recorder, and his stomach instinctively tightened. 'What's that?'

'I'm just going to ask you a few questions and all I want is for you to answer them honestly. I know you're afraid of letting down your guard, Ward, but I promise you that I'm not going to do anything to jeopardise your career or your privacy.'

His jaw tightened. 'I'm not afraid of anything.'

She seemed to be stifling a smile. 'Sorry, yes, reluctant is the word I meant to use.'

Suddenly he wanted to get the hell out of there. He'd told himself this was just another interview with just another person from the PR world. Granted, this particular person wasn't like most of the others, but he was familiar enough with this stuff to understand the rules at least, if not the game itself.

He could handle this. He *was* a professional.

He guessed now he should feel lucky to have this chance – to be here, able to sit with someone like Hannah, who, it seemed, really did want to help him salvage his career.

Thanks to her straight-talking, he'd been forced to acknowledge that in an alternative reality, he could be some working stiff who had to punch in and out of an office every day chasing a brass ring, and answering to an endless array of middle managers about one meaningless report after another while they timed his lunch breaks. Just like his mom always wanted.

Instead, he was living his dream. Not someone else's. He didn't have to fit inside a nameless, faceless box that some corporate overlord dictated. Though to be fair, Panthers owner Craig Sumners pretty much fit that bill. Still, Ward's office was the rink. His job description required a set of skates, a helmet, a couple of smelly gloves and a badass exterior. He was even allowed to start fights at work. But lately, he had been stupid enough to think that he was invincible.

Hannah's brutal assessment of him had brought him to his senses. He knew he had to be extremely careful around her though, because he'd already seen she was the kind of person who managed to get people to let their guard down.

He didn't want to let his guard down. Especially not with her.

All you need to do is stay focused and watch what you say. And chill. She's not some kind of witch. She's just a publicist who happens to be very good at her job. And most important of all, she wants to help.

'Let's start with something easy,' Hannah began, and again there was something about her that made him feel as if they were the only two people in the world and he could tell her anything. He swallowed hard.

Focus, man. Focus. 'Shoot.'

'Were you always athletic? When you were in high school, were you team captain, stuff like that?'

He took a deep breath and shook his head. 'When I was in high school, I was about as *un*athletic as a guy could be. I was skinny and awkward and I got bullied more often than I care to remember. My freshman and sophomore years were nightmares too. Then over the summer before my junior year, something happened. I think that all the hormones that were supposed to kick in earlier finally had their moment, and the next thing I knew, I was starting to fill out. That gave me the confidence to try out for a couple of things. I didn't make the football team or the baseball team, but I landed on the ice with the hockey guys – and that's when I fell in love with the game.'

He looked at Hannah and was surprised to see her frowning.

'What's wrong?' he asked, anxiety instantly flaring.

'It's just that – well, I didn't expect to find out that you were bullied. I had you pegged as one of those popular jock types who had a golden time in high school. Homecoming King and all that.'

Ward snorted. 'Nope, high school was a mess – even when I started doing well in sports. I had zero confidence and always felt like an outsider.' He found himself trying to figure out just what it was about Hannah that made him open up like this, travel down side paths he normally stayed away from. He'd always managed to stay away from publicly discussing his high school days. Too many unpleasant memories to be found there.

She was dangerous, actually.

Everything he'd built could so easily fall apart if Ward wasn't careful. He'd spent years studying; watching and learning what kind of person he needed to become to get to where he was and with just a couple of missteps, it could all come crashing down.

That couldn't happen. He needed to ensure that mask stayed on good and tight.

Because now, people looked up to him. Women wanted to be with him, men wanted to be him – and neither would if they could truly see the real him.

Behind it, he was a fraud – a phoney. All that bravado, all that swagger that he'd perfected over the years . . . at the end of the day, when the cameras were gone, Ward was home all by himself, wishing he could find someplace off the field he belonged – or a way to look at his reflection in the mirror one day and not hate what he saw.

Chapter 24

HANNAH

'Dare I ask what crisis you're dealing with now?' Zoe answered by way of greeting after the call rang only once.

Hannah laughed into the device as she ambled down Sixth. 'For the first time in forever, I think I'm ahead of a crisis, shockingly enough.'

Today had gone far better than she'd expected. She'd hoped to have McKenzie open up a little, but he'd gone even further. When he'd started to talk about his high school days, and then the tough, domineering coach that shaped his early playing years, there had been an openness and vulnerability to him that she'd suspected was there all along but he was so far reluctant to reveal.

She thrived on people opening themselves up to her, and letting down their guard. She understood that it was a gift they were offering and made certain never to abuse the privilege either. When Ward had talked about those early years, she'd seen in his eyes that vulnerable, immature kid he used to be.

Which made her want to uncover so much more. She needed to take her time though, and be doubly careful to ensure she didn't scare him away. But weirdly, the more she got to know this guy — the real one — the more of a conundrum he seemed to be.

'So it seems like I have a client who is finally willing to work with me and a neighbour who doesn't want to set me on fire,' Hannah said, having filled in her friend on recent events. 'All in all, a win, yes?'

'Which is usually when the other shoe drops, no?'

She stopped in her tracks, ready to argue the point and, in doing so, caused a powerwalking, smartphone-wielding stockbroker to collide with her, practically knocking her over. 'Feck, sorry,' she gasped, which earned her an insolent glare.

'Goddamn phone-zombie tourist . . .' the man barked, before unironically returning his attention to his own device and picking up the pace.

'You OK?' Zoe queried.

'Yes, I'm just starting to remember where I am. I forgot how rushed everyone is here.'

Her friend clucked on the other end of the line. 'Regretting the decision to relocate, are we?'

Hannah let out an involuntary shiver, her thoughts briefly transporting her back to LA and the reasons for her escape. 'Nope. I just have to remember that people are less . . . zen in these parts.' She started walking again, trying her best not to dawdle lest she cause a proverbial pile-up on the sidewalk. 'So,' she continued, 'about the other shoe dropping . . . oh, you of little faith, but I'm thinking positive. I honestly feel like I've turned a corner. Things are looking up.'

'What's the strategy then?'

Hannah heard the smile in Zoe's voice, and she suddenly missed her friend, badly. She wished they could go to a bar and have a brainstorming session over a bottle of wine like they used to after a long day's work.

'As far as the hockey player goes, I need to get the thinking cap back on now that he's feeling agreeable to working with me instead of against me. And I need to make sure I get results, so he *remains* agreeable.'

Easier said than done though. The joys of choosing a career managing people.

With that, Hannah turned her thoughts to her neighbour.

'And as far as Ed in P-1 goes . . . well, I just need to not rock the boat. He'll be in my rear-view mirror once Courtney's back in six weeks anyway. Until then, I just need him to *not* call the cops because he believes I'm breathing too loud.'

Zoe sighed heavily on the other end of the line. 'Crotchety old grump. I mean, how does a guy like that even *live* in New York if they don't want people around them? Seriously, go move out into the country, buy a house in the woods and become a proper hermit like the Unabomber.'

Hannah laughed. 'Let's hope he's nothing like the Unabomber, or even my Rice Krispie buns won't save me.'

'So,' Zoe continued, changing the subject, 'it's Friday night. What's the plan? Any hot dates on the horizon?'

Hannah snorted. 'Ha. I have more than enough on my plate at the moment.' But Zoe made a good point. It was the weekend and she didn't know her colleagues at the New York office well enough yet to socialise with them, plus she was still hesitant about making connections until she could be more confident about what they did or didn't know about the reason for her transfer.

The idea of returning to the apartment and tiptoeing around in case of upsetting her neighbour didn't appeal either. Nor did eating alone again. As wonderful as Courtney's place was, Hannah figured that maybe this week she had at least earned the right not to burn or obliterate another ready meal.

'Actually, I think I'm going to take myself out,' she decided on the spot. 'Have a glass of wine, some nice food and do a bit of brainstorming.'

'Heard anything from Rob?' her friend enquired then, her tone changing. 'You'd tell me, wouldn't you?'

'Not a dickie bird,' Hannah muttered truthfully, still a little unsure how to feel about it.

'I'm *really* hoping that's one of your weird Irish expressions meaning no, otherwise I might just have to fly over to talk some sense into you in person.'

'Ha. No need for straight-talking on my part. I'm way over all that, honestly.'

Hannah hoped her friend couldn't tell that she was spinning a tale.

Now all she needed to do was believe her own narrative.

Having treated herself to a meal and a couple of glasses of wine at a French bistro at 63rd and Park, Hannah returned to the apartment still feeling a little lonely and out of sorts. She waved to Bruno the doorman as she headed through the lobby and tapped her foot as she rode the elevator up to her floor.

Upon exiting, she paused in the hallway listening for any sign of activity in P-1, briefly considering knocking on the door to see if Ed would answer. Given their recent impasse, it felt like the time might be right to introduce herself directly and put a face to the name. And she also wanted to see if reality aligned with the picture she had painted of him in her head. Raising a tentative hand, she then backed down at the last minute. After all, she had promised him peace and quiet so knocking on his door out of nowhere on a Friday night would surely set back the progress she had made.

So instead, Hannah continued down the hallway and opened the door to P-2, shutting it gently behind her. She listened for a second. The apartment was deathly quiet. No errant technology on the fritz or roaming animals, which made her sigh in relief.

But also served to highlight her current solitude, especially in such a big and buzzy city. It was still early days with regards to making friends at work, plus in truth she kind of welcomed the peace and quiet after such a tumultuous year. But if she didn't start putting herself out there more, she ran the risk of ending up much like her neighbour.

Which definitely seemed like a depressing prospect.

Going into the kitchen, she opened the Sub-Zero fridge and grabbed a bottle of Pellegrino before extracting a glass from one of the kitchen cabinets.

She wondered how Ed had become the way he was – ornery, angry at the world, presumptively stuck in the past. He seemed to be homebound and, from what she could glean so far, only seemed to have his nurse as a visitor, which amid a city like this seemed so bleak. If she were in his position, Hannah figured she would welcome the chance to talk to other people and to feel like there was still a world outside those walls. Heck, she felt like that right now.

Well, they said the opposite of depression was connection, so since she and Ed were both pretty much lonely in New York at the moment, maybe their little faceless to-and-fro was the perfect way to offer one another a lifeline.

Hello P-1,
I appreciate your understanding of the situation. Nothing seems to be going haywire with the tech over here since, so maybe the situation has solved itself.

Which also applied to my working week as it turns out. A stumbling block I was facing with a difficult man who was a bit of a tough nut to crack is beginning to sort itself out too. He needs my help but is very much . . . let's just say, stuck in his ways. So I took myself out to a nice dinner tonight hoping to get some thoughts flowing, but I'm afraid that didn't happen. All was not lost, though, as I had a divine mushroom risotto and a to-die-for chocolate soufflé. (And just in case you think I'm the type of person who takes pictures of their food to post online, I can assure you that I do not. I'm far too interested in eating!)

But being new to the area, I'm not sure where else is good around here. Maybe as a local, you could provide recommendations? No pressure, I don't know if that's your thing or not. Admittedly, I'm not much of a foodie, and outside of the no-bake I sent over, not much of a cook either.

Hannah wanted to sound breezy and chatty and perhaps appeal to his empathetic side by mentioning her lonely dinner and that she had a few struggles of her own. Nothing compared to his of course but . . . She tapped her fingers on the makeshift countertop, unsure of what to say next and, with that very motion, remembered something.

Tomorrow was Saturday, the day the marble installers were due. Probably a good idea to give him a heads-up about that in case of any noise or ruckus in getting the materials up here or having the countertop fixed in place. Considering he was already so averse to construction noise.

Which leads me to the reason for my note. There's a small work crew coming tomorrow so there might be a little noise. Nothing major, just a couple of guys to install a new countertop.

Rest assured, I'll be here to supervise and ensure things go as smoothly (and quietly!) as possible. I've been told it will only be a couple of hours at the most. And you'll be especially relieved to know this is the very last of the upgrades. No more construction work.

She signed off by telling Ed that his understanding throughout the entire remodelling process was deeply appreciated and that she'd go out of her way to ensure he wasn't disturbed any further.

Hannah grimaced and folded over the note.

Fingers crossed.

Chapter 25

WARD

Ward woke up feeling grumpy. He couldn't quite explain it, but his recent optimism had suddenly disintegrated into thin air. It was eight o'clock on a Saturday morning and already he could hear hustle and bustle everywhere. It seemed as if everyone else in the city had started their weekend with gusto and were up enjoying the bright spring sunshine.

A knock at his door sounded and he grimaced, annoyed that he needed to start his with another training session. His knee seemed to throb in response and the storm cloud over his head grew larger. The last thing he wanted to do was be subjected to Shelley's borderline physical abuse. Yet another no-nonsense female unwilling to deal with his shit.

As if Pretzel wasn't bad enough.

Exhaling, he went to open the door and Shelley breezed in with barely a hello.

'Man, it's a madhouse out there today,' she commented as she threw a duffel bag containing workout gear on the couch.

'In this town what else is new?'

Ward settled down on a yoga mat, and she began her usual machinations on him with a variety of stretches. He did his best to push on through the pain but it wasn't easy today and it showed on his face.

'This hurting?' she asked, digging an elbow into his glute.

'No,' he growled. 'Everything is wonderful.'

She eased off ever so slightly but continued with consistent pressure as if recognising that he still needed to be the tough guy.

'So,' she asked then, evidently trying to distract him from the discomfort, 'Johnny tells me you're working with a publicist now?'

This earned her another growl. 'Yeah, what's it to you?'

Shelley flung her ponytail over her shoulder as she transferred her elbow to Ward's right glute and dug in. He was tense all over. 'I'm just . . . surprised to tell you the truth. You don't strike me as the PR-hungry type.'

'I'm not. But I'm being forced to work with this pain-in-the-ass girl. Story of my life.'

Recognizing the not-so-subtle dig, Shelley rolled her eyes, pushed his body to the ground and grabbed his left knee, stretching it high in front of him.

'Well, whoever she is I'm sure she's great at her job, but no one's a miracle worker. Did you know that I work with a lot of pro athletes and none of them whine as much as you do?' She pushed his leg harder, lengthening his hamstring.

'She knows what she's dealing with. I told her straight-up that I wasn't going along with any lame-ass bullshit, so she's coming back with a strategy, something I can work with.'

Shelley nodded as she released his leg and began stretching the other.

'Like I have a strategy personalised to your needs. I guess her job and mine are not so different. I'm trying to help you improve physically and she – what's her name?'

'Hannah.'

'Hannah is trying to improve you reputationally. Both of us

treating two very different sides of WildCat Ward McKenzie.' She grinned. 'If you ask me, she has the tougher job, *way* tougher.'

'Ha. Very funny.'

'Well, a little advice for what it's worth: just let the girl do her job, trust her judgement and don't expect instant gratification either. Results take time. You didn't get to the level you're at professionally overnight, did you?'

'No,' he agreed, thinking about his relatively slow and steady career trajectory, and praying that all the hard-earned gains he'd made over the years weren't now in the rear-view mirror.

'Don't expect any public messes you've made to disappear overnight either. It took time to build up that macho bad-boy image of yours, so it's going to take some work to rehabilitate. Just like what we're doing with your body right now.'

Case in point, Ward groaned as she moved on to his hip flexors.

'Yeah, but even with your help, I still have some control over this. I feel like I don't have any over that PR bullshit.'

'True, but that's also probably the way it needs to be. You got yourself into this mess – someone else has to get you out of it, but the main thing is you have to be *willing* to put in the work too, Ward. Just like you're doing with me. Show this girl some mercy and meet her halfway. Make an effort to prove to her, Hannah, that you have an open mind – and for Chrissakes, don't look for instant miracles either. Rome wasn't built in a day. We're all only human.' When he rolled his eyes in response, Shelley laughed. 'Even you.'

Chapter 26

HANNAH

Hannah got out of bed early in preparation for the marble installers to arrive.

Given his history with this stuff, she sorely hoped next door wasn't upset by the news that there would be more work happening again today, and uttered a silent prayer that all would go OK and that the job would indeed be a one-day thing as promised. And most importantly, any noise and disruption would be kept to a minimum. Keeping the neighbour happy was quite the tightrope but she was more than willing to use all the interpersonal skills at her disposal to keep the peace and ensure her cushy living situation wasn't put at risk. Tools of the trade and all that.

She switched her phone back off silent mode and flicked through her message notifications while toasting a bagel and sipping a mug of tea.

Then turning her attention back to the matter in hand, she brought up Courtney's original welcome note, of which she'd taken a snapshot on her phone for reference.

'Calacatta marble . . .' she mumbled out loud, typing the words into the online search bar, and bringing up relevant image results so she was able to verify that the right stuff arrived.

Nice.

Nodding approvingly at the cream-coloured ivory stone threaded with distinctive silver veins and flecks of gold, she glanced up at the space around her. It was what she would choose too, given the opportunity. Courtney truly did have great taste. Her curiosity piqued, Hannah then opened up another browser window to check the price.

'Yikes,' she gulped, eyes widening at the results. 'Seems I'm more of a Formica girl . . .'

As if on cue, a loud knock sounded on the front door and she jumped off the stool, hurrying to answer. Seems the marble guys were early. Well, with any luck maybe that meant that they would also finish early and the remainder of this beautiful spring day would be her own.

'Installation for Wilde?' a workman in a pair of jeans and a t-shirt emblazoned with a company logo greeted her upon opening the door.

'Sure, hi. I'm Hannah, the house-sitter.'

The man shrugged as if he could care less about who she was or why she was there. 'Whatever. Got some papers to sign first.' He shoved a clipboard at her and took a pen from behind his right ear, offering it to her.

Hannah cautiously took both items and bit her lip. 'OK, but I need to verify that it's correct first. Before I sign anything, I mean.' Courtney had stressed that the stone pieces needed to be bookmarked, which from what Hannah could tell, basically meant that the markings of each piece were a perfect mirror image of each other. 'Those are my instructions – from the owner,' she said, trying to sound authoritative against the worker's gruff demeanour.

He huffed, clearly annoyed, shifting his weight from one foot to the other, then swept his arm behind him to the empty hallway.

'You think I'm gonna drag a tonne of stone all the way up here just to drag it all back down if it's the wrong stuff?'

Hannah grimaced. His voice was echoing down the hallway. The renovation work hadn't even begun yet and already there was a racket!

'Well,' she said diplomatically, lowering her voice in the hope he'd take the hint, 'I suppose it would be a bigger problem if you installed something that wasn't quite what your customer ordered and then had to reinstall everything to make it right?' she countered, trying to keep a neutral face. 'That sounds like a very expensive mistake — not that I know much about marble installation. You're the expert.'

The guy sighed heavily; he knew she was right. Verify first, or potentially double the work. 'All right. All right. But you get where I'm comin' from, yes?'

'Of course, I do. And I'm just following orders. I need to check first before I sign for it. That's all.'

In response, the worker rolled his eyes. 'Lady, I've been doing this a long time—'

'How about this?' she cut him off amiably. 'I'll come down to the loading bay or wherever your truck is parked, and take a quick look. I'm sure it's the right stuff; I'm not questioning the quality or workmanship. I simply want to do my due diligence, just as I'm sure you always want to do a good job for your clients, yes?'

'Yeah, yeah, whatever. OK. Follow me,' he said as he started to stomp off, his footfalls landing hard on the hallway floor, all the while steadfastly refusing to use his indoor voice. Assuming he had one. 'Just so you know though, the cargo area of this place ain't as fancy as the parts you people use.'

You people. 'Like I said, I'm just the house-sitter.' Since he believed that she was one of the building's well-heeled residents, Hannah hoped that this explanation might help level the playing field a little.

She dutifully followed behind, getting into the service elevator at the other end of the hallway and riding it down and out back to the building's loading area, whereupon he led her to a large truck with the same company logo emblazoned on its side. Upon instruction, another member of the work crew duly removed a covering to reveal the marble underneath. Hannah turned her phone's flashlight on, looked at the work order on the clipboard and then glanced at the picture she'd screenshot earlier, comparing it to what she was seeing now.

All checked out and the stone looked even better in real life, richer in texture and tone, and so unbelievably soft and luxurious to the touch.

Confirming as much to the foreman, she thanked him again for allowing her to confirm and that all was good to go. She signed the delivery docket, then got out of the truck, took the elevator back up to the penthouse floor, and propped the door of P-2 fully open to allow the team access in and out.

And as she did, Hannah spied another note on the ground. Her heart fled to her throat, hoping that it wasn't another complaint from Ed prompted by the loud-mouthed foreman at the door just now.

Good to hear that the building work is finally over. I personally don't believe in upgrades if everything works just fine as it is. But that's me.

Hannah smiled, exhaling in relief that the message was cordial. Even if he couldn't resist adding in one of his typically ornery remarks.

While the marble guys did their thing, she took her laptop into the bedroom, taking the opportunity to catch up on email and other work stuff while she waited and, more pertinently, attempt to make a start on a more coherent strategy for Ward McKenzie's grand transformation.

But nothing especially interesting or original jumped out, other than testing the waters with a run-of-the-mill puff piece based on what little information she'd gleaned from their last meeting.

Much to Hannah's relief, the installation finished without fuss, and having said goodbye to the crew, she snapped a picture of the finished job and quickly sent it off to Sara, certain that she and her boss would be keen to see how it all turned out.

The end result was indeed dreamy. The luxurious countertop stretched all the way down to the floor on both sides, which the foreman described as a waterfall finish, adding an extra layer of finesse to the already breathtaking kitchen upgrade. Hannah decided that if she ever won the lottery and bought a place of her own, she'd upgrade the *entire house* with this stuff.

As the photo swished off, heading into the ether and its intended destination, a brainwave hit; her train of thought echoing and perhaps even prompted by Ed's written words from earlier.

I personally don't believe in upgrades if everything works just fine as it is . . .

Inspiration striking fast and hard, she took out her phone and quickly hammered off another missive, this time to a different recipient.

Possible to meet today? I have an idea.

Chapter 27

WARD

Ward sauntered down Fifth Avenue to the address Hannah had provided, and when he spotted the store she was standing in front of, his expression immediately became guarded.

'*This* is your big idea?' he asked, defensively shoving his hands in his jeans pocket.

'You said you were on board. Time to prove it.' She offered him a winning smile and held out her hand. 'The first step in our great Ward McKenzie upgrade. Hand it over.'

He groaned. 'How did I know you were going to say that . . . ?' He pulled the Nokia out of his pocket. 'This thing and I go way back, you know.'

Barking a laugh, she took the device from him. 'I'm honestly surprised it still works. It even *looks* like a hockey puck.' She shook her head. 'At some point, the service will just stop, so let's pull the plaster off and get this over with. Come on.'

She turned on her heel and opened the glass door of the famed flagship Apple store.

Ward sighed and took a few slow steps forward, a slight smile playing across his lips. 'I'm assuming I don't have a choice . . . '

'Not even a little one. Time to stop the dinosaur act – if you still want a career, that is.'

Inside, an Apple Genius had already spotted the flip phone and zeroed in on his mark, knowing a sale and a new monthly subscription were easy pickings.

Ward threw her a rueful glance over his shoulder, though she noticed that, despite himself, his eyes flickered with intrigue as he turned the latest phone model over in his hands, considering its sleek design.

'Your fans are going to love this,' she told him. 'Finally, we can get you a direct line to them so you get to control the narrative.'

Or more to the point, I do.

'I don't see why I can't just use one of my team shots. Isn't that the point? People know me as a pro player, right?' Ward complained when, afterwards, he and Hannah grabbed some food in a quiet, non-descript diner a few blocks away.

But today, his remonstrations didn't sound so much whiny but rather playful, and this more relaxed version of him was the one she recognized from that first day in Frank's.

The very one that had made her completely tongue-tied.

She'd commandeered his shiny new phone and was currently in the process of setting up social media channels, adding a profile pic and whatnot. Her fingers worked expertly as she focused her attention on the screen. Having snapped a few candid pictures of him in situ at the restaurant, she was now editing accordingly.

'That's where you're wrong. Everyone sees you *only* as a hockey player. It's the only way they know you – and I think we can both agree that image isn't altogether positive. What we want them to see is the human side of you. The guy beneath the hockey uniform.' Then Hannah winced a little, wishing the words she'd chosen didn't sound quite so . . . suggestive.

But luckily he didn't seem to notice her embarrassment.

'I hate that social media crap, everyone screaming for attention like a bunch of performing seals. Look at my house, my vacation, my kids, my stupid dog . . . Who the hell cares?'

'It's not the same. You're a public figure, yet from what I can tell you've never even attempted to connect with your fans. Think of all those kids growing up dreaming of being you, idolising you, grown men and women too,' and as she briefly met his gaze, Hannah realized he was watching her face, as if studying her reaction. 'For some reason,' she added archly, 'regardless, you're a hero to lots of people.'

Then just as quickly, the mask was back. 'That shit is for narcissists. I don't need anyone blowing smoke up my ass.'

So Hannah changed tack. 'Look, what we're trying to dismantle is this negative, toxic macho image of you that's been perpetuated so far. Nobody thinks to question whether it's true because there's never been a counterpoint. Which basically means that you've never had any say in how people perceive you, Ward. You've left it all to other people, the media or whatever, so they're always the ones in control. Not you. Which surprises me, to be honest, because if there's one thing I've learned about you it's that you prefer to do things on your own terms.'

He seemed to think about this for a second, and when he nodded gruffly, she figured her words had landed. Selecting a shot she liked and making it his profile picture, she then handed him back the device. 'So take back control.'

'OK, but what do I even do with this thing?' He held the phone like it was a ticking time bomb. 'All sounds straightforward in theory but what the hell do I say?'

'Just whatever you're comfortable with but keep it on brand.

I've watched some of your post-game interviews, you're good at that and your passion for the game shines through. So talk about sports, comment on other games, players or whatever. But in a *nice* way, which goes without saying, I hope.'

He grinned. 'No trash talk. OK, I can be nice when I need to.'

'You sure about that?' Hannah laughed. 'But if you're ever uncertain, probably easier to think about what you *don't* say. Definitely no wading into commentary on politics or culture wars, no matter how tempted you might be. Think of that stuff like the kids' table at a party otherwise filled with adults. You don't want to be whining and squabbling in the corner with a bunch of toddlers, trying to solve an argument with rational thinking. Nope, just stay sitting at the grown-ups' table, OK?'

She'd also learned that Ward seemed to appreciate analogies far better than non-specific generalities.

'No whining either – got it. So should I uh, say something now?'

'No time like the present.' Hannah looked up and glanced around. 'I like this place. It would be fun to tag it. John Doe . . . not for long maybe. Here, let me get you started.'

She grabbed the device and as she went to take it, his fingers briefly brushed her skin and an unmistakable shiver flashed through her. Just the new device still warming up? Or something else?

Reluctant to meet Ward's gaze for fear that he'd felt it too (or hadn't), Hannah swallowed, and her hands quickly went back to work, crafting Ward's first-ever social media 'post' with all applicable hashtags.

'Seriously? I have to let people know about everywhere I go

now too? I'm just a hockey player, Hannah. No one's gonna care about where I'm eating. And just so you know, no *way* am I taking pictures of my goddamn burger. I mean what's even the point of that?'

Biting back a grin, she tsked and dropped his phone back on the table, afraid to risk any more tactile contact before picking up hers, intending to loop in some celebrity bloggers and sports reporter connections on the news that famously introverted (or more to the point antiquated) Ward McKenzie was now on socials.

Let the fun begin.

'You're wrong in that regard too. I mean, no, of course, you don't need to take pictures of your food. But a big part of curating and improving your personal brand is by lifting up others,' she countered. 'It's a shame you didn't grab your handle years ago, though. Kim Kardashian doesn't need to put a number after hers.'

Ward snorted. 'The very *last* person I want to emulate.'

'What? You have a problem with being a billionaire adored by millions?' she chuckled. 'David Beckham then?' He rolled his eyes and Hannah warmed even more to her theme. 'OK, maybe Travis Kelce more your style . . . actually, we could even try to set you up with a pop princess . . . '

He shot her one of his famed daggers looks and she burst out laughing. 'Nope, lunch I can give you, but my personal life is off-limits.'

His voice was light yet she knew he wasn't kidding. 'Regardless, once we get you verified, everyone will know it's you.'

'Verified,' he repeated eyerolling. 'As if some blue tick suddenly makes me a worthy person. Do intelligent grown-ups honestly buy into this crap?'

'Absolutely!' Hannah laid the phone back down on the table between them and he stared at the shiny device as if already itching to pick it back up.

'Holy Hell,' he muttered. 'Talk about the kids' table, I can't believe I've joined a bunch of babies reliant on a tech soother.' She didn't reply – her gaze fixed on reply notifications already coming in on her own phone and Ward snickered. 'Case in point. You know, I'm actually insulted now. So much for my ladykiller charm . . .' Before she could respond, his device duly lit up and dinged with multiple notifications. 'What the . . . ?'

Reaching out, she snagged it off the table. 'Whoops, sorry about that. Let me just . . .' She tapped on the screen and nodded, then passed the phone back to him. 'All good. Just switched off your screen alerts. That gets old very fast.'

Brow furrowed, he again looked down. 'What the hell just happened, Hannah? How do I already have . . . five hundred followers . . . six . . . eight . . . it just keeps growing. You set this thing up like two seconds ago. Who are these idiots?'

Hannah guffawed. He truly was a different breed. 'They're not idiots, they're *interested* – lucky for you. Analogue news alert, Ward – this is my job.' She chuckled. 'ESPN just tagged you. So did the Bleacher Report. And any moment now, TMZ is about to pass comment on your choice of lunch venue . . .'

As if to illustrate what she'd just said, the guy who'd seated them at their table on arrival called out from behind the counter.

'Hey, man, thanks for the shout-out! This is gonna be *great* for business.' He was holding up his own phone, now displaying Ward's very first social media post; a shot of him in the same spot he was sitting in right now.

Hannah's eyes twinkled. 'Congratulations, Ward. *Now* you're famous. But with great power comes great responsibility,' she warned. 'Remember what I told you, and for your sake and mine, I'm begging you, please do *not* mess this up.'

Chapter 28

WARD

Ward needed to unwind. He'd been spending way too much time in his head lately, and if there was one lesson he'd learned in therapy, it was that the worst thing in the world for him was having to deal with all the clutter in his head.

His muscles ached and he knew it was because he'd been weaning himself off the painkillers. The smart thing for him would have been to go to a professional to deal with his problem, but both he and Johnny had decided if word got out that he had an inkling of a drug problem too, his career would be over for sure.

Do not mess this up . . .

Shelley was doing a great job with him though. She pushed him when it was called for and backed off when she sensed he needed some room.

'You're lucky you were smart enough to know you couldn't handle this on your own,' she'd told him. 'Some people think they have things under control, and before they know it, they're on the edge of falling through the cracks and ruining their lives. You had enough sense to know you needed help – and then showed you were *really* smart by coming to me.'

One of the other things she'd taught Ward was when he was feeling caged in, he needed to get out and get some fresh air.

'Take a walk. The worst thing you can do is stay home and spend time with your thoughts. That's when people are at their weakest. That's when things start to go wrong for them.'

So now, Ward found himself wandering along the city streets past midnight. It was a clear evening and there seemed to be even more stars out than usual. He moved at a solid pace, just wanting to burn off that restless energy, needing to be out in the open.

After about ten minutes though, he realized he had no idea where he was. Although he hadn't taken any turns and had simply gone straight ahead, now he was in a part of the city he wasn't so familiar with. The buildings around him were empty and trashed, and there were all kinds of shadows moving in the alleys and narrow spaces between structures.

He turned around to head back home but when he looked, the sidewalk was gone – replaced by a dirt path into some woods. His heart pounded.

What the hell was happening to him? Had he already done damage to himself with the pain pills? Was his grasp on reality slipping?

He started to run, then. No destination in mind. All he knew was he needed to keep going, needed to break free from whatever was invading his mind.

He was terrified.

He ran along the sidewalk ahead of him but that suddenly twisted down an alley and when he tried to stop, he couldn't. His feet propelled him ahead and he shot all the way down, slamming into total darkness.

'You're a failure,' came a voice – cold, dark, relentless. 'You're nothing. Your new *fans* will soon find out that you're weak and insignificant. You'll never be one of the great ones – and that means you'll soon be forgotten. It'll be as if you'd never existed.'

Something grabbed him, then. Something cold and filled with a hatred so powerful that Ward cried out in terror – before snapping awake in bed.

Nightmares were common when weaning from painkillers, Shelley had told him. The brain did all kinds of weird stuff.

'Sometimes the dreams are so bad that people would rather take the drugs instead of dealing with whatever boogeymen their minds conjure up. You got to be on your guard all the time, Ward – because you might find yourself backsliding without even knowing it's happening.'

He got out of bed, went into the bathroom and flicked on the light, staring at his reflection in the mirror for a moment. Then he splashed cold water on his face and towelled off, trying to gather his wits about him.

As he climbed back into bed, he thought again about what the voice had said and a wave of fear went through him.

They'll soon find out that you're weak and insignificant. You'll never be one of the greats . . .

Ward burrowed beneath the covers, wishing he wasn't so certain the voice was speaking the truth.

After he'd woken from the nightmare, he hadn't been able to get back to sleep. He'd tried to distract himself by watching a middle-of-the-night marathon rerun session of *Murder She Wrote* on the TV situated above his bed, but even J.B. Fletcher's sharp-witted shenanigans hadn't been enough to distract him from the memory of the dream.

You'll never be one of the greats . . .

It was true, of course – Ward McKenzie would never be known as a truly great hockey player. He was a solid centre and a battler, for sure, but he'd always wanted to be more. In truth, his entire life was spent in pursuit of being better – more athletic, more popular, having more girlfriends. From his first week of college, all the way through his professional career, he'd made a point of trying to do what he thought people expected him to do. *Be better.*

Being regarded as a womaniser was something he used to take pride in because it gave him kudos. Of course, the girls he got with knew how to play the game too. They weren't looking for anything serious – they were just in it for the fun and the clout of bagging a pro athlete. At one time, that was enough for Ward, too.

Now getting up, he groaned and reached for his phone to check the time. Pawing around for a bit and not finding the small flip device his hands were so accustomed to, he suddenly remembered the shiny new thing. And groaned again, realizing that his newfound influx of followers and associated attention must have been the trigger for the dream. Great. As if his ego wasn't frail enough, now it was already falling into the validation-from-strangers trap too.

Or worse, performance anxiety stemming from his growing ease with Hannah?

Be better.

'Shit.' He had overslept, according to the phone it was almost ten – the exact time Shelley was scheduled for another training session.

Ward sat upright in bed and pulled on a t-shirt at the same moment he felt Pretzel brush against his leg. He shot her a dirty look. 'And I suppose you want to be fed now, too? You could have at least woken me up.'

He quickly changed clothes and shuffled from his bedroom to the front door, the cat following in his wake.

'Hold on, hold on, just a sec,' he called before undoing the lock and throwing open the door. Sure enough, he found Shelley on the other side, tapping her foot impatiently.

'Up late scrolling?' she greeted, a sardonic smirk planted on her face.

Ward sighed and turned away from her, heading toward the kitchen.

'I'd like to pretend I don't know what you're talking about,' he retorted. 'But to answer your question, no, I was not doing that. And I don't intend to any time soon.'

'We'll see. An occasional jump down the rabbit hole can be relaxing as hell,' she shrugged, nonplussed. 'Anyway, congrats for going live on socials. Big move for you.' She smiled. 'That picture in the restaurant you posted. It was good.'

'I don't get how you even know this stuff. And I didn't post anything,' Ward said, going into his pantry to get Pretzel her breakfast. 'That was Hannah.'

His thoughts drifted to the weekend and as much as he wanted to throw some snarky comment out at Shelley about the whole situation, he realized he couldn't. The fact was, he'd had fun on Saturday – Hannah had a knack of making everything more appealing and, despite the pitfalls, he had to admit he was impressed by how fast his newfound digital fame had grown. Course, he would never admit that out loud – not to anyone.

Shelley duly finished setting up the mat and some other equipment on the floor of his living room. 'I threw you a follow too, just so you know.'

'So did, like, ten thousand other people it seems,' he replied. 'Social media is peak stupid. I seriously don't know why anyone cares about what I have to say.'

The trainer rolled her eyes. 'You don't have to love it or spend your life on it. Just use it to your advantage.'

'So should I follow you back or something?'

'Your call. But since you're now a blue ticker, you probably should maintain some level of exclusivity. You know, follow your teammates, coaches, other players, the team's account and all that. Ward McKenzie's not going to interact with just any Joe Blow.'

He made a face and handed Shelley his phone. 'I'm also not an elitist jerk. Pull up your profile or handle or whatever the hell your corner of that crazy world is.'

She did and handed the device back to him.

'Nice picture,' he complimented, studying her profile and hitting the follow button. Then he frowned. 'You have a kid?'

'Yep, five years old. What, I don't seem the maternal type to you?'

He looked flustered. 'Sorry, I didn't mean anything by it. I was just surprised, that's all, Johnny didn't say.'

'Why would he? But for the record, Zeke is why I do this stuff for guys like you. My baby's my world.'

'Sounds like you're a great mom.'

God knows his own mother had never uttered those words about him, and somehow this added information gave him a whole new level of respect for Shelley. There was no guy in any of the photos so he could only assume she was a single mom.

He didn't want to let her down. In much the same way he didn't want to let Hannah down now either.

Ward shook his head and handed Shelley back the phone. Who the heck was this shiny touchy-feely version of himself all these new females in his life were turning him into?

'Wow. So I'm Instagram official with WildCat McKenzie,' she

teased, throwing her dark ponytail playfully over one shoulder. 'Though you really should take the time to make some more relevant connections too – like I said, with teammates and fellow professionals. Don't think people won't analyze who you're following and why. Especially women. And judging by the number of message alerts you have, I'm willing to bet some puck bunnies have already slid into your DMs.'

Ward scoffed, then realizing she was being serious, looked back at the phone, clicking on the message icon.

'Seriously?' He briefly started scrolling and his eyes widened. 'This is nuts. I don't even know what to do with this. Why would girls put themselves out there like that to a total stranger – and before you say anything, I *am* a total stranger to these women. No matter how much they think they know me because they saw me on the ice.' He quickly glanced at a photo of a blonde bombshell. 'Although,' he mumbled, flashing her a mischievous grin, 'maybe this thing's not so bad after all.'

'Well, I'm no PR expert, but I can guarantee Hannah is *not* going to like it if you start responding to those messages – or even looking at the photos. They can tell if you've opened it, you know. Don't go getting too click-happy.'

Ward grimaced and dropped the phone like it was a ticking time bomb. This was a whole new world for him and he still didn't know how to feel about it. 'OK. Will you just delete them for me or whatever without clicking on them? Or show me how to do it? When we're done training.'

They both got down on the floor to start their session.

'So have you decided what you're going to post about?' Shelley asked conversationally. 'Some cat pics maybe?' She was relishing having fun at his expense.

'I am *not* posting about Pretzel.' He glanced over to where she was now greedily gulping down her breakfast.

'People love cat content though,' she continued as he started a set of crunches. 'Or actually, maybe sharing your training progress would be good? We could shoot something right now. I'll stay off-camera and record some footage while you stretch and whatever. People would love to see that your head is back in the game. And that you're working hard to get better – get back on the ice. Panthers fans especially.'

And maybe management too.

Grunting a final crunch, he considered her suggestion. It wasn't anything he hadn't done on camera before. And yeah, it would be good for his employers and teammates at least to know that he truly was taking all of this rehabilitation stuff, physical and otherwise, seriously.

'I like it. Sounds "on brand", as Hannah might say,' Ward said with a wink, figuring she would surely approve.

Chapter 29

HANNAH

'How did you do it?' Zoe demanded.

Her head still fuzzy after yet another crazy day at the office, Hannah's brow furrowed and she shook her head. 'Do what?'

'Blow McKenzie up on social media for the *right* reasons this time?'

'Slight exaggeration,' she replied airily. 'He's only posted once at the weekend – and actually, that was me posting for him.'

'No, yesterday he posted a video of himself working out. It's everywhere. He looks HOT.'

Confused, Hannah put the call on speaker and pulled up Ward's socials. Sure enough, a video clip had been published across all platforms and, in the footage, Ward was holding a plank on his elbows and toes. Hard to tell from the background, but it looked like he was doing a one-on-one session with a trainer.

She watched, impressed, as he expertly held the pose for over a minute, barely breaking a sweat. Workout aside though, the video was an out and out thirst-trap. She couldn't help but notice the muscles visible on his back under the cloth of his t-shirt. Or the careful sculpting of his biceps. *Glutes aren't bad, either*, she noted, gulping a little. It was clear he was in great shape – and of course had spent a lot of time in his life taking care of himself.

But she wasn't supposed to notice things like that.

Then a voice sounded off-camera — the person shooting the footage and Hannah was startled a little at the realization that his trainer was female. For some reason, guilty of a type of reverse sexism, she had automatically assumed that he was working out with a guy. That someone like Ward would only work out with another 'bro'.

The off-camera trainer offered words of encouragement, and Hannah strained her ears, trying to listen closer to the voice, which was smooth, sultry and very definitely in control. Automatically she painted a mental picture of the woman she couldn't see. Sexy, assured and in great shape — probably with six-pack abs too — and she didn't know why this unsettled her. But before she could ponder it further, Zoe brought her squarely back to the present.

'Hannah? You still there?'

Clearing her throat, she refocused.

'Yes, sorry. Was just watching . . .'

'I know, right? Proper thirst-trap. I'm actually shocked you didn't have something to do with it.' Which made Hannah jump to the thought that Ward's trainer may well have been the brains behind the video. Fitspo influencer-type. 'You know,' Zoe continued, 'if *that's* the kind of messaging you're going for — and let me tell you that I and the nation's female population wholeheartedly agree — there's a whole world of opportunities for you to run with.'

Hannah felt her attention redirect as her mind also churned with new possibilities. 'Well, technically he's still in recovery so it's not like he can offer training clinics if that's what you're thinking . . .' she mused.

'How about a couple of live Q and As? He could answer fans' questions about his fitness in real time. Talk about his approach and the challenges and setbacks he's faced as he recovers from injury, how not to overdo it and stuff. Would really get people behind his journey back to fitness. You know how much the public *loves* recovery stories.'

Excitement surged through Hannah too at the various possibilities. Yes, this truly was something she could run with. And she couldn't deny that this considerably less toxic display of Ward's masculinity was appealing. In more ways than one.

'I think it's certainly something he could get behind anyway,' she mumbled, deep in thought. 'Making himself more accessible to the public has been the crux of his reticence, but this is good since it doesn't involve anything personal per se. He's already said he wants to be known purely as an athlete and that it's all about the game, about competing . . . well, this is right in line with that.'

Eager to chat through the finer details of such a strategy with him and also wanting to ensure that she could stay on top of the messaging, Hannah said goodbye to Zoe, promising to reconnect soon.

She then called Ward, wanting to congratulate him on his unexpected initiative, and while she was at it, take the opportunity to suggest another PR angle she'd planned to help boost a podcast she'd booked for him to record tomorrow.

But the call went directly to voicemail and her thoughts drifted again. Why was his phone off? The sexy voice of his female trainer popped to the forefront of her brain, as did something he'd said the other day at John Doe's.

My personal life is off-limits.

'Get it together,' she admonished herself. 'It's none of your business what the guy does with his trainer or anyone for that matter. In fact, why do you even care?'

The question stopped her in her tracks and she shook her head as if trying to dislodge the intrusive thought. Plus the image of Ward's taut bare muscles moving in rhythm . . .

Stop it, Hannah shook her head. She'd go ahead and check back in with him later.

Easier to ask for forgiveness than permission, was one of Zoe's favourite mantras and since the first element of her strategy seemed to be working OK, she could safely assume he'd be on board with the next part too. He was trusting her now, which was a great sign.

Hannah then made a call to a features editor at the online site Sports Starz wanting to know if he'd be interested in a personal piece.

'You bet,' Tom Whitmore enthused. 'WildCat McKenzie's one of those guaranteed click jockeys – put that bad boy's name in the headline and your eyeball rate's always going to go through the roof.'

Hannah sighed. That 'bad boy's name' was precisely what needed to be dismantled. Sure, a piece like this might result in lower engagement than the clickbait stuff, but it would demonstrate that Ward had matured. And bolstered by his newfound social media attention, something like this would surely help counter all the accumulated stories about his affairs and the drinking and brawling. A tall order, but the only thing Hannah could do was give it her best shot – and see where it went.

Emailing Tom the piece, plus an accompanying candid shot of Ward taken that day at the shelter which she'd kept on file for such an opportunity, she mentally crossed her fingers, hoping for lots more eyeballs of the forgiving kind this time. And couldn't help but smile at the photo, one that she herself had snapped of him unawares.

This would show the world a very different side to Ward McKenzie for sure.

Later, she exited her office and hailed a cab, heading back to Courtney's apartment, her mind swirling with various other ideas for the hockey player's rehabilitation strategy. As always, once her brain found an opening, the ideas kept on coming.

Zipping upwards in the elevator to the penthouse floor, she tried his phone again – but the result was the same, voicemail.

My personal life is off-limits.

Could there be a significant other in his life that Hannah wasn't aware of? Like the woman who shot that video. Well, if there was, she needed to know about it. For one thing, romance could provide even more positive press fodder and if she arranged some pap shots of him doing more wholesome couple activities, it would go a long way toward flipping the script on the womaniser image.

Strange though, once he'd let his guard down Hannah wasn't quite convinced that Ward truly was a philanderer either. Unfortunately, she'd had enough experience with narcissistic males to recognize one when she saw it, and that element of his image never really rang true. Hence her confusion about the two very different sides to him, the hard man image he'd so carefully curated, or the more recent vulnerable guy who made her feel almost protective of him.

Was that it? Hannah wondered. Was what she'd been feeling around him more to do with protective instinct than anything more . . . problematic? Because she would never in a million years be attracted to such a blatant womaniser.

Come to think of it though, any of the women with whom Ward had been associated previously had shown up readily in the media – which indicated that a lot of those dalliances were perhaps set up, showmances even. She wasn't sure, but it was possible that he himself might have been responsible for building up that love 'em and leave 'em narrative. Because the more time she spent with him, the more convinced Hannah became that he was anything but a playboy.

Once she'd reached her floor, she headed down the hallway, casting a glance at Ed's door as she passed. Her neighbour had been quiet of late and she wondered what he was up to. But her idle concern turned to curiosity the moment she entered the apartment and on the floor lay another note.

Think of the devil . . .

Hey P-2,
Pretty quiet over there for the past while. You doing OK?

Hannah had to smile. Apparently, Ed had been wondering about her silence just as much as she had been about his. And she snorted at the irony of him pointing out the absence of noise.

I suppose I shouldn't be complaining about that, right? After all, I've been doing nothing but telling you to keep it down since the moment you moved in.

'Well, at least he admits it,' she commented, eyebrows raised at this unexpected bout of honesty and self-awareness.

Based on the lack of racket, I'm guessing that you are now fully settled in. Or, you've been busy doing your social media crap or whatever. Yes, yes, I know what that is. I'm not a total caveman – even though I act like it sometimes, I get it.

I also get that I sound like a grouch most days – and have given you a hard time, which I'm realizing now might be undeserved. And so I am trying to be a bit more accommodating and open-minded. I've been dealing with some health stuff lately, and pain tends to put a man in a bad mood. And yeah, I've been told not to take it out on the people around me but most of the time I forget that advice. But I am trying.

At those words, Hannah's heart truly went out to the guy. Her thoughts drifted to her granddad once again, reminding her that it was a lot for an older person to contend with when the body started to break down and work against them.

Her grandmother had died five years before her husband, and until Granddad passed away, he had been entirely housebound and had a very hard time walking. With the result that he had been extra-cranky and bored out of his mind too. He'd also needed a home-help nurse on occasion, but at least he'd had his family. All the family and extended relatives too had made sure to visit as often as possible to keep a close eye on him and make sure he knew he was loved.

She didn't think Ed had that and it surely wouldn't be fun to be alone most of the time. Especially in such a big and bustling city like this. She'd already experienced a taste of that herself in the short time she'd been here.

Don't get me wrong. I'm not looking for sympathy here.

Hannah smiled again as if Ed had just admonished her for her private thoughts.

Just admitting some truths about myself. Once a guy gets to a certain age, it really can be like trying to teach an old dog new tricks. We are stubborn, and like you said before, set in our ways. But I guess that the only constant is change and I've been discovering that a bit for myself recently, and still trying to wrap my head around it. I probably don't have to make things as hard on everyone as I do, but I've always been focused on keeping my head down and working hard, so when I can't do that, I find myself a bit at a loss and then I get cranky. That's where I've been lately. You just happened to show up during that time and I've taken the brunt of it out on you, so to speak.

Sounded like he wasn't enjoying retirement either, she mused, thinking that it must be a huge adjustment too. To be a hard worker your whole life and then suddenly be stuck at home and feel like time is moving on without you.

She wondered what he used to do for a living. To afford a place like this it had to be something fancy, like a lawyer, banker or doctor. Or someone in the entertainment business. Yet for some reason, none of those fit. His words didn't give off a fancy, white-collar vibe or a confident showbiz type. Something about the way Ed talked about himself seemed much more down to earth. 'Save for the Penthouse on the Upper East Side,' she mumbled, feeling even more confused by the picture of her elderly neighbour she'd conjured in her mind.

It's an adjustment, going from useful to useless. Everyone wants to feel like they matter, that they're doing something good in their life. Anyway, enough rambling from me.

Obviously you are much busier than I, and have things to do. I didn't say it before, but thanks again for keeping the noise down. Weird thing is, now the silence is starting to get to me.

As you've probably already figured out, I can be hard to please . . .

Now she had even more questions, but one thing Hannah felt for certain about was that her neighbour seemed to exist in a state of limbo. The problem solver in her craved the opportunity to help him.

But how?

It certainly did sound like he was indeed lonely, and a bit stuck too, she surmised, as she considered his small admissions. Which automatically made her think of Ward McKenzie and the problem-solving Hannah was literally being paid to do on his behalf. Another man heading toward the end of his career – much to his chagrin. Ward was precariously close to being fired from the team and set adrift from the game he loved. Unlike her neighbour, the player wasn't stuck per se, but he was indeed walking a tightrope of sorts and he too needed to regain his purpose.

Hannah vowed to write back to Ed later once she'd gathered her thoughts and perhaps make him another batch of Rice Krispie buns to help cheer him up a little.

Given his latest correspondence and the olive branch offered within, it also felt like the time was right for the two of them to meet in person.

Chapter 30

WARD

When Bernie's name showed up on Ward's Caller ID later that evening, he fully expected his agent was about to congratulate him on a job well done on the training video. Which had since truly blown up far beyond even his own limited expectations. Shelley was right. People were interested in watching him work out – who knew?

Or watching him suffer, more like.

Regardless, it could only be a good thing to have people talk about him in a positive way for a change, instead of laughing at him falling down drunk in the park. So maybe there was something to this PR stuff, after all.

'Hey, Bernie,' he greeted, a smile in his voice. 'What's up?'

'Even the fact that you asked tells me that you haven't heard about Sport Starz?'

'Yeah, I know the site, but I don't know what you're talking about.'

'I'm talking about Ward McKenzie's newfound . . . softer side,' his agent stated then chuckled. 'You haven't seen it then.'

An all-too-familiar feeling of dread formed in the pit of his stomach. *What now?*

'How bad is it?' he asked gruffly. He held the phone away from his ear and stared at it as if willing the offending article to jump out. He had no clue if it was possible to check for what Bernie was talking about without hanging up.

When his agent spoke again, there was a more thoughtful tone to his voice. 'Well, on the one hand, it puts you in a good light, so that's a good thing, right?'

'Tell me what's on the other,' Ward grunted, striding across the room to dig out his laptop.

There was another pause, this one longer than the first.

'It also puts you into the "cute and cuddly" category, and I'm not sure if that's quite the image we were going for.'

He groaned. 'What? How could you let this happen to me?'

'Me? What are you talking about? I just wanted your image cleaned up enough to keep you from getting thrown off the team. I'm not the guy who decided that he needed to start being all sensitive and open about his feelings. What were you thinking?'

It had to be some touchy-feely bullshit Hannah had pitched based on their chat at his old place that time.

Damn it.

Ward should have known better. The problem was when he was around her, he just naturally seemed to open up to her. She seemed to be genuinely interested in him too – not the public version of him, but the actual man he was. He recalled their playful interactions that day she'd persuaded him to switch out his phone, how he'd found himself feeling so at ease that he'd effortlessly, stupidly let his guard down around her, to the point that in the diner, it even felt like flirting.

Man, he was an idiot. Of course he should have realized that some of what he'd told her would become fodder for his goddamn rehabilitation programme. But he thought Hannah was better than that.

'Can you at least give me an idea how bad this is?' he asked, bashing at laptop keys, until finally clicking through to the Sports Starz site. And when he saw the image accompanying whatever crap that was written, Ward stopped short.

A picture of him that day at the animal shelter, holding a bunch of kittens. He wasn't sure who'd taken it but he *definitely* hadn't posed for it with the photographer. It was a candid shot of him looking away from the camera and cracking a smile. He remembered doing so despite himself when one of the feistier kittens had swiped at this hand.

'Let's put it this way – the Sports Bros podcast guys are already having a field day. Joking that everyone already knew that you loved puss—'

'Got it. Thanks.' Ward gritted his teeth.

'I'm thinking that you might want to have another talk with Hannah and tell her that, yes, we want to soften your image, but not turn you into a freaking marshmallow.'

'Yeah,' he agreed. 'I'll handle it.'

Hanging up, Ward immediately checked through his social media notifications to assess the extent of the damage.

Huh. Good thing Hannah had switched screen alerts off, otherwise the thing would've been lighting up like a Christmas tree. Some faint ribbing here and there, but it wasn't all that bad. Still, it was bad enough that he was guaranteed to get some heavy-duty blowback in the locker room.

But then he also noticed a couple of missed calls from Hannah earlier. He called her back, but since it was late, it just went straight to voicemail.

'Hey,' he growled, leaving her a message, 'you and I need to have another talk. When I said comic book, I didn't mean Yogi-freakin'-Bear. Call me. Asap.'

Chapter 31

HANNAH

Hey P-1,

It's P-2 over here checking in. I hope you've been feeling better lately and that life is treating you kindly. I'm working with someone right now - a client who's also been dealing with some health issues, so I totally understand what you're going through. It can be incredibly difficult to truly know what to do when you aren't facing it yourself - outside of being supportive and empathetic - so please understand that I am sending nothing but good, healing vibes your way.

And actually, I have something to thank you for. You might not realize it, but your words inadvertently gave me some inspiration of late, valuable inspiration that helped me in my own professional life. I'm always looking for sources of inspiration and appreciate the advice from those older and wiser than me. So thank you, it's much appreciated.

It was only when Hannah was in the middle of her microwave spaghetti, still thinking about Ed's comment about being useful, that a thought struck her. That perhaps by appealing to his wisdom and generational experience she might go some way toward helping him feel that way again.

And the truth was that he *had* given her some inspiration lately, given it was his remarks about 'straight talking' and 'upgrades' that had kicked off the first stage of her plans for Ward McKenzie's image overhaul. So she wasn't lying.

But re-reading her words, she worried momentarily that Ed might well suspect that she was sucking up instead of taking it as a compliment. And was again reminded of the co-op board dispute and impending lawsuit.

That wouldn't do.

No, she decided then. She hadn't said anything untoward. She was just being a friendly neighbour and it could only help Courtney too in the long run if she returned and the guy next door's attitude toward her had made a complete 360 transformation.

Hannah folded the piece of paper and taking a plate of Rice Krispie buns that were so fresh the chocolate was still a little wet, she headed for the door, hoping that Ed was home so that she could say all of this in person. If not, she'd leave the note to let him know that she understood. And the treats too.

But just as she was about to leave, her phone buzzed on the kitchen countertop, indicating an incoming text. As was her habit, she switched it to silent in the evenings and the current slew of missed notifications validated her decision.

But spying the origin of the most recent message, Hannah realized this was one she couldn't ignore. Heart in her throat, she set the plate back down and clicked on the message, opening it fully.

Hey stranger . . . LA hasn't been the same since you left.

The blood rushed to her face, and she felt light-headed. Words from someone she'd truly believed was in her rear-view mirror.

She quickly tossed her phone back on the counter, but Hannah knew it was too late. The sender would have already been alerted to the fact that she'd read the message.

And the follow-up merely confirmed it.

I need to see you.

Chapter 32

WARD

'Well, hello. I swear you only come out of wherever it is you hide when you want to be fed.'

As if on cue, the cat mewed and Ward figured that was a direct order. He leaned down, grimacing ever so slightly at the action.

Placing some food in Pretzel's bowl and offering breakfast to his feline friend, he once again felt his mood grow dark about the latest coverage and the fact that Hannah still hadn't returned his call from yesterday. But it was late when he called so maybe she switched her phone off outside of work hours or something. God knows the damn thing bugged the hell out of you, wanting to be picked up, stroked and played with. Something he'd already known, of course, hence his refusal to 'get with the times'.

But like it or not, he was part of the collective now. Well and truly assimilated.

Despite himself, he chuckled. Maybe Hannah was actually the Borg Queen in disguise. As if on cue, his tormentor buzzed – but another name popped on the caller ID, and Ward's foul mood instantly returned. For a moment, he debated not taking it, sending it to voicemail. But he knew that would only delay the inevitable.

When Irene wanted to talk to him, she didn't rest from her mission *until* she did.

Stringing together a colourful line of expletives usually reserved for when he was on the ice, Ward grabbed the device and connected the call.

'Morning, Mom,' he said sharply. 'What's going on?'

A tsk ensued on the other end of the line.

'Well, isn't that a way to greet your mother? You know, one day I'm not going to be around and you're going to have to find someone new to treat like garbage.'

He rolled his eyes at the dramatics and rubbed his right temple – few things could provoke a headache like his mom.

And her timing was always sublime. He breathed through his nose, trying to bring his blood pressure down. No point in starting a fight. Best to simply figure out what she needed and why she was calling, and then hang up. He'd become practised at handling her over the years, if never quite successful.

'Sorry,' he mumbled. 'Just tired. Have a lot going on these days.'

On the other end of the line, Irene suddenly crooned the tone of her voice becoming sing-songy. 'I see that. Your Aunt Helen just forwarded something she saw online that would make any mother proud.'

Ward bit his tongue, recognizing the not-so-subtle dig.

As if rising to the ranks of a pro hockey player was something to be looked down upon – like it hadn't required determination, commitment, and yes, even talent. It wasn't like Ward skated in a beer league, for Chrissake. Or was some overweight has-been, trying to hold on to his high school glory days.

As if Irene too had not been elevated beyond her previous station in life as a low-income single mom because of *his* success. Ward had already ensured that she'd have it easier financially as she got older. And yet she still insisted on making calls like this – all to make him purposely feel shit about himself.

Though as to why a shot of him holding a bunch of kittens should put her nose out of joint he didn't understand. But he had never in his life understood Irene's thought process, so, hey.

'What – so you're reduced to soft porn now?'

Huh? Ward felt his grip on the phone tighten and he had the sudden desire to break the damn thing in half just to end his mother's torment. He inhaled deeply, counting to four before exhaling. 'It was fun,' he said evenly, doing his damnedest not to take the bait. 'I actually ended up saving a stray that was about to be destroyed and . . .'

She ignored him. 'Oh, you mean the animal shelter thing. I know you certainly didn't come up with that crap. So who did?'

Completely confused by the direction the conversation had taken, (to say nothing as to how the 'porn' thing came into it), Ward's brain hurt. Regardless, he knew that if he mentioned to Irene that he was working with a publicist to improve his reputation, his mother would pee all over it.

But then how did he describe Hannah, if not for the fact that she was his rep? And yes, it was her job to improve his reputation. A task that she seemed to have embraced wholeheartedly.

Despite his annoyance at her sharing the kittens' pic, Ward couldn't deny the level of consideration she had given him thus far, nor the time and effort. The continuous words of encouragement too, even as he wanted to tear the whole experience apart.

Something his mother was attempting to do right now with her not-so-subtle insults and backhanded compliments.

Apple doesn't fall far from the tree, huh?

But Ward decided he wasn't going to allow Irene to trash

Hannah's good work on his behalf. Before he could think further about it he answered simply, 'A friend. A friend of mine arranged it. And she did a good job.'

'And is this friend going to appear in the next video? Or are we just gonna see more of you half-naked huffing and puffing while flexing your muscles?'

And then it dawned on Ward that his mother was referring, not to the kittens pic, but to the training video Shelley had filmed of him. *Soft porn?*

His entire body cringed so badly he wanted to lie down and die.

'Jesus, Mom, it was a workout video to show my fans how my progress is going.'

'Well, Aunt Helen seemed to think that it was one of those sites where weirdos pay you to get naked, but what do I know?'

And if Helen thought that, who knew how many others would too? Ward winced with mortification.

He'd fucked this up already, hadn't he? No wonder Hannah wasn't answering. He'd blown her strategy with his very first foray into this stuff. Why didn't he run it by her – the expert – instead of letting Shelley talk him into it? He didn't think his trainer meant any harm and was only trying to help, but man, had that backfired.

Christ. Ward wasn't sure if he could show his face in public again, let alone online. And to think he was worried about the locker room ribbing about the kittens' pic . . . the guys would have a goddamn *field day* with this.

'So is this . . . friend,' his mother drawled. 'Another one who's gonna get her wits about her in due time and run off screaming to another city?'

Amid all her other insults, the low-blow comment about

Melanie made Ward feel as if he had been physically slapped, and fresh anger rushed through him.

'Always a pleasure hearing from you, Mom,' he managed to reply before his temper got the better of him. 'But if what I'm doing upsets you so much, maybe send back the cheques I keep mailing. And tell Aunt Helen to mind her own damn business.'

He ended the call and slammed the phone on the countertop, not caring if the stupid thing broke into a thousand pieces. If he had been on the ice this would have been the exact moment he bodychecked an opponent and upended a guy onto the boards.

But he couldn't do that. Much as he wanted to, he couldn't act out or worse, lash out. That wouldn't do him any good, and it would put him on the wrong side of Hannah again too.

As it was, he'd done enough.

Ward pulled at his hair as if the action could rip out the conflicting thoughts and emotions his mother had provoked. Then picking up the phone, the latest source of his humiliation, he navigated to his socials and promptly deleted the stupid training video.

Don't mess this up.

Worried now that Hannah had seen the video clip, taken it as yet another stupid stunt and written him off as a lost cause altogether, he called her number again, desperate to explain that it had been an ill-advised move that hadn't stemmed from him.

And more importantly, that it was gone.

Though he knew enough about the internet to know that this stuff was never truly 'gone' and these things always came back to haunt you. Regardless, Hannah would know what to do, how to handle this, how to *rescue* this.

Assuming she still wanted to.

He would be seeing her today anyway at that podcast thing, but still disconcerted by Irene's take on that stupid video, Ward wanted to reassure himself – or more to the point – wanted *Hannah* to reassure him, that he hadn't messed up. That he hadn't blown it already.

Still, she didn't pick up. He checked his watch. The working day had already begun now so the only reason she wasn't answering had to be that she was screening her calls.

Damn . . .

Again, he was forwarded straight to voicemail whereupon Hannah's smiling voice told him to leave a message.

And for the second time that morning, Ward slammed his brand-new phone down on the countertop, his mood once again dark as pitch.

Chapter 33

HANNAH

Hannah needed the kind of advice that only a best friend could give. But she hadn't been able to reach Zoe last night.

Although she was pretty sure what that advice was going to be, she admitted to herself as she looked blearily in the mirror while applying that morning's make-up. She'd barely slept and her face showed it.

I need to see you.

Last night, three more dancing dots immediately appeared onscreen under that message, signalling a follow-up.

As she stood at the marble countertop, inches above her discarded phone, watching and waiting for the words to appear, Hannah realized she was holding her breath. The fresh batch of goodies destined for next door and all intentions of a cordial introduction were immediately forgotten, as she struggled to figure out what this out-of-the-blue communication from her ex could mean.

Their break-up and the aftermath hadn't been . . . pretty to say the least but when she had put in for the job transfer and moved across the country, that had been the end of it. Or so she'd thought.

So what was Rob's intention in seeking her out now? Had he flown here to New York to see her? Maybe try to win her back?

The soft boop sound of another incoming message had quickly put her out of her misery.

Chilling in NYC for a few days before the championship – it's at Bethpage this year. Thought we might get together for dinner or a drink while I'm in town?

Of course. The golf tournament was coming up soon. Hannah wasn't sure whether to be disappointed or relieved.

And spent an age trying to figure out how she did feel, or more to the point, how to respond to his invitation.

Last night, she certainly didn't want to reply immediately, not until she had a chance to think things through properly. Plus she was so agitated it felt as if someone had just turned the heat up by twenty degrees, so Hannah moved into the living room and opened the window, suddenly desperate for some air.

Then heard another follow-up message come in.

Leaving the phone untouched on the countertop so that it would go into sleep mode, and thus Rob would figure that she was no longer online, she slunk down on the sofa and kicked off her shoes, popping one of the goodies originally destined for Ed into her mouth.

She was no longer in the mood for neighbourly relations, or indeed tiptoeing around outside in the hallway, not when her mind was in such turmoil. She could always drop them off in the morning, but in the meantime, no point in letting them go to waste.

The switched-off phone remained silent, but Hannah couldn't relax, expecting it to buzz again any second. Not being able to check was torture though, so she got up and decided to distract herself by pouring herself a glass of wine. Then retreating to the sofa, she grabbed her laptop and began mindlessly scrolling online in the hope of clearing her head a bit until she could better think straight.

An email alert popped up, but she ignored it, determined not to be drawn into her work inbox and potentially more drama with a client. She had more than enough of that to contend with as it was. But the email alert reminded her that there was actually a way to covertly check Rob's messages without revealing on his side that she was currently online.

Safe in the knowledge that those damning blinking dots wouldn't give her away this time, Hannah took a mouthful of wine and then clicked into iMessage, quickly running her gaze over her ex's latest words, trying to figure out the meaning behind them.

You were always my lucky charm, after all.

OK, so he wanted to get together while he was in town. To what purpose? To apologize, explain himself, try to win her back . . . or in the hope of a roll in the hay for old times' sake? She didn't know how she felt about any of those possibilities but what Hannah did know was that she really did need to speak to Zoe. Her friend would help her make sense out of all this, or more to the point, make sure she saw sense.

Since Hannah was still reluctant to retrieve the phone for fear that Rob would know she'd read his latest missive and was still ruminating over how to respond, she typed out a quick text to her friend via the messaging app instead.

Can you talk?

With iMessage, there was no way to know if Zoe was available, which of course was exactly why Hannah was using it. But when she didn't respond or call back immediately, she figured that her friend had to be in a meeting, in the car, or maybe even on a flight.

Which meant Hannah was stuck. OK, she thought, taking a deep breath and another gulp of wine. Maybe she needed to just put this whole thing to bed here and now by sending her ex a quick, easy-breezy reply, instead of obsessing over it like a teenager.

The obvious was something non-committal like; *Sure, check back in with me when you're in town* or some such, but that didn't feel right.

As if nothing had happened. As if everything she'd been through in the interim meant nothing, and the lengths to which she'd gone to put the necessary distance between them by moving her entire life out of LA were entirely trivialised.

Those older hard-done-by feelings flooded right back, and miffed that she had to deal with all of this again, just when she was feeling that she'd successfully put it behind her, Hannah threw back the last of her wine and began typing a response that didn't let Rob so easily off the hook.

But while intending to compose a short response of a few choice words that left him equally confused as to *her* true meaning, before she knew it, she'd started pouring it all out; how much she had sacrificed, how his actions had humiliated her and how hurt she'd been, relieved to be able to unburden it all on someone right then since Zoe wasn't available. And of course, safe in the knowledge that she was never going to send it.

Because while she'd so often been tempted, she would never dream of revealing any of her true feelings to Rob, unwilling to give him the satisfaction of knowing just how much he'd hurt her. Better to let him continue to believe that she was above any such dramatics and that the conclusion of their relationship was a matter of course and a mutual decision.

Make it so.

Hannah harrumphed. Aware that her glass was now empty and, definitely in the mood for another, she stood up and headed for the fridge for a refill, satisfied to have safely got it all off her chest at least.

Despite that, sleep still hadn't come easily.

And this morning, in the cold light of day and absent the wine buzz, she was again fixated on Rob's unexpected contact and, more to the point, what Zoe would surely say once she heard about it.

She was still afraid to check the phone for fear that Rob had sent through anything else that might distract her and she needed to get her act together pronto, because she was already running late for her first appointment at a podcast studio downtown with Ward McKenzie.

In the midst of it all, she hadn't returned his call from yesterday but despite her intention not to get drawn into work stuff last night, she had quickly checked on the Sports Starz piece before going to bed and was satisfied that this more personal piece of coverage had done the job.

And happy to see that they had indeed used the adorable kittens' picture as an accompaniment, which would surely help win hearts and minds.

And speaking of . . . that stray had made another appearance last night, though thankfully hadn't set off any noise or alarms, other than those in Hannah's own head. She'd got another fright when, after refilling her wine glass, she'd returned to the sofa and spied the cat idly wandering across the coffee table like it owned the place. Must've come in through the open window again, but this time Hannah wasn't taking any chances, or indeed wasn't in the mood for a visit, so she'd promptly shooed the feline back out the gap and hopefully to wherever it called home.

Now, she struggled to put on her eyeliner correctly and smudged it.

Damn. Doing her best to repair, Hannah then decided she didn't actually give a hoot about the way she looked this morning and hurried out, hoping she could easily grab a taxi down to Soho. Whereupon she was meeting Ward for a pre-recording with a hockey podcaster, something he had expressed actual enthusiasm about when she'd pitched the idea that day at John Doe's while his guard seemed to be down. A rare win.

'Yeah, I prefer radio and podcast stuff,' he'd told her.

'Why's that?'

He'd shrugged and flashed that lopsided grin that could melt butter. 'No cameras. Or any of that hair and make-up crap.'

Ironic since it wasn't as if he had a face made for radio.

Now, as she hailed a cab outside her building, Hannah mentally reprimanded herself. The last thing she needed to think about was McKenzie's butter-melting smile.

Surely she'd already learned her lesson.

Chapter 34

The cab finally came to a stop and Hannah checked the time. She was *very* late. Quickly paying the driver, she jumped from the car and immediately spotted Ward standing outside the address of the studio. She rushed to meet him and there was no denying he looked irritated.

'I called you twice yesterday,' he grunted by way of a greeting. 'And texted earlier to check if I was in the right place. I wasn't even sure if you'd show up.'

'Why wouldn't I show up?' Hannah glanced down at her phone for the first time that morning. Since last night, she'd been treating it like a ticking time bomb. 'I'm sorry. I switch my phone to silent mode after hours and forgot to take it back off this morning. It's been blowing up . . . and my cab driver was a chatterbox. So much traffic, too,' she lied.

'Really? I didn't hit much.'

'I'm coming from a different part of town though,' she replied. Her voice was snappy, which was unlike her.

'Like I said, I called you,' he grunted. 'After you posted that article that made me seem like some kind of pathetic loser. And what the hell were you thinking with that picture?'

His all-too-familiar petulance, especially given the night she'd just endured, was the last straw, and despite her best intentions, something in her snapped.

'Oh, for crying out loud, not this again. You think that because you revealed a little warmth, a little humanity, it makes you a loser? Let me tell you something, Ward McKenzie, the strongest, most incredible men I've ever known have all been comfortable with who they are, regardless of how anyone else views them. If you think showing a little vulnerability means that you're a loser, well, maybe that just proves that you *are* one.'

All at once she noticed her hands shaking and cursed herself for losing control. Ensuring smooth sailing might be Hannah's job, but right then she'd had just about enough of trying to keep people – mostly troublesome men of late – in check.

To say nothing of very little sleep.

'How the hell can you say that?' Ward shot back. 'There are already freakin' memes about me and those cats.'

'There's also a lot of people who thought it was one of the best things they've seen lately – a tough guy like you not being afraid to show your sensitive side. Step out of the Stone Age, McKenzie. You don't always have to play the macho jerk.'

'Just because I don't like people making fun of me doesn't mean I'm a macho jerk.'

'As long as you know who you are, who the hell cares what anyone else thinks?'

'Come on. It's more than that and you know it. Guys on the team, to say nothing of opponents, are going to think I'm weak. They're not going to take me seriously.'

'If that's your biggest concern, then you're not seeing how even *that* can work out in your favour.'

He frowned. 'What are you talking about?'

'If your opposition thinks you're weak, they're going to underestimate you. So you use that to your advantage. No idea how you didn't learn *that* on the ice.'

He seemed to think about that, concluding that she might have a point.

'It's just . . . you said you'd run this stuff by me and you didn't,' he murmured, shoving his hands in his pockets. 'That wasn't cool. Neither is ignoring my calls by the way.'

Hannah inhaled deeply and did her best to count to ten, worried that she'd lose it altogether if she wasn't careful. It wasn't uncommon for clients to think that her entire life revolved around them and their needs alone, but this guy really was starting to take the biscuit. Still, she had no choice but to try to smooth things over. This was her job after all.

'Like I said, I'm sorry. I had some other stuff to deal with last night.' She exhaled, suddenly deflated. 'I didn't sleep the best and . . . well, I'm just not feeling great today.'

In that moment, he seemed to suddenly notice her dishevelled appearance; messy eye make-up, half-applied lipstick and general downbeat demeanour all round.

'Hungover?' he teased, his tone turning light as he realized the opportunity to potentially needle her for once. 'Makes a change.'

'Hardly. I mean, no, I'm not hungover. I'm . . . just discombobulated . . .'

'OK, I have *no* idea what the hell that means.' Then Ward's expression transitioned from playful to genuine concern and his green eyes searched her face as if looking for clues as to what was throwing her off. 'Hey,' he said softly, touching her elbow gently, 'I'm sorry. If you need to talk . . .'

He was staring at her with an intensity that made her stomach do flip-flops. Hannah didn't know if it was because of her current confusion about Rob or if it was just because the more time she spent with Ward, the more drawn to him she seemed to become. Which was doubly dangerous.

'It's fine, honestly. For the record, I actually did try to give you a heads-up about the piece yesterday, but couldn't reach you. In any case, Ward, I can't run every single element of the strategy by you, or I'd never get anything done. You need to trust me too. I already said I wouldn't pursue anything you weren't comfortable with. And I honestly didn't think you'd lose it over a bunch of helpless kittens.'

'Like I said, I'm sorry. But speaking of running things by . . . did you see that I posted something online – a video?' He looked so hesitant and unsure of himself now that she softened afresh.

'Yes. An inspired idea and something we can really build on too. I already have a few ideas and—'

'I deleted it.'

She stared at him. 'What? Why? Your first post, proper post, I mean, and it went viral too! People are going crazy over it, Ward, why would you—'

'It was cheesy and dumb and it wasn't even my idea. Shelley my . . . friend, figured it was a good move at the time but I changed my mind. That's not how I want to be seen.' He looked away briefly and Hannah knew there was more he wasn't saying. And she couldn't help but wonder again about this 'friend'.

My personal life is off-limits.

Regardless, if Ward truly didn't want to go down the fitness video route, for whatever reason, then there was nothing she could do to persuade him.

He looked back at her again. 'Anyway, I'm sorry for being a dick just now. Guess I sometimes forget I'm not the only asshat client you've got to deal with. Are you sure you're OK though? Anything I can help with?'

Hannah shook her head. The last thing she needed to do was talk about her private life, or previous relationship mistakes, with him. *Her* personal life was off-limits too. Especially to this particular client.

'It's grand,' she insisted, trying to sound offhand. 'Nothing that a better night's sleep won't fix.'

Ward nodded reluctantly and then his lips twisted up in a half-smile. 'So that whole loser speech . . . did you just blurt that out off the top of your head or were you rehearsing it because deep down you knew I'd chew you out for releasing that picture?'

'A little bit of both,' she admitted with a grin. 'I'll be honest – I had an inkling you might not be fully on board since you're such a tough guy and all.' She met his gaze briefly and was relieved to see that he wasn't quite as annoyed as he pretended to be. 'But I was curious to see how the online reaction panned out. Based on the response so far, I'm starting to think that, thanks to us both, we're finally making progress and are a lot further along the road to having that image of yours reformed, no?'

He snorted, shaking his head. 'At what cost, though? Don't get me wrong, I appreciate everything you're doing, truly I do. Guess I just still need some persuading that the image we're trying to project is real.'

Hannah frowned and she spoke gently, addressing him seriously this time. 'Ward, I suspect somewhere along the line somebody convinced you that you're less than, for whatever reason. They're wrong. The fact is – that guy in that picture, that one split second at the shelter when you dropped the macho mask – is exactly who you are. Yes, you're a pro athlete and you're tough and you're strong, and all the rest of it. No one is denying that. At the same time, there's a tender more vulnerable side to you, too. One that you were kind enough to reveal to me on occasion. But you need to lower the deflector shield,' she said gently, deliberately using a *Star Trek* reference to help hammer the message home. 'People respond better to the real you.'

Ward stared directly at her then and after a beat, asked, 'Do *you?*'

The huskiness in his voice sent sparks shooting through her and she looked away, no longer able to withstand those penetrating eyes. She laughed nervously, well and truly discombobulated now.

'Who wouldn't?' Then tucking the phone back into her pocket, Hannah swallowed hard and pasted on a bright smile. 'Now, come on, let's get in there and keep up the good work.'

Chapter 35

'Block him,' Zoe commanded sternly.

That afternoon, Hannah managed to bring her friend up to speed about her ex's messages.

You were always my lucky charm, after all

Because she'd accessed the last one covertly on her laptop, as far as Rob was concerned she wouldn't have seen it 'til this morning, rather than spending half the night awake and ruminating over every word.

A million alternate responses still jostled around her brain, all conflicting, but as much as she wanted to be honest in her response, deep down Hannah knew the easy-breezy 'gimme a call when you get here' reply was the safest choice. And after that, come what may.

'Did you hear what I said?' demanded Zoe, who had a scary knack for reading Hannah's mind. 'Don't even reply. *Block* him. That's the only option. He's trying to get under your skin again. Remember what happened last time. You haven't forgotten, have you?'

'Of course not. It's just . . .' She bit her lip.

'No. No "it's just" . . . Aw, please tell me that you haven't responded.'

Hannah cringed afresh at the wine-infused essay-length

confessional still sitting in iMessage. 'I haven't responded,' she admitted truthfully.

Yet.

'Good. Don't. Rob Kendrick is *no* good for you. You are better than that.'

In her heart, Hannah knew her friend was right. She wanted to follow her advice – she truly did. What did they say the definition of insanity was again? Making the same bad decision over again and expecting different results.

She took a deep breath and steeled herself. 'I know you're right. About everything. I promise I'm not going to do anything stupid.'

'Good,' Zoe answered. 'Because if you do, I'm gonna . . .'

'You're going to do *what*? Fly all the way over here and slap some sense in me?'

'If I have to.'

Hannah laughed. 'Well, if that's what it takes to get a visit . . .' she teased, which earned her a guffaw in return.

'All right, all right. I guess I should be relieved things aren't so bad that I need to step foot into that cesspit. Guess where I'm heading now?'

'No idea.'

'I'll give you a clue. Huevos Rancheros à la Polo.'

Hannah's mouth actually watered like one of Pavlov's dogs. 'The Pink Palace? I *hate* you.' What she wouldn't give just then to be in the Beverly Hills Hotel with her friend eating breakfast in the sunshine at their favourite Polo Lounge poolside table. She could visualise the blue skies and palm trees already.

'I'll get an extra portion in your honour. Especially since I'm not paying. Speaking of . . .' she continued, 'I've been following all the recent coverage on McKenzie. It's good.'

'Yeah, and a podcast he just recorded is excellent. He'd never admit it, but he is a natural at this stuff. You can tell when he's enjoying himself – he was this morning – and that will show through to the audience. I'm looking forward to it airing.' She paused for a moment. 'Although, I think I might owe him a bit of an apology.'

'Why's that?'

'Well, I was feeling a bit . . . out of sorts after the Rob thing last night and I was late and irritable. I snapped at him a few times. Started to take some of it out on him, which wasn't fair. I mean, he's been really good to work with lately. Going along with my ideas, showing up on time, not falling down drunk, even seems to be occasionally enjoying himself. There are still some teething problems and a few hiccups too. But, he seemed to get that I was in a bad mood today and my mind was elsewhere . . . and was actually really sweet to me . . . '

Hannah's voice trailed off, remembering Ward's kind eyes and genuine concern in Soho earlier, and her stomach did that flip-floppy thing again. After the podcast recording, he'd even suggested they grab a coffee if she needed an ear and only for the fact that she had another client appointment lined up, she was sorely tempted. But knew deep down that it was way too dangerous.

'I'm not going to have to have a "Come to Jesus" talk with you about this guy now too, am I?' Zoe drawled.

Her friend's tone very quickly brought Hannah back to earth.

'What? Feck, no. What are you even talking about?' she argued, sounding indignant at the very suggestion, but also secretly glad that her friend wasn't in the office with her. She was blushing.

'You sounded awfully . . . dreamy there for a sec.'

'That's ridiculous,' she retorted quickly, squaring her shoulders.

'It's not like that at *all*. I was just saying, he was being . . . normal, which makes a nice change. That's it.'

'I mean I don't blame you. The man is *hot*. But . . .'

'Don't go there, I know. Anyway, I'd better get back to it; enjoy your Beverly Hills breakfast and know that I'm not in the *least* bit jealous.'

Hannah's phone was pinging even as she spoke.

'Liar. Catch you later.'

I had no idea you felt that way.

Hannah's first reaction upon reading a new text that had just come in from Rob was complete confusion. What did he mean?

Until she scrolled up and spied the wall of words preceding it and her hand flew to her mouth in horror. *Oh my god!*

Suddenly the room began to spin as Hannah realized that the boozy in-depth confessional she'd written last night – instead of still sitting innocently in draft on her laptop – had somehow ended up in her and Rob's message string!

Which meant her ex had read every single word and was now privy to all her honest, unfiltered thoughts and emotions regarding their relationship. To everything she'd laid bare.

But . . . but . . . *how?*

Had she inadvertently pressed send amid last night's wine haze?

But no, she'd only had a couple of glasses at the most, and she'd only written it all in the first place as a form of emotional purge. And more importantly, safe in the knowledge that she was *never* going to send it!

Her thoughts scrambled to make sense of it. Was there some feature on iMessage she didn't know about that automatically sent messages after a specified amount of time or something? Regardless, Hannah was so mortified she could barely think straight.

Now Rob knew *everything*. She could no longer hold her head high and play the part of the strong and mature ex, all drama completely beneath her. From his point of view, the message surely came across as unhinged.

Oh no, oh no. So much for easy breezy . . .

Then she considered the response he'd just sent. Short and sweet. *I had no idea you felt that way.*

He was obviously taken aback, and no doubt confused too, by this out-of-the-blue emotional outpouring when one of the things he used to say he loved about her was how she always kept her cool. Until that one time, of course. And while it was difficult — impossible almost — even then Hannah had done her utmost to save face, she'd had little choice but to automatically switch into damage control mode. Like she always did when things went awry.

So what now? How could she rescue *this*, or more to the point, should she even try? Ultimately there was really nothing she could do, was there? Rob knew exactly how she felt now, and thus would surely have no choice but to recognize and appreciate her reasons for leaving.

The question was, what would he do about it?

He was coming to the city for the tournament soon, so time would tell. And if he wanted to meet up, they could discuss it all then. Until that point, Hannah guessed she had no choice but to leave the ball in his court. But how oh how had she lobbed that deeply embarrassing volley? It was mystifying.

Swallowing hard as she tried not to reread every mortifying word, Hannah swiped right of the message to ascertain the sending time. Yes, it was indeed last night, not long after she'd finished writing it. So she must have inadvertently hit the enter button on her laptop somehow, which had let the cat out of the bag, because however advanced technology was, it didn't spontaneously press buttons of its own accord . . .

Then, recalling her train of thought, plus the last time she'd thought tech had a mind of its own in the form of Courtney's media system, the realization hit.

Cat out of the bag . . .

Or more pertinently, the very animal that had idly wandered across her laptop last night while she went to refill her glass.

Chapter 36

P-2,

Thanks for your note. I'm actually proud to think I helped with your work issue. It's good to feel like I have something to offer these days.

I'm sure, by this point, you think I'm simply a pain in the ass. Hell, you might even be regretting moving in next to a guy like me but take heart in the idea that I won't live forever.

I've been doing a lot of self-reflection lately – and I appreciate that you have been so courteous to keep me alerted of your plans. I don't know if I would have done the same if I were in your shoes. I'm sure that says something about my character as well as yours.

No doubt you've heard a lot about me from others, mostly complaints, but at the end of the day, I don't think I'm a bad guy. Truth be told, I don't think about how others view me at all. Mostly because I don't care. Never have. You know what they say about opinions. However, the world is a whole different place from when I grew up, and right now it's all about feelings and self-awareness and being kind to everyone, even the assholes.

So since you say you're having some men struggles, at work or in life in general, maybe this might help. A few classic truths, if you will. Brace yourself.

Plus it might help the two of us understand one other better too.

1. Most guys value recognition for their abilities, achievements and contributions. Feeling respected is a powerful motivator and when you start to get the feeling you're being brushed under the rug, it pisses you off. That's where I have been existing lately and it's not fun.

2. While it may not appear to be the case with me, I can assure you that guys also value connection with other people, even if society likes to suggest otherwise. Yes, we express this need differently compared to women, but we still want to be supported by the people in our lives. It's hard to feel happy when you feel ignored or taken for granted.

3. We have to have a purpose. Doesn't matter what it is . . . career, family, some hobby, whatever. It's important. But it has to be authentic. Not contrived or for validation. Probably the biggest problem I have with the way the world works now. Everything is fake – all made up for show to impress other people. I value truth.

4. Yes, we men can be emotionally complex. Might not look like it on paper, but we are capable of a wide range of emotions. But again, the world looks down on guys who emote too much. So, a lot of times instead, we just shut down – and are judged for that too.

5. We have just as much drive for success as anyone – regardless of age. We still want to win. But the older you get, the more that gets overlooked. The older you get the more you get forgotten about.

6. Guys like me oftentimes get lumped into that category especially. That we are focused only on ourselves and selfish. I suppose this can be true at times, but I believe in helping other people – and I've slowly come to the realization that maybe you do too.

Well, that's a lot of words, I know. But I wanted to thank you for being so considerate lately and letting me know you care. And to tell you that the same applies in return. If you happen to need advice on anything else, let me know and I'll try my best to help.

P-1

PS There's a board meeting at the end of the month and I'm gonna ask them to pull back on the legal stuff. Try to persuade them that maybe you're exactly the kind of person this place needs, after all.

Oh wow.

Hannah's eyes filled with tears once she'd finished reading Ed's latest note, found beneath the door when she got home from work. Given the week she'd had, it truly couldn't have come at a better moment.

She'd heard nothing from Rob since. The golf tournament was this weekend though, so maybe he'd decided to wait until he was in town before reaching out to her again.

Or not at all.

As it was, she'd had little choice but to set aside her monumental embarrassment, which Hannah was almost certain had been predicated by that errant wandering stray. She'd kept all windows closed in the apartment since then.

Her client list was growing larger by the day, as were the number of alerts on her phone and the size of her workload. While yes, she was keen to impress at the new office, she was now starting to regret her earlier enthusiasm and agreement to tackle such a time-sucking client list.

In short, the pressure was starting to get to her.

So to know that Ed next door had finally come around, and she had one less thing to consider and was safe in the knowledge that she could remain in Courtney's apartment without worrying about further neighbourly missteps, was a huge relief. She was sure the influencer in turn would be over the moon that Hannah's little overtures had essentially smoothed the way for her problematic lawsuit to disappear too.

Finally, something was looking up.

She read back through the note (though this one was more of a letter), touched and intrigued too by Ed's list of truths about men.

Six classic truths, mirroring the Classic Six in which they both resided. She chuckled, wondering if that was intentional; she'd already got the sense that he was a wry and witty old soul, and a lot smarter than he pretended to be.

Regardless, she fully intended to use some of these intergenerational nuggets of wisdom when it came to the men in her life, her ex too. Maybe some straight-talking to Rob had been long overdue and the cat had done her a favour after all?

One male in particular for whom the majority of Ed's advice resonated though, was of course, Ward McKenzie. A bit of a relic himself by all accounts, though Hannah truly was getting a much better handle on the hockey player these days.

Perhaps too much, she mused, blushing afresh, as she once again replayed in her mind their heated encounter outside the podcast place that morning, when at one point during their bickering she was almost certain (hopeful?) that Ward was going to kiss her.

But that was crazy, wasn't it? She barely knew the guy. To say nothing of the fact that he was off-limits. No, her stupid imagination was working overtime, as was Ward McKenzie's more down-to-earth appeal, much the same way it had that day she'd bumped into him at the coffee place.

The tough-guy macho facade she could handle. It was the softer, vulnerable, more human side – the real him – that made her feel so discomfited. And since this very side was the one Hannah was actively working to bring to the forefront, she knew she'd better snap out of it, fast.

She'd worked hard enough to disentangle herself from the disaster she'd been central to on the other side of the country.

So what she needed to do now was focus her efforts on getting Ward McKenzie's image in shape and further down her list of priorities.

And try her damnedest to ensure that she didn't get caught up in any similar messes this side too.

Chapter 37

WARD

When Ward saw Johnny enter the diner, he waved him over, standing up and giving his friend a solid hug as soon as he arrived.

'How's it going, Mr Sensitive?' Johnny asked, grinning.

'Wow. Just jumped right in on that, huh?'

His friend's laughter boomed as he clapped Ward on the back, slid into the booth, and sat down. 'Hey, you wouldn't respect me if I didn't give you a little hell now and then, right? Shelley says that you're doing really well with the rehab.'

'I haven't had a pill in weeks and I've even cut back on the beer. That girl is determined to break my body, Johnny. She's a tyrant.'

'That's why she's the best. But speaking of tyrants, what else has PR Girl got planned for you these days? Maybe sign you up for a slumber party with some orphans or something?'

'Hilarious.'

'You've gotta admit, though – she's doing wonders. You're a completely different man now, thanks to her – at least, as far as the public goes. For those of us who know you, you're still the same old jerk you've always been. Anyway, what was so important that you had me give up my golf round?'

'What can I say? I miss seeing your ugly face, that's all.'

Johnny shook his head. 'You know better than to try to play that game with me. What's going on?'

Ward sighed, looking down into the cup of coffee in front of him. He was spared from answering right then when a waitress came over to take their order.

After requesting coffee and a plate of hash browns and two eggs over easy, his friend said, 'Come on, man. We've known each other too long. Just tell me.'

Ward took a deep breath. 'I'm worried.'

'I get that,' Johnny said, nodding. 'You're under a lot of pressure and it's hard to stay upbeat when you know that you might have pushed your luck too far. But I think it's gonna be OK. That PR girl of yours seems to have a way of turning mud into gold. I'm pretty certain Coach Lewis and the top brass will be happy and you're going to come out of this intact. And thanks to Shelley, get back on the ice fighting fit and better than ever.'

'It's not about that,' Ward ventured nervously. 'It's about Hannah.'

'Who?'

'PR Girl.'

Johnny raised his eyebrows. 'What do you mean? I thought you said you were on board with her stuff these days.'

He exhaled and dropped his gaze to the table. 'I am, but I also think . . . she's getting to me.'

Ward had been fully prepared to blow up at Hannah that time over the shelter picture she'd posted. But when she'd turned up at the podcast thing, just being back in her proximity made him feel better already, and completely diffused the anger he'd been carrying.

What was it about that girl that did that? He was one of those people who could usually maintain a good solid head of steam for a long time but when it came to Hannah, he just couldn't bring himself to stay angry. Part of it, he knew, was that she was a genuinely good person. He got that. He'd been around enough phonies to spot them a mile away but Hannah was the real deal, a decent human being.

And then when she admitted she'd had other stuff to deal with too, he'd felt like crap. He got the sense that it wasn't just work either, there was a distinct whiff that something personal was going on with her.

But worst of all that day, when she'd briefly blown up at *him* instead with that 'loser' talk stuff with so much heat in her eyes, for one crazy moment, Ward had actually considered just grabbing and kissing her, just to see what happened.

'Getting to you, how? Too much PR stuff?'

'Worse. I'm beginning to think about her. Too much, *way* too much.'

At that, Johnny burst out laughing. His laugh was loud and long and Ward just sat there as several other patrons in the diner turned their attention to the two of them. Eventually, he ran out of steam and the laughter faded.

'You done?'

His buddy snorted and for a moment, Ward thought he was going to start laughing once again. He didn't, though. Instead, he took a deep breath to get himself under control. 'OK, well, I guess it's only natural that you'd wind up getting yourself caught up like this – after all she's female and you're . . . well, you're you know.'

'What's that supposed to mean?'

Johnny raised his eyebrows.

'You're kidding, right? Don't forget I know your history. And I saw that workout video that was all over the place too. You're a one-man *Magic Mike* movie, dude.'

'Gimme a break.'

'I know that you've built up the reputation– and I also know that you've never really gone out of your way to change it either.'

'What about Melanie?' he retorted.

'What about her? Once she moved to Chicago, that was the end of it. You didn't act too broken up over it so I just assumed she was just another one from the parade that happened to last longer than most.'

It had been way more than that, but Ward had never been comfortable sharing his emotions with anyone. Growing up without a father had somehow convinced him that it was his job to be the man of the house and he'd also learned that showing emotion around Irene only earned him a lecture about how it was a 'hard world out there and you'd better make damned sure no one sees that you're soft'.

A life lesson that his first coach had drilled in even harder. *Never show 'em you're weak.*

'Maybe. Here's the thing, though – how the hell do I stop thinking that way about the damn girl when we're supposed to be working together?'

His friend thought about it for a long moment, then finally said, 'You're gonna have to work that one out on your own, bruh. But the last thing you need now is to toss in that hand grenade. Seems like that *damn girl* could well be your last chance. Whatever you do, don't fuck it up.'

Chapter 38

HANNAH

Hannah sat at her desk, scrolling through the headlines from a fundraising event at the St Regis Hotel the night before.

Another score for Ward McKenzie.

The athlete had been a big hit at the KidsCare Foundation benefit. He'd been part of a silent auction that had raised over fifteen thousand dollars after a wealthy donor bid on him for a series of private hockey lessons and one-on-one coaching for his son.

She sought out the accompanying media shots and swallowed hard at the sight of him. The tux she'd arranged was off-the-rack Dolce but looked tailored to perfection on his strong body, and while these days he didn't rely on the cane so much, she'd also suggested it as an accessory to give an additional dapper touch.

And to remind his burgeoning legion of admirers that he was still on his recovery 'journey'.

The man of the moment was due to arrive at the office soon for a debrief on everything else she had planned for him. And based on what she'd just learned from his agent, potentially a very nice surprise too.

Hannah smiled. It had been a busy time. There was no denying that things were seriously starting to turn around for Ward now and public perception had gone through a major shift. They had since fallen into an easy partnership and had established a good cadence working together. There had been no more public missteps or stupid outbursts, and to his credit, Ward had been following her directions and guidance, and their work was paying off.

He seemed way more comfortable with the social media side now too, provided that whatever he shared was in line with and on-brand with his sports image.

While he rarely posted anything personal, he'd even taken the initiative to tag Frank's coffee place one time, resulting in a deluge of fresh custom, and Hannah knew that helping his friend's business meant way more to him than any personal online clout he'd amassed.

She just hoped all Frank's newbies thought to bring cash.

Once the bulk of the messaging revolved around sports, didn't encroach on his privacy or paint him as someone he didn't believe himself to be, Ward was cool. So Hannah did her best to colour within those lines – and despite those initial false starts, all seemed to be working out.

After that little slip outside the podcast place, she was also doubly careful not to lower her own guard or reveal anything more about her personal life to him.

This needed to remain a one-sided game. Life in general seemed to have settled down too, much to her relief.

Despite (or more likely because of) her cringeworthy iMessage confessional, Rob had since completely ghosted her and she'd heard nothing from him regardless of his being in the city for the golf tournament.

And while a part of her heart broke all over again, and her ego was well and truly crucified, she also figured it was for the best. There was no future for them now, never had been really, and those recent overtures from him were surely just blatant attempts at an easy booty call while he was in town.

You were always my lucky charm.

Maybe the cat did her a favour after all.

Following a few promising nights out on the town with a couple of office colleagues, whom Hannah was hopeful might in time become friends, she and Ed next door had since fallen into a friendship of sorts too, which meant her formerly pitiful social life was also looking up.

And while they still hadn't come face to face, at least these days there was an easy neighbourly camaraderie. Sensing that Ed was far more comfortable with anonymity since he'd never once suggested any in-person encounters, Hannah was careful not to force the issue.

No more noise complaints or threatening notes, no more wayward deliveries – all of that had been sorted – and he, in turn, seemed considerably more reassured about having her next door. She was gratified that their interactions, which often now verged on banter, provided him with a bit of companionship and an outlet that he didn't otherwise have, cooped up all day in his apartment.

At her very core, Hannah was a helper – and whether it was developing branding strategies for wannabee influencers, athletes with reputation problems or helping a homebound elderly man feel less lonely – finding ways to smooth things over had always given her the most joy.

Make it so.

Though now that she thought about it, she hadn't heard from Ed for a while. She made a mental note to check in soon and bake him some more treats – if, for once, she got home from the office at a reasonable hour.

The line on her desk buzzed, announcing Ward McKenzie's

arrival, and when a few minutes later he appeared in her office, Hannah looked up.

He took a seat across from her, but seemed to have regressed to his older glummer self – and not at all like the dashing man-about-town beaming back at her from the PC screen after yet another successful public outing.

'You OK?' she asked by way of a hello.

He slumped down. 'Too much standing around last night, I think. Leg's bothering me,' he mumbled. 'And I got home later than I wanted to.' He scowled, wincing a little. 'I was supposed to join some guys from the team to practise some light training today; see how things are shaping up, but I called it off. I'm tired and then I had to trudge all the way down here too.'

Hannah swallowed guiltily, uneasy at the prospect of setting his recovery back because of something she had done. *Again.*

'Ah, I'm sorry about that,' she replied earnestly. 'I didn't know about the practice. And as for coming here, next time just tell me if you're not feeling up to it, OK? I could just as easily have come to you.'

He met her gaze and after a beat, his green eyes softened. 'Nah, it's OK,' he conceded. 'I rescheduled the training thing for later in the week. Just felt a bit stiff, you know?'

'Probably the dress shoes too,' she commented, glancing at his trainers. 'I know how I feel after a night in four-inch stilettos.'

He finally smiled. 'Yeah, well, at least you're something to look at.'

Hannah's mouth went momentarily dry, and she felt a blush rising to her cheeks. Quickly, she reached for her laptop and turned it around to face him, hoping it would take his attention off of her face. Dangerous ground.

'Seriously, though,' she stammered, quickly moving on, 'look at this coverage. The media shots are so good. You look great.'

He leaned in to get a closer look at the screen and two lines appeared in between his eyebrows.

'I look like a bozo. And now I'm giving hockey lessons to some rich jackass's kid. I dunno, Hannah, I felt like a pet monkey or something.'

'It's three lessons, and the kid's just seven years old. And you don't have to do it until you are fully fit and back on the ice again. Plus, you raised so much money for a very *good* cause, remember? You might have to give lessons to a rich kid, but the money you raised will help a lot of *sick* kids.'

While he had never truly opened up about it, Hannah had done enough research on Ward to find out that he hadn't had the easiest time growing up. She supposed there might be a bit of a projection as to why anything that helped less fortunate kids was always something he could be more easily persuaded into, but she would never dream of asking him about it.

'Yeah, I know, I know. I guess you're right,' he admitted.

Hannah also knew that conceding someone else could be right about something was equally hard on him, so she didn't labour that either.

'So,' she continued, smiling. 'A great success all round.' She saw him shift in his seat and he averted his eyes, this time looking at the wall. 'What's up?' she asked, realizing he had something else to say.

He shrugged again. 'I don't know. I mean, yeah, great that some money was raised and kids will be helped. But rubbing elbows with some of those people . . . it feels so phoney. The fancy tux, crazy money being thrown around, that's just not my scene.'

'But it was all for a good cause . . .'

'I'm just afraid people are going to think I'm a sell-out now. I've never hung with that crowd. Feels like I'm doing it for the wrong reasons like it's all about me getting papped.'

'No one is going to think that. You're Ward McKenzie. Tireless grinder who's just as capable of scoring as making an assist allowing a teammate to take the spotlight. You did a good deed last night. Others in your position do that stuff too . . . Gretzky, Iginla, Phaneuf,' Hannah listed on her fingers. Working with him, she had little choice but to become well-versed in ice hockey — but she also knew that he liked being reminded that some of his sports heroes and counterparts put themselves out there too. 'Those guys are all genuine community-minded success stories who give back. No one suggests they do it just for publicity, just like no one would suggest the same about you.'

He sat up a bit straighter then and Hannah knew she had scored a point in her favour.

'You're right. All in all, it's the outcome that counts, right?'

She offered him a thumbs up. 'Exactly. And speaking of outcomes . . . ' She beamed, ready to raise the real reason she'd wanted this debrief in person. 'I spoke to Bernie and he's thrilled with how everything's going. To the point that he got a call from Craig Sumners, asking if you'd attend his wife's charity benefit happening soon.'

Ward groaned. 'What? How is my having to kiss-ass at yet another fundraiser a good thing? I thought you said this was going well. I've been breaking my butt with all this PR stuff to get the top brass back onside. And now Sumners wants me to jump through even more hoops?'

'That's the thing though, it's not just you. The whole Panthers squad is invited and lots of media too, it seems. Very big affair, at the Plaza Hotel. Bernie gets the sense that there's more to it than meets the eye and that the event is merely a platform for something bigger. Something public. And if that something gets even more eyeballs on his wife's favourite charity then all the better.'

'Aw, you know I hate that stuff, Hannah. I don't belong there.'

She laughed. 'No one belongs there, Ward. Everyone's just pretending they do.'

'Wait—' he narrowed his eyes as if only now registering what else she'd said '—the whole team will be there?'

'Yes. Now, I don't want to pre-empt but, according to Bernie, the board is happy, *very* happy with how well your rehabilitation, both personal and physical has been going. And he's wondering if this might well be the perfect opportunity for a big announcement. Return of the prodigal son, maybe?'

'Seriously?' Ward's face lit up and it was amazing to see. Being welcomed back into the fold was all he wanted, the only reason he'd allowed Hannah to let him in, and the perfect culmination of all the work they'd been doing this last while.

She knew that the Panthers' owner Craig Sumners was a wealthy philanthropist but he was also a very savvy businessman, known for his theatrical flourishes with anything team-related. If he wanted the whole team to be there and Ward too, it was a pretty good bet that something major was planned. She just hoped that Bernie's instincts were right and that it was a grand public welcome back for the rehabilitated player. But not knowing the intricacies of sports boardroom shenanigans, Hannah couldn't conceive of what else it could be.

'OK, OK, yes . . .' Ward's gaze raced excitedly around the room as he seemed to be coming around. 'Maybe that is good. I mean, I'm not thrilled about having to wear the monkey suit again but needs must, I guess.' He shrugged but his face now glowed with excitement and expectation.

'Well, that's another thing . . . ' Hannah began steeling herself, certain he wasn't going to like *this* part. 'Like I said, it's a pretty grand affair at the Plaza. All the other players were told to bring a plus-one, and Bernie wants you to do the same. All part of the responsible, mature, fully rehabilitated new you. And before you say it, I know, I know . . . your personal life is off-limits, but if there happens to be someone who's at ease with all this, or maybe used to rubbing shoulders with such people or . . . '

But far from rejecting the idea outright, Ward seemed to be thinking it over. 'Actually, there is,' he said, grinning, and Hannah wondered why she felt so deflated at this, his admission that there was indeed a significant other in his life after all. 'Someone who knows *exactly* how to handle it.'

Obviously someone used to the public eye too. That woman in the fitness video?

Then Ward flashed his heart-melting smile directly at Hannah.

'I get that it might be beyond the call of duty, but when you think about it, who better?'

Chapter 39

Dear P-1,

You've been awfully quiet lately. I'm hoping that it's just because there's fewer things about me to annoy you, and not because you're feeling poorly or anything. Meant to say before, that if ever you're feeling unwell or in poor spirits let me know and I'll pop over with some of my world-famous lamb stew. Don't want to boast but I've been told in the past that my recipe is capable of literally saving lives. (Slight admission, it comes from a can and I just add fresh cream, but it's offered from the heart and that makes all the difference.)

Sorry I haven't had the chance to bake much recently – work has been crazy plus some new demands on my social life, but I promise I'll get back to it soon. I think I'm going to add some macadamia nuts to the chocolate next time to liven things up. You OK with macadamia nuts? Some people don't like them but I love them.

Baking is the best distraction and unfailingly helps keep my mind off my problems. Well, they're not really problems, more dilemmas, I suppose. (Yes, I know – a dilemma is a kind of problem too before you point it out.)

OK, I'm rambling now. Just checking in again to make

sure you're doing OK. And to say that if ever you do need anything, (or want to see a friendly face?) I'm right next door.

Sincerely,

P-2

PS: I hope you do like macadamias. I know in California people certainly have strong opinions about them and take them very seriously indeed.

P-2,

Well, obviously I have strong opinions about macadamias, though I wouldn't go so far as to take them as seriously as Californians do, or that they do themselves. Truly the most pretentious of all the nuts, I always imagine them walking around with a cane and wearing a monocle. Peanuts, on the other hand, are the greatest nuts in the world. When your back is to the wall, you can bet the peanut is going to be there to help you out.

Thanks for checking in on me, by the way. That was very thoughtful of you. I had a bad run of health recently but am feeling much better these days.

P-1

PS: Lamb stew from a can sounds . . . weird. Let's just stick with the good stuff.

P-1,

Well, well, well I found your take on macadamia nuts to be interesting. Mostly because it's Mr Peanut who wears a monocle and has a cane. Not only that, but peanuts are not nuts at all as it happens. They are actually legumes.

P-2,

Ha! I can't believe you fell for it. Of course I know it's Mr Peanut that's the fancy-pants legume. Just trying to keep you on your toes. Can't wait to try your latest macadamia-flavoured formula whenever you find the time to make it amid your important high-flying social stuff, and naturally, I will report back as to whether or not you've hit the mark.

And with a view to your dilemma-problems, try me. Happy to add some perspective if I can. Plus, now I'm nosy.

★

'I don't know about you but every so often I get the feeling the world has gone completely nuts,' Zoe muttered without preamble upon answering Hannah's call.

Thinking of her and Ed's most recent correspondence, Hannah had to smile. 'I know that feeling.'

'So, spill. Is the reason for this call something to do with McKenzie?'

'What makes you think that?' she asked, a little taken aback at her friend's perception.

'Because you've never talked about a client as much as you talk about that guy. I'm actually starting to feel a little jealous.'

'That's because I was having such a hard time getting a handle on him,' she argued. 'He was a kind of an enigma at first.'

'Huh. Still getting the sense that this guy isn't just another client though, is he?'

Hannah opened her mouth to protest but then closed it,

frowning. 'Honestly, I'm not entirely sure how to feel. He kind of still is an enigma. Tries so hard to keep up this tough guy act. But when I'm with him and he lets his guard down, he's so different.'

Zoe let out a little laugh. 'Welcome to the world of men. Most would rather cut their right arm off than admit they have feelings or any sort of vulnerability. I don't know if it's an evolutionary thing, or if they're just plain stupid – or maybe a combination of both.'

Yet again harking back to one of Ed's 'classic truths', Hannah shook her head. 'I know Ward certainly isn't stupid. But he has put me in somewhat of a bind now . . . ' She went on to recount how he had suggested *she* accompany him to the upcoming event at the Plaza.

Back in her office, she honestly hadn't been sure how to answer, and then he got embarrassed and uncomfortable and so to prevent things getting awkward, she'd agreed, despite every cell in her body worrying about history repeating.

'Stop. Don't even mention that worm's name in my presence,' Zoe rebuked when she told her this.

She laughed. 'You're not here though.'

'Doesn't matter. Look, my experience with men is a little bit deeper than yours and I could always spot the ones who aren't worth it a mile away. Kendrick was never a keeper. Problem is, from what you've been telling me, the jury's still out on McKenzie. I think you need to figure out which side of the guy is the real deal – the one you've moulded him into, or the embarrassing loser the world used to know. Regardless, a night at the Plaza sounds like fun, so ignore me. And what makes you think it would be awkward?'

Hannah exhaled. 'Well, I didn't say anything at the time, but a while back, when I was still trying to get him to trust me, we had this . . . moment.'

'What kind of *moment*?'

'It was around that time I got those texts from Rob, so I was out of sorts and I kind of took it out on Ward one day, and got angry with him. And even though he's a world renowned hothead, he backed down—'

'Well of course he did,' her friend interjected. 'I too made that mistake at first, underestimating you as a mere gust of wind, when in reality once something gets you going you're one helluva tornado.'

Hannah laughed, not sure she'd quite agree with that description, especially when she made a point of rarely flipping her lid.

'And then . . . well, things felt a bit . . . heated and I know it's crazy but at one point, I honestly thought he was going to kiss me.'

'And why would it be crazy if he did? Especially if things were, as you say *heated*.'

'What? He's a client, Zoe. You should know better than anyone that I can't go there.'

Her friend groaned. 'You know, I wish I had your kind of professional dilemma just once. Heat is *good*! Most of my clients are old enough to have taken Cleopatra to the Egyptian prom. And you're complaining that Ward McKenzie wants to take you to the Plaza.'

'I'm not complaining. I'm just not sure if it's the best idea that's all. I mean I'll go – in a professional capacity obviously,' she stressed for Zoe's benefit. 'But there's no way I'm going to endanger my job or our client relationship because of my personal feelings.'

'Aha, I knew it! Didn't you just hear what you said? So that means you *do* have the hots for McKenzie. Here's what I think,

Cinderella: go to the ball and watch with pride as your client enjoys his moment in the sun being welcomed back to the Panthers. McKenzie's happy, the New York office is thrilled with a job well done etc. Then, you can drop the account and – safe in the knowledge that there's no longer a conflict of interest – you're free and easy to jump the wildcat's bones and live happily ever after. The End.'

Chapter 40

WARD

Ward ran the vacuum cleaner over the same spot on the carpet for the fifth time and finally just got down on his hands and knees and picked up the small furball that must've been Pretzel's.

Great. What was the point of having an expensive machine that couldn't even pick up a small piece of debris? He had half a mind to demand his money back and then remembered that he'd been paid to promo this thing and had actually got it for free. It bothered him that his name was being used to promote an obviously defective piece of equipment that people were going to pay their hard-earned money for, but Hannah had arranged this plus a whole other selection of endorsements, so he had to pretend it was the greatest thing since sliced bread.

Man, was he tired of pretending. He couldn't wait for all this bullshit PR stuff to end so that he could go back to the way things used to be. He seriously hoped that next week's event would in fact be the end of it and he was being welcomed back to the team in a blaze of glory.

But despite Hannah's optimism, Ward had a feeling that things weren't that simple. She didn't know Craig Sumners like he did. If the team owner wanted Ward back on the team, he didn't have to make a big public song and dance about it. There was more to this, he was certain of it. Which was probably why he'd come right out and asked Hannah to go along with him on the night.

As backup.

'As a work thing, obviously,' he'd insisted after, to save his embarrassment and also so she wouldn't think he was hitting on her or anything. Ward sighed. As much as he wanted to sometimes. Most times. But he knew better than to rock the boat when things were on the right track, and she'd done so much to get him to this point.

He was almost afraid to get his hopes up about being welcomed back to the team, so he also knew that if things didn't go as planned, having Hannah there would keep him on an even keel.

It was complicated too because he also recognized that what he felt for her wasn't just attraction. She simply had this way of keeping him grounded somehow. A way of teasing out an inner, *better* side of him so that he didn't have to feel so guarded all the time.

Lower the deflector shield . . .

And that was doubly scary, because Ward didn't know what he'd do when all of this public makeover stuff did come to an end, and there was no longer a reason for Hannah to be in his life.

So he was in two minds. While getting back on the ice had been all he'd ever wanted, achieving that pretty much meant that he'd be saying goodbye to Hannah. Having overcome their initial teething problems, he'd since come to almost depend on having her around. A little too much if he was being honest about it.

But maybe she enjoyed being around him too, and their easy relationship would continue? Probably not. Women like her didn't babysit guys like him unless they were being paid to do so. And yet, a part of him was almost certain that he and Hannah were more than that – more than just client and publicist.

But what did he know?

Went without saying that maintaining relationships had never been his strong point. Take Melanie for instance. An incoming call broke him out of his ruminations then and Ward tapped the earbuds he was wearing to block out the hoover noise.

'Hello, stranger.'

The voice was low and throaty and immediately made his stomach tighten. *Seriously?*

It was almost like his thoughts alone had summoned a ghost.

'Mel . . . hey. How are you doing?'

'I'm good,' his ex replied, 'and from what I've been reading lately, it seems like you are, too.'

He chuckled. 'Don't believe everything you read.'

'How's the injury coming along? Physical therapy helping?'

Still numb with surprise, he sat down on the couch and leaned back against the cushions. As much as he hated to admit it, even hearing her voice brought back so many feelings that were hard to control.

'Yes,' he replied, 'it's coming along good.'

There was a long pause and then she added, her voice tentative, 'And are you coping OK with the pain?'

He'd gone through the pain meds issue once before when they were still together. She'd been there for him – probably more than he had any right to expect her to be, and for that he owed her a debt of gratitude. Hell, he owed Melanie a lot of things.

'I'm off the pills now,' he told her. 'Johnny set me up with a trainer who's making sure I stay on the straight and narrow.'

'Wow, glad to hear it,' she said. 'Out of all the people in your life, Johnny's the best. The two of us always had something in common.'

That caused him to raise his eyebrows. 'Really?' he asked. 'What do you guys have in common?'

There was another long pause. 'We both always want the best for you, obviously.'

Out of all the words that could have come through his earpiece, Ward hadn't been expecting that.

'Forgive me if I find that hard to believe, considering that I haven't heard from you in months.'

'Well, work has been keeping me busy and I wanted to take some time out too. See what was going on with me and how I was feeling.'

'Right. Well, just in case you're interested in what *I* was feeling, I was feeling like you just walked out of my life and left me hanging. I was feeling like everything that you and I had been through didn't mean a damned thing. I didn't mind when you moved away, Mel, I understood that was something you had to do. But you cut all ties with me. You didn't answer my calls, didn't reply to my texts. Hell, you even blew off Johnny who you suddenly seem to like so much.'

There was a long pause and Ward wondered if he'd gone too far and she'd set the phone down.

Finally, Melanie spoke again. 'I was scared, to tell you the truth. The thought that there might be something real between us scared the hell out of me.'

'It scared me, too,' he admitted softly.

'So I know that when you get scared, the first thing you do is put as much distance between yourself and what's scaring you. That's what I was afraid was going to happen with us. I was afraid that one day, you were going to wake up take one look at me and decide I wasn't what you wanted. I figured that you'd get bored and move on to the next girl. Like you always did.'

'You didn't know that, though. And you never gave either of us the chance to find out.'

'I know,' she admitted, 'and that's totally on me. I take full responsibility for that. Things are different now though. Things have changed.'

'How?' he demanded. 'What's changed?'

'Well, for starters, it seems that *you've* changed,' she pointed out. 'I've been keeping up with all the stuff about you lately, seeing the pictures. I don't know what got into you, but I gotta admit that I approve.'

He shrugged. 'Bernie had a PR firm handle things for me and I guess they've gone a little bit overboard trying to change my image.'

'I don't think you can say "trying" anymore, Ward. They've done it. When I left, I was pretty certain that you'd just go back to your boozing and partying days and revert to the guy you were before we got together. And for a while, seems like that's what happened. Yet somehow you managed to get your act straightened out.'

'Yeah, well – a lot of the credit for that needs to go to my ballbreaker publicist.' Melanie laughed and Ward found himself smiling at that achingly familiar sound.

'So was she the one who took that picture of you grinning like a fool with those kittens?'

'Yep, that was Hannah.'

There was a pause. 'Hannah?'

'Yeah, that's the name of my publicist,' he said, a little defensively.

'Interesting . . .'

'What's so interesting about that?'

'Nothing – it's just I don't think you've ever really shown that side of yourself to anyone, not even me. You've always kept the walls up. Looks like Hannah's managed to work miracles.'

Ward snorted. 'I've been working on myself, too. If I want to get back on the team I need to have this squeaky clean image, and that's what I've been doing.'

'Of course. Is she cute, by the way?'

This was where he had to be careful, he knew. It could very easily turn into a minefield he didn't want to navigate. 'Doesn't matter,' he replied his tone glib.

'So she is important to you then,' Melanie stated quietly.

'What makes you say that?'

'When I asked you if she was cute, you didn't answer the question.'

Now Ward felt annoyed for some reason. 'Mel, is there a purpose to this conversation or did you just decide to call and give me the third degree for no good reason?'

She exhaled. 'Well, I suppose the purpose is that I'll be in town next week. And I was wondering if we should maybe get together. For old times' sake.'

Chapter 41

HANNAH

Dear P-1,

So like I said before, I'm dealing with more of a personal dilemma this time, and since you are older, wiser and more experienced at this stuff, I figured you might have some insight.

My entire life, I've never been good with matters of the heart. No matter how hard I try, I just never seem to get it right. For as far back as I can remember, every time I thought that I had found a boy that liked me, and that I liked in return, it turned out a disaster.

Sean Williams was my first crush. He sat beside me in school and had this shy little smile and, when he looked at me, turned my insides to mush. Turned out, though, that the only reason he was even looking at me was because my best friend Laura's desk was right next to mine and he was trying to see past me to look at her.

Next, I was desperately in love with Mattie McDonald. He was tall and on the football team and everything about him was just perfect. When I finally got the nerve to actually talk to him, he told me that if I lost some weight and did something with my hair, he could probably talk one of his friends into asking me out.

College brought me to Jake Flynn. He was smart and clever and said all the right things at all the right times. He made me feel as if I was the only girl that he could truly be himself around – and then I found out that he'd been himself with many other girls at the same time he was with me.

And that brings me to my ex – who I thought at the time was someone I was going to spend the rest of my life with. Handsome and charming with the world at his feet, he could have had any woman he liked, yet he wanted me. Or so I thought. Turns out he only wanted what I could get for him and once he'd got it, I became insignificant.

And now to add to my long line of failures, there's this new guy and even though he hasn't said anything, I think I've been getting some vibes. But again I'm just not sure if I'm reading too much into things. The problem this time is that he's off-limits. So even if there was something, I have no choice but to set my feelings aside. I need to protect my heart. Career too.

I've tried talking to a friend for advice, of course, but maybe there's something about getting an entirely objective (and anonymous!) point of view. Completely understand if you find all of this stupid and shallow and I'm sure now you're sorry you asked.

P-2

Dear P-2,
First of all, flattering as it is that you come to me for advice, referring to me as older and wiser makes me sound as if I'm

ready for a nursing home. While recent health issues have left me a little fragile, I'm not quite ready to be put out to pasture just yet.

Secondly, advice on matters of the heart is where I truly fall down. There might be a few things I know how to do in this world but being in a successful relationship surely isn't one of them.

This much I do know – and once again this is coming purely from a male perspective – men are the apex cowards of the world. We've got these walls up for our own protection. When we're around women, we tend to say and do stupid things – and so those stupid things make women think that we're simple.

It's hard to open up about our feelings to other people – especially when we don't know how they're feeling about us. Safer to just wait until they tell us how they feel, instead of us making the first move.

So, if we're not absolutely sure how someone feels about us, most of us aren't going to say a word because we're terrified that we're going to come across as pathetic or stupid, or in case we get shot down.

No man wants to be shot down.

Women have always been much more in tune with how things truly are. Men just kind of plod along, making stupid mistakes, and if we're lucky, don't do too much damage along the way. Me, I've made my fair share of mistakes and have lots of regrets too. And as for someone being off-limits? Story of my life.

I doubt I've been much help to you, sorry. The one thing I

can tell you is that confusion in matters of the heart remains
a conundrum across all generations.

Your hungry neighbour,

P-1

Chapter 42

WARD

Ward saw Johnny smirking at him from the corner of his eye and he turned away from the mirror and glared at his friend. 'You got something you want to say?'

Johnny grinned and shook his head, barely able to keep the amusement out of his voice. He'd dropped in to wish him luck before the event, both hoping that tonight would herald Ward's official Panthers return.

'It's just . . . I've never seen you like this, man. You've been standing in front of that mirror for ten minutes just looking at yourself all twitchy. It's like you've almost become . . . civilized or something.'

'You want to take this outside, I can show you how quick I become uncivilized, pal.'

This time, Johnny couldn't keep the laughter in and he threw his head back and bellowed with complete abandon. 'Easy, buddy,' he said, holding up his hands in mock surrender. 'There's no need to go all *Terminator* on me, OK. I'm just saying this is a side of you that I've never seen before – that's all.'

'Yeah, well, if it were up to me, I wouldn't even be going to this stupid fundraiser. But Bernie and Hannah both seem to think it's all pointing that way.'

'That's why PR Girl's gonna be there? For the cameras and stuff?'

Ward didn't want to admit to his friend that he'd asked Hannah as his plus one. No point in giving Johnny yet another reason to make fun of him.

'Exactly. Seeing as my fall from grace was pretty public, she wants to ensure my return to the fold is too.'

'All about keeping the illusion alive, huh.'

Illusion.

The moment Johnny said it, Ward's gut tightened.

That's exactly what all of this was, wasn't it? An illusion. Him and Hannah's easy-breezy relationship, all the attention she'd been paying him, her apparent insight into who he truly was. It was all about keeping up appearances, purely designed to fit into the story she was selling the public – about how Ward was now a changed man, ready to play by the rules and be a Good Boy.

Tonight was a form of unveiling; a shiny new Ward McKenzie who'd left his wild side in the past and was now heading towards a bright, carefully orchestrated future.

'What's wrong? You got that look on your face.'

'Nothing's wrong. I was just thinking about something, that's all.'

He'd been thinking about ripping the monkey suit off and walking away but couldn't do that either if he wanted to get back on the team. So again, he had to go along with the charade.

'You sure? You got that very same frown you get right before you hit someone.'

'I'm good,' Ward insisted. 'I just want to get this whole thing over with tonight, that's all.' He decided to change the subject. 'So hey, Melanie called and told me she wants to meet.'

Johnny's eyes widened. 'Why? What's going on?'

'I'm not completely sure but I got the feeling she thinks she might have made a mistake by ending things.'

Johnny broke out in a grin. 'That's great, man.'

'Uh, yeah. I mean, I guess it's a good thing. Problem is – well, I'm not sure what I want anymore. I'm finally in a place where I'm beginning to get my head on straight and I don't want to risk going down the rabbit hole again.'

Johnny was silent for a moment. 'I see what's happening here,' he said.

'Good. Maybe you can tell me, then.'

His friend raised an eyebrow, laughing. 'Oh, come on. You want me to spell it out for you? You're cooling on Mel because you've got PR Girl squarely in your sights now. You already admitted you had the hots.'

Ward flinched despite himself, and he hoped his buddy didn't see it. 'Hannah? That's ridiculous. Like you said before, way too risky when she's supposed to be making me look good.' He made a great show of straightening his bow tie.

'If it's that ridiculous why do you get that goofy smile on your face whenever you talk about her? Or you let her lead you around some fancy store like a back-to-front version of *Pretty Woman?*'

He was referring to the fact that Hannah had personally helped him pick out his tux for tonight instead of sending stuff over to Bernie's like she did for previous formal outings. They'd gone to the Armani store on Fifth and had been invited into a private room away from the main store because she knew how much he hated shopping. She'd assured him that this experience wouldn't be like trolling the racks at a regular department store – and that it would be painless.

'You might even enjoy it,' she'd teased.

And he had. It hadn't been a chore. It had actually been kinda cool. Hannah had given him feedback and advice, she had encouraged him to try some different styles he never would have in a million years to the point that tonight it didn't feel so much like a performing monkey, but a guy who had made something of himself.

Just like she always did, Hannah made Ward feel like the kind of man he wanted to be.

And he was terrified that soon enough, she'd see through him and figure out the man he actually was.

Chapter 43

Later, Ward waited by the fountain for Hannah at Central Park South, nervously moving from one foot to the other as he watched a parade of monied New Yorkers emerge from limousines that, in this part of town, had surely only travelled a couple of blocks.

Despite all this showy stuff, he had a bad feeling about tonight. It still made no sense to him as to why the Panthers' owner had insisted they all be here tonight for his wife's fancy benefit.

Sumners had a reputation for doing whatever it took to get whatever he wanted, and Ward knew he'd steamroll right over anyone who got in his way. Before his anxiety could work him into another funk, however, he spied Hannah gliding across the road towards the hotel. He hadn't seen her car pull up and it seemed like she hadn't seen him yet either.

The sight of her stopped him in his tracks.

He wasn't sure just what he'd been expecting, but when he saw her in a glistening midnight blue dress that fitted like a dream, and silver stiletto heels accentuating her slender calves, his brain just about went into sensory overload, the sight of her rendering him almost paralysed.

Look, he already found her attractive. That much was painfully apparent. But having only ever seen her look good in more casual day-to-day attire, he wasn't at all prepared for what a godamn heartstopper she was when she decided to go all-out.

'Jesus,' he muttered, under his breath as he moved to the Plaza entrance to catch up with her on the steps. 'I really am in big trouble here.'

Chapter 44

HANNAH

The moment Hannah saw the expression on Ward's face, she knew she'd made the right choice.

Back at the apartment she'd tried on and discarded a floral Kate Spade midi dress she'd initially thought might work, and while the print was fun, it just wasn't sophisticated enough for a night at the Plaza. Nor was anything else in her minuscule collection of more lowkey workwear. Especially when her plus one was going in Armani.

Then, recalling that there was an incredible closet full of couture right in the room next door, and that Courtney herself had encouraged her to go nuts . . .

Even though the dress felt like liquid silk on her skin, Hannah already knew she'd still worry for the entire night about damaging this glistening Vampire's Wife number. She was still marvelling at the fact that the dress had actually fit considering the size-difference, a testament to the designer's flatteringly fluid choice of material. It was a shame the brand was now no longer in operation, so wearing such a gown was a rarity in more ways than one.

Ward was just staring at her as she went towards him, watching her every step in her silver heeled sandals, and when she finally stopped, he looked her up and down with a glint in his eyes that was unmistakable.

What Hannah hadn't expected though was how incredibly gratified his reaction made her feel. Given the circumstances, she thought he'd be entirely focused on the night ahead. To say nothing of the fact she was supposed to be here in a professional capacity. So the heat in his gaze raised all kinds of uncomfortable questions that she'd have to examine more closely at another time.

Right then, though, she kind of wanted to just stand there and relish watching him try to form a coherent sentence.

'This OK?' she asked, unable to keep from smiling. 'I needed to look the part.'

He cleared his throat then and said, 'You look . . . incredible.' There was a raw huskiness to his voice that made her pulse quicken and she shook her head as if trying to banish any unwanted thoughts.

And Hannah was definitely having unwanted thoughts. Or were they?

Ward extended an elbow, his gaze never straying from hers. 'Well, I guess we should head inside and hope we survive the ordeal ahead — although, I've gotta admit, having you here looking like that . . . it might not be the torture I was imagining.'

'Was that actually a compliment?' She laughed. 'You caught me off-guard by not making some smartass remark for once.'

He duly escorted her into the hotel and they followed the throng of people past the Palm Court and onwards to the Plaza's renowned Grand Ballroom. She'd always loved this hotel, a classic monument to the city's gilded age, and she found herself torn between needing to keep things on a professional footing as Ward's publicist, and wanting just to kick back and enjoy the occasion as his actual plus one in this iconic New York location.

To distract herself, she glanced around at the other guests. Everyone there seemed to be in their element, moving easily through the crowd, stopping and having casual conversations about subjects that mostly involved making money or losing money, or moving to New Zealand before the New World apocalypse took place.

The other hockey players all seemed easy and confident, though most had the same cocky arrogant demeanour that reminded her of her early days with Ward. Their dates all wore expensive couture *they* clearly didn't need to borrow, though sadly their faces each looked to have been stretched by the same surgeon.

Some of them looked in her direction, then quickly away when she made eye contact as if easily dismissing her as not one of them, despite the dress. Evidently she wasn't pulling it off as well as she'd hoped.

Ward seemed to notice her unease because he gently touched her hand. 'What's it feel like to be on the other side of the curtain this time? You push us poor suckers out there in the spotlight, while you're lucky enough to get to fade into the background.'

'You're right,' she whispered. 'This is . . . scary.'

'Believe it or not, you get used to it. I gotta admit, though, there have been times lately when I wonder if it wouldn't be better just to walk away and try to have a normal life.'

His statement caught her by surprise. 'What? You love hockey, Ward. You could never just walk away from it.'

'The game I love, yes, – it's all the bullshit that comes with it I can't stand. I love the game because it's one with clear and simple rules that make sense and I can understand. All this fake, ass-kissing stuff?' He waved around the room. 'This is what I don't get. Like I told you before, it feels like another game but one where everyone else knows the rules except they're not written down anywhere. Or if they are, they haven't given me a copy.'

Hannah truly began to understand what he meant. There he was among so-called friends and still people were looking in their direction and having whispered conversations.

'I suppose it is hard being the centre of attention all the time,' she said. Hannah had always preferred being behind the scenes, helping others into the spotlight, then watching from a distance and vicariously sharing in their moments. When it turned in her direction though, her instinct was to run for the nearest exit.

Ward gave her a quizzical look. 'Are you kidding? I'm not the centre of attention. Tonight, all those people are looking at you.'

She shook her head. 'You're wrong. No one even knows who I am.'

'That's just the point. Nobody knows who you are and they're all wondering: "Who is that gorgeous creature with that bozo? Is she someone famous? I think I might have seen her at the Emmys last year." You're causing a stir, Hannah.'

Causing a stir . . .

That . . . wasn't good. She flinched and quickly moved away from him.

'You OK?' he queried, noticing her sudden change in demeanour.

'It's nothing. I suppose I'm just not used to people staring at me.'

He raised an eyebrow. 'You came dressed like that, and you weren't expecting to be stared at?' His gaze held hers and there was no mistaking the heat in his eyes this time.

Oh god. She couldn't falter. Not again.

'Let's go inside.'

A little later, after the gala dinner was over and a jazz band started up, Hannah found herself out on the ballroom floor in Ward McKenzie's arms and, despite her misgivings, she couldn't imagine anywhere better to be.

The first thing she'd noticed when he'd insisted they share a dance was how *solid* he was. It felt as if she were being held by a mountain. The next thing that struck her was how good he smelled. She didn't know what scent he was wearing tonight, but it was intoxicating.

Though she might have been a little intoxicated anyway, due to the champagne.

It didn't surprise her that he was a good dancer either. She'd seen footage of him on the ice before the injury and, despite his bulk, he'd always seemed so effortlessly graceful.

'How's the knee?' she asked, and instead of replying, he playfully spun her around.

'You tell me.'

'Show off,' she muttered laughing.

There was an unmistakable but surprisingly easy chemistry between them tonight, and she found herself enjoying the occasion far more than expected. When Ward let his guard down he really was fun to be around. She'd anticipated that things might be a little awkward between them given the confusion surrounding her apparent role here. But now it felt as if the professional element had completely faded into the background and Hannah was very much in plus-one mode and having the time of her life.

Just then, the music suddenly stopped, bringing her thoughts back to the present, though she realized that her dancing partner didn't seem to notice and was still her holding close.

Following a brief introduction and a heavy round of applause, revered Panthers' owner Craig Sumners trotted up to the mic. Hannah glanced back at Ward and reluctantly stepped out of his arms, giving his elbow an encouraging squeeze.

Here we go . . .

Chapter 45

WARD

When Ward saw the boss take to the stage, microphone in hand, he knew he should feel excited that maybe the moment he'd been waiting for had arrived but instead he felt annoyed. And doubly annoyed that Hannah had released herself from his arms and the fun they'd been having had been cut short. He'd been enjoying himself so much that he'd almost forgotten the reason he was here. Or hoped that was the reason.

But when the team owner made eye contact with him then, there was a dark glint in Sumners' gaze that made him certain he was right to worry.

'Uh-oh,' he muttered quietly.

Hannah glanced at him. 'What's wrong?'

'I'm not sure,' he admitted, 'but something tells me that I'm not about to like whatever the hell is about to happen.'

When Sumners saw that he had everyone's attention, the Panthers' owner began to speak, his voice firm and confident. 'First of all, on behalf of my lovely wife Barbara and myself, thank you all for coming here tonight. Benefits tend to bring out the best in people and tonight is no exception.' Then he chuckled. 'Though I suspect that might be about to change.'

There was polite, if somewhat confused, applause.

'Now, when I first took ownership of the Panthers, I don't mind admitting that I had no idea what I was doing. All I knew was that I wanted to be a part of something special — a part of New York history. This team has always been revered for its sporting prowess, passion, and success, but is also known for bringing entertainment and sometimes controversy to the game. And concerning the latter, no player has done more for that than our very own returning hero WildCat Ward McKenzie, who I'm happy to see here tonight.'

Ward felt all eyes turn on him and, despite Sumners' words, his instinct was to turn around and get the hell out of there. Instead, he stood in place when he felt Hannah's hand slip into his, giving him another reassuring squeeze. Reflexively he tightened his hold, as if it was some kind of lifeline. 'Now, we're all aware that our boy has suffered some physical injuries lately, but by all accounts is recovering nicely, and we're keen to have him back on the ice soon.'

Hannah looked up at him, flashing a delighted smile, and Ward exhaled. OK, he was coming back. He'd done it. The board hadn't given him the axe after all. Sumners had just confirmed the news he'd been waiting all this time to hear.

He knew that by rights he should be over the moon, so he wondered why he wasn't feeling that way. Probably because Sumners had simply issued the news so offhandedly and without any great fanfare. Which suggested he wasn't finished with what he had to say just yet.

No, something was off.

He leaned in close to Hannah and whispered, 'That's not it, there's more.'

Almost as if he'd overheard, Sumners then turned his full attention in his direction. 'Of course, besides injury, we're also all aware Ward has had some . . . recent challenges too; issues that he has worked very hard to overcome. His behaviour could even have been considered problematic by some, but like always, he was man enough to take all that criticism and face it head-on.'

His stomach tightened and he braced himself. All these cringe niceties aside, by the way Sumners was looking at him he was certain that a major bombshell was about to be dropped – and it was the kind of blast designed to cause maximum damage.

'I'm sure you've all seen some of the press lately and I gotta say some of us have had to do a double-take to see our Panther playing around with kittens. While we knew the PR people had to tame our wildcat a bit, we didn't expect him to be neutered.'

There was a burst of laughter from the crowd and Ward's face flushed. Hannah grabbed his hand again and entwined his fingers tightly in hers as if the pressure could contain the humiliation burning up inside of him.

'In other news, as some of you may already know, Coach Lewis recently alerted us of his retirement and I'm sad to say will be leaving us after the playoffs,' he stated and Ward frowned.

Coach Lewis was leaving? He couldn't conceive of playing under someone other than his beloved mentor who'd been at the helm since before he'd signed with the team. The big man had always looked out for all his players, both on and off the ice. He was even the one who'd encouraged Bernie to do all this image overhaul stuff to keep Ward from falling out of favour with the top brass. Granted the team's winning streak had suffered of late, but Coach Lewis was Panthers through-and-through and a battler too. He truly couldn't imagine the old man throwing in the towel and walking away of his own accord.

So did he jump? Or was he pushed?

'Rest assured we're already on the case and have put plans in place to help usher in a new era – a changing of the guard, if you will,' Sumners went on, pretty much answering Ward's unspoken question. If they already had someone lined up then yeah, poor Coach had been unceremoniously axed. 'So to ensure that next season we get some of that old predatory fire back in the team's belly, and return to the greatness we all so richly desire, I'm excited to introduce to you all tonight – our brand-new head coach of the New York Panthers, the legendary . . . Jefferson Prince!'

You have got to be kidding me . . .

As thunderous applause exploded all around him, Ward pulled away from Hannah's grasp, then turned and all but ran out of the banquet room.

He couldn't do this. Not again.

Chapter 46

HANNAH

Hannah was about to go after Ward, but still uncertain as to what was going on, and deeply confused by his reaction to it, she couldn't help but stay where she was. Her attention was drawn to the heavyset guy in his late fifties heading up to stand beside Sumners, apparently the Panthers' (and Ward's) brand-new coach.

After some brief backslapping, and once the applause died down, Jefferson Prince took the microphone from Sumners and boomed, 'Well, judging from the sound of that welcome, it's good to know there's still some real men left in the game.' More rapturous applause.

Hannah grew uncomfortable at the sudden change of atmosphere; there was now an edge to it that was akin to a political rally.

She stood there, confused. Who was this guy?

'Thank you, thank you,' Prince continued, flashing a set of brilliant white teeth. 'Glad to see that I'm among friends here. When Craig called me up about this job, he said that he remembered a time when being an athlete meant something, signified that you were different, possessed a talent others lacked, and people looked up to because they knew you were different. Faster. Stronger. *Better*.

'Then, times changed – the world changed – and they said sport needed to change, too. Suddenly athletes were expected to be caring, compassionate and filled with marshmallow goodness and unicorn-sprinkled tenderness.'

More resounding laughter and applause, and Hannah felt a bit nauseous at the nasty undertone in the guy's words.

'Well, I don't know about you, but I want to go back to the way things were, folks – back to when a man was a man and didn't wear dresses, back to when nobody but nerds gave a damn about what a friggin' pronoun was, back to the days when an athlete could live his life on his own terms off the field without having to worry about whether he was going to be "cancelled".

'Some of you might not know this, but I was Ward McKenzie's first coach after he went pro, so I guess you could say I'm the man who turned him into the badass predator we all know and love. And now that power duo is reunited! No doubt about it, by the time I'm done, WildCat McKenzie will be back bigger and better than ever. Back on the ice with the Panthers where he belongs, and back in the world of *real* men.'

Hannah couldn't find him in the lobby or anywhere else in the hotel, so she hurried outside and quickly spied Ward across the road pacing on the sidewalk by the park's south entrance.

The streets were quiet and largely traffic-free at this time of night, so she hurried across with ease, approaching with some hesitation, deeply cognisant of this latest public humiliation.

And doubly annoyed that she (albeit on the instructions of his agent) had played a part in it by encouraging him to attend tonight in the first place, and thus helped set up his participation in that nasty reputational flogging. His instincts had been spot on all the same.

He'd worked so hard to turn himself around and rehabilitate

his behaviour on the advice of a coach who understood that it was doing him no favours, only to be returned into the arms of a man who it seems stood for pretty much everything toxic about pro-athlete culture.

As Hannah got closer and got a better look at his face, her heart dropped at his pained expression and the raging maelstrom behind his eyes. She reached out and gently touched his arm. 'That guy, he was your first coach, the one you talked about before?'

He nodded, the hard set in his jawline brimming with anger, and his hands clenched as if ready to punch through the low sandstone wall.

'I knew it, I fucking knew it was some kind of set-up. I could never trust Sumners as far as I could throw him, and now I wonder if this whole image rehabilitation thing was a smokescreen all along too.'

'What? How so?'

'Sumners never had any intention of dropping me. He just enjoyed me and Bernie dancing to his tune, pretending he gave a crap about my public image, all the while using tonight's so-called welcome back as the perfect vehicle to bring in Prince after firing Coach Lewis.'

'No, Coach Lewis *was* truly concerned about your future – Bernie told me that. They certainly didn't set you up, Ward, no one who cared about you would do something like that,' she reassured him, although after what just happened, she knew that wasn't true in Sumners' case. The man was successful for a reason, primarily because he was a cut-throat vulture who, unlike Ward, knew how to play many different games. The way things had gone down in there certainly did feel like a public ambush, and she couldn't blame Ward for being angry.

'Come on, let's take a walk,' Hannah suggested, linking her arm in his and guiding him down the stone steps and into the park. Though it was late, the path closest to the streets was well-lit by the overhead lantern lighting, and the trail was illuminated even further by nearby buildings surrounding the space. The trees and glistening light reflections in the dark lake had a natural calming effect, which she hoped might work its magic on Ward.

'I can't do this, Hannah,' he said after a beat, his body still shaking with anger. 'I can't work with JP again. He has this way of getting right under your skin, making you feel worthless . . .'

'Maybe yes, when you were younger and still figuring out who you were. But you're a different person now, a grown man. Not some kid that's so easy to mould into whatever tough-guy messed-up idea he has, or thinks the world has. I heard him talk back there after you left. He's a relic, Ward. From a bygone age.'

'Nah, I know the guy. He won't rest until he breaks me. That's how he operates. You heard what Sumners said. The wildcat's been *neutered*?'

His jaw clenched so tightly she thought it might explode and she winced inwardly, reminded of the fact that much of her recent efforts in helping him tone down his old ways was responsible. And that Ward himself had expressed concerns that his new and improved nice-guy image might be going too far.

'He was talking about you as a player, trash-talking like they do before a game to rile players up. That's what I got from it. Seriously, all they care about is what you do on the ice, and your skill as an athlete has *nothing* to do with who you are as a person, Ward. Don't get confused again. Remember that's why you were so adrift in the first place, unable to step into your own shoes. Off the ice, Prince or Sumner don't own you. As long as you can perform, that's all that matters. And you can and you will, I know you will. Back better than ever, isn't that what you want too?'

'I don't know . . .' They reached the Gapstow bridge and moved to cross it, arms still linked. Glancing at Ward as they turned in the faint light, Hannah could still see so much uncertainty written on his face.

He paused in the middle of the humped stone bridge, staring down into the inky water, and as she stepped back, she shivered a little, the evening chill now starting to seep into her bones.

Ward noticed and immediately took off his jacket, wrapping it around her. 'Here.' His hands rested on her arms for a little longer than was strictly necessary and unable to stop herself, Hannah moved ever so slightly closer to the warmth of his body.

Because of the cold or . . . something else.

The atmosphere suddenly changed then, emotion still heightened, but in a different, more charged way and she could feel the weight of his gaze on her face.

Afraid to meet it, she looked back at the cityscape, the beautifully illuminated Beaux Arts hotel building like a postcard amid the trees in the near distance. She couldn't help but imagine how picture-perfect they must look now in silhouette, two figures standing so close in the darkness in the middle of the humped stone bridge, the twinkling Manhattan skyline spread out behind them.

'The important thing is, you're on the way back to doing what you love,' she told him, scrambling to get back onto safer territory. 'Exactly what you wanted. That was the game plan, remember. It doesn't matter what they say or do from now on. They can't change you as a person, and if they try, *I'm* here now, remember? Those two don't scare me and I'm certainly not going to stand by and let them undo all our hard work. You haven't yet seen me when I'm angry.'

She chuckled, trying her utmost to lighten the mood, but Ward's still-downcast expression suggested that he remained unconvinced. 'Make no mistake, I'm still here to keep you on the straight and narrow.' Hannah turned back to him then and stared at his face, now urging him to meet her gaze. 'I'm right *here*,' she insisted gently.

Then as if by rote, her hand moved to his cheek and she softly caressed his tight jawline. She couldn't help it. The hopelessness in his eyes was agonising and she needed to do something to take it away.

Ward finally moved his gaze back from the lake to meet hers, his eyes deep green pools still full of emotion. His hand flew up to touch hers and he rested it there for a moment, before pulling her close and into his arms, gently resting his head on her shoulder.

When he turned his face inwards and she could feel his warm breath on her bare neck, Hannah shivered again. But this time she wasn't shaking from the cold.

'Come home with me,' he whispered, pleading. 'Tonight. I need you.'

Her entire body was screaming at her to turn her face to meet his, signifying her assent. There was truly nothing more she wanted right in that moment than to feel Ward's mouth on hers, wrap her arms around him and allow him to take her anywhere he wanted to go, and everything else beyond.

But . . .

She broke free from his embrace, quickly standing back. 'I can't.'

'Can't, or won't?' The hunger in his gaze was intoxicating and Hannah knew that if he got closer again she wouldn't be able to resist it. Her body was humming as he picked up her hand and gently ran a finger along the edge of her wrist. It felt like fire on her skin. She needed to get this under control.

'You're . . . a client.'

'And what if I wasn't?' he countered, emboldened by the palpable energy between them, and the fact that she hadn't moved away again. He knew the effect he was having on her. Any hesitation or pretence was now long gone. They both knew exactly what was happening; what they both wanted, something that had been building all this time, yet quietly repressed, and that was dangerous.

Somehow, Hannah made herself step back further from the wall and wrapped her arms over her chest, as if to warn herself off.

'You *are*. And this is crazy. You've had some champagne, and it's been a weird night . . .'

'It's not that and you know it,' he argued, and of course he was right.

Hannah wouldn't look at him though. 'It's just, there are boundaries around this, rules. Like I said you're a client and I'm a professional. Plus . . .'

'Plus what?' He took a step closer again and it took every last ounce of willpower Hannah had not to sink back into his embrace.

'I've been dealing with some stuff . . . and I'm not ready for . . . anything. I was hurt by someone, still am,' she spluttered, shaking her head as if close to tears. She couldn't think of any other excuse sufficient enough to put a stop to this, and so she purposely played it up, wanting him to believe that she was still getting over her ex.

It worked.

'Oh. Oh, crap, I'm sorry. I didn't mean . . .' He immediately stepped back, putting the necessary distance between them, much to the relief of her trembling nerve endings. 'I'm sorry, Hannah. I'm an idiot.' Embarrassed now, he ran a hand through his hair. 'I got it all wrong, I should never have . . . Christ, I'm a fucking idiot, I really thought that you—'

'It's OK.'

'No, no it's not. I shouldn't have pushed or insisted.' He walked back and forth along the bridge, agitated afresh. 'I'm sorry if you felt pressurised, it's just yeah, the champagne . . . and I was upset and my head was all over the place. Christ, what a fucking night . . .' Then he dug out his phone. 'Here, let me call you a taxi. What part of town do you live in, and oh crap I shouldn't even be asking you something like that after . . .'

Hannah moved to catch up with Ward as he strode off the bridge and back onto the path out of the park, evidently believing he'd completely overstepped. She wanted to reassure him that wasn't the case, and it was after all *she* who'd initially reached for him in that way. But she couldn't do that, for fear that if he touched her again, this time she wouldn't be able to help but follow through once and for all. And however much she wanted to, she couldn't let that happen.

Ward *was* a client, and after tonight, he needed her more than ever.

It was a line they couldn't and shouldn't cross for a reason. As it was, she guessed that he was merely seeking a different form of comfort, a brief roll in the hay to block out what had happened at the event, a meaningless, distracting interlude before he figured out what to do next.

And that would be impossible if they crossed that boundary and went back to his place. Hannah would never be able to work with him again. Despite thinking that the announcement of his return to the Panthers meant this was all over and her job was more or less done, if anything, the work was only just beginning.

She couldn't leave Ward to deal with the fallout on his own. Not with her insight and deeper understanding of his mindset and vulnerabilities, or the danger of falling back into old patterns if the pressure got too much. She cared about him too much to let that happen.

And so she wouldn't – for Ward's sake, and her own too.

She'd had a moment of weakness, sure, but at the end of the day, Hannah wouldn't be so stupid as to risk everything she'd done to put her past behind her, and all the changes she'd made since starting over after LA.

Only to put herself right back into the same situation.

Chapter 47

So, I can't believe I'm even writing this, but . . .

Hannah noticed that some of Ed's words had been crossed out and scribbled over 'til whatever had been there was completely illegible as if he'd needed to get his thoughts in order before he continued.

I can't believe I'm writing this, but here we are. Seems I have a dilemma of my own.

Smiling with anticipation and no small part curiosity, she took the note over to the sofa, tucking her legs beneath her to get comfortable. It felt good to have something different to focus on, after the turmoil of the last week.

Following their 'moment' in the park, Ward had once again clammed up, retreated back into himself, and had been formal and distant with her ever since. Pretty much back to how he used to be when she'd first encountered him.

What's worse, it seemed someone from the paparazzi had spotted the two of them slink out of the Plaza separately and nabbed a shot of them heading into the park in the darkness, the online gossip sites running the headline **Back in the Den – Returning Panther McKenzie Scores with Mystery Woman**, beneath a grainy shot of her leading him down the steps.

While his face was clear beneath the street lights, luckily Hannah was slightly ahead of him and in side profile, and thus pretty much unrecognizable to anyone other than herself, thank goodness. And Zoe, of course, who was having a field day teasing her ever since.

Having made some meaningful inroads at work recently, the last thing Hannah needed was a misstep like this to undermine her.

She and Ward hadn't spoken again of that night though, other than she reiterating that the plan hadn't changed and that going back to the Panthers under Jefferson Prince did not mean an automatic return to his old self-destructive ways.

But he remained unconvinced and, she guessed, still a little embarrassed (or maybe even annoyed?) following her brush off. But how could she complain since she was the one who'd insisted on professional boundaries? To his credit, he'd insisted on seeing her off safely in a cab once they were back on the street, uttering a low-key goodbye and another apology as she drove off and he waited to catch the next.

It all felt like such a mess once again though, as if she and Ward were right back at square one. To say nothing of the fact that the New York office was busier than she could have imagined, with more client demands piling up by the day.

So to say she welcomed any opportunity for distraction from work pressure was an understatement.

As you can probably tell, I've been on my own for a while. Not alone per se but . . . well, you know. Nothing lasts forever. Life had other plans. Always does, regardless of what we want or hope. And after the last time, I pretty much figured that stuff – relationship stuff – wouldn't happen again for me.

Hannah read the paragraph again and put a hand over her heart, touched by his candour. Was he divorced? A widower, maybe? she pondered, suddenly imagining Ed in his wheelchair in the cemetery reverently laying flowers on a grave.

Life had other plans . . .

Her thoughts again drifted to her grandfather. He had outlived Hannah's grandmother by years. They had been together since they were teenagers and had married after he returned from a military stint during the Second World War. Married for almost seventy years with five children and a slew of great-grandchildren including herself, and with family around them at all times. Neither had been lonely at the end – not by a stretch. And they had been the love of each other's lives; Granddad certainly hadn't been looking for a second shot at romance when he was in his nineties.

So clearly Ed wasn't of similar age to her grandfather, nor as old and frail as she'd assumed.

So I guess what I'm trying to say is that I met someone special, and thought I was reading the signals right, but it's a mess

Who was this woman? she wondered then, enjoying the mystery. Someone he met at the doctor's office or the hospital? Maybe a widow or divorcee who lived in the building? Or maybe even his nurse? Hannah's mind swam with possibilities.

The note continued, **We haven't known each other that long. Truthfully, we come from completely different worlds** . . .

Again, he'd written a few more words before crossing them out and scribbling over them. Evidently, he had a lot on his mind and wasn't sure how to articulate those thoughts as they came.

Me being me, of course, I started things off on the wrong foot.

'Of course, you did . . .' She smiled, reminded of their own bumpy start.

That being said, I really don't know what to do at this point. I care a lot about her and want to tell her how I feel. But I would hate to show my interest in someone like her and not have it reciprocated, which is the most likely outcome. She's pretty incredible and I'm afraid of looking stupid.

'So you think she's too good for you? I'm sure that's not true.'

Goes without saying I'm out of practice with this stuff, and the older you get the harder it seems to be.

In her mind's eye, Hannah tried to picture Ed and his wife — a long-married couple who expected to be together forever. Until forever didn't happen and now he lived alone in their home in a very different world.

But new relationships were harrowing no matter what age you were, she reflected wryly. She shuddered at the thought of still having to try to navigate this stuff in her advancing years. Terrifying.

So this time, I guess it's me asking for some advice. How do I *not* make a fool out of myself?

The last question made Hannah laugh out loud. She was the last person he should be asking this.

> No pressure. I just figured I might be able to benefit from some female insight since I truly don't seem to know what I'm doing and which end is up.

How to tell him that I don't know what I'm doing either, she pondered.

She was flattered that he had come to her for advice in return though. The anonymity of their back-and-forth conversations allowed an intimacy that she was certain wouldn't have been possible had she and Ed ever met face to face.

Jumping off the stool, she went to seek out her pad of paper and a pen.

'OK, Ed, I'll try my best,' she mumbled, aware of the irony of trying to give relationship advice to a senior, while her own experiences in that regard were always a raging disaster.

What was that saying again? Ah, yes . . . those who can't *do*, teach.

And with that, Hannah started writing.

> Firstly let me say that I'm flattered that you thought to approach me for advice in return. Though I'm sorry to hear that you've been going through life on your own for a while . . . loss of any kind is so painful. However, it's exciting that you've met someone you feel you'd like to get to know better.

Hannah wondered momentarily if the woman in question was, in fact, his nurse or carer which might make things very awkward for him if she shot him down. Better not to overanalyze and just keep the advice general and unspecific.

> And good on you for potentially putting yourself out there. Though I know it can be scary, too . . . and believe me, I understand how hard it is to face the risk of rejection. Let me begin by reminding you there isn't a one-size-fits-all approach to love – and I have had my share of relationship disasters. So I'm by no means an expert (putting that disclaimer out there just in case).
>
> However, I think that if you approach this or any situation from an honest place, that's always good. Authenticity in anyone – male or female – is appealing and I've learned through experience to run a mile from anyone who pretends to be someone they're not. From what I already know about you, I can tell that you already live by this rule. And while it's good to speak your mind and be able to come straight out and articulate what you want, I do think that when it comes to matters of the heart, we all do better by treading a little more carefully . . .

Hannah grimaced, trying her best not to sound blunt.

> Feels to me that if you communicate openly and honestly, and aren't sending too many mixed signals, the object of your affection will quickly figure out that you can be trusted. And that after all is the basis of any great relationship.
>
> And once trust and respect is established, I think you can risk being a little braver or bold. Fortune favours the brave. Get her attention by doing something that catches her eye . . . but don't try too hard either.

Rob popped into Hannah's brain unbidden then, and she reviewed the previous statement before adding to it.

But under no circumstances do anything self-serving. You can be bold without making the other person feel awkward or on the spot . . . or worse, embarrassed. No faster way to send someone scurrying in the opposite direction.

'Or the other side of the country,' she muttered wryly.

I'm going out on a limb since I don't know any background but I'm assuming you run in similar circles and have some shared interests. Always remember to respect space and boundaries.
Ultimately, I think if you approach the situation with the best of intentions (as I'm sure you will) and take your time, it's likely that when you finally do pluck up the courage to take things further, you'll have success. And even if you don't, you can walk away knowing that you did everything right, and were true to yourself. Kind and respectful, a true gentleman. While you think the rules might have changed since the last time you put yourself out there, no matter what age you are, the basics truly haven't. Deep down, everybody just wants someone to love and cherish, and to get the same in return. What you seem to have forgotten, is that you already know you're capable of achieving that.

Hannah smiled then, deciding to call on the ever-reliable advice of her own long-time fictional mentor, which she felt was perfectly suited for the task at hand.

Now go boldly and make it so.

Chapter 48

WARD

Pretzel purred contentedly on the couch next to where Ward sat with his laptop open. ESPN was on the TV and two talking heads were offering their round-up on that night's games, including the Panthers' less-than-stellar performance against Dallas earlier in the evening and lots of chatter about their new coach. While their analysis should have commanded his attention, he was barely listening.

He couldn't get his mind off of Hannah, how goddamn stupid he'd been and how badly he'd misread the situation, completely confusing her attention as attraction.

You're her job, his inner voice reminded him. *She's* paid *to pay attention to you.*

He shook his head as if doing so would dispel his humiliation and he could conjure up an alternate reality. But what exactly? he pondered. One in which Hannah had come back here with him and they'd . . .

No, he realized, it was more than just physical, so much more. He'd been so sure there was something deeper growing between them, was certain of it; otherwise she wouldn't have reassured him that she'd be there for him, or let him hold her like that.

Though she'd rejected him in the end regardless, hadn't she?

He replayed that scene over and over again in his mind, the look on her face when she'd told him she'd been hurt by someone and was still getting over it. Ward wanted to tear the asshole limb from limb whoever he was. Hannah didn't deserve to be hurt like that. *He* would never hurt her like that, or any way. Not in a million years.

Or would he? Wasn't that his pattern? Fall for a girl and then love-bomb her, until just when he thought she was feeling the same way, she took off and left him for dust. Like Melanie had. He'd since told his ex that he didn't think there was any point in hooking up when she was back in town. That's all it would've been too – a meaningless, pointless hookup.

Because he didn't feel the same way he used to about Melanie. The way he felt now about Hannah.

Jeez, this was torture. Women were torture. How did he always end up going from one bad situation to another? Granted at least Hannah had the sense to blow off his advances, though Ward did know enough about women to know that she'd been . . . thinking about it.

But ultimately he'd got it wrong. And she was a woman of principle. Someone who kept to her boundaries. Played it straight and between the lines. His mind continued to drift and he scratched Pretzel behind the ears absently, trying to regain control of his thoughts and the flurry of conflicting emotions he was feeling right then – about everything.

While he was relieved to know that his Panthers future was secure, he was still dreading the thought of having to work under JP again. But Hannah was right about that too, he wasn't some stupid kid anymore and Ward just had to stick to his guns and ensure right from the get-go that he wasn't going to be pushed around.

People could say what they liked but this wildcat was still in full possession of his claws. Mostly.

Ward then looked at the actual cat as if Pretzel could provide some inspiration, but she just stared back at him in disdain.

He figured he was antsy because he felt so removed from Hannah again now. He had got so used to opening up, dropping the mask and being himself around her. And again he wondered about the asshole who'd hurt her before she came here to the city. Recalling her mention once that she'd got an office transfer, he figured the relationship breaking up must have been the reason why. Some dude in LA then.

Conscious of how much Hannah knew about what made him tick, and how little he knew about her in return, Ward glanced at the laptop.

It could be considered overstepping and invasive, a form of snooping even. But Hannah herself was the one who kept saying that the internet meant nobody's life remained secret anymore, and pretty much everything was laid bare for the world to see.

So it wasn't as if he was being a creep or anything . . .

Pulling the device onto his lap, he fired up a search engine and typed in her name, hoping to hit on her socials, though given what he knew about her, plus her line of business he figured she was a private settings kind of girl. Still, you never knew.

It was a form of self-sabotage, of course, but yet Ward wanted to get a bead on the kind of guy who had captured Hannah's heart. When lots of results bearing her name popped up, he modified the query, adding Lotus PR to the end of the search string.

And there she was.

Hannah's gorgeous face with her hair tied up and huge blue eyes in a professional bio shot beneath a link to the company website,

LinkedIn page and other business-related socials. No personals, which meant unfortunately for him no real insight as to what she liked to do, or what she enjoyed outside of work.

But then something at the top of the search result caught his attention. A YouTube video with the headline: **Kendrick Catches a Birdy.**

Ward clicked on the link and the clip opened up to the scenic backdrop of some golf course by the ocean somewhere, and that pro golfer Rob Kendrick standing on the grass, celebrating a shot. He was pumping his fists and high-fiving his caddy.

A reporter approached to get his thoughts on the triumph.

'How does it feel, Rob? It's been a while since your last big tournament win – what are you thinking right now?'

Grinning to the camera, satisfaction danced in the golfer's baby-blue eyes. The sunshine glistened off his blond hair, his skin was tan, and his arm muscles rippled under his orange Nike golf shirt. Typical privileged Ivy League prick. He looked every bit the winner, a total champ at the top of his game. His whole demeanour screamed young, vibrant, and on the up. Ward could hear the crowd of onlookers screaming with delight and felt a reflexive stab of envy as he recalled what it was like to win on that level, to feel unstoppable.

'Well, John—' the golfer grinned at the reporter as he walked off the green and headed to the crowd '—I gotta tell you, it feels great. This is what I've been working towards and I just felt it today, you know? Everything was working. All of it came together. Honestly, I feel on top of the world.'

'Congratulations on an incredible game. So how are you planning to celebrate?'

Something sparkled in Kendrick's eyes then – a hint of mischief coupled with menace, Ward recognized. He didn't know much about golf but he already knew in his bones he disliked this smarmy asshat. In sport, you learned to size up people within a split second, and his instincts were screaming right now that this guy was a dick.

'You know what? I'm not going to tell you; I'll show you.'

The golfer moved ever so slightly to the left of the frame, beckoning to someone off-camera. He reached out, his words garbled, clearly trying to persuade someone into the frame. A muffled voice could be heard protesting, but Kendrick persisted, his shit-eating grin only intensifying as he became more determined.

Finally, he yanked a figure into the frame with him, a woman with her back to the camera. Wrapping his arm around her waist, Kendrick pulled her close, leaning her backwards in a dramatic flourish and kissed her.

Showboating . . .

Ward's lip curled in disgust. It was obvious the girl didn't want to go along with it either and he felt bad for her.

Yup, his intuition was dead on. Guy was a narc of the highest order.

'There you have it, folks,' the reporter grinned raising an eyebrow, 'PGA tournament champ Rob Kendrick, causing a stir here today in more ways than one.'

And as the camera panned away from the golfer and his reluctant squeeze as she wriggled out of his grasp, Ward frowned again. His vision blurred and he blinked, refocused and tried to zoom in on the woman, whose deeply uncomfortable face was now suffused with scarlet blush.

The woman on the screen was Hannah.

Chapter 49

HANNAH

Hannah was in the middle of a pleasant dream. She was in the stands at a sporting event amidst a roaring crowd. Something significant was happening; it was a clutch game and the teams were tied with just minutes to spare on the clock. It was cold though, the whole arena was frigid and her mind wasn't registering what game was being played until the dream came into full clarity.

An announcer on a loudspeaker was calling out Ward's name, and then Hannah saw him sailing onto the ice after single-handedly turning the game with a bottle-knocker, his knee fully healed, his face alight with triumphant delight – his passion for the sport palpable.

He was home, a returning hero.

He took off his helmet, shaking it at the crowd, and everyone went wild. She jumped to her feet and joined in, feeling proud, knowing she had helped with this, that he was once again able to play the sport he loved and the fans were eager to celebrate him. Looking every bit the winner that she knew him to be.

Then from the ice, his green eyes searched her face out and when he finally found her, he raised his stick in salute. She waved shyly as he flashed a mischievous knowing wink and even as she slept her stomach did a pleasant little flip.

However, just as Ward started to glide off and take control of the puck, moving on the ice with renewed determination, there was another noise.

A persistent ding dong.

Confused, she searched the arena to try to figure out where it was coming from, but to no avail. Then the sound turned to a loud knock, and Hannah felt herself being pulled back to consciousness, no longer in the cold hockey arena but warm in her bed.

Feeling discombobulated – and somewhat disappointed to have been so rudely interrupted amid such a pleasant dream – she blearily sat up in bed, shaking her head free of the cobwebs of sleep.

There was the knocking again. She grabbed her phone from the bedside table to check the time.

Had she overlooked a scheduled delivery for Courtney or something? she wondered, surprised at the early-hour interruption.

The Peacock chairs and other remaining furniture had arrived last week, so no she didn't think there was anything else. And regardless, everything would have first gone through downstairs with either Julie or one of the doormen. Nobody else had access to the penthouse floor.

Nobody except . . .

Hannah jumped from the bed and threw on a robe over her pyjama pants and shirt, glancing in the mirror to check her reflection. Her face was puffy from sleep and her hair was matted across her forehead.

Great, Ed decides that first thing in the morning is a good time for an introduction? Or maybe he wanted to discuss in more detail the relationship advice she'd given him.

Talk about timing . . .

Though she did know many seniors liked to rise early. Her

granddad used to be up at six every morning like clockwork, a hangover from his military days. But she really would've appreciated a heads-up. Brushing the rogue strands from her face and wiping the sleep from her eyes, she rushed from the bedroom and through to the entryway.

More pounding. It was borderline demanding now and Hannah's heart started to race with worry that maybe there was some sort of emergency in the building.

She had a sudden vision of Ed being wheeled out on a stretcher after a heart attack or a bad fall or something. Pictured emergency crews lined up in the hallway, trying to revive him, and she felt her blood surge with panic. Maybe it wasn't a visit at all, maybe Ed needed help and the paramedics wanted her to provide something crucial?

'Coming, coming!' she called out.

Reaching the door, she put her eye to the peephole – after all, she was a single woman living alone in New York. Regardless of the top-notch security and doormen in the building that prevented randomers on the street from wandering in and accessing the uppermost floors, you could never be too cautious.

However, as she focused her vision to see who was on the other side of the door, Hannah felt the little hairs on the back of her neck rise, realizing that the peephole was blocked – as if someone was purposely shielding themselves from her vision.

Her bare arms chilled with goose pimples and trepidation and she glanced at the locks on the door – the chain was engaged and the deadbolt turned to its correct position.

'Who is it? The peephole is blocked – and I'm not answering if I don't know who's there,' she called out.

And then she heard laughter. Familiar laughter.

'Relax, it's me.'

Her heart jumped into her throat as she realized she knew that voice and she looked back through the spyhole, this time with disbelief and no small measure of confusion.

On the other side was a tanned, blond and ridiculously handsome man holding a bouquet of roses.

Chapter 50

WARD

Ward had watched that damn clip at least ten times – hell, probably more like twenty. It had inspired a whole new range of emotions in him, mostly anger-related. Right from the get-go it was clear that Hannah had been extremely uncomfortable – and Kendrick clearly hadn't given a damn that he'd put her on the spot. The opposite actually. He'd relished her discomfort.

Jealousy too, because there was no denying the fact that she and that dickwad were indeed a couple. And finally, confusion.

Because upon checking the Lotus PR client list and Kendrick's own Wikipedia bio, it was apparent that the golfer was a company client.

So much for professional boundaries . . .

Once he'd successfully pulled his attention away from the video clip, Ward spent more time tumbling down the online rabbit hole, trying to find out as much as he could. Unfortunately, there wasn't a whole lot outside of that lame stunt Kendrick had pulled on camera. And it wasn't altogether clear when or why the relationship ended. Or if they were still together even, which really irritated him. Worried him too.

'I was hurt by someone.'

Hannah also said she was still trying to figure stuff out, but that

258

didn't necessarily mean it was over and she'd told Ward nothing that even suggested that.

He took to scrolling through Kendrick's socials then, looking for pictures or mentions of him and Hannah together. But knew that if he found any, he was simply torturing himself even further.

Instead, he pulled up the PGA Tour schedule, feeling his curiosity intensify. Unlike some of his teammates, golf was not a hobby of his in the off-season and he didn't watch it either. Too damn slow, boring and dweeby. So he had very little awareness of what went on within that sport.

But the moment the schedule loaded on his screen, he felt his suspicions tingle.

This year, the PGA Championship had been held at Bethpage Golf Course on Long Island – a mere hour outside of Manhattan. And Rob Kendrick had been playing in the tournament last month. Round about the time that Hannah had arrived late at that podcast thing, looking dishevelled and distracted, and sexy as hell.

Ward felt himself clenching his fists.

Now he knew why she was late and her make-up all mussed up. Clearly, they'd reconnected while he was in town.

His imagination suddenly ran rampant as he replayed Kendrick and Hannah's bodies melded together in that video, the familiarity of the intimate moment on national TV plain for all to see.

His torment deepening, Ward had the sudden urge to call her up and ask about it. He wanted to know if she was still with Kendrick. *Needed* to know. What exactly they were to each other? And more importantly, why had she been so willing to break boundaries for that client and not him? Though he probably wouldn't have the guts to add that part. But if he was going to continue to trust Hannah, Ward needed to know.

Whatever went down between them that led to Hannah coming here from LA, it was almost certain that they'd reconnected anyway. After all, how many times had he looked up some old fling for a hook-up while travelling for a road game? If there was one cliché true about pro athletes of any stripe, it was that it was all too easy to have a puck bunny in other cities. No-commitment dalliances were par for the course.

Though Hannah wasn't a hook-up, he mused darkly, resolving to call her first thing tomorrow and ask her straight up what the deal was. She wasn't a puck bunny – or whatever the golf equivalent might be.

But mostly because this wasn't just jealousy on his part.

Smarmy video stunt aside, Ward knew it in his bones that Kendrick was bad news. And for her own sake, Hannah needed to stay a million miles away from a dick like that.

Chapter 51

HANNAH

Rob sauntered into the apartment like he owned the place and made a big show of presenting her the flowers before shoving his hands in his pockets, a knowing smile on his face as he took in Hannah's state of dishevelment.

'Sleeping in this morning?' he teased, all the while taking in the space and offering an appreciative whistle. 'Nice digs. Very nice. Quite the *bachelorette* pad . . .'

'How the hell did you get up here? The doorman . . .'

'Is a *huge* fan,' he interjected and yes, of course, she should have guessed that Rob's charm ensured that the waters parted for him wherever he went.

Which presumably explained how he'd found out where she was living too. No doubt a quick call to someone in the New York office would have easily done the trick. Especially when the rumour mill had ensured that many in Lotus PR were aware of his and Hannah's history . . .

Two years before, Rob had signed with the LA office after winning his first big Major and was looking for ways to boost his brand.

'Less Rory McIlroy and more Grayson Murray,' he'd told them, grinning. 'I want to cause a stir.'

Hannah initially had no qualms about taking him on as a client. Blond and blue-eyed, Rob hailed from San Diego, and had that easy, laid-back Californian charm that wooed his fans (especially those of the female variety), appealed to sponsors, and made him a quickly revered figure on the PGA tour. He had charisma and star power written all over him and she'd been excited to be the person who propelled him to new heights.

Needless to say, that charm ended up working far too well on her too.

From the outset and by mutual agreement they'd decided to hide their relationship – it was not a good look, professionally speaking. Even though the agency didn't have any strict company policies against dating clients, Hannah was deeply mindful that it was something you simply shouldn't do if you wanted to be taken seriously.

Rob seemed happy enough to go along with her need for secrecy and, for a while, things felt comfortable and steady – they kept a low profile as a couple and simply enjoyed being in each other's company.

Not long after Hannah moved in with him, however, she noticed that his growing success started to go to his head. He began craving the cameras more and more and expressing contempt for younger up-and-comers or more talented seniors who attracted larger crowds on the tour.

And then one day Rob went rogue – and did so without a thought or inkling of concern about what it might do to her career.

When he unexpectedly pulled her into a camera shot after winning a tournament at Torrey Hills and kissed her on national TV before muttering in her ear, '*This* is how you cause a stir,' Hannah couldn't believe he could publicly humiliate her like that.

While there in attendance in a professional capacity, suddenly she was thrust into the spotlight and their relationship immediately laid bare.

Of course, it wasn't a bad look for him; he craved the cameras and the headlines. But her ethics and professional integrity were soon under question. Rob was the talent, after all. He had nothing to worry about. He was the one who paid her for her services.

Soon the media – and worse, people in her industry – were making tongue-in-cheek comments about exactly what 'services' Hannah was providing. She'd endured the whispers, seen the disdainful looks from colleagues at the agency and felt the awkwardness when she walked into a room and all talking ceased.

She had never in her life felt so humiliated. So cheap and small.

Which was why she'd left LA for New York and a brand-new start where nobody would point and whisper. And taken a stand with Rob, telling him that she wanted to end it, stupidly believing that he'd admit to his mistake and find a way to rescue their relationship, to fight for it even.

But that hadn't happened, so Hannah had had little choice but to assume that their time together meant nothing to him, that she meant nothing to him.

Buoyed and supported by Zoe, who to be fair had expressed from the outset that there was nothing about Rob Kendrick that couldn't be fixed by a brick to the head, Hannah had vowed to move on, hold her head high, make a fresh start elsewhere and forget all about him.

She believed she had done that quite successfully too until recently, whereupon that pesky cat had inadvertently ensured that her ex knew her true feelings, and all the hurt and shame she'd endured in the aftermath.

And had promptly ghosted her after, all promises of a reunion while he was in New York for the tournament suddenly forgotten.

Yet, inexplicably here he was now in Courtney's apartment, standing right in front of her.

Hannah put the flowers on a side table against the wall in the entryway.

'I'm sure you know this place is not mine. And it's early actually.' She self-consciously brushed her fingers through her hair and tucked a few errant strands behind her ears. Glancing down, she quickly realized the front of her robe was open, her silk pyjamas exposed, and she wasn't wearing a bra. She wrapped the robe around her body and tightened the sash.

Then looked up and met Rob's gaze. As if reading her thoughts, his eyes flicked ever so briefly along her body, his gaze lasting a moment too long.

Swallowing hard, Hannah crossed her arms. 'Why are you here?'

He shrugged and turned on his heel, striding silkily through the apartment like a tiger.

'I wanted to see you,' he said, non-committal, as he strolled over to the window, taking in the expansive view of the park beyond the glass. 'Quite the vista.' And again, as if he owned the place, blithely lifted the sash window, letting in some fresh morning air.

'Yes,' she replied distractedly. 'But again, what are you doing here? And why now when you were in the city last month and I didn't hear a word?'

He turned to face her, and his expression transitioned from playful to serious.

'First of all,' he began, 'I owe you an apology for being the biggest idiot in the world.'

She stared at him, not sure what to say to this and also how he had deftly side-stepped her question. Though she could probably guess exactly what Zoe would say if her friend were here.

'I know I messed up, and it kills me that I hurt you. I realize now what I did was inexcusable. That message . . .'

'Why did you need me to spell it out though?' Hannah asked, perplexed. 'Surely you must have known what that little stunt would do to me professionally?'

He sighed. 'I honestly wasn't thinking at the time,' he admitted. 'I was just on top of the world and I wanted to share that with you. With everyone.'

He certainly sounded sincere. As she stared into his baby-blue eyes, all the great times they'd had together came flooding back. Then remembering how he could so easily turn on the charm when he wanted something, Hannah headed into the kitchen and placed a pod in the Keurig, determined to keep her composure. Forget the tea, she was definitely going to need coffee for this conversation.

'That message was weeks ago though,' she reiterated. 'And you said you'd be in town for the tournament last month. I know you were. So why not come and see me then? Why now?'

Rob's eyes softened and he did the puppy dog eyes thing.

Don't fall for it, she warned herself.

'I wanted to come and see you when I was at the tournament, babe. But honestly . . . I didn't know what to say. I hated how we ended things and I needed to think about . . . next steps.'

Next steps? As if her feelings were to be considered as part of some kind of *strategy*? There was more to this visit than met the eye, she was sure of it. She turned to face him, determined to say her peace but keep her cool.

'Well, now you know why I left. You disrespected me. You

humiliated me on live TV. You thought of yourself only. You didn't care a whit about what the fallout would be for me or my career, how I would be judged by my colleagues, my boss, and my clients. You made me look like a fool,' she finished softly.

He slowly crossed the space between them, pausing ever so briefly by the door to her bedroom. He glanced into the room and took in the rumpled sheets and the mattress, the bedsheets likely still warm. Looking back at her, Rob's eyes twinkled suggestively, and she knew exactly what he was thinking about.

She straightened her shoulders and did her best to remain non-plussed.

'I know what's on your mind,' she challenged. 'And I can tell you here and now *that* is not going to happen.'

He chuckled and moved closer. 'See, it's stuff like that. You get me, Hannah. You *know* me.' He took a few more steps and studied her from the opposite side of the kitchen island, where her phone rested since the night before. 'That's why we were so good together. And could be again.'

Putting a hand on the device, Rob idly spun it around on the marble top in lazy circles. The movement woke the screen and she glanced down to see a slew of notifications, patiently awaiting her response. And right at that moment, almost as if the other party was aware she was in the vicinity, it started to buzz with a fresh incoming call.

Frowning, Rob snatched the phone and looked at the caller display. The smile dropped and his blue eyes now sparkled with something else as he stared at her.

'McKenzie . . .' he spat darkly. 'I honestly didn't believe it but . . . Are you actually serious, Hannah?'

Then all at once, she realized why he'd suddenly shown up at her door like this, a mere week after those paparazzi shots of her and Ward in the park. He'd evidently seen them and recognized her.

Rob didn't want Hannah, but he didn't want anyone else to have her either. He'd always been the kind of guy who needed to be top dog and couldn't stand the notion of anyone snapping at his heels. As a fellow sportsman, he presumably viewed Ward as a more worthy rival and was now looking to reassert dominance.

Realizing all this, Hannah wasn't sure whether to feel disappointment, or relief. She grabbed at the phone, trying to snatch it back. But it was no use. He was taller and faster, and he easily pulled it back out of her reach, sauntering away toward the living room window.

'Rob, stop it,' she insisted, holding out a hand. 'Give me that. I need to take that—'

Glancing back and smirking at her helplessness, Rob accepted the call.

'Good morning . . .' he greeted, haughty superiority oozing off him. She moved for the phone again, but he brushed her off. 'I'm afraid Hannah can't talk at the moment,' he mocked in a suggestive growl. 'She's a bit . . . indisposed.'

Chapter 52

WARD

Ward squeezed the phone tight as the line went dead. He glared at the device and resisted the urge to smash it against the wall. Jealously and protectiveness flared in tandem – hot and intense like a fire. His vision tunnelled and he felt as if a red mist was descending upon him.

He was right. She was still seeing Kendrick. There was no mistaking the voice, not when he'd heard it on that video clip he must have watched a hundred times.

And she was with him *right now*.

He slammed the phone onto the coffee table, which made Pretzel startle. Quickly composing herself, she looked at Ward with disgust and sprang from the couch, leaving the room. But he wasn't paying attention to the cat.

Hannah had just spent the night with that guy. They'd probably just crawled out of bed. Or by the sounds of it, were still in it. An unbidden image of Kendrick and Hannah together intruded his brain and his fists clenched at the notion. Then snapping out of it, he shook his head, trying to make sense of it all.

There are boundaries.

Kendrick was still one of Hannah's clients. Obviously those

boundaries didn't prevent her from falling into bed with *him*. She had bent those rules for that . . . that dick.

He tapped his fingers on the coffee table, trying his damnedest to make sense of what he was feeling. Was it primarily overprotectiveness? Or just territorial. Was he jealous of Kendrick because he had something he wanted. Or because he genuinely thought that Hannah was making a bad decision?

He hated feeling this way, hated feeling so helpless and out of control again. All he'd wanted to do was focus on getting back on the ice, getting healthy, getting his career back. Everything back on an even keel.

Hannah had helped him do all that. She had calmed him, grounded him, encouraged him. Made him feel, rightly or wrongly, that she truly cared about him, the person. Not just the athlete or the image.

But that was obviously all bullshit.

Right then, Ward wished that he had never met her. That Bernie hadn't insisted that he needed to revamp his goddamn reputation. He would have been able to fix his knee, stay off the pills and get back on the ice.

And yes, Hannah had helped him, improved him even. Ward couldn't deny that. He marvelled at just how well she seemed to get him. How great she had been at creating a strategy that fit his personality just so. She understood him. She *cared*.

Ward cared too. Hannah deserved a whole better than that guy, regardless of whether or not that person was him.

Plus he wanted her approval. Craved it. And now some other guy was getting that and a whole lot more too, he thought darkly, despondent and angry at the world once more.

Certain that he'd messed up. Again.

Chapter 53

HANNAH

'What the hell was that?' Hannah exclaimed angrily.

Rob raised his eyebrows, a smirk playing at the corners of his mouth and casually handed her back the phone as if nothing had happened. He oozed smugness and in that moment she wondered what she had ever seen in him.

He shrugged. 'I was just messing around.'

'Messing around with my—' she began before grabbing the phone and reclaiming it. She looked down at the screen. Yes, it was a call from Ward that had been safely disconnected and her thoughts spiralled, wondering what he must be thinking.

Especially when Rob had made it sound just then that they were . . . She felt her face flush – with embarrassment and anger too.

None of it was lost on her ex, who watched her closely.

'Why does it matter? I was just joking – just having fun. I'm sure your *client* will understand . . .'

His words were thick with sarcasm and she looked down at her feet, ashamed at what he was trying to suggest.

Rob studied her as if he could see right into her mind and knew everything she was thinking, everything she was feeling.

'So answer me. What does it matter what he thinks, Hannah?'

he chided, his tone feigning innocence. 'I mean, he is just a client, right?' His blue eyes darkened. 'Or have you been helping him with some *physical* therapy too? Wouldn't be the first time.'

'He is just a client,' she retorted, but even as she tried to insist to Rob that there was nothing between them, of course it wasn't true. She remembered when she had first bumped into Ward that day at the coffee place. How flustered he had made her. Recalled all the times it had felt like he had been flirting, being playful with her. The undeniable spark she'd been working so hard to suppress.

And then, of course, that night in the park.

'It's none of your business anyway,' she muttered but he was looking at her closely and whatever was written on her face seemed to confirm what he was accusing her of.

'Seriously? You go from *me* to banging some washed-up loser hockey player?' His eyes sparkled dangerously.

'I'm not and he's not washed up.' For some reason, she felt doubly irritated on Ward's behalf at this description. 'But more to the point, it truly has nothing to do with you regardless. We aren't together anymore, Rob. We are so not together that I put two thousand miles between us,' she stated.

'But we could be. We could again. It's not too late for us. You told me yourself how hard it was to walk away. And you know how much I want you.'

Before Hannah could even register the action, Rob had circled her waist, slipping his hands beneath her robe. She felt their warmth as they pressed against the silk of her pyjamas and she pulled away, pushing at his chest. But he was strong and his grip tight and she struggled to break free, her panic rising. She didn't want this. But still, he persisted. Finally, her body acted instinctively. She pulled her knee up and planted it firmly between his legs, meeting its intended target.

In some situations, diplomacy had its limits.

Rob howled like a wounded animal but released her and Hannah took the opportunity to jump away. Hands shaking, she grabbed her phone, pulled up the emergency call button and held the screen up for him to see.

'Get out,' she warned. 'I mean it, get out or you can explain to the police what happened. I will press attempted assault charges against you. I swear to God, we are finished. I want nothing to do with you. I never want to see you again. Do you understand?'

She realized she was trembling as the adrenaline flowed like a river through her veins. When they had been dating, he had never been like this. He had never made her feel unsafe.

Clearly, something about him had changed. He had become used to getting *exactly* what he wanted whenever he felt like it.

'As if,' Rob scoffed, but now his eyes glistened dangerously, and Hannah felt seriously scared. He truly did believe he had the upper hand here and she couldn't be certain he *wouldn't* be able to smooth-talk the police too, she worried, thinking hard. She wondered if there was some other way to extricate herself from this. Could she call downstairs for help? Alert Ed next door even? But it wasn't as though a feeble old man could do anything, she thought, fraught with desperation.

Again it seemed as if Rob could read her thoughts.

'So make the call then,' he dared menacingly, taking a step toward her. She had seen an inkling of this darker side of him before, witnessed him aim his ire at other people when things didn't go his way. But that was often how it went with talent. They were so used to everyone blowing smoke up their backsides that they could get away with behaving like toddlers. He had never been like this with *her* before though and now it scared her. 'Or maybe you should call your latest squeeze and ask him to come to your rescue? He has form in that way, I hear. Let's hope his right hook is better than his stick work.'

Should she call Ward back? Hannah wondered suddenly, but to what aim? It wasn't as if he could crash the door down and come to her rescue. To say nothing of the fact that he didn't even know where she lived.

Rob kept closing the distance between them and instinctively she moved backwards step by step, until she was up against the marble countertop with nowhere left to go as her ex loomed ever closer. This was one situation Hannah felt helpless to de-escalate.

Then all of a sudden came a chirruping sound of sorts, and she struggled to process what was happening when, out of nowhere, the stray cat appeared alongside her on the countertop. Then jumping onto the stool closest to Rob, it hissed, raised its paw and swiped at her ex in one quick motion, raking its claws across his cheek.

His hand flew to his face in shock and then he pulled his fingers away to assess the damage, staring at them in disbelief.

'What the . . . ?' he gasped, and then looked from Hannah to the cat, trying to process what had just happened. 'You have a friggin' cat?'

'Get out, Rob,' she cried, her voice faltering with a mixture of fear and relief. 'I mean it. *Leave.*'

The unexpected interruption seemed to be enough to make him come to his senses. 'You're not worth it,' he spat. 'You've never been worth it. Look at you, a pathetic cat lady all alone in an apartment you don't even own and could never afford. You're nothing without me. A nobody.'

Hannah raised her chin defiantly. 'If I'm such a nobody then why are you here?' She levelled her gaze at him, composure slowly returning. 'And I forgot to mention it, but this apartment has a state-of-the-art security system, including motion-activated CCTV.' She smiled at the uncertainty in his expression as he tried to second-guess whether or not she was being serious. 'Never come here again, unless you want that footage to be leaked to the press. And I'm sure you're well aware that I can make good on that threat – you know, for a nobody.'

The cat's intervention had also granted her the presence of mind to think of something that would get him to back off, something she could use against him. His precious ego. There was no internal CCTV activated while she was staying here of course, that would be creepy, but he didn't know that.

She saw concern dance across his face then as Rob finally concluded that she might well have the upper hand here, and even a trump card. She could damage him personally and professionally in a heartbeat. His eyes darted around the space, as he thought hard, clearly seeking out the hidden cameras, reality dawning at what they'd just captured.

Then seemed to come to a conclusion.

'Like I said, you're not worth it.' Rob put a hand up, finally conceding defeat, and much to Hannah's relief, retreated to the door.

When she was certain he was gone, she reinstated the locks, then came back into the kitchen in search of the cat. Who'd since settled itself on one of the wicker Peacock chairs and was now casually licking its fur as if it was no big deal; all in a day's work. 'I have no idea where you came from or who you belong to, but thank you,' Hannah said, crouching down to massage its ears. The cat leaned into her hand and elicited a deep purr. 'Good shot, too. Well played.'

Chapter 54

WARD

W ard had been dodging Hannah's calls for days now. And then he started to avoid Bernie's too – according to his agent's voicemail, she had got in touch to pass on the message that he'd been asked to present an award to a teammate at this year's NHL ceremony happening at the end of the month.

Whatever . . . they could set the whole town on him and put in alarms with the NYPD and FDNY if they liked. He didn't care. He just couldn't bring himself to speak to her . . . and he had plenty little to say to his agent too after Bernie had thrown him into Sumners' den without warning, inadvertently or otherwise.

In fact, Ward had nothing to say to anyone. People in general were welcome to talk to his ass, or his voicemail at least. After all, he had things to do. He'd spent the morning watching the most recent PGA Championship on replay – or rather, watching one player in particular. Hoping to establish whether his instinct about this guy was correct or merely clouded by jealousy.

Not that he realistically could do anything about it if Hannah was still with him, but Ward needed to know.

And so he studied, like he always did with people.

'Amazing shot,' gasped the TV commentator now. 'But only if

he can chip his ball and miss that bunker, which has proven tricky for the best of them during this tourney.'

'Agreed, Carl. And even though Kendrick is second on the leader board at the moment, it's apparent that he's been somewhat off his game this time.'

Ward snorted, narrowed his eyes at the screen and made a silent prayer. He didn't believe in manifesting, but if he could retrospectively will the asshat's ball into the sand by the power of mind alone, there's no way he would pass up the opportunity.

On the screen, the golfer and his caddie consulted, deciding on the best approach. Then Kendrick sidled up to the ball and made a few dweeby practice strokes. The sunlight glinted off his blond hair, and Ward sat forward and leaned in towards the screen, studying the guy's face.

Yup, the kind of face you wanted to punch.

Kendrick pulled his club back and made the shot, deftly hitting the ball. Its trajectory propelled it up, up, up – and then the spin took it straight down. Right into the bunker.

Ward jumped up from the couch and let out a whoop as if he himself had just scored a Stanley Cup winner – instead of actively rooting against another athlete in a TV replay of a tournament that finished weeks before.

'Keep those shots coming, jackass,' he muttered.

Speaking of . . . Ward glanced at his crystal rocks glass. It was empty. But a miss like that deserved a celebration.

He went to pour himself another two fingers of bourbon as his thoughts returned to Hannah and he wondered if she'd been there at the tournament. He scowled at the notion that she might even have been there on the sidelines, cheering for Kendrick and encouraging him.

At the very same time she'd been encouraging *him*, but in an altogether different way.

Ward conceded to himself now that he wasn't just sitting there like a loser watching the replay just to wish bad vibes on Kendrick, but also trying to figure out if he and Hannah truly were still together or had been, back at the time the tournament took place here in New York. He'd been scanning the crowds whenever the cameras panned around the course and hadn't seen her. But that didn't mean she hadn't been there.

The significance of Kendrick answering his call to her, and what it suggested, had sent Ward into an even deeper spiral than the one he'd already been struggling to climb out of since that night in the park. The humiliation of that evening overall still burned; public embarrassment aside, it was a night of reckoning overall. With Hannah, he'd missed the signals – or worse, misread them altogether. Had taken her interest, enthusiasm and generosity toward him to mean something more.

Again.

When or if he did feel up to working with her again, and while he figured it was none of his business – no, he knew for sure that it wasn't any of his business – on some level, Ward was interested to see whether she would address Kendrick answering her phone like that.

But maybe she didn't care. After all, why should she be embarrassed or concerned about what Ward thought if she and the golfer were together?

She prided herself on being a professional through and through, despite this latest evidence to the contrary, but perhaps he'd read that all wrong too? Maybe she'd got the transfer to the New York office so that there was no longer a conflict of interest, and so she and that dickwad could continue seeing one another.

It was about the only reasonable explanation he could think of. But then that night in the park when she'd said she'd been hurt, how did that tally?

Probably just trying to let him down gently, Ward concluded, cringing at the notion that she was simply taking pity on him. Hannah might well care about him as a person and empathise with his situation, but at the end of the day, all he was to her was a client – nothing more than a pay cheque.

But he'd made a mistake and confused all the attention she was paying him with something else. Unused to people besides Johnny giving a shit about him as a person, Ward had latched onto Hannah like the stupid loser he was.

So until he got a full physio signoff on the knee and was able to get back on the ice and do what he did best, he was going to do the second thing he did best: hole himself up in his place, shut out the world and drink.

And cheer when Kendrick hit another dud shot.

Ward kicked his feet up on his coffee table and sat back, sinking into the sofa. Until his relaxation was interrupted by a knock on the door.

He got up, shuffled listlessly to the entryway, and looking out the peephole, recognized his visitor and groaned. He could just pretend he wasn't home, but if he did that, she would just keep knocking and wouldn't leave until he opened up.

'How's it going?' he greeted blearily.

Shelley's arms were folded across her chest and she tossed her ponytail over one shoulder, eyes dark and glittering.

'*How's it going?* For real? You're not answering your phone and you missed our last two sessions. For someone who wants so much to get back on his feet, you certainly aren't acting like it. And the fact that I have to trek all the way over here – *twice* – and you're not here, pisses me off. I'm not your babysitter, McKenzie. I already have a kid.' Coming inside she inclined her head to noise from the TV. 'And since when do you like golf?'

He shrugged. 'Yeah, so what?'

She pushed past him then, her attention turning from the TV to another point of interest in the room. 'Actually, better question,' she said sharply, scooping up his glass of bourbon. 'What the hell is this? It's eleven a.m. and you're *drinking*?'

Not waiting for his response, Shelley held up her arms and marched back out the door. 'That's it. I'm done.'

'I don't need a lecture,' Ward grunted, still dragging his feet when, a little later, Shelley frogmarched him down the street.

'I'm not giving you a lecture,' she retorted. 'That already happened. We're done with lectures and are taking a walk. *That's* what we are doing now.'

It was a beautiful morning. Birds singing, the sun blazing – everywhere there was hustle and bustle. But Ward didn't register any of it. Some of the cobwebs in his head cleared as he remembered why they had left his apartment to venture out and do – namely, get coffee and freshen him up a bit.

'Just around this corner here.'

When they entered Frank's, the cosy space was much busier than normal, thanks in no small part to Ward's initial social media shout-out, and Shelley slipped her arm through his since he was still a little wobbly.

'So, what's good here?' she asked, staring approvingly at the pastry display.

But Ward was distracted by a familiar sound coming from the

280

top of the order line and instinctively felt the tiny hairs on the back of his neck stand at high alert.

'See? I remembered,' a woman said, laughing, handing over a ten-dollar bill.

Finished with her transaction, she turned to leave. Their eyes locked and Hannah blushed a deep, heavy crimson; much like she had that first day they met – right here in this coffeehouse.

Chapter 55

HANNAH

'Oh, hi.' Hannah smiled awkwardly. 'I didn't expect to see you . . . I mean, I do come here a lot since . . .'

But despite all that had happened in the interim, she felt even more uncomfortable now than when she'd crashed into Ward that day and sent him sprawling.

'Hey.' He quickly averted his gaze and looked at the ground.

'Everything OK?' she inquired, studying him. He looked awful. 'I haven't been able to reach you lately and I wanted to check in about prep for the NHL presentation thing. Knee still holding up?'

'Sure, I've just been . . . busy.'

Ward shifted a little, glancing to the side, and it was then Hannah realized that he wasn't alone, and a woman's arm was threaded through his.

A gorgeous twenty-something brunette in workout gear with dark eyes and a flawless olive complexion, she looked every last iota of the Classic Athlete Other Half.

Ah. So *that* must be what had been dominating so much of his time lately, to the point that he hadn't been returning her calls.

'Hi there,' she greeted his companion enthusiastically, watching them together, her gaze alternating between their faces.

'This is Shelley . . .' Ward began, awkwardness thick in his voice.

Hannah extended her hand in greeting, slightly slopping her coffee in the process. 'Oh shite . . . er, um, just hold on.' She grabbed a paper napkin off the counter and placed the coffee cup down as she tried to wipe her fingers dry. 'Hannah,' she replied pleasantly, and a smile of recognition broke out on the girl's face. Extracting her arm from Ward's, she grasped Hannah's hand in an enthusiastic greeting. To the point that she was worried her fingers might break.

'Great to meet you,' Shelley greeted in return, her voice low and throaty and which Hannah immediately recognized as the one behind the camera in Ward's famous fitness video.

Aha.

'I have to tell you, everything you have been doing for Ward is wonderful,' she continued. 'Seriously, nice work; you had a job cut out.'

She searched the girl's face for any sign of insincerity or discomfort but found nothing. Shelley didn't offer any explanation of who she was either as if it was obvious that she and Ward were together. Hannah felt foolish for worrying about his reaction to Rob answering his call. She had been self-conscious over nothing because even though she'd turned Ward down that night in the park, he'd simply brushed himself off, taken it in his stride, and resumed whatever he had going on with *this* gorgeous creature.

She was stunning, almost Amazonian in stature, and while Shelley also seemed lovely and self-assured, Hannah got the sense that this confident, no-nonsense lady would not take kindly to anyone cheating on her, and thus decided she would not like to get on the other side of her if wronged.

As this flurry of thoughts raced around Hannah's brain, she forced herself to come back to the present moment – and noticed that Ward was staring at her. So she made a conscious effort to even out her features.

'Thanks and it's lovely to meet you too . . .' she beamed at Shelley, then made a show of checking her watch. 'But I'd better rush, I have an appointment with a client,' she added. Hannah had nowhere to be at that particular moment, but she needed to remove herself from the café and away from Ward and his stunning companion. Then she turned to him but didn't make eye contact. 'Like I said, we need to touch base about preparations for the NHL ceremony. Wardrobe and all that. Big red carpet affair for sure. Huge. I know it's not your thing but . . .'

Shelley punched his arm playfully. 'Don't make Hannah's job harder than it has to be. He told me about the experience you all had at Armani. For the record, he enjoyed it, even though of course he'd never admit it.' She rolled her eyes conspiratorially, evidently all too aware of Ward's contrary reluctance.

'Well, even better that we ran into each other today then too,' Hannah chirped, the thought occurring to her. 'Assuming you'll be his plus one for the night, Panthers' management would be more than happy to pick up the tab for your outfit too.' She winked. 'They have a Bergdorf account so I could meet you guys there sometime this week and go through some options?'

Shelley's eyes widened with delight and Hannah congratulated herself on that little brainwave. What girl wouldn't want someone else to fit the bill for something fabulous to wear at a glitzy red carpet-ceremony?

She wondered why Ward hadn't taken Shelley as his plus one to the Plaza that time, then figured that maybe she was camera shy or that he didn't want the press 'up in his business', to use his words. And also couldn't help but wonder what she had made of that gossip paparazzi photo of him with his 'mystery lady friend' in the park. Maybe Shelley didn't care a whit either way, and stuff like that was par for the course and simply the price you paid for being with a pro athlete.

Something Hannah had come to realize far too late.

Bidding the couple goodbye, she reminded Ward once again to call her to go through arrangements for the event, and then headed back out onto the street, happy to put some distance between her thoughts and the encounter.

But still curious about Shelley, she took out her phone and brought up Ward's socials, scrolling to his follow list, which despite her continued encouragement remained in the double digits, even though he now had hundreds of thousands of followers.

The people he had deigned to follow were mostly teammates, sports sites, ESPN etc and then she saw it.

Shelley Winters. Private profile, so whatever her profession, it seemed she wasn't a woman who courted the limelight either. Ward didn't even follow Lotus PR. But he followed Shelley because clearly she was important to him. An important, albeit thus far concealed, part of his life. Whom Hannah had just strong-armed into accompanying him to a very public event.

She winced.

My private life is off-limits.

Not anymore.

Chapter 56

WARD

Later that week, Ward sat on the plush sofa in the private shopping area at Bergdorf's, where he and Shelley had agreed to meet Hannah.

He tapped his foot impatiently while his newfound plus-one giddily perused racks of clothing suggestions provided in advance by the personal shopper.

'Hannah seems cool,' she'd commented that morning after the encounter at Frank's, as she and Ward had meandered down 72nd Street, sipping their respective coffees.

Having sobered up considerably – both due to the jolt of caffeine and the random run-in, he'd simply nodded and mumbled something non-committal. He hadn't wanted to talk about it – he had too much to think about when it came to Hannah.

'You never explained who I was back there. You *wanted* her to think that you and I were together, didn't you? That's why you didn't say anything when she mentioned the awards thing.'

'Forget it.'

'No, seriously. I saw how you were with her. She's a lot more to you than just your publicist, isn't she?'

'Shelley, I'm serious. Don't go there.'

'OK, but I still think you should've told her we weren't together.'

She scoffed. 'As if! Even though I'm kinda glad you didn't, since it seems I get to play Cinderella for a night.'

'Yeah, thanks for rolling with that. I really do need a plus one so if you're sure . . .'

'Are you kidding me? A free dress and a red carpet event? Do you even *know* how long it's been since I got glammed up?'

Now in the store, he had to smile as Shelley gasped, gently caressing the soft embroidered sleeve of one of the tux choices. 'Woah, now I know how Julia Roberts felt . . .'

'I hate this stuff . . .' he grumbled, wondering where Hannah was. She was running late. These days, she seemed to always be running late. Too distracted by Kendrick probably.

'Oh, stop whining,' Shelley chided, without looking at him. 'And stop with the foot-tapping too, it's annoying. She isn't that late.' She glanced at her watch. 'No need to send out a search party.'

But Ward still felt uneasy.

He was grateful to Shelley for agreeing to come along to the awards thing, albeit if it was just so she could get her hands on a fancy dress and a night hobnobbing on the Panthers' dime. But now that she knew his secret . . . had *guessed* it . . . he worried about keeping up the ruse that they were together in front of Hannah.

Assuming she gave a rat's ass either way.

But the truth was that he was kind of grateful to his trainer for the moral support too. Every time he'd got trussed up for this stuff, he ended up looking like an idiot or making a fool of himself. At least with Shelley on his arm, someone else he trusted to keep him on the straight and narrow at the best of times, all should be cool.

'Now *this* is nice . . .' She held up a sleek velvet emerald tux.

'Very Harry Styles at the Grammys,' she observed, tilting her head in admiration.

Ward snorted. 'Isn't that the guy who wears dresses and pearls too? Not the look I'm going for.'

'Of course, I forgot. Ward McKenzie is *way* too macho to get in touch with his feminine side.'

'It's the NHL awards, Shelley. I don't think me showing up dressed like a girl would go down well with the team.' Although he'd consider it if it meant pissing off JP.

'Let's just wait to see what Hannah says when she—'

At that moment, the aforementioned bustled through to the personal shopping area, looking a bit frazzled. She seemed completely out of sorts and distracted too, as if she had a million things on her mind and this appointment was just one more stupid item on her to-do list.

'Sorry, I know I'm late. Apologies.' She smiled at Shelley and went to embrace her. 'Hi! Great to see you.' Then her eyes rested on Ward. 'You OK? You don't look happy.'

'I'm fine,' he answered, even as he felt the blood start to pump harder in his veins simply because she had entered the room – and at the way she now seemed to be appraising him, reading him. 'Shelley was just looking at some of the stuff the Bergdorf's person pulled.' He shrugged. 'Seems she's a Gucci girl.'

'Oh yes, I *love* this, it's perfect,' Hannah agreed, walking forward to touch the luxurious fabric. 'A bit easier than last time.' She grinned at the other woman. 'Clearly, you have great taste.' She chuckled. 'Or you're much better at keeping him in line than I am, more like.'

In response, Ward seemed determined not to meet Shelley's eye and ignored the knowing smile on her face.

'It's nice, I guess,' he muttered. He got up from his chair and retreated unwillingly to the changing room.

Hannah looked at Shelley, a look of disbelief on her face. 'Seriously, why couldn't I have met you months ago?' She winked. 'My job would've been a whole lot easier.'

Chapter 57

HANNAH

The following week, Hannah regarded herself in the mirror and did a quick assessment. She had pulled her hair up into an elegant and understated chignon. Her make-up was evening-appropriate and subtle, with just a bit of sparkle in her lipstick and a tasteful smoky eye.

Aware that this time at the NHL awards, she was once again relegated to being very much behind the scenes (and happy about it) she'd opted for the Kate Spade, a cute dress in its own right, and low-key enough not to show up the red carpet showstoppers. Practically her uniform for black-tie events like this – perfectly suited for the occasion, but only to fade into the background.

The capacity in which she'd always been to Ward McKenzie, after all, a supporting role.

Her thoughts turned immediately to Shelley and how incredible she'd looked trying on the fuchsia Carolina Herrera gown and towering black patent Louboutin slingbacks she'd chosen at Bergdorf's when they'd moved across the road to the women's store. A show-stopper that hugged her incredible curves, made to be photographed. True leading lady material.

She and Ward would look perfect together in front of the cameras tonight.

And this was what Hannah wanted, after all, the culmination of everything they had worked for. A glitzy professional event ahead of a glorious return to the squad, presenting an award to a teammate and looking the picture of health, knee fully healed. And even better, his first official public outing with the stunning lady in his life by his side, both sparkling in front of the cameras.

So why did it all feel so . . . flat?

Vowing not to think about it for fear that her psyche would take her places she truly had no business going, Hannah squared her shoulders, exited the bedroom and headed toward the kitchen, whereupon she had left her phone and a utilitarian crossbody bag. Plus a collection of one-sheets on Ward's confirmed return to the team for handing out to the press.

A car was arriving shortly to take her to the venue, a gorgeous event space one hundred stories above twinkling Manhattan in one of the Hudson Yards skyscrapers.

Ward and Shelley would be arriving later, in just enough time to walk the carpet and talk to the press on the ground level with other celebrity attendees before heading straight up to the event. Whereas Hannah's evening needed to start considerably earlier in the media tent.

Her phone pinged on cue, signalling the arrival of her ride, and that she needed to scoot. Taking a deep breath and steeling herself for the evening, she headed for the door, only to be met with a last-minute snafu.

Another note.

Hannah stopped in her tracks, debating whether or not to read it now or wait 'til after the event. She hadn't heard from Ed for a while, and was concerned he might've heard some of the ruckus with Rob that night and been annoyed by the noise. Despite the thaw, he was still a cranky old man who could turn from hot to cold in a heartbeat.

No, she didn't need any more distractions. With all that had happened lately, her emotions were fragile enough and tonight she really needed to be on top of her game.

Whatever this was, it could wait.

Chapter 58

WARD

Ward waited for the limo to stop before he jumped out to open the door for Shelley. Waving goodbye to her mom and her cute-as-a-button five-year-old, she exited her place in the Bronx looking nervous – a first for her, he noted chuckling.

She fidgeted with the bodice of the dress a little before moving her hand to her shining tresses, tapping her hair gently to check whether everything was staying in place.

'Do I look OK?' she asked him tentatively, and Ward gave her a lopsided grin, totally unfamiliar with this side of her.

'You look incredible.'

This had all turned into something that they hadn't planned, but he was glad to have her by his side. There was never any denying that Shelley was a showstopper – and it wouldn't be hard for her to play the role of pro athlete girlfriend tonight – she fit the mould, for real or otherwise.

The driver pulled away and headed back towards Manhattan to the Hudson Yards venue where Hannah was waiting for them.

He glanced out the window at the city streets, thinking about the night ahead. He wasn't entirely sure yet how he and Shelley were going to backtrack when all was said and done, especially after appearing in front of the press together, but he would think about that later.

He chuckled inwardly. But he was *really* interested in what Johnny would have to say about it once his buddy saw the pictures show up.

Shelley interrupted his musing.

'So this red carpet thing . . .' she began. 'I'm not gonna lie, I'm nervous. All those cameras flashing – people shouting, this is not exactly my wheelhouse. What should I do? How do I stand? I've only ever seen celebrities on TV. I never thought I would be the one doing this stuff – especially since I'm not a celebrity.'

'Red carpets are bullshit,' Ward grunted.

'Wow. Thanks for calming my nerves.'

'No, I mean, yeah, they are actual bullshit. Nothing but a circus, and award ceremonies are fake and scripted too. I'll be with you all the time though, so all you have to do is smile, take a step, look at the cameras, smile and then repeat that about a thousand times. That's all there is to it.'

Shelley exhaled. 'So, just fill the role of your arm candy. I'm still nervous though. What if I trip?'

'Are you kidding me? You can hold a plank far longer than anyone else I know. You won't trip.'

'Or if someone asks me a question? Like some reporter asks how long we've been . . . dating or something?'

'Just smile and play dumb,' Ward answered bluntly. 'They're more likely to ask you what you're wearing. Or *who*, for some stupid reason.' He rolled his eyes.

'So should I . . .'

'If you're worried about anything, just let Hannah handle it. That's what she's there for.'

But his words made him wince inwardly.

He pictured Hannah feeding some fabricated story about him and Shelley to the press – and realized he didn't want that either.

The whole thing could run away far beyond tonight and turn into something he couldn't row back on, could no longer control. That wasn't fair on Shelley either.

Damn, this was all such a mess . . .

'Hey, I'm sorry. I know this is a big deal for you. And I know I'm probably not saying the things I should because I have done this shit before. It will all be OK, though. Likely, the attention won't even be on us, they'll mostly be focused on the winners and we can just breeze through and go upstairs and take our seats,' he told her, trying to sound more reassuring. 'The night will be over before we know it and then we can figure out how to . . . um . . . break up.'

Shelley nodded, feeling happier. 'Right. Yes. It will be over before we know it.'

'Yeah. And you can always rely on some idiot to show up and start showboating on the red carpet – there's always some rookie desperate to attract the cameras and take the focus off everyone else. That's what we want. Or someone with some hot pop star on their arm, and no one is going to care about us.'

Shelley smiled, looking appeased, but maybe also a little disappointed, Ward noted. 'So, fingers crossed for a showboater, then?'

'Yeah. Someone who *wants* to be the centre of attention. Trust me. On nights like this, there's always one.'

A little later, the limo driver cleared his throat and called from the front seat, 'Mr McKenzie? We've arrived.'

The car pulled up at the edge of Hudson Yards Plaza and Ward turned his attention to the outside.

There was a bustle of activity beneath the iconic heart-shaped Vessel copper sculpture in front of the main building. Production people hurrying around, professional handlers shuttling clients to where they needed to be and photographers hoping to catch a glimpse of celebrity attendees before they headed into the holding tent that would lead them through the media area and then upstairs for the ceremony.

Ward had visited the residential part of this development when it first opened, checking out one of the impressive condos on sale at the time. The real estate agent had taken him to the tallest building and the Edge viewing sky deck, which offered the obligatory panoramic one-hundred-storey views over Manhattan, and a glass 'floor' directly over the skyscrapers beneath, which the tourists went crazy for and Ward had to admit was pretty cool.

Tonight's award ceremony would be held in the same building's Peak restaurant event space on the 101st floor, allowing sparkling night-time views of the city.

Now in the plaza, onlookers and autograph hunters waving shirts and phones, crammed in for a spot by the velvet rope line. It was organised chaos.

'OK, deep breath,' Ward said to himself as much as Shelley. 'We only have to walk a few yards into that tent right there.' He pointed. 'Hannah's waiting for us in there. The red carpet stuff will be happening inside the building before we head up to Peak for the event. Then everything will be more controlled.'

While he normally hated this stuff, he couldn't deny that he was incredibly fortunate to be a part of all this, and Shelley's nervousness had also reminded him that this life of his was nothing to take for granted.

Despite all the confusion he was feeling about Hannah, he had plenty of reasons to be grateful; a healed knee, his professional future assured, and tonight, a beautiful woman by his side.

He and Shelley had become unlikely friends over the last while.

She'd been a fantastic support to him, giving the occasional kick in the ass when he needed it, and she deserved a night to remember. So Ward resolved to forget about his stupid personal bullshit and just concentrate on making sure she got one.

His gorgeous companion nodded, gulping a little. 'OK, cool, just a few yards to the tent. And then . . . Hannah and control.'

'Exactly.' He grinned, still amused at this side of her. 'You ready then?'

Another high-pitched laugh. 'As ready as I'll ever be.'

Ward put a comforting hand on Shelley's and reached for the door handle. 'All right then. Showtime.'

Chapter 59

HANNAH

Standing just inside the reception tent erected beneath the foot of the Vessel – the copper beehive structure beautifully illuminated by night – Hannah watched limo after limo and town car after town car pull up outside the plaza by the river; celebrities and sports glitterati emerging from within.

This was her first time working an event at this particular location, and while she hadn't yet been up to the skyscraper, she was already impressed by the venue, likely chosen to ensure that the very coolest of the great and good would show up. Then again, she knew from experience that when it came to limelight-seeking celebs, it wasn't a tall order to get them to show – for anything – when press or cameras were involved.

Ward McKenzie being about the only exception to that rule. It was almost endearing.

Even if it had made her job a whole lot harder.

She glanced down at her phone to track the car shuttling Ward and Shelley, which should be pulling up . . . right now.

Craning her neck to see through the crowds, Hannah slinked through the mass of handlers and security people and exited the tent. She wanted to be sure that they saw her the moment they stepped from the car, so she could swoop in and take charge.

She watched as one black car moved away from the plaza, enabling another to pull up in its place. The backseat door on the far side of the car opened and sure enough, there was Ward. Her stomach did that ticklish little flip thing again and a smile found its way to her face.

The Gucci suit Shelley suggested had fit like a glove even in the changing room and the shade perfectly complemented the green of his eyes. Now freshly shaven, he cut a dashing silhouette and looked every bit the star. Vitality oozed from him – and there was no denying that he was more than ready to get back on the ice. No cane in sight and he had a spring in his step as he got out and moved to the other side of the car. The crowd yelled their delight and he even raised a hand in salute.

Wow, wonders would never cease.

As the limo driver opened the door for the other passenger, Ward extended an arm; a second later, Shelley emerged from the car, sparkling in Carolina Herrera.

His date smiled as he stood, theatrically directing her hand into the crook of his arm, looking every bit the doting boyfriend. Shelley glanced around at the crowd as she got her bearings but her smile never faltered. If she was nervous, she didn't show it.

They looked incredible together, Hannah thought, taken aback by how wistful she felt. Perfectly camera-ready.

'Exactly how it should be,' she whispered under her breath as she headed forward to meet them.

'Guys!' she called out, immediately flipping the switch and going into professional mode. 'Hey there,' she greeted. 'You guys look amazing. Shelley, honest to God, *wow.*'

The other girl looked down at herself and her face flushed with pleasure. 'Thank you! I mean, I don't think I've ever seen anything like this before in my life, never mind worn a dress like this. This is like prom night on steroids.'

Hannah laughed, sort of wishing she didn't like Shelley so much. But it was impossible not to. 'Well, you look gorgeous,' she assured her, before glancing at Ward and realizing that while she had been complimenting Shelley, he had been studying *her*.

'You look great too,' he commented, and Hannah felt the din of the crowd melt away as if it was just the two of them.

'Thank you,' she replied evenly, her eyes moving to Shelley, who seemed oblivious. In her mind, there was no way she compared in any universe. 'Looking good yourself.'

The trance was quickly broken as Hannah felt her cell phone buzz in her hand, reminding her to spring back into action.

'Right, follow me.' She directed them through the plaza and past the waving onlookers. 'Shelley, pass me your clutch when you get inside, then you don't have to think about it while you pose.'

Evidently nervous all the same, Shelley bobbed her head agreeably and handed over the small blue crystal Judith Leiber Couture evening bag shaped like a crescent moon – a last-minute purchase by Ward that day at the store. Her phone buzzed again but Hannah ignored it until they were good to go.

Ward and Shelley followed in her wake, winding through various other publicists and handlers and red carpet arrivals, as they made their way into the holding tent. 'It will be less crazy once we get inside . . .'

The phone vibrated again, begging for Hannah's attention.

Where's the bloody fire? she thought, wondering what could be the issue, since shepherding her client and his date through this event was her only priority tonight.

But just in case it was one of the event organisers and there was a change of plan in the awards running order or somesuch, maybe she'd better check. Hannah juggled the clutch and the one-sheets she was holding and brought her phone's screen to life.

To see five missed calls and a flurry of messages . . .

Clicking open the most recent text, she once again felt her stomach react – only this time it dropped like a stone as opposed to floating like a butterfly.

It simply read, Turn around.

Chapter 60

WARD

With Shelley on his arm, Ward trailed just behind Hannah, trying to keep the smile plastered on his face as they entered the holding tent.

'This place is crazy,' she remarked, just loud enough for him to hear.

He snorted. 'Like I said, a circus.' He glanced in her direction. 'You doing OK so far?'

'Yes, just don't let go of my arm, OK? I really am afraid I'm going to fall.'

He patted her hand and offered an encouraging smile. There was no denying Shelley was a trooper – everything she was doing tonight was way above and beyond what she'd originally signed up for.

'I won't let you fall,' he assured her gently.

The gesture wasn't lost on some paparazzi posted on the steps outside the Vessel and they started to hoot and howl, shouting in Ward's direction.

'Hey, McKenzie, who's your date tonight?' . . . 'Ward, introduce us to your girlfriend!' . . . 'How'd a five like you land a ten like her?' . . . 'Is this your mystery lady in the park? Introduce us to the girl who finally tamed the wildcat . . .'

Shelley looked at him wide-eyed, wavering just for a moment but he jutted his chin out, nudging her on.

'Just ignore them and keep walking. Follow Hannah.'

He turned his attention to Hannah's back as she purposefully navigated them through the melee out front and into the tent, then noticed her step falter ever so briefly. Trying to juggle what she was carrying, he saw her check her phone – and hesitate at whatever she saw there. It was barely noticeable, but something had grabbed her attention that Ward instinctively knew didn't have anything to do with this event.

She pulled up the hem of her dress just a little as if she had got her foot stuck in the material and he put his other arm out to steady her.

'Hey, you OK?' he asked, concern evident in his voice. And when Hannah glanced up to register his hand on her arm, he saw that her face was ghostly white beneath her make-up and it wasn't from the glare of the overhead spotlights. She looked spooked. But by what, he couldn't tell.

She gave a quick nod and shook her head stiffly, unwilling to meet his gaze.

'Yes, all fine. Just keep on this way,' she intoned.

Ward furrowed his brow in concern and no small measure of curiosity about what seemed to have unsettled her like this especially when she was always the epitome of cool, calm and collected. He reluctantly withdrew his hand as she moved off, determined to move deeper into the crowd.

'She OK?' Shelley asked, her smile fading as she watched Hannah go, keeping track of where she was leading them.

He shook his head absently. 'I actually don't know . . . ' He inhaled sharply and edged her on once again. 'Let's keep up.'

Shelley put her smile back in place and Ward did his best to appear relaxed as they moved through the reception area and the outside media chatter faded into the background.

Then Hannah stopped walking and turned to face them.

He noticed that some of the colour had returned to her face, even as her eyes danced nervously around, paying attention to the people that surrounded them it seemed.

Studying faces, he observed.

The crowd was still considerable, but in here it was just the red carpet players; sport stars, celebs and their respective dates with handlers and security close at hand. Hannah would give cues as to where to wait, when to step out onto the carpet, when to turn to face the cameras and media line, and which press member to talk to thereafter.

'OK,' she began. 'So, just a few people in line up ahead. You guys ready?'

Ward noticed she was being deliberately perky, despite her obvious distraction and as they waited, kept throwing errant, concerned glances all around as if scanning the crowd for something.

Or someone.

But every time he attempted to track her gaze, she seemed to refocus on him and Shelley ensuring that they paid attention to what she was instructing.

He knew something bad was at play at that moment though; he just wasn't sure what.

'Seriously, Hannah . . . is everything . . . ?'

But she cut him off. 'All right you two,' she prompted, giving them a terse smile. 'We're up.' Hannah then bent down to the small train at the back of Shelley's dress, fanning it out for maximum impact. 'You feeling OK? Nothing uncomfortable? Lipstick still good? Yes, I can see it is. Hold on, there's a fleck of mascara just right here . . . '

Shelley murmured her thanks, but Ward could tell that his companion was in her own little world just then too, steeling herself and mentally preparing for her moment in the spotlight.

Assured that his date was good to go, Hannah turned her attention back to him.

'And you,' she said, giving him a once over. 'No doubt you're fine,' she added playfully, her face softening as she looked at him from head to toe. 'Not your first rodeo, after all.'

While he did feel calm until now, Hannah's voice was full of nerves which really unsettled him. He peered at her curiously.

'Never mind me. You sure you're OK?' he pressed. 'You seem . . . tense.'

She tsked him and waved a hand at the suggestion, but again, her eyes darted off to the right.

'I'm fine. You know me.'

'That's exactly it. I do,' he said softly, privately. 'And you're *not* fine.'

But before he could press any further, one of the organisers beckoned to Hannah. Their turn to walk the carpet.

'OK, here we go. Now both of you . . . smile. Relax. Ward, help her out, take her hand and put her at ease. You really do both look amazing. Just *perfect* together.'

Her gaze met his then for just a beat too long and he saw something in her eyes, which made his pulse quicken, but for a different reason this time.

Fear.

But then Hannah shushed them away. 'What are you waiting for? Now . . . go.'

Chapter 61

HANNAH

Her phone was being bombarded. It was buzzing incessantly while she dealt with Ward and Shelley and as they took to the carpet. She stood back out of sight, sweating with anxiety as she scrolled through them.

Beads of moisture started to form on her brow line, and she felt herself grow hot in her clothes. She had the urge to find the nearest bottle of cold water and pour it over her head.

You look great tonight.

You know we should be together.

Why are you ignoring me?

You know I miss you.

You know I do everything out of love.

I don't like how we left things.

Why do you have to overreact about everything?

I came here tonight especially because of you.

I made time in my schedule.

You have never built me up. Ever.

You're totally ungrateful, you know that?

All persistent and demanding, even the ones where he professed his so-called 'love'.

Hannah knew well Rob didn't love her. Not even a little. Never had. He wanted to control her. She was a shiny object that he thought he could have any time. But had since figured out he couldn't anymore – and that's why he continued to pursue her like this. Even when she thought he'd got the message in no uncertain terms at the apartment.

No one said no to Rob Kendrick, after all.

And now it seemed he'd finagled his way into this event tonight, no doubt using his 'athlete star power' to bag an invite. But did he do it to get to her, or was he just having fun toying with her because he knew she'd be here working with Ward?

If you don't talk to me, you're going to regret it.

Hannah waited by the press line doing her job to the best of her ability while her client and his date stood in front of the cameras, smiling and posing up a storm. Shelley had very quickly shaken off her nerves and they were doing a great job together – but admittedly Hannah was having a hard time being fully present.

She hadn't spotted Rob yet, but it was clear he was close – and he could see her. She felt a bit like a gazelle being toyed with by a lion. What was his move here? Was he there purely because of her, or was he just using her proximity to mess with her head? Because he could. CCTV or not, he also knew Hannah well enough to realize that she wouldn't have followed through on that threat. But what was his endgame? Did she have actual reason to be afraid of him? She turned her attention back to the red carpet and saw Ward glancing in her direction, even as the glare of the overhead spotlights obscured her in shadow. Offering what she hoped was a winning smile, she flashed an awkward thumbs-up and encouraging shake of her head.

But his eyes trailed from her gaze and turned toward the press tent entrance whereupon his expression darkened. Whatever distracted half-smile he had been wearing a moment before instantly disappeared.

Hannah furrowed her brow. He needed to snap out of it. OK, so he hated this stuff and was likely now tired of all the calling and requests to turn this way and that, but the red carpet crawl was two minutes at most. Any good pictures already taken were surely going to be overshadowed by him looking like he was ready to spit nails.

And the media noticed.

Ward looked pissed so the cameras urgently snapped with even more abandon. The sports reporters in particular knew that glare, typically reserved for when WildCat McKenzie dropped the mitts and decided to throw an opponent into the boards.

Even as his red carpet companion continued to smile and pose, oblivious to the change in mood, it was obvious that something behind the press line had stolen his attention.

Come on, Ward. Don't do this to me now.

Hannah's anxiety intensified as he continued to glower at something unseen.

'What's going on with Ward, Hannah?' one of the events team asked.

Distracted, she turned to face the guy, readying herself to give some sort of halfway believable excuse, like he was just tired or his knee was giving him trouble. She opened her mouth to speak, trying her best to think on her feet and cover for him – but before she could form a syllable, her attention was once again directed elsewhere.

A hand on her elbow and the grip was commanding . . . demanding.

Hannah didn't need to turn to figure out who the hand belonged to.

She jerked her elbow away from Rob as if his touch had just burned her skin. He wore the same winning smile typically reserved for the cameras, but his eyes danced with malicious pleasure.

'What are you *doing* here?' she asked, all the while trying to appear natural and unaffected. The last thing she needed now was to sully Ward's press with her dramas.

'Thought I might find you here,' he replied with faux sincerity. He cast a glance toward the step where Ward stood, frozen in place. His right arm had since dropped from Shelley's waist and she too seemed to be trying to make sense of the sudden change in mood. Her eyes flittered nervously from him to the press line and then back to the calling photographers.

Rob narrowed his eyes at Ward as if sensing the challenge. 'Looks like lover-boy is a little jealous . . .'

Hannah felt confusion flood her brain. But Ward had no idea that she and Rob were even connected. Her ex hadn't introduced himself that morning on the phone and Hannah had never mentioned it either. Had she?

What in the world . . . ?

She snapped to attention as she felt the eyeballs of others move in their direction. The press had also seemed to realize the subject of Ward McKenzie's ire was none other than another celebrity attendee, pro golfer, Rob Kendrick. And wait . . . wasn't McKenzie's publicist the same one Kendrick had kissed on camera at that golf tournament earlier this year?

The flashing cameras suddenly began to zero in on them too, as if sensing that something was going down.

'Rob,' Hannah hissed at him, trying to keep her face calm, 'this is *not* appropriate, you know that. You can't possibly want press so badly that—'

But he closed what little space there was between them and rested his hand on her lower back, non-too-gently pulling her closer.

'It's not polite to avoid my messages,' he spat through gritted teeth, and seeing the dark glint in his eyes, Hannah felt very afraid.

She felt the heat of the flashing lights on her and her vision blurred as her composure slipped. She instinctively stood back from Rob, trying to extricate herself from his grip, but to no avail. The clutch she was holding for Shelley slipped down her arm and the motion also dislodged the pile of one-sheets from her hand, which scattered to the carpet beneath her feet. Far from releasing his hold on her, he roughly jerked her back.

'Rob, please—' But before Hannah could utter another word, she was swiftly released from her ex's tight grip.

'Get your hands off her.' As if out of nowhere, Ward was there grabbing Rob's arm and yanking it off her.

Her ex flew backwards and momentarily stumbled, before righting himself and looking around, trying to assess who in the crowd might have seen him being manhandled. He quickly got his answer as a wave of cameras flashed in unison – lenses suddenly trained away from the red carpet and right in his direction.

'You OK?' Ward muttered but Hannah was still too dazed to reply. Ward had placed himself directly in front of her, blocking her from Rob, and the golfer immediately recognized the square off. He jutted his chin in response, but it was evident that he had not anticipated such a public showdown. Her ex thrust his chest out defensively, trying to look bigger than he was. While both men were professional athletes, Ward was built for physicality and altercation. After all, it wasn't as if golfers were ever encouraged to develop a gloves-off mindset while on the links.

Rob sniffed sarcastically. 'What's it to you, McKenzie? Can't see how this is any of *your* business.' He glanced over to where Shelley stood, still rooted in the spot at the red carpet side of the media line, all press attention now turned in the other direction. 'And why would a dude who can pull *that* sort of tail worry about *this*?' He pointed a finger at Hannah and snorted a derisive laugh. 'Unless . . . ' he added nastily, clearly for the benefit of the rapt media present, 'is little Miss Hannah another side piece then? Mixing work and pleasure like she's known to do. Get paid and get laid? I should have figured . . . '

'Keep her name out of your mouth, asshole . . . ' Ward glowered. He turned back to check on Hannah who remained there shocked and speechless, her face painted a deep crimson.

Taking advantage of the fact that his head was turned, Rob moved quickly and punched Ward on the left cheek. Ward stepped backwards a little, into a row of cameramen clicking gleefully. But he recovered quickly, fire blazing in his eyes. And dark delight peppered his face as if this was exactly the invitation he had been waiting for.

No one dared sucker-punch Ward McKenzie.

In one deft movement, and with a wry smile, Ward casually discarded the jacket of his suit, pushed up his sleeves and charged forward.

The wildcat's claws were out.

His first punch landed squarely on Kendrick's nose and his mouth twitched at the satisfying crunch of bone and cartilage under his fist. His opponent squealed and swung a return with one arm, while reaching for his face with the other.

Through it all, the cameras flashed – and Hannah felt frozen, watching in dismay. Yes, he might have been trying to defend her honour, but she knew all of her hard work – everything she had tried to do to repair Ward's image – and salvage her own career, it was all going down the tubes right now. It was Rob's own fault for daring to attack, there was no *way* a guy like Ward would let that go, and now everything was completely out of control.

Her mind swam, desperately trying to make sense of it all. Ward had clearly understood she was unsafe just now, but how did he even know about her and Rob?

It was that phone call. Of course, it was.

'Oh my God!' Shelley exclaimed, suddenly appearing beside her. 'What's going on? What do we do?'

Open-mouthed, she looked at her, speechless.

'Hannah, do *something.* Aren't you supposed to be a fixer? Fix *this,* stop them.'

But her mind was a blur, even as she heard another punch land. Rob had somehow been able to get a blow in, hitting Ward in the stomach. Not that it had stopped him – in fact, it had barely fazed him.

She turned back to the other girl, whose expression had turned from pleading to annoyance.

'Oh, for Chrissakes . . . ' Shelley rolled her eyes, and storming off in her Louboutins, promptly raced into action, leaving Hannah in her dumbfounded trance.

She grabbed at Ward's shoulders, trying to pull him off of Rob, who was definitely at the losing end of the scuffle. His nose was bloodied – and almost certainly broken. His right cheek was already swollen and turning purple, and his previously white dress shirt was now stained with blood. Hannah just didn't know whose blood. 'Ward, *stop* it,' Shelley demanded. 'This is bad for you.'

The press was simply eating the drama up and Hannah looked around for security to break things up.

But Shelley's presence was at least enough to get Ward's attention. Her face full of colour and her eyes shooting cold, angry daggers, she growled, 'This is *not* the circus I signed up for. What the hell is wrong with you?'

Of the two men, Ward had, of course, fared much better. His shirt was untucked, a few of the top buttons ripped off and part of his broad chest was exposed. He sported a split lip that didn't seem to bother him in the slightest as he continued to hover menacingly over Rob, looking eager and dangerously close to jumping back into the fray.

Hannah was just relieved that the other woman's intervention had calmed things.

Until Rob made the fatal mistake of manhandling Shelley then, trying to swat her out of the way. As soon as he lay a finger on her, her eyes narrowed and then all hell truly broke loose when both Ward and his date hit back in tandem.

A couple of security goons eventually stepped in to break things up once and for all, and Hannah was finally moved to action.

'Enough,' she gasped, trying to catch her breath. 'How could you *do* this?' she cried, directing the question at them both.

While Ward seemed to briefly come to his senses and looked chastened, her ex didn't appear in the least bit admonished. Still conscious of the press close by, the golfer tried to figure out a way to spin the fact that he'd just got his ass kicked, not just by McKenzie but a *girl* too.

He climbed to his feet, gingerly touching his broken nose. 'Oh, come on, you love the drama, babe. Don't pretend you don't.' He smirked. 'We can laugh about it later,' he added mischievously as if

Hannah was in on it. 'And McKenzie, I'm suing your ass. Expect assault charges.'

'Bring it on,' Ward countered, taking another step closer. 'I'll gladly whoop yours anytime asshole.'

Hannah then turned back to face him. 'And you . . . ' she began as her heart hammered in her chest, but then realized she didn't know what to say. She looked up to meet his green eyes, still glittering with emotion. She was so angry with him, yet at the same time thankful that he had stepped in. But tonight had surely put the final nail in the coffin of his career . . . and hers too.

After all of her . . . *their* . . . work.

Now, Hannah knew she would be little more than a punchline in the PR world. There wouldn't be a third time for her to strike out, that much she knew.

'Ward . . . I . . . ' she began, swallowing hard. 'I . . . I can't work with you anymore.'

Then turning on her heel as the cameras continued to gleefully flash and record every last humiliating moment, a laughing stock once more, Hannah slunk away into the crowd as quickly as she could, desperate to disappear.

Chapter 62

WARD

'What in the hell were you thinking? I mean, just *look* at this!' Bernie bellowed as he pointed angrily at the flat-panel TV on the wall of his office.

Onscreen, the Rumble on Red as the media had since deemed it, played out in all its glory – Kendrick's opening punch, Ward's retaliation and subsequent ass-kicking of the golfer, then Shelley entering the fray in her designer dress and heels like the badass she was.

Slumped into a chair on the other side of his agent's desk, Ward sat in stony silence, refusing to look at the TV. After all, he had been there. He had lived it – why did he need to watch it again?

But no matter, the press continued to eat it up. It was the only thing that ESPN and FOX Sports and every single other sports network, YouTuber and gossip site had been talking about and replaying ad nauseum for the past twenty-four hours. The NHL ceremony and award winners were merely cast aside as afterthoughts.

The media reaction had been intense – but Ward had a hard time caring. He flexed his bruised right hand and reflected on the sensation of first-connecting his fist with Kendrick's smug-ass face. The recollection was deeply satisfying and he smirked at the memory.

'Something funny?' barked Bernie. 'Is there some sort of joke I'm missing out on right now?'

He glanced up and met his agent's furious gaze, then quickly rearranged his features.

'I really don't think you truly understand the gravity of this situation. I'm serious. You're in deep shit this time, serious shit. This is not a good look—'

'It was just a fight. It's not like I haven't been in any before.'

Bernie snorted. 'That's how you're justifying this? That you've been in fights before? OK, maybe yes, you have. On the ice. During a *game*. Or a boozy night out. *Not* on the red carpet in front of two hundred cameras. With a fellow pro athlete who is going to sue you from here to eternity.'

'That asshat hit me first,' spat Ward.

'And so you pummelled him? The ass-whooping you gave him, do you think that was *justified*? You look unhinged.' Again, Bernie pointed at the TV.

Ward glanced over and took a deep breath. He had to admit, that footage wasn't awesome, especially since it appeared that Kendrick wasn't fighting back – or certainly not with the same intensity that Ward was delivering. Which had been kinda disappointing at the time too, to be honest. *Loser.*

'Look, Bernie,' he continued, 'that guy—' he jerked his chin toward the screen '—is a prick. He was grabbing Hannah, gripping hard on her arm. And she was pulling away. I saw it. I didn't like it. That's why I went over – and told him to get his hands off of her. Everything after that is on him.'

Bernie sighed and collapsed heavily into his office chair, dragging his hands through his hair, and leaving behind little spikes. He looked like he hadn't slept last night, which, of course, he hadn't since he was once again in damage-control mode. He threw his head back and looked at the ceiling for a moment.

'So, you were just being a knight in shining armour, then? Is that what it was?' he asked, sarcasm clear in his voice. 'Did it ever occur to you that maybe that was an issue best left for your publicist? That maybe it was a lovers' quarrel that was none of your business?'

Ward looked away, purposefully avoiding his agent's gaze.

Of course, it had occurred to him that it wasn't any of his business. But he also realized that he had developed a serious blind spot when it came to Hannah. He wanted her business to be his business.

When he remained silent, Bernie pressed on.

'And speaking of Hannah, what does she have to say about all of this? Huh? Did she ask you to butt in like that? I'm pretty certain she wouldn't thank you for it – not for making such a public spectacle of her private life.'

Ward felt like he was under a microscope, and he shifted uncomfortably in his seat.

'She quit, OK? She said she can't work with me anymore.'

Truth be told, Hannah's declaration the night before hadn't truly registered with him in the heat of the moment. However, once he'd returned home (the event organisers insisting that it was best he forget about presenting the award and just attend to his bruises), taken off the torn shirt and started seeing the coverage flood in, the scuffle completely overshadowing the event itself, the reality of the situation began to settle in.

The fact that Hannah might be serious about what she said didn't sit well with Ward. After all, his intentions had been pure – he knew she was being roughed up by Kendrick and he'd swooped in to defend her. That guy was bad news.

But what if yet again he had misread the situation? he wondered now. *What if what went down was simply a private matter, a heated exchange between a couple in a relationship – and it really was none of his business? And his jealousy toward Kendrick had maybe distorted his perception.*

Nah, he wasn't stupid. Ward knew a narc when he saw one and could only hope that Hannah saw it now too.

It wasn't like Ward hadn't tried calling her at least ten times since. And while he was trying to play it cool on the outside, now as he sat here in his agent's office being admonished, he had to admit that he was worried.

Not necessarily about the intense public scrutiny or potential aftermath, but that he had ruined his relationship with Hannah. That there was a real possibility that she truly had washed her hands of him this time and might well go back to Kendrick regardless. That he had got it all completely and terribly wrong.

Again.

The thought made him feel sick.

'Oh, well isn't that just the freakin' cherry on top . . .' exclaimed Bernie, throwing his hands up in the air and bringing Ward back into the present. 'And after all of the good work she did. Jesus, do you have any self-awareness at all? Are you able to even fathom that your actions have consequences?'

'Of course I do,' he retorted, jumping out of his chair defensively. 'I just couldn't stand by and let her be roughed up like a ragdoll, OK? She doesn't deserve that, don't you get it? She's special, Bernie. She's—'

Emotion was thick in his voice and Ward's impassioned reaction was not lost on Bernie, who had known his client for more years than he could honestly remember. And now recognition dawned.

'Aw crap,' Bernie said, shaking his head. 'Why didn't I see this before? That's it, isn't it? You have something going on with Hannah? This is all some crazy love triangle shit, isn't it?'

Ward squared his shoulders and jutted out his chin. 'No, there's nothing going on, it's just . . . I didn't want to see anything bad happen to her, OK?'

But Bernie wasn't buying it.

'You know I've known you way too long, right? You're a skirt chaser. *Everyone* knows you are. And this just solidifies your image. Bad boy womaniser – getting involved with another guy's girl. That's what working with Hannah was supposed to turn around, but you dragged her right into it, huh? Knight in shining armour, my ass.'

He opened his mouth to defend himself and also to insist that Hannah hadn't done anything wrong, hadn't crossed over any professional lines and she shouldn't be blamed for anything, but Bernie cut him off.

'You know, everything I arranged for you was contingent on you turning things around. Your recovery, getting off the pills . . .' When Ward looked up sharply, his agent shook his head. 'You think I didn't know about the pills? That's part of it too but only a part. Getting you back on track was also tied to the public deciding you aren't an asshole – that you don't have anger management problems, that you aren't a toxic knuckle-dragger. And for a while there, I thought you truly were turning things around. But now you have successfully managed to throw away everything in a matter of minutes by kicking the ass of a pro golfer . . . a PGA champ in the prime of his career . . . and it seems becoming involved in some imbroglio with the publicist I arranged for you. Who quits after you pick a fight with her boyfriend on the red carpet! Who knows what the hell else is going on, what else could come out . . .' Bernie paused, catching his breath, as impassioned with rage as Ward had been on the TV a moment ago. 'Man, you know you and I go way back,' he continued, 'but I just don't know anymore. After all this, don't expect Panthers' management to welcome you back with such open arms anymore – Craig Sumners is already in my ear. This kind of stuff is bad publicity. He's not happy. No one is. They will likely buy out your contract because they have to, but don't expect to be a part of the squad ever again.'

At these words, Ward's face fell.

Could his career really be over this time? This kind of stuff was right up Jefferson Prince's alley, after all . . .

He shook his head. 'Sumners is not going to cut me now,' he started, thinking if he put the words out there, he could make them true. 'Not after that big public welcome home.'

'He might not have a choice,' Bernie replied darkly. 'He and Prince might be OK with this kinda macho bullshit but the sponsors won't. And you know no one else is going to touch you either. There's not going to be a team out there willing to take on a player so volatile and unpredictable – no one wants their brand hurt by a loose cannon.' He sighed once again and looked at Ward, his face finally softening. 'And really, man, when that happens . . .'

'What?' Ward barked, trepidation in his voice at his agent's tone.

'Then I'm going to have to take Hannah's lead. You've become a lot of work lately. And eventually, a guy like me has to question if the juice is worth the squeeze.'

Chapter 63

HANNAH

Hannah was sick of explaining. She was exhausted from having to repeat the same story over and over. And especially weary from having to plead her case with every higher-up in the New York office. To say nothing of the fact that she was utterly mortified at having her private life thrust out into the open yet again.

No matter what she said, or what explanation or viewpoint she provided, no one at Lotus HR was going to take her seriously now. Not after what had happened before with Rob. This was just another example of her messing up – a walking case study of how *not* to be a public relations professional. It was mortifying.

The day after, Hannah was told to stop everything she was doing for her current portfolio and instructed in no uncertain terms, that she should stay entirely out of the public eye nor speak to any member of the press. The firm's damage control and crisis management arm had gone into overdrive, trying to clean up what had happened, which included putting her on a leave of absence for an undetermined amount of time and informing Ward and his agent that the company was severing their contract.

All in all, a nightmare. Now, she was huddled in a pair of cotton pyjamas on Courtney's couch under a blanket, all the blinds shut tight in the apartment to keep out the light of day and mute the sounds of the street below, where millions of happy New Yorkers went on about their days, their lives not in shambles and their futures bright.

Her phone buzzed again, and she glanced at the screen. Private number.

She knew Lotus wouldn't mask its identity if someone from HR was calling to deliver a verdict.

That meant press, she thought, *or Ward. Or Rob. All of whom had been calling and messaging relentlessly in the aftermath and whom Hannah did not want to talk to right now. Or ever.*

But a troublesome thought played at the edges of her brain.

Hannah knew she would survive if she never spoke with a member of the press again. She also was perfectly fine with keeping Rob in her rear-view mirror for the rest of her life. In fact, if she never had to lay eyes on him again, she would consider it a success.

But Ward . . . A fresh ache settled in her chest when she imagined never speaking to him again, or seeing him again, or hearing him complain or tease her . . . or laugh.

Even though she was still spitting feathers with him for his part in her latest humiliation. Hannah kicked the sofa with her sock-clad foot and threw her head under the blanket as if doing so would make her problems disappear. But if anything, the darkness under the covers amplified the confused thoughts that ran rampant through her mind.

How had such public drama found her again?

She was supposed to control the narrative after all – not allow chaos to follow her around like an uninvited sidekick.

And what the hell had got into Ward? Why did he fly off the handle like that?

That she couldn't make sense of. OK, so Rob had grabbed her, and evidently sensing her discomfort (or fear?), Ward had intervened. But to continue it after . . . that was beyond just standing up for her, it felt almost personal. Like Rob was an opponent in a high-stakes game.

She had been shocked – still was, frankly. But there was something else there, too, now that she examined it. A thrill of satisfaction. Didn't Rob deserve what he'd got? Hannah didn't condone violence, but even so, her answer was . . . maybe.

Her ex had needed to be put in his place for a while – and to think he was going to get away with sucker-punching Ward McKenzie . . . Despite herself Hannah felt an instinctive flicker of desire.

She no longer cared about Rob, of that she was now absolutely certain. But what about these other feelings? The jolt of butterflies from having Ward defend her honour? Her thoughts turned to how he had effortlessly thrown off his jacket and rolled up his sleeves, emerald eyes glittering as the Wildcat readied himself to pounce. She shivered deliciously.

Seemed she wasn't the only one who felt that way.

'That was HOT! And I have never and I mean *never* wanted to shake a guy's hand so much in my life. And then some.' Zoe had phoned agog within minutes of the news breaking out, convinced it was the best thing she'd ever seen. Until remembering that it wasn't so entertaining for Hannah.

'I'm coming over on the next flight,' her friend assured, but Hannah managed to persuade her not to. She didn't feel up to talking, and for the moment, just wanted to be alone for a while until she was ready to think about what to do next.

Regardless of his intentions though, she still couldn't condone

Ward's actions. Though she couldn't deny how him defending her so gallantly had made her feel.

Oh, for goodness' sake stop it! She threw her head back against the cushion propped behind her and then heard a demanding cry.

A moment later, a light weight settled at the end of the couch where her feet were and made the journey up to her chest. A pair of speckled blue eyes met her gaze head-on and the cat tilted its head slightly as if to say, 'What's the problem *now*?'

Hannah raised her eyebrows. 'I think you must sense when I'm in crisis since you always seem to turn up when I need a friend.' Then, realizing she was going crazy, she shook her head. 'Or maybe I *am* turning into a crazy cat lady.' Her thoughts then turned to her next-door neighbour, thinking at this point she too could subscribe to the appeal of becoming a recluse.

The note that appeared before she'd headed off to the awards ceremony had not been from Ed, but a written apology from Bruno. The doorman was inconsolable that he'd allowed Rob to sweet-talk him into letting him upstairs, her ex insisting that calling ahead to announce his arrival would ruin the romantic surprise he'd planned.

While Hannah couldn't deny that she was annoyed about it, Bruno was such a sweetheart that she could hardly be angry with him. So while Hannah was pleased that the ruckus with Rob hadn't changed Ed's mind about her, it didn't help that her entire New York move had descended into complete disaster and her future still hung in the balance.

Feeling dejected and emotional, she pulled the cat closer to pet its ears and ran a finger down its silky back. For once it didn't shrink away or baulk at the contact, and instead purred under her palm, pressing into it.

The simple show of affection was all it took for her to succumb, and she sat in the dark with the animal and allowed herself a little sob, as she contemplated the mess that was once again her life.

Chapter 64

WARD

Ward was sure that he was starting to wear a trench in the hardwood floors of his place from pacing back and forth. Pausing, he picked up his phone for the hundredth time and glanced at the screen.

Several missed calls – press, Johnny, a couple of nosy teammates, his mom – but nothing from the only person he wanted to hear from.

He went to his call log and selected the last person he'd contacted an hour ago . . . and then an hour before that. Not surprisingly, it went directly to Hannah's voicemail – again.

He let out a growl of frustration and resumed pacing.

By now he felt like he was going stir-crazy. For the past few days, he'd laid low – taking the advice of Bernie. At this point, it was the least he could do in the hopes of salvaging his career. However, he didn't know how much he could take remaining holed up at home like this. It felt like the walls were closing in on him.

If only she would talk to him. He could deal with the fallout of everything else if she would just return one of his calls or messages.

Stopping his pacing, he headed into the bathroom and looked at his reflection in the mirror. The bruises were fading – the one on his jaw was probably the worst still, but at least it had started to go from deep purple to a green-tinged mustard yellow. His split lip wasn't as visible and was now pretty much scabbed over.

'Whatever,' he shrugged. 'Not the worst I've been.'

He headed out of the bathroom and grabbed his jacket hanging by the front door, his gaze drifting to Pretzel's still-full food bowl, trying to recall the last time he'd seen her. He'd been so distracted with his current predicament that he honestly couldn't remember.

Vowing to search for the cat later, he shrugged the jacket over his arms, put on a baseball cap and jumped in the elevator, heading down to the ground floor of his building.

Ward needed to move. He craved some fresh air. Needed to be out and among the living. Hell, grabbing a beer wasn't a bad idea, either. Having run through a list of watering joints in his head, he decided on Horn's Hook Tavern nearby. It was a chill and relaxed spot and no one there was likely to pay much attention to him or give him any grief.

Pulling open the front door, he walked into the dimly lit setting and took a seat at the bar. He immediately recognized the bartender and nodded his head in greeting. A moment later, once Joe was done pulling a beer for another customer, he approached.

'Hey, man, long time,' Joe greeted, offering him a fist bump. 'The usual? How's the knee?'

Ward nodded. 'Thanks, Joe. Better. And yeah. Tall one.'

As he poured he looked over and smiled. 'Good thing you didn't relapse after that stunt with the golfer. Man, that was great. Always thought he was an asshole.' He placed the beer in front of Ward and smacked the counter. 'So, what's the deal? What the hell happened? Just been off the ice for too long and needed to kick some ass?'

The corner of Ward's mouth turned up. 'Something like that,' he replied with some satisfaction.

'Your girl, though . . .' Joe whistled his appreciation. 'Where'd you find her? Smokin'. And damn, a fighter too. Nice catch.'

Ward sighed and decided he didn't need to perpetuate his so-called relationship with Shelley any more than he had already.

'She's not "my girl". My trainer actually. She was doing me a favour that night, that's all,' he told Joe. 'PR shit.'

The barman barked a laugh. 'Nice! So, was going tag team on Kendrick's ass part of your PR strategy then, too? That sucker punch; who did he honestly think he was messing with? Dude dumb enough to screw with you deserved a beat down.'

Ward took a sip of his beer and pushed his ballcap back a bit on his head, getting comfortable. 'Definitely *not* part of the strategy. And as much as I agree with you, unfortunately no one else seems to.' Quickly, he gave a brief overview of the truth – that his hockey career was likely in a nose dive and he was being viewed as human kryptonite with Panthers' management and across the league. 'I'm a "loose cannon" apparently,' he snorted.

The barman shook his head in response. 'Man, that's no good – really, that sucks. I mean, that'd be the day that I let someone sucker punch me and they get away with it.' He tilted his head and narrowed his eyes at Ward thoughtfully. 'So why'd Kendrick do it then? The first punch I mean? Everyone has been wondering what started it all.'

Ward considered the bartender and then shrugged, figuring it couldn't hurt to tell a watered-down version of the truth.

'I saw him grabbing a friend of mine. Being rough. I didn't like it and warned him off. That's just not how you treat a woman, you know?'

'Hell, no,' Joe agreed. 'I would never let someone lay hands on any woman – doesn't matter if it was my girl, my mom, my sister, my great aunt, my pain-in-the-you-know-where neighbour Barb, or a perfect stranger. If they did, they'd get what's coming to them too.'

Ward smiled, appreciative that Joe got it. 'Yeah, not everyone sees it like that.'

'And now you're being *cancelled*, I guess,' the barman said, shaking his head bitterly. It was a statement, not a question. 'Even though the other guy's the asshole.'

Sipping again, Ward muttered, 'Yup.' He took a deep breath. 'I suppose I've had a good run of it,' he added sadly, even as his thoughts conjured Hannah's face, instead of his time on the ice – and that hurt him more.

'Sorry, man. Those rich pretty-boys always somehow manage to come up trumps. This one's on me.' He pointed to the beer.

'Thanks.'

Joe tapped the bar twice with his left hand and then went back to his duties, grabbing a bottle of vodka and serving another customer while Ward's eyes drifted to the television screen high in the corner next to the bar.

ESPN was playing, like it usually was in a place like this. On the screen, some talking heads on SportsCenter were covering something from the night before in the NBA. He watched with minimal interest, idly reading the closed caption dialogue simply for something to do.

Whatever tidbit was being covered ended and instead switched to footage, yet again, of the fight on the red carpet. Ward groaned. When would this stuff let up? It had been days already. He tugged his hat down tighter on his head taking a long pull of his beer, readying himself to leave.

I don't need to see this again.

But then the coverage broke away from the brawl and returned to the studio, where the words 'Breaking News' flashed across the screen, this time beneath Rob Kendrick's face.

Suddenly interested, Ward motioned to Joe. 'Hey . . . mind turning that up?'

Crap, he hoped the ass hadn't since made some big public announcement about pressing charges or something.

Joe glanced up at what he was watching and smirked. 'Ha! You looking to go round two? Don't punch my TV, OK?'

'I'll do my best to keep it together,' he mumbled as Joe turned up the volume.

On the screen, one of the news reporters was talking. 'Questions have been swirling today about the head-to-head face-off late last week involving NHL All-Star Ward McKenzie and PGA Champ Rob Kendrick at the NHL Awards. And while we aren't entirely clear on what spurred the red carpet rumble, some brand-new information about one of the parties has since come to light . . . '

Chapter 65

HANNAH

'Well at least I'm out of my pyjamas,' Hannah muttered to the cat as she slipped on a pair of jeans and a t-shirt. 'That's progress, is it not?'

While she still was living under a form of involuntary house arrest – and existed in a state of limbo with her job – she had at least opened up the blinds, taken a shower, and started picking up after herself around the apartment. The sting of the very public embarrassment was there still, but Hannah recognized that she couldn't keep acting like a mushroom.

Plus, it now seemed she had a cat to look after. Since first coming to her rescue that night with Rob and now in the aftermath of the red carpet bust-up, it had been her near-constant companion. Sitting with her, watching her with its inquisitive eyes, curling up next to her in bed at night.

Hannah had to admit she didn't mind the company and its presence made her feel less crazy than when she was alone and talking to herself, wallowing in her own despondency.

'Are you hungry?' she asked and then smiled. 'Of course, you're hungry. You're always hungry. Thank goodness you can get cat food delivered here – along with everything else.'

Hannah padded her way barefoot into the kitchen, the animal

following curiously behind her. As she went to put a tin of Fancy Feast into a small dish, her phone pinged.

TURN ON ESPN RIGHT NOW . . . Zoe demanded in all caps.

Her stomach leapt with trepidation.

Oh God, now what? Hannah's thoughts immediately turned to Ward and fresh worry pulsed through her veins. She had been following the headlines and was aware that things right now were *very bad* for him – like career-ending bad. She didn't know how it could get any worse.

Rushing into the living room, she clapped her hands and switched on the media system, grabbing the remote control to find the channel.

But instead of Ward's face splashed across the screen above a Breaking News banner, she saw Rob's. Turning up the volume, she felt doubly intrigued as she plopped down on the couch.

'Celebrated pro golfer, Rob Kendrick, has been known since the beginning of his career for his charismatic smile and perfect swing. Crowds flock to his tournaments to witness the prowess of this golfing sensation and sponsors have clamoured to be associated with the latest rising star,' the announcer began.

'However, behind Kendrick's polished exterior and neatly pressed golf attire hides some disturbing behaviour . . . now brought to light after the golfer's recent public altercation with hockey player Ward McKenzie.'

The screen cut to a clip of the fight, but instead of cutting straight to the two men's fisticuffs like previous clips, this one started with Rob's unprovoked sucker punch, and Hannah grimaced afresh at the memory.

'In recent days, this network has received some new information from varied sources within the tight-knit golfing community,

332

which led our team of reporters to investigate further. In our effort to substantiate the claims, we have uncovered accounts of inappropriate behaviour on Mr Kendrick's part towards WPGA tour members, female staff members, tournament organisers, and romantic partners. Let's hear first hand now from WPGA pro and four-time U.S. Women's Open Golf Champion, Emma Stirling.'

Hannah's mouth dropped as the screen cut to the well-known sportswoman sitting at the press conference and flanked by two other women, one of whom she recognized as Emma's manager.

The golfer briefly tucked a lock of her silky chocolate hair behind her ear before turning her cornflower-blue eyes directly into the camera with steely resolve. She cleared her throat as she spoke into a bank of microphones.

'I'm here today to let the golfing community and the general public know that Rob Kendrick is a predator,' she stated decisively. 'For the past several months, he has harassed and stalked me after initially exposing himself to me in the Pebble Beach clubhouse during a charity tournament last year. Since then, he has sent a barrage of inappropriate texts and even shown up uninvited at my home in Calabasas. On one occasion, he followed me on a routine trip to the grocery store, grabbing and threatening me.'

Her manager patted her on her back, whispering encouragement, while the other woman who Hannah now figured was an attorney stood sentry by Emma's side as she continued.

'My intent in coming forward today is to say that Rob Kendrick should be held accountable for his behaviour. While I am not entirely sure what happened at the NHL Awards, I can only suspect that it had something to do with Rob's sociopathic behaviour – and that he likely picked the wrong target this time. Beyond the physical, Rob Kendrick's general treatment of women needs to be made public. He is dangerous and doesn't understand the meaning of the word "no" . . . to my mind, he is a threat.' Emma glanced down, composing herself before she looked to the cameras again and added, 'Also, to Ward McKenzie, let me just say, you're a hero.'

Emma offered a weak smile before the media present went crazy with questions before the coverage cut back to the SportsCenter desk.

'Outside of Stirling's impassioned statement, other women have also since come forward and the PGA has today announced that it's launching a formal investigation into Kendrick's conduct. In the interim, he has been suspended from the PGA. Already some sponsors, including Nike, Rolex and Mastercard, have stated they will also be severing ties with Kendrick immediately with the assertion that their organizations, "Believe women". While this story is still developing, it does appear that the #MeToo Movement is about to lay claim to yet another high-profile sports figure,' the announcer finished diplomatically. 'However, the question remains, what happened at the NHL Awards and why? Did we get it all wrong about Ward McKenzie? Far from a Zero, could he actually be a Hero?'

The piece ended with the broadcaster now singing Ward's praises over footage of career highlights and past accolades, while Hannah remained in shocked silence.

It hadn't been just her – she hadn't been Rob's only target.

Of course, you weren't – and it all makes total sense now, she thought in disbelief. While this was devastating for her ex, for whom she had no sympathy, she also knew how the press worked.

If ESPN was the first to begin rehabbing Ward's career and image, then all other outlets would jump on that bandwagon. Two things were for sure. Rob was going down . . . hard. But Ward was going to be OK. She was certain of it.

Zero to Hero overnight.

More than OK, she thought, heartened. He was going to get it all back — everything he'd been working toward, everything he wanted.

And deserved.

Chapter 66

'So, Hannah, this whole mess . . . thanks for bearing with us while we figured things out,' Wes, her Lotus NY boss, grimaced at her from the other side of his desk a few days later. 'I know you have probably felt a bit . . . in limbo. I'm sorry about that, but I'm sure you can understand the firm's position, considering.'

She nodded, determined to keep her chin up. 'Considering . . .' she repeated.

'So, here's the thing. It's taken some back and forth and whatnot – lots of mixed opinions but we've decided we want you back on the job. What with this whole Kendrick thing, the agency has decided to part ways – we understand you are no longer involved with him, and count yourself in the ranks of what those other women have been saying. If you know what I mean,' he stuttered, much to Hannah's amusement. 'Plus you were doing so great with McKenzie so we appreciate that maybe we were too . . . hasty in severing things. People are just loving him right now and with him getting back on the ice too, well, we want to harness all of that star power. And that's where you shine.'

Hannah sat up a bit straighter in her seat. She had figured as much once Wes called her into the office. If they wanted to fire her, they would have done it over the phone and washed their hands of the matter.

'I see . . .'

336

He smiled at her. 'So, we're good? All water under the bridge? Look forward and not backward? I really mean that, Hannah, you're great with McKenzie, and if anyone can encourage him back with us, it's going to be you. You *get* him. You *understand* what makes him tick. And honestly, he's the type of guy Lotus wants to represent. He's a *good* guy.'

That he was, and yes, Ward deserved all the good things that were coming to him now. But she knew that she couldn't do what Wes was asking of her. She could win him back as a client, sure; all she would have to do was return one of his many calls. It would be as simple as that in theory at least.

But like she'd informed Bernie the day before, she truly couldn't work with him anymore.

Professional conflict of interest aside, there would now certainly be an emotional one. Shackling herself to Ward as a client would be like putting her heart in its own self-made prison. Though she didn't tell his agent *that*.

Now as she walked through the front doors of the building, she knew exactly what the next item on her to-do list would be – move out of Courtney's apartment, figure out what her next step was . . . and determine where exactly she would land after.

Thankfully, she had a little money saved to last her a bit before she thought about what to do career-wise, but really what she craved the most right now was peace and solitude. She wasn't sure where she was going to go, but she knew that wherever it was, it needed to be away from New York and from Ward McKenzie.

Maybe she could head home for a bit and see her parents – it had been ages since she'd crossed the Atlantic for a long overdue visit. No place like home, after all?

Or Vegas, like Zoe had suggested. 'We'll go to Caesars, blow it all on black seventeen, lay by the pool for a day and then go see Mindfreak. Ask Criss Angel if he could maybe shove a razor blade down Rob Kendrick's throat.'

Hannah was tempted, mostly because she'd love the opportunity to reunite with her friend, but also knew Zoe was busy with her own life and work commitments, and in truth had already spent more than enough time holding Hannah's hand in the aftermath of her last crisis.

Before she could think any more about any definite course of action, she spied Julie behind the reception desk, sorting through some papers. Hannah approached the building supervisor and delicately cleared her throat, making her presence known.

The other woman looked up and gave her a kind smile, her eyes softening in sympathy and Hannah winced inwardly. Clearly, she too had seen the news coverage and put two and two together.

'Hannah, how are you doing? Honestly, Bruno's still completely inconsolable that he let that . . . well you know, upstairs unannounced. More so now. Never meet your heroes, I guess. You doing OK?'

Unable to pretend, she grimaced. 'To be honest, things could be better. I've . . . been laying low. And I've already told Bruno that I don't blame him. At all. Completely honest mistake. He wasn't to know.'

'Pretty wild though, huh? Anything I can do to help?' Julie asked genuinely, her concern evident.

'Well, now that you mention it . . . ' She took a deep breath and exhaled. 'I'm going to be leaving soon . . . '

'Oh, I'm so sorry to hear that.' Julie reached forward to pat Hannah's hand where it rested on the counter. 'We all loved having you here. But I guess I understand too, considering.' She shook her head. 'Honestly, who'd have guessed that you guys even knew each other, let alone worked together. What are the chances?'

Hannah bit her lip, keen to move off the topic of Rob. 'Everything has been . . . a lot.' She shook her head to stay on track. She didn't need to lay her entire sob story on the super. 'Obviously I'll alert Courtney's people, but I suppose if you and Bruno could maybe keep an eye on her mail and deliveries and whatnot? You know she gets a lot of stuff. No furniture or build-related deliveries scheduled as far as I know.' She went through the mental checklist she had been compiling in her head since she'd made the decision to vacate. 'It's just I don't want any mail or packages to disturb Ed again. Since things are on such an even keel now.'

Julie nodded her head in understanding. 'Of course. Though I'm guessing he's all sunshine and rainbows at the moment too. It would take a lot to bring him down. Though of course, *you* know that better than me.' She laughed, which Hannah thought was a curious response, considering. 'You know, you really did work wonders with him,' she added, with a twinkle in her eye. 'He's a whole different guy these days.'

Hannah grimaced. 'So maybe my time here wasn't a complete disaster.'

'Not in the least,' Julie agreed. 'And of course you have my word that Bruno and I'll keep an eye on P-2-related activity until Courtney returns.'

Thanking her once more, Hannah promised to say goodbye before she left for good and then headed back up to the penthouse floor. The elevator opened and she headed down the hallway, casting a glance at P-1 as she passed.

Inside, she was immediately greeted by the cat. Placing her bag on the kitchen counter, she started scratching the faithful feline's head before heading to the cupboard and grabbing another tin of Fancy Feast, opening it up and placing it on the floor.

Resting her head in her hand, Hannah watched it eat, now wondering what to do with it when she left. She obviously couldn't lock it in the apartment to fend for itself, nor could she leave the window open for it to pop in and out as it pleased.

'You have to belong to someone, can you possibly tell me who?' she asked the animal, who simply blinked in response. 'It would be so much easier if you could talk.' The cat turned its attention back to its food, apparently deciding that its future feeding and housing situation was Hannah's problem. 'I think I might miss you though,' she mumbled. 'You've been a good friend to me this last while.'

She momentarily thought about calling back down to Julie to find out if anyone in the building had mentioned or reported a missing pet. But just as quickly decided against it, once again fearful of causing more problems or creating unnecessary headaches when all seemed so settled just now. Then another thought occurred to her.

It was risky, but at this point, what had she got to lose?

Grabbing a piece of paper and a pen, she sat back down at the counter.

OK, so he might go crazy again and refuse to have anything to do with the cat. But at the very least, she definitely owed her neighbour a goodbye.

P-1,
I'm sorry I haven't written lately – I've had a lot going on and have been keeping to myself. Been dealing with some really challenging work stuff, which spilled over into the personal. Which sadly is why I'm writing today.

She was tired of reliving the sorry saga over and over in her head and worse watching it all unfold repeatedly in the media, but she had been so open with Ed up until this point, it felt wrong not to be honest about why she was leaving the building.

It's time for me to leave this place. Now, before you throw a going-away party . . .

Jokes aside, I just wanted to say that I have so enjoyed our back-and-forth while here, it was nice to have a confidant and sounding board, and finally someone appreciative of my baking talent (or lack thereof). I'd like to think that we got to know each other a bit too. So I didn't want to leave without saying goodbye.

I suppose you're wondering why I have decided to go then.

The truth is . . . I have screwed up. Big. Huge. Enormously terrible. I originally moved here from Los Angeles because I needed to start anew. But somehow my problems followed me across the country.

I was running from a bad relationship – one I now realize I shouldn't have been in in the first place. My idiot ex went so far as to show up at a big event here in the city and start a public fight in front of all of the cameras with a (now former) client of mine. All you have to do is turn on the TV if you want to see what I'm talking about. He's a scary guy and he even showed up here uninvited one time . . .

I'm getting off track. Sorry.

But I'm not leaving to get away from him this time. Seems he's finally got his comeuppance. I'm leaving because I made the same mistake.

And have fallen (again!) for someone I shouldn't have.

Except this other man is a world apart from my ex, one of the best I've ever known. If it weren't for the fact that he needed my professional help, I would have never met him . . . and I definitely wouldn't have fallen in love with him. I would feel like a fool if he knew about how I felt about him – especially since he's with someone else.

So I need to leave because it would be a special type of torture to know that I might just run into him getting coffee one morning, or bump into him elsewhere by accident. For as big as this city is, you and I both know it can also be very small.

The one thing I am happy about though, is that I know he's going to be OK. He doesn't need my help anymore – his star is on the rise and everything I'd ever hoped for him has come to fruition. The world finally sees him as I do.

I owe some of that to you, believe it or not. A while back you gave me some key advice (and dare I say practice?) in handling ahem . . . *unique* men. So thank you. But now, I have one more thing I need to ask of you – a parting favour.

There's this stray cat that's been coming around since I've been here – getting in through a window or a vent or something. Honestly, I'm not sure. It just pops in and out whenever it feels like it. Remember the unknown culprit who set off the media system that time? Two guesses.

It must belong to someone in this building or another close by. The problem is, I have been feeding it, so I'm concerned about its welfare once I'm gone.

Do you think you could maybe keep an eye out for it? I have some food that I can leave outside your door if you agree. Again, I'd really appreciate it. It's been kind of a friend to me too lately, and since I know for sure you have a good heart it would help ease my mind.

So that's about it. It truly has been a pleasure corresponding with you like this, Ed. I hope you have a great life and that the special person you mentioned appreciates you.

My one regret is that we didn't get the chance to meet in person. I just hope I was a good neighbour to you while I was here. And if not, please don't take it out on Courtney when she returns. She's a sweet and incredibly generous person who was good enough to lend me a place to lick my wounds after my last disaster, and if you take the opportunity to get to know her as you and I have, I know she will be an even better neighbour in the long run.

So that's it. Not exactly sure where I'm going to end up next but know that I will always think of you fondly. And perhaps our paths may even cross again sometime. In this town, you just never know. Only in New York.

P-2 (The Temporary Version)

Another loose end tied up, but Hannah was surprisingly emotional as she signed off. Her nerves were frayed to pieces these days.

She looked at the cat, who was now finished eating and had been sitting on the floor, staring up at her as if wondering what she had written.

'He's a bit of a grump who takes time to warm up to, but I'm sure he'll do the job until your owner comes looking for you, or you just decide to make your way home. Or maybe you two will be the perfect match.'

The cat offered an uninterested sniff in response.

Folding up the paper, Hannah stood and stretched, feeling antsy.

Getting some air and ridding herself of all this anxious energy would do her good. Or else she'd just hole up for the night with a bottle of wine but then have a raging hangover to contend with on top of everything else.

'I'm going out for a walk,' she told the cat. 'You do – well, whatever it is that you do when I'm not here – and I'll see you in a bit.' Reaching down, she gave it a gentle scratch behind the ears before heading out the door.

Approaching the door to P-1, Hannah cast a final glance over the words before slipping the note under the door, wondering why she felt so wistful about saying goodbye to someone she'd never met.

Chapter 67

WARD

'So now that everyone's decided you're a hero and not a knuckle-dragging goon, I've received an influx of new clients. Seems people think *I'm* the mastermind behind your . . . um . . . stamina.' Shelley's eyes twinkled with amusement and Ward, no matter how down in the dumps he still felt, couldn't help but smile.

Today's session was their last since he was now back training with the team and they'd arranged to meet in the park for a gentle jog.

'Obviously,' she added, standing in her running gear, stretching and bouncing on her feet as she warmed up, 'I'm setting the record straight with my clients in no uncertain terms that you and I have a business relationship only. Call it my own PR strategy.'

'Well, I'm glad something good came out of it in the end. Did Zeke get to see his mom kick ass on TV?'

She laughed and playfully punched him on the shoulder. 'He keeps replaying it over and over. And plenty of good has come out of it. You're fighting fit and will be back on the ice right in time for the playoffs. Even better, the world loves you, I'm so happy for you.'

Kendrick's sudden plummet from grace had truly led to a massive about-turn, with Ward now being placed on a pedestal and heralded as a Gallant Defender of Women on pretty much every media outlet. Even his mom had grudgingly admitted she was impressed, a first for sure.

And while he'd publicly emerged the victor and his image was completely transformed, like Hannah had always intended, it all felt empty and lacking. Because Ward didn't have her to celebrate it with. All he had wanted when he first met her was to fix the knee and get back to playing – and he had all of that now and even more, but it felt hollow.

Shelley stopped stretching and crossed her arms over her chest, her smile fading. 'She's still not talking to you, is she?'

He glanced away, pretending to be interested in a dog walker wrangling a six-pack of pooches down the sidewalk, then shook his head.

'Not returning my calls,' he said. 'Obviously thinks I'm the one responsible for destroying his career – even though the asshat did that to himself. And if she's still with him after everything . . .'

Shelley pursed her lips. 'You honestly think she's still with him? Not a chance. She didn't seem happy with him that night, and anyway, who would stay with a guy like that after what's come out? Hannah's not an idiot. And yeah, of course she was mad at you, who wouldn't be? I was ready to kill you with my bare hands for putting me in that situation *and* in a goddamn Cinderella dress too. But controlling your image was Hannah's job, so all the work she did went right down the drain. I don't blame her for being upset,' Shelley surmised. 'Embarrassed too, I guess, though I get now that you were doing her a favour.'

Ward nodded and ran his hands through his hair – and the pair started on a light jog in the direction of Bethesda Terrace.

'I know that and I've tried to apologize. Don't get me wrong, I am definitely not sorry for kicking his ass. I knew I didn't misjudge that; he was obviously hurting her so I wasn't sorry even when the kangaroo court was calling for my head instead of his. And grabbing you too? Asshole deserved everything we gave him.'

'Damn straight.' Shelley kept pace next to him as they turned on East Drive. Cherry blossoms adorned the surrounding tree branches, creating a floral carpet beneath their feet as they ran. 'Nothing to apologize for there.'

'Except for making Hannah's life harder,' Ward admitted. 'Right from the get-go I made things difficult, sometimes impossible for her. I complained about every last thing. I never thought for a second that she might have stuff to deal with too, and had another dickwad making her life hard. And she didn't deserve that, especially when she's so good at what she does and took the time to understand what I was comfortable with. She . . . got me.'

As they reached the bottom of the steps, Ward stopped in his tracks and Shelley ran a couple steps ahead before realizing she had lost him. She looked back to see him leaning over, bent at his waist, hands on his knees, his head facing the ground.

The water sparkled in the sunlight as the angelic statue on top of the fountain watched over the space like a silent sentinel. A gentle breeze carried with it the laughter of nearby picnickers and the distant hum of city life, but all of it was lost on Ward.

Shelley walked over and put a comforting hand on his shoulder. 'So then, go and get *her.*'

Chapter 68

Returning from his run, Ward headed through the foyer of his building and to the elevator, in need of a shower. He felt much better after the workout though, and the talk with Shelley, heartened that maybe Hannah hadn't gone back to Kendrick despite all.

But then why was she still not returning his calls?

Getting into the elevator, he pressed the button for his floor and turned around to face the lobby, glancing down at his phone to check it again. Then looked back up just as the elevator doors were closing, only to see someone who looked remarkably like Hannah passing through the lobby and toward the double-door exit. Even from behind he'd recognize her anywhere.

She hadn't seen him, but his heart soared, and a flurry of emotions burst in his chest. Had she come here to see him? Finally calmed down enough to talk to him? Maybe she would tell him that she had ended it with Kendrick? Or hopefully, had a change of heart about taking him back as a client. What could all this mean?

Ward jerked an arm in between the closing elevator doors in the hope of stopping them. But it was too late and he pulled his hand back just in time to save it from getting smashed as they sealed themselves shut. That was all he needed, exit busted knee, enter broken hand.

Tapping his foot, he willed the elevator to go faster so he could ride it back down again and try to catch up with her. He needed to hear her voice and see her – more than he felt like he needed oxygen. But something else was wriggling its way around his brain like an invasive worm. And then it dawned on him.

How did she know where he lived?

Yes, he had a few real estate investments in the city, places he rented out, places that made him money – but she'd never visited him here. They'd always met somewhere else, taken separate cabs, left in different Ubers. Could it be just a coincidence then that she'd been there? Maybe she knew someone else in the building? And hadn't come to see him at all, he thought despondently.

But regardless, he had to see *her.*

Reaching his floor as he impatiently pressed the button to go straight back down, when he heard a noise that hadn't touched his ears for several days.

A meow.

Ward had come to understand her various vocalisms and immediately recognized it as Pretzel saying, *So where the hell have you been? I need feeding.*

He'd since thrown out the untouched days-old food in her bowl and now he felt torn. Who knew where she'd been or the last time she had the opportunity to eat something? She was his responsibility after all.

'Now of all times, you show up,' he grunted, looking for something to hold the elevator doors open since he'd already pushed the down button. He grabbed a nearby console table and positioned it in place between them. 'OK, hold on, but we need to be quick.'

Then dashing to the cupboard for a bag of Meow Mix, he quickly dumped some kibble into her food dish, realizing that with

349

each passing second, he was losing the chance to catch up with Hannah. He dropped the bag of food on the floor resolving to deal with it when he got back.

But as he moved the console table out of the way and back alongside the internal door to the hallway, something else caught his attention, a piece of paper beneath it.

A note.

He snatched it up, and got back into the elevator, noticing Pretzel watching with interest as he waited for the doors to close, ignoring her food. He wondered idly if she'd been using it for one of her jaunts, but then dismissed the thought, feeling like an idiot. While Ward loved the fact that he could just jump on and off directly through to his place and it kept him from having to interact with other residents, cats couldn't push buttons, could they?

He recognized that everyone else thought he was aloof and he had a reputation as a bit of a curmudgeon, which he didn't do anything to dismantle because it ensured his privacy. That had been a saving grace, in recent days, especially when the media had been throwing him around like a tidal wave. Freshly impatient even as the car made its descent, he stabbed again at the L button for the lobby, one of only three on the panel – L, P for Penthouse, and E for Emergency.

Feeling fidgety he glanced at the note, opening it up and scanning it as he waited. He didn't have time for this now but was always curious as to what his neighbour had to say.

While he'd been initially peeved at the idea of a celebrity influencer moving in next door, especially one who seemed to court the media attention he himself detested, he'd gradually come to enjoy their interactions, and also grudgingly come to the conclusion that the girl next door wasn't such an airhead after all.

The kid was nice actually, and Ward had been grateful that she seemed equally happy to keep things anonymous. Despite his initial suspicions, he soon discovered they had much more in common than he'd thought. Intrigued by some of her earlier correspondence and attempts to win him over, he'd looked up her socials and found that she was actually quite cool, into financial stuff like himself and not just some vacuous poser.

Like Hannah always said, appearances could often be deceptive.

As he scanned through the page, his eyes widened when Courtney mentioned something about leaving. It couldn't be because of him, could it? Had she seen or heard something about the fight with Kendrick maybe, and become spooked about having him as a neighbour after all?

Then Ward stood frozen, as he zeroed on some of P-2's other words.

And alarm bells exploded in his head.

A place to stay . . . romantically involved with a client . . . idiot ex . . . stalking . . . big event . . . a fight in front of all of the cameras . . . current (now former) client . . .

He felt himself breathing faster as suddenly rapt, he pored over every last line. Until he came to the biggest bombshell of all.

I'm leaving because I messed up − again. I've fallen in love with someone else I shouldn't have.

Time stood still.

But before he could ponder it any longer, the elevator doors opened and while he had only left this space mere minutes before, it felt as if the world had tilted on its axis since he'd seen Hannah exit through the spinning doors ahead.

None of this made sense.

'Not possible,' he muttered to himself. 'You're projecting, you're going crazy.'

Striding briskly through the lobby, note still in hand, Ward headed straight toward Bruno standing near the entryway.

'Aha! Here's the man I wanted to see!' The doorman smiled. 'I have a delivery for you, just signed for it. I was going to bring it up on my break.'

But Ward was shaking his head. 'Great, but that woman, the one who just came through here a couple of minutes ago . . .'

Surprised by the urgency in his voice, Bruno's face flushed with worry, it was clear something distressing was afoot. 'What woman?' He looked around the empty lobby space as if searching for a hint.

'She just walked out, literally two minutes ago, right after I came back from the park. Dark hair. About five foot six or so. Pretty. Really pretty.' Ward looked expectantly at the doorway as if Hannah might suddenly reappear out of thin air.

'Oh, you mean Miss Ryan?'

Hearing the name confirmed made everything come into focus. Hannah hadn't been here in this building by chance. Far from it, it seemed.

'She lives here, then? She's a resident?' Ward pressed.

Bruno looked at him strangely, like he'd suddenly sprouted wings and a tail.

'Does she *live here,* Bruno?' he demanded, already knowing the answer.

'Well, of course, I mean technically speaking – but not for much longer it seems. Julie told me she's vacating soon in preparation for Miss Wilde's return.'

Ward honestly thought he might pass out.

'Courtney Wilde? The influencer?'

'Yes, your neighbour, in P-2. Miss Ryan has been housesitting the penthouse while Miss Wilde's been away in Europe. I really would've thought you already knew this . . . I mean, since you and Miss Ryan work together *and* live side by side.' Bruno looked at him curiously. 'Edward, are you sure you're feeling OK?'

Chapter 69

Ward was still reeling as the reality of the situation sank in and the implications of it all came crashing down on top of him. Hannah was living in this very building, had been *staying* next door in P-2 this entire time.

Hannah *was* P-2. Not Courtney.

He had been spilling his guts to her over and over, and she in turn, had been baring her soul to him.

But now that he knew, and once he'd started to connect the dots, things started to make sense . . . the assumption that he was old-fashioned and curmudgeonly, the cat that had decided to make its home in both places, the 'advice' he had supplied in the guise of helping her win over a 'difficult' male associate.

Hannah though, was presumably still operating in the dark. She had no idea who was on the other side of their shared wall. Worse yet, she seemed to believe him to be in love with Shelley and had made plans to move out and who knows, maybe leave the city altogether.

Then, of course, the best part.

She's fallen in love with me, he mused incredulously, unable to believe the words even as he kept reading them over and over. But Hannah didn't know that she had it all wrong about Shelley either. Didn't know that he was in love with her in return. Or that there was nothing more he wanted than to be able to tell her that.

Yet, if he revealed the truth and the crazy mistake they'd both made about each other's identity, what would happen then? Wouldn't she feel embarrassed? Maybe feel like he abused her trust, maybe even set out to deceive her on purpose. Manipulated even?

If he walked out his door right now and went next door to knock on hers without any warning or explanation, he would look like a stalker, just like Kendrick. Same if he took to lingering in the lobby, waiting for her either to leave the building or enter it. She was far more likely to be spooked than won over.

Ward swallowed hard, recalling with embarrassment the many times he'd approached next door, angry and annoyed over trivial, insignificant stuff and taking out his frustrations, causing Hannah additional grief on top of what she had to deal with day to day. He shook his head with frustration – what a self-centred ass he'd been. And to think that all this time he was trying to reach her, to explain about the shit he'd done, she had been mere steps away.

But if he was somehow given the chance, he swore he would make it all up to her and then some.

He needed to do this the right way though. He only had one shot. Especially when it seemed the clock was ticking.

Having considered various other angles and approaches, he figured there really was only one way. He glanced over at Pretzel. 'To think that you've been squatting over there all this time, while I've been over here wondering how to get her attention . . .'

He could only surmise that the cat had been traversing between the decorative window ledge running along the front of the penthouse level and jumping in and out of the openings where possible, making herself at home wherever took her mood.

Ward knew what he was about to do was a major gamble, but

he was hoping that Hannah's curiosity and unfailing good nature would get the better of her.

'OK.' He exhaled, bracing himself for the slotshot of his life. 'Here goes.'

P-2,

Firstly, I'm sorry to hear that you're leaving. I honestly cannot even tell you how sorry. I know things haven't always been smooth sailing with me, and that I've likely caused you a headache or ten since your arrival. For that I apologize, I truly am sorry – I would hate for you to leave and not know that.

Secondly, I know of the stray you're talking about. You're very kind to watch and worry about a pet that isn't yours. I'll make sure to keep an eye out for it, no worries on that score. Believe it or not, I know a thing or two about cats.

I also agree that we have become unlikely friends and the fact that you went above and beyond to be kind and so nice to me when you'd surely been warned about my ways, says a lot about you and the type of person you are, decent, honest and considerate.

The world needs more people like you.

Also sorry to hear about your recent professional and personal struggles – and heartbreak especially. Truth be told, I've been facing the same thing myself – I've told you as much, but I'm beginning to feel hopeful.

I do in fact watch TV, and I believe I know what you're talking about. If that's what you've been dealing with, well, let me just say that your asshat ex got his comeuppance fair and square. And maybe worth mentioning that in my humble opinion, no man goes to bat like that for someone, unless he cares about her deeply too.

So I'm pretty certain your guy feels the same about you.

Could you maybe be looking at things the wrong way? Trust me, I've made a mistake like that before. Thinking that the person I love is with someone else, when the opposite is true.

Like you said, we have a lot more in common than we thought.

And you are right, your (former) client is going to be OK – professionally speaking. Removing the client label is the best thing that could happen.

You say I've given you good advice before – there's a real chance I'm right this time, too.

In any case, considering all we've shared this last while, it feels wrong to not put a face to the name before you leave. If you feel up to it, maybe we could meet for a quick coffee?

Let me know if you're open to it. Anytime tomorrow is good for me. You pick the place. Really doesn't seem right to part ways without having the chance to truly say hello before we say goodbye?

Hope to see you soon,

P-1

Chapter 70

HANNAH

The following morning, Hannah wandered hesitantly down the street and around the corner for her unexpected 'blind date'.

Standing outside the meeting spot she'd selected, she looked up, taking in its unassuming facade, and automatically smiled, remembering her first visit there.

This place was the perfect location to meet Ed. It was close by so not too tricky for her neighbour to get to, absent of any accessibility hurdles. It was also easy-going and considerably less stuffy than many of the more high-end eateries around here, and quieter too.

Despite Ward's early promo efforts, business had since tapered off and gone back to normal, tap-and-go Millennials apparently unimpressed at the proprietor's steadfast refusal to bend to technology.

Hannah smiled. Since she already knew Ed certainly wasn't a Starbucks kinda guy, maybe he and fellow technophobe dinosaur Frank would hit it off and if he didn't already, Ed might even keep frequenting this place once she was gone?

She was still taken aback that now, after all this time her curmudgeonly neighbour wanted to meet, and while in truth she wasn't especially up for being sociable, there was no way she was going to turn him down. He had obviously come to value their faceless companionship a lot too.

So the notion that this meeting might have a dual purpose in helping her lonely neighbour make a new friend made Hannah feel less guilty about her out-of-the-blue announcement that she was leaving at such short notice.

She was curious too about the insight he'd provided in his latest missive about Ward and Rob's public showdown and the suggestion that maybe she'd misinterpreted. But she could certainly agree with his assertion that Ward's current status as a former client was the best thing for all concerned. There truly was always something so wise and reassuring about Ed's words.

Now she wondered momentarily if she was subconsciously tempting fate by deciding on such a meeting spot. 'No,' she reassured herself. 'It's old school, just like him.'

Last night when she'd picked up Ed's note on return from her walk, she'd written a quick response thanking him for the invitation, saying she would meet him here tomorrow at eleven.

And just so you know who to look for, I'm mid-thirties, chestnut-hair, about five-three or so. I'll head in early to grab us a table. Excited about meeting in person.

Even though he hadn't provided a physical description in return, she was pretty sure she would be able to identify Ed when he came through the door; an older male with mobility issues, a gruff exterior and inferiority complex that concealed his inner child and good heart.

Huh she thought now, *sounds familiar . . .*

Hannah took a quick look at her reflection in the window of

Frank's coffee house, fluffed her hair, then opened the front doors and strode in. Squinting a little to get her bearings, she glanced around the café's current patrons, trying to discern whether Ed had beaten her there.

'Hey, Frank,' she called out to the smiling proprietor, who was as always behind the counter, manning the place on his own. Looking longingly at his fresh produce display, she grabbed a free table for two by the window taking the far side so she could keep an eye on the door for her neighbour's arrival.

'What can I get for you?' Frank asked as he approached.

'Just a flat white, please.' As much as she wanted one of his legendary cannolis, she figured it would be rude to order something before Ed's arrival. But given his sweet tooth she thought he'd be only too happy to join her.

'You got it. Anything to eat?'

'I'm actually . . . waiting for someone. I'll let you know.'

Hannah felt herself jumpy with nervous energy. It really was kind of like going on a blind date. She truly had no idea if she and Ed would hit it off in person, which was also why being anonymous all this while had made it so easy to communicate. So she hoped things didn't feel awkward face to face.

Frank headed off to fill the order while Hannah tapped her hands on the table, feeling fidgety. She picked up her phone and glanced at the time.

It was now a little after eleven. She hoped he wasn't having trouble finding the place or negotiating the street in his wheelchair or mobility aid, or whatever he used day to day. And now she wondered if it had been a bad call not just to meet in the lobby of their building and go from there. But that would have been way too awkward. This way, much like a blind date, either one could come and go as they pleased.

Just then, the door chimed and Hannah perked up to check out the new arrival but the person, a guy in a baseball cap, was much too young. Then looking properly at the face beneath the ballcap, she felt the room start to spin.

Ward had just walked in.

Shite . . . Hannah grimaced and automatically started to slump in her seat to fade away from view, even as her heart instinctively fluttered at the mere sight of him.

But if she truly thought about it, wasn't there a subconscious part of her that had chosen this very place, considering their history? She wasn't sure and she just sat there, hoping that he might just grab his usual takeout and wouldn't notice her, but it was too late. Frank approached her table with her order right as Ward passed by.

'Hey, man, how you doin'?' he called out, bringing attention directly to where she sat. As Frank set the cup down in front of her, Hannah muttered a thanks but could already feel Ward's gaze on her as he closed the distance between them.

'Great, Frank, how about you?'

'All good, man, all good.'

Swallowing hard and staring at her hands as Frank moved away, Hannah finally transitioned her attention to his piercing green gaze.

'Hey, Hannah,' he greeted quietly.

She shifted in her seat even as she felt her face grow hot.

'Hi, um . . . what are you doing here?' she stuttered.

'Just grabbing coffee. This is one of my favourite places, but I think you already know that,' he answered, and now she worried that he might think she was here hoping to bump into him or something. Like some psycho stalker.

But of course that didn't make sense since she was the one who'd been avoiding *his* calls.

'So how are . . . things?' Trying to compose herself she briefly raised her gaze to his, before glancing again at the door. This was incredibly awkward. Especially if Ed were to appear now and they were all forced to exchange pleasantries or something. Hannah wasn't sure how she'd introduce either man to the other without raising a lot of questions on both sides.

Ward seemed to follow her line of sight. 'Are you meeting someone?' He motioned to the empty seat in front of her.

'Actually, yes, I . . .'

But he was already sitting down. 'Is it a date?' he teased, making Hannah's heart pound in her chest. 'I'll move when he gets here.'

'It's . . . not a date. Just a friend . . .'

He studied her face. 'Saying some goodbyes maybe?' he asked softly.

Hannah opened and closed her mouth, feeling momentarily confused until it dawned on her. Bernie must have told him about her plans to leave the city, her excuse not to have him back as her client.

'You could say that,' she confirmed, feeling a bit sheepish now for being too cowardly to fill him in herself.

'I've been trying to call you, Hannah,' he said then, his voice growing softer, causing her to look up at his face, still covered in bruises. His eyes sparkled like emeralds.

'I know.'

'You haven't called me back. Never even replied to my messages.'

'I know,' she repeated. What else could she say?

'I'm so sorry for what happened, I know I should have controlled my temper and shouldn't have made a scene. I embarrassed you in public and made things hard for you, I recognize that. But no way could I stand by and watch you being pushed around like that. Can you accept my apology?'

Hannah took a sip of her coffee and then wiped her palms on her jeans. Her hands were sweating. She did not want to have this conversation with Ward. There was no way she would get out of it with her heart intact.

'You know, my friend, who I'm meeting, he's likely to be here any second . . .'

'Do you accept my apology?' he pressed. 'Honestly, Hannah, I know you and Kendrick have a history, but . . .' Then he trailed off. 'I know I don't have any right to ask and your relationship is none of my business, but I just need to know, after everything, are you OK? With him I mean?' She'd still been glancing at the door, but his heartfelt tone brought her back to the present. 'You're important to me,' he continued earnestly. 'Your happiness is important to me. And now I'm worried that I put you in a difficult position.'

'Well, it wouldn't be the first time, would it?' she remarked, the words out before she could stop them, but catching sight of his expression she relented. 'I was just teasing. I get that your intentions were pure. You were just trying to be the good guy – no, you *are* the good guy.'

Ward leaned forward in his seat, waiting for her to say more.

Taking a deep breath, she added, 'Yes, I forgive you.'

Of course I do. How the hell could I not when you're looking at me like that?

'Thank God,' he said softly, emotion thick in his voice. He put his hands on the table and Hannah had the sudden urge to cover them with her own but knew that would be wildly inappropriate. Yet somehow the mood between them had shifted, something had intensified, and she glanced at the door again, now wishing that Ed wouldn't show up after all.

'Anyway,' she said, her voice becoming light as she realized she needed to wrap this up, 'all's well that ends well. Rob got what was coming to him. Your career is going to be fine, better than fine, since the whole world now adores you.' She smiled and then added, 'I just hope you and Shelley are—'

'I am *not* with Shelley,' Ward interjected quickly. 'Let's clarify that once and for all.' Hannah furrowed her brow, suddenly confused. She opened her mouth, additional questions on her tongue, but he stopped her. 'I have never been with Shelley,' he said, his tone measured, searching her face for a reaction. 'She's my personal trainer, a friend who agreed to come to the ceremony as my plus one after you pretty much strong-armed her into it that day here. You assumed we were together for some reason . . . *You* created that narrative.'

Did she? Hannah searched through her memory trying to put the string of events in order, and realized that he was right.

'I was happy to go along with it, though,' Ward admitted. 'I was embarrassed after that night in the park and ashamed too. Especially when you'd told me you were with someone, with Kendrick.'

'But I wasn't, I mean we'd split up by then but it was all a bit messy and confusing still and then he turned up at my place unexpectedly and . . .'

She felt herself start to ramble and truly hoped that Ed didn't decide to show up now because at this point it would be a seriously unwelcome intrusion. She got the sense that she and Ward were on the verge of something important, and she needed an answer to her next question.

'Why?' she asked, her voice no more than a whisper.

'Why what?'

'Why did you want me to think that you were with Shelley?'

'Because I was afraid, Hannah. I already crossed a line that night in the park. And I was terrified of losing you, not as my publicist or a friend but . . .'

Her eyes met his and she knew without a doubt that he was telling her the truth.

'Oh . . .' she breathed as the weight of his admission weighed on her heart.

Then Ward stood up. 'How late is your friend running?' he asked, suddenly changing the subject so fast that her thoughts spun back to the present. She'd almost forgotten she was here to meet someone else.

'Quite a bit to be fair.' She too looked absently at the door.

'Well, I guess I'd better get going. Again, I'm so sorry for all the trouble I've caused. Just know that I appreciate everything you've done for me and I wish you didn't need to leave. I especially hope that my actions haven't caused you to want to do that. You're a special person, Hannah, and you deserve so much better than someone like Kendrick.' She nodded, unsure what to say, and Ward continued. 'I'm sure that the guy you're waiting for knows how lucky he is to have you in his life.'

'Apparently not since he's decided not to come after all,' Hannah mused, a little let down, but also somewhat relieved that Ed hadn't appeared.

Her emotions were all over the place and she didn't think she could take any more surprises, nor handle idle pleasantries.

'Well, at least it meant you and I got the chance to say goodbye.'
As he turned to leave, Ward tentatively reached across and rested a
hand on hers. 'See you round, Hannah.'

She barely managed to utter goodbye in return she was so
overcome by the significance of what he'd revealed to her. He cared
about her too. Yet what was she supposed to do? Run out on the
street after him and fling herself into his arms?

Hannah sat there for a few moments longer, uncertain if she was
still waiting for Ed or deciding what to do about Ward.

But before she could think any more about either scenario,
Frank reappeared at the table with a plate, on top of which sat one
of his famous pastries, the same one she'd chosen the very first day
she'd come here.

She glanced up in surprise. 'But I didn't order . . .'

The older man nodded toward the door. 'Ed did. He came in
before you arrived and asked me to give this to you when he was
gone.'

'He did?' Hannah looked at him, mystified. *Ed had been in here
already?* How had she missed him? But Frank just shrugged and
moved away.

Still reeling, she stared down at the plate and then noticed a
piece of paper sticking out from beneath the cannoli.

Another note.

Hey Cannoli Girl. Good to finally meet in person.

Seems like you and I both made assumptions about a lot
of things from the get-go. Believe me, I had no idea either
what was going on until I read your goodbye note.

While I hope what I told you just now makes sense, there's
so much more I need to say. And a lot of time to make up for.

But I thought I'd start by paying you back for all those Rice Krispie treats you made for me. Good thing I already know you like this one.

Edward McKenzie

PS: I'm heading home now if you'd like to chat some more. I have a feeling you'll know exactly where to find me . . .

Chapter 71

Ed . . . Ward . . . Edward . . . they were the same *person*?!!

But . . . *how* . . . ?

Still reeling, Hannah had stared at the note for an entire minute or more, stunned by what she was reading, or more to the point, the implications.

Her brain just couldn't fathom the enormity of the notion that Ed and Ward could be one and the same. That she and Ward had been communicating anonymously all throughout the time they worked together. Had been living right next door to one another.

Without either of them knowing, it seemed, since Ed (Ward) had admitted in the note that he was clueless until her goodbye letter.

Was it actually possible . . . ?

And yet weirdly, it kind of made sense somehow. How Ed's advice seemed to work so perfectly for Ward, how his stubborn, old-fashioned ways pretty much mirrored the athlete's contrarian personality . . . to the point that at times it did feel to Hannah that she was dealing with the same kind of person, albeit of a generational difference.

Because she was.

She knew that Ward had various homes in the city but how had she never passed him in the lobby, or seen him in the elevator . . .

And then remembered how Julie had mentioned P-1 had its

own private elevator, and that Ed (and Ward) was fastidious about his privacy . . .

She also recalled the strange looks Bruno and the building supervisor had given her sometimes when she talked about Ed, commenting on his age and grumpy personality. But she'd been led to believe that from Courtney's first letter when she'd called him the 'old guy next door'.

When of course to that generation, anyone over the age of twenty was practically geriatric . . .

But now Hannah cringed when she thought about how much of herself she'd revealed in those notes, inadvertently or otherwise.

Ward knew exactly what she thought about him and, worse, even how she felt, almost right from the beginning. Good *and* bad. She had bared her soul in those notes, grateful for the opportunity to open up to someone who it seemed was equally happy to remain anonymous.

Hadn't Ward done the same though? she reasoned, feeling a little less vulnerable. Hadn't he too laid bare his own reservations, his lack of confidence in matters of the heart?

And all the while he'd been talking about her. Or so she'd recently learned.

If she hadn't spoken to him just now she'd have assumed he was referring to Shelley, or the ex who'd moved away to Chicago. But no it was her, it was definitely her.

He'd made that crystal clear by setting it all up with Frank beforehand, the cannoli and this final note.

I think you'll know exactly where to find me . . .

Taking a quick bite (it was way too good to ignore) Hannah stuffed the note in her pocket, paid and said goodbye to Frank, then hurried back out onto the street, still dazed and utterly confused by what she'd just learned.

Yet excited too.

Back in the building, she waved a quick hello at a smiling Bruno, who if she didn't know better looked to be in on the whole thing, despite Ed/Ward's protestations to the contrary.

Which was his real name by the way? She'd only ever known him as Ward, how he'd always been known as a professional. And since she'd only dealt with him in that capacity why would she know any better? Perhaps he went by Ed day to day, using a variation of his real name like some actors or other high-profile public figures did to help preserve their anonymity.

Which was why she was completely confused when Frank had referred to him that way just now. And of course, she and next door had only ever addressed one another as their apartment numbers, P-1 and P-2.

It was all too surreal to take in properly but Hannah knew that she needed to see him now, was desperate to find out the answers to all of her questions and presumably answer some of his too.

There's so much more I want to say.

Finally alone in the elevator, she exhaled and gripped the wall for support, all of a sudden uncertain as to what to expect when she reached the penthouse floor.

And suddenly concerned that she'd read the note all wrong. It wouldn't be the first time she'd completely missed the mark, would it? But no, there was no reading between the lines this time. He had been pretty clear. He was going home and now Hannah knew exactly where that was.

Had done so all along.

When the doors pinged open on the penthouse floor and she

stepped out into the hallway, something registered in her brain – something she had never before seen.

The door to P-1 was open, daylight spilling out from the inside, some of it partially obstructed by the shadow of a lone figure standing in the doorway. Hannah stopped in her tracks and looked over at the entrance to P-2, her brain feeling like a bowl of mashed potatoes.

A soft meow came from the open doorway and the cat appeared, wrapping itself around its master's legs and looking at Hannah with an expression that suggested, 'Duh, do you get it now?'

Hold on . . . she had another sudden revelation. *Was that the mangy stray from the shelter Ward had got so worked up about? The one that was doomed to be destroyed* . . .

'Hey, P-2,' a voice said softly, and she glanced up to meet Ward's gaze as he leaned lazily on the doorframe.

Hannah opened and closed her mouth, unsure what to say. She pointed a finger at him and the cat and then back again down the hallway. 'You . . . you . . .'

'I know,' he said, with a rueful smile. 'But I didn't find out until yesterday.'

He stood up straight then and began to approach her cautiously, as if still gauging her reaction, cognisant that she was still in the middle of an information overload.

'But Ed . . .' she whispered, pointing at the door. 'He's old and he can't get around and had a nurse visit some days and . . .'

'Edward is my full name, but I've been Ward since Jefferson Prince decided it went better with Wildcat. I go by Ed to my friends. As you know, my knee was busted, hence my need for strength and conditioning visits from Shelley. I believe you've already met Pretzel. And *you're* the one who always said I was a relic from a different time . . .'

371

Pretzel? She squinted at him. 'You never told me your real name was Edward,' Hannah admonished weakly as he continued to get closer.

'You never asked.' His green eyes were intent on her face and she tilted her head up, still trying to make all of this make sense. But suddenly she was within striking distance of his chest, and she could feel the heat of his body as he moved ever closer. 'And you read all my notes, all my thoughts and personal stuff.'

'Not your notes – our notes. *Our* thoughts and personal stuff, Hannah. This whole time. It was both of us.'

She felt herself sinking into his embrace as if it were the most natural thing in the world. Yes, she hadn't been the only one expressing what she was feeling and experiencing, Ward too had confessed that he was falling for someone but was scared to tell her how he felt.

And that someone had been her all along.

Appearances can often be deceptive.

'Seriously, how long . . . how long have you known? That it was me over there?' Hannah glanced back at the other door.

Ward gently brushed a hand down the side of her face, and she felt herself tremble.

'I only just figured it out too. From your goodbye note yesterday, plus I had just seen you in the lobby and asked Bruno about you . . .' He shook his head and she could tell it all seemed just as crazy and incredible to him. 'Putting it all together, it kinda made sense though,' he added chuckling. 'But do you honestly think I would have been such an ornery old bastard if I knew the woman I'd fall in love with – who I've *fallen* in love with – lived right next door? Hell, I would have torn down the drywall to be with you.'

Then Ward bent his head and gently touched his forehead to

hers. His skin felt like fire and she sank into his embrace, safe in the feeling of his strong arms around her.

After a beat, she pulled back.

'Just for the record, you do realize you're no longer my client,' she teased, a mischievous smile playing about her lips.

'Nor will I be at any point in the future.' He traced her lips with his finger. 'Because that would be highly unprofessional . . . '

'So unprofessional,' she murmured.

Then he straightened up as if a thought had just occurred to him, but his eyes twinkled. 'So you're really leaving New York, huh?' He glanced down the hallway towards P-2, a devilish twinkle in his eye.

She looked at him dubiously. 'I think you already know I'm not going anywhere.'

'Oh yes, you are.' His voice was husky, and scooping her into his arms, Ward effortlessly lifted her off her feet and back toward his doorway. 'If you think for a second that wall can continue to separate us, you are sorely mistaken. And no more notes either,' he ordered, crossing over the threshold with her; Hannah was only too happy to oblige. 'Time for some long overdue face-to-face.'

And with that, he kicked shut the door of P-1 behind them.

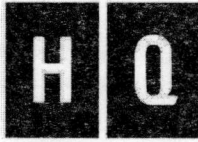

ONE PLACE. MANY STORIES

Bold, innovative and
empowering publishing.

FOLLOW US ON:

@HQStories